LEARNING TO LOSE

LEARNING TO LOSE

A Novel

DAVID TRUEBA

TRANSLATED BY MARA FAYE LETHEM

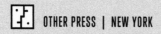 OTHER PRESS | NEW YORK

This work has been published with a subsidy from the Directorate General
of Books, Archives and Libraries of the Spanish Ministry of Culture.

Production Editor: *Yvonne E. Cárdenas*
Book design: *Simon M. Sullivan*
This book was set in 12 pt Fournier by Alpha Design & Composition of
Pittsfield, NH.

10 9 8 7 6 5 4 3 2 1

LIBRARY OF CONGRESS CATALOGING-IN-PUBLICATION DATA

Trueba, David, 1969-
    [Saber perder. English]
    Learning to lose / David Trueba ; translated by Mara Faye Lethem.
        p. cm.
    Originally published in Spanish as Saber perder in 2008.
    ISBN 978-1-59051-322-4 (pbk.) — ISBN 978-1-59051-388-0 (e-book)
1. Teenage girls—Fiction. 2. Traffic accident victims—Fiction. 3. Soccer
players—Fiction. 4. Fathers and daughters—Fiction. 5. Fathers and sons—
Fiction. 6. Guilt—Fiction. 7. Fear of failure—Fiction. 8. Interpersonal
relations—Fiction. 9. Madrid (Spain)—Fiction. 10. Psychological fiction.
I. Lethem, Mara. II. Title.
    PQ6670.R77S2313 2010
    863'.64 dc22

                                                      2010006933

For Cristina Huete,
FILM PRODUCER

Canto a noite até ser dia

But in my arms till break of day
Let the living creature lie,
Mortal, guilty, but to me
The entirely beautiful.

—W. H. Auden, "Lullaby"

CONTENTS

part one

IS THIS DESIRE?

1

Desire works like the wind. With no apparent effort. If it finds our sails extended, it will drag us at a dizzying speed. If our doors and shutters are closed, it bangs at them for a while, searching for cracks or slots it can slip in through. The desire attached to an object of desire binds us to it. But there is another kind of desire, abstract, disconcerting, that envelops us like a mood. It declares that we are ready for desire and that we just have to wait, our sails unfurled, for the wind to blow. That is the desire to desire.

Sylvia is sitting in the back of the classroom, in the row by the window, in the penultimate seat. The only kid behind her is Rainbow, a Colombian kid who's wearing the official track-suit of the Spanish national soccer team and dozing through the day's classes. Sylvia turns sixteen on Sunday. She seems older, rising above her classmates with her detached attitude. Those same classmates whom she now scrutinizes.

No, it's not any of these. None of these mouths is the mouth I want brushing against my mouth. I don't want any of these tongues tangled in mine. Nobody here has the teeth that are going to nibble on my lower lip, my earlobe, the bend of my neck, the fold of my stomach. Nobody here.

Nobody.

In class Sylvia is surrounded by bodies that aren't fully formed, incongruous faces, ill-proportioned arms and legs, as if they were all growing in haphazard spurts. Carlos Valencia has appealing tan forearms that stick out powerfully from beneath his T-shirt, but his arrogance is off-putting. Sepúlveda "the Dullard" has the delicate hands of a draftsman, but he's goofy and spineless. Raúl Zapata's body is flabby, definitely not the one Sylvia wants to receive onto hers like a wave of flesh. Nando Solares's face is overtaken by zits and sometimes blends into the stucco wall. Manu Recio, Óscar Panero, and Nico Verón are nice, but they are little boys; the first one has a peach-fuzz moustache, the second only speaks in fits and starts, and the third is now shoving two pencils into his nostrils to make his buddies laugh.

"The Tank" Palazón goes out with Sonia and puts his arm around her waist and smacks her ass with his sausage-fingered hand in a possessive gesture that Sylvia abhors. "Skeleton" Ocaña is malnourished, has grown rampantly, and has a lisp; Samuel Torán only thinks about soccer, and she'd have to turn into a ball to attract his foolish brown gaze. Curro Santiso is already, at fifteen, obviously the property registrar, drab accountant, or financial adviser he will become, completely uninteresting. "Blockhead" Sanz is out of the running because he doesn't just tend toward homosexuality, he oozes with it. He's got enough problems sidestepping ridicule from the macho kids who exaggerate his swishiness, hounding him and pushing him with their shoulders every time they cross paths. Quelo Zuazo lives on an unexplored planet and "Cocky" Ochoa treats high school with the same passion a nuclear engineer could muster up for studying in elementary school. Pedro Suanzes and Edu Velázquez are both Goths, loners with long hair and black clothes, given a wide berth due to the suspicion that they're plotting to murder the rest of the class in some painful way. "Hedgehog" Sousa is an Ecuadorian with spiky hair and a wall lizard's laugh.

And then there's Rainbow, nicknamed for the many different colors he wears, almost the full spectrum.

The sun that comes in through the window and rests on the desks is sometimes more interesting than class. Sylvia would love to pole-vault over her age. Be ten years older. Right now. Get up without permission, move through the rows of desks, reach the door, and leave her life behind. In spite of everything, Sylvia still hasn't achieved Rainbow's perfect indifference. Sitting behind her, he sometimes plays with his pen cap among the thick jungle of Sylvia's curls, as if he dreamed of finding a toucan or some other exotic bird beneath the mat of black hair. Sylvia doesn't like her hair. She'd rather have the adopted Byelorussian Nadia's blond locks or Alba's straight hair. They were two of her best friends at school. The good thing about hair is that at least you don't have to see it all the time. Unlike your breasts. Two years ago, Sylvia secretly prayed they would grow; she now suspects that her prayers were answered, to an extreme. As if wishing for rain brought floods. She doesn't dare take a step without her 38C bra, a garment that she's always found orthopedic. On the street, she puts up with constant lustful stares focused on them, in gym class she listens to Santiso and Ochoa joke about their uncontrollable bouncing, and in every conversation there is a moment where they monopolize all the attention, space, and time. When she chooses a T-shirt or a sweater, she is competing with her tits. If they take center stage, the rest of her is ignored. Sometimes she jokes that it's a drag to always arrive a minute after her boobs. Her friend Mai reproaches her for buying loose shirts instead of form-fitting ones. Would you rather be flat like me, no one can tell the difference between my chest and my back. But Sylvia suspects that Mai pretends to be envious just to make her feel less self-conscious.

Others had sat at that same desk before her, enveloped in the same bittersweetness, that desire to desire. The Instituto Félix Paravicino was founded in 1932, expanded in 1967 with an impersonal concrete extension that insults the beauty of the original brick one, and in 1985 went from being an all-girls school to coed. In the old building, the staircases are wide with intricate braided patterns on the floor and a wooden railing with an addictive curve that thousands of young hands caress each day. In the new building, the stairs are narrow and have a terrazzo floor, like you'd find in a bathroom, and a handrail made of cheap pine with a glossy varnish. The old building has wide French windows, where the glass is set into wood with iron latches that turn with a pleasant friction. In the new building, the windows are aluminum, with handles that creak when you pull them. The hallways of the old building are spacious and light-filled, with art nouveau tiles. In the new one, they're tight, dark halls punctuated by tiny hollow wood doors. When someone goes from one building to the other, it's like an aesthetic slap in the face; if the world's progress were judged solely based on the expansion, we are clearly headed in an appalling direction.

On Fridays Sylvia finds the succession of classes even more unbearable. Doña Pilar, history, first thing. Nicknamed "I Was There" because no matter how distant an event she describes, she seems old enough to have lived through it. They say she managed to suppress her death certificate to make it look like she's still alive. In the family vault, they've given her an ultimatum: they'll hold her spot for a couple months more. And Dionisio, the English teacher—his eyes shine brighter than the students' do when the bell rings, even though he doesn't seem to have anything more exciting awaiting him than the sports section, or maybe one of those Internet sites where chicks get it on with horses. Carmen, the Spanish teacher, has a nervous problem with her jaw and can only speak for ten minutes; the rest of the class is devoted to syntactical exercises. During class she brings her hand to her jawbone as if it were about to detach from her face, and even though she seems to be in constant pain, her students insist it's all due to her voracious oral sex practices. Don Emilio, physics, tirelessly travels down the aisles between the desks like he's trying to break an Olympic record. His students imagine him arriving home proudly: honey, today I did four and a half miles in four classes. Octavio, math, has a bushy moustache and neck paralysis, and leans to the right stiff and unstable, as if an intense wind were blowing from the other direction. He is the only one who sometimes gives them the pleasure of interrupting class to talk about real life, commenting on a TV show or a curious news item, or helping them to calculate what inflation means when applied to their teen interests. Any chance of a second's break from classwork feels like a party. Last year they used to leave the newspaper on his desk to tempt him into commenting on it and squandering class time. Sylvia has the feeling that her teachers have given up any other existence beyond being teachers. When she sees them on the street, they are unrecognizable, like a doctor out of his office. Like once when her mother told her about going to the theater and being greeted in a friendly way by someone in the next row, not realizing until the third act that it was her dentist.

But Sylvia doesn't have a much higher opinion of her classmates. The class is a chorus of yawns. At the breaks, they rush off into groups, as if they were afraid of being alone for even a second. In the cafeteria and the schoolyard, they congregate in front of a magazine or a cell phone screen and exchange short text messages between loud off-key laughs. And then there's the jocks, for whom class is intolerable bench time before continuing the never-ending game. In the schoolyard, six simultaneous soccer games are being disputed, one of them played with a tennis ball in a shrunken version of the game unfit for the nearsighted. Sylvia and her girlfriends can't let their guard down, because someone is always practicing their aim by kicking a ball at their asses or bellies, and they have to pretend it doesn't hurt while the others laugh. Those who haven't managed to infiltrate any of the main cliques wander invisible through the school grounds like chameleons concealing their loneliness. And there are the ones who take their schoolwork seriously, exchanging materials in the library and often staying in the classroom during recess.

Sometimes, when a teacher finishes an explanation and asks if anyone has any questions, Sylvia has a desire to raise her hand and say, yes, could you start all over again from the beginning? I mean from the very beginning, from birth, because I don't understand a thing from any of these almost sixteen years I've been alive.

Summer is over. A couple of weeks ago, on the first Saturday after school started, Sylvia went out with her friend Mai. She met a guy and they got drunk on beer. She had started drinking just three months earlier. They danced together sweatily in the heat of the packed club, and Sylvia ended up with her back against the bathroom wall, her gaze fixed on a broken tile the color of cinnamon, his saliva near, his breath, and his nervous hand that after failing to open her bra forced its fingers into her panties. The bathroom was dirty, the boy was named Pablo, and it was impossible to understand what he was saying into her ear in damp whispers because of the deafening music. It wasn't easy to get away and run through the bathroom, dodging puddles of piss, to get some air on the street. When she looked up, he was watching her, stock-still, from the opposite sidewalk.

He wasn't gonna be the one, either.

Luckily Mai took her home and managed to erase the trail of smoke, beer, and confused desire. Don't obsess. Virginity is all in your head, said Mai. You lose it by thinking, and by jerking off, honey. You're not a virgin, Sy, you've just never been with a man.

Mai lived six blocks from Sylvia, although they'd only started hanging out in high school. She was a year older, but they shared the same corner in the cafeteria, which was like a sort of bunker Mai kept people out of with lashes of her sharp tongue. Only a select few had access to her world. Sylvia had modeled her own taste on Mai's firm criteria. Thanks to Mai, she'd worn her first short skirt and her first black tights and thick-soled boots, although she still hadn't dared to wear T-shirts without shoulder pads because of her scandalous bust. They had bought a silver ring together in a craft market and Mai had placed it on Sylvia's thumb. She started writing her name with a *y* like Mai had suggested and listening to decent music. For Mai music was divided into decent and all the rest. Mai had drilled a small silver hoop through her nose, peed standing up, and had been smoking since she was thirteen.

Last summer Mai had hooked up with a guy she met in Ireland, while she was there studying English. She spent all of July fucking, as she declared to Sylvia in laconic e-mails. "Sy, I'm a new woman. Yes, a new woman!" she wrote one day. When they saw each other again at the airport, Sylvia felt that Mai was indeed a new woman. The pimples on her chin had disappeared, she had streaked her black hair with red, and her new bangs covered one eye, the one she called her ugly eye. She had tattooed a vine with razor-blade leaves around her left ankle and now she showered almost every day. It seemed to Sylvia that Mai's mouth was more fleshy, her lips more voluptuous. But the real transformation was in Mai's laugh. She no longer laughed with her typical twisted contempt. No. Now boundless chortles bubbled up from deep inside her, a true, open laughter that to Sylvia smelled of sex and satisfaction.

It's as if my pussy had finally become a full-fledged part of my body. Not like before, where it was more like a subletter in the apartment downstairs. Then she told her about Mateo. He's from León, so I didn't practice much English.

Sylvia listened to Mai talk about her relationship and she felt something strange. She hadn't yet identified it as desire whistling beside her ear.

In the pigsty, which was what Mai called her room, filled with CDs and clothes bought at street markets, there was no space for romance. But now every Friday she hopped on a bus to spend the weekend with her guy in a big old house in Bierzo. You're going to turn into a red-cheeked village girl, Sylvia would tell her, the joke covering up her fear that they would grow apart.

Dani joined them at the cafeteria table. He was in Mai's class and their friendship had sprung up spontaneously. One day Mai was tirelessly humming a song, backed up by her made-up English lyrics, and Dani touched her on the shoulder and held out a worn sheet of paper. In the margins, he had written the words to the song. Up until then, she hadn't spoken more than two monosyllabic words to Dani, with his thin silver glasses and evasive gaze. The song was by a group from Denver headed by a sinister guy who performed sitting in a wing chair surrounded by his musicians. It was called "Let's Pretend the World Is Made for Us Only" and Dani joined just that world Mai claimed to live in, the one she had built up around herself.

That Friday Mai cuts her last two classes to catch the three-thirty ALSA bus for León. Sylvia sees her walking away from school with her headphones beneath her hair, her butch swagger, and her big black boots that match her exaggerated eye shadow.

At the end of the schoolday, Sylvia bumps into Dani. Actually, she had been waiting to bump into him, after pacing nervously in front of the bulletin board in the lobby. Satur, the porter, reads the sports news and nods his head to each teacher who leaves; to the students, he gives only a considered disdain. At the back of the hallway is an enormous painting of the monk the high school is named after, a reproduction of a portrait by El Greco, with a slogan engraved in stylized letters: "Be neither so arrogant as to presume to be liked by everyone, nor so humble as to give in to the discontent of a few." The students' eyes had run over the sentence a thousand times without really getting it, or even paying it much attention.

Sylvia fakes running into Dani by accident and he looks up from the magazine he is reading, one of those bibles of teen taste.

Hey, Dani, Sunday's my birthday. Oh, yeah? Happy birthday. I'm having a little party at my house . . . Mai's coming. And a few other people. You wanna come? Dani doesn't answer right away. Sunday? Yeah, in the afternoon, on the early side. Around four-thirty, five. Um, I'm not sure if I have plans.

They walk along the street. Cars two rows deep and the sound of honking horns. The northern exit of the school has traffic jams on Fridays. The junction of avenues is presided over by a Corte Inglés department store, triumphant like a modern cathedral. A blond American actress with a suspiciously perfect nose encourages autumnal spending. Dani's jeans fall from his waist, their bottoms frayed at his heels. Sylvia is convinced that her lips are too thin and she tries to make them look bigger with an expression she's practiced in front of the mirror two thousand times, the slightly open mouth.

Will there be potato chips, Coca-Cola, sandwiches? he asks. Yeah, of course, and a clown that blows up dick-shaped balloons. Sylvia adjusts her backpack on her shoulder. Are you gonna come? Dani nods. Sixteen, right? he adds. Yup, sixteen. An old lady.

Sylvia's hair floats up over her shoulders as she walks. She is wearing it down and as she steps off the curb it rises weightlessly and then drifts back to its original position. Dani heads toward the metro. As they say good-bye, she's about to tell him the truth. There is no party. It's all just a stupid tactic to get him alone. But she just answers his ciao with an identical one of her own.

Sylvia walks toward her house. There is a slight breeze that hits her back and pushes a curl toward her cheek. As she always does when she's nervous, Sylvia chews on a lock of hair, walking with it in her mouth.

2

Aurora broke her hip in a completely unspectacular way. Getting out of the bathtub, she lifted her leg over the edge and suddenly heard a small crunch. She felt a slight shiver and her legs turned rubbery. She fell slowly, with time to brush the tips of her fingers along the wall tiles and prepare for the impact. Her elbow hit the fixtures, causing a cold pain, and a second later she was lying down, naked and overcome, on the still-damp bottom of the bathtub. Papá, she wanted to shout, but the sound came out weak. She tried to raise her voice, but the best she could do was emit a repetitive, well-spaced-out lament.

Papá . . . Papá . . . Papá.

The murmur reaches the little back room, where Leandro is reading the newspaper. His first reaction is to think that his wife is calling him for another one of her ridiculous requests, for him to get down a jar of spices on a too-high shelf, to ask him something silly. So he answers with an apathetic what? that gets no reply. He leisurely closes the newspaper and stands up. Later he will be ashamed of the irritation he feels at having to stop reading. It's always the same: he sits down to read and she talks to him over the radio or the ringing telephone. Or the doorbell sounds and she asks, can you get it? when he already has the intercom receiver in his hand. He goes down the hallway until he identifies where the monotonous call is coming from. There is no urgency in Aurora's voice. Perhaps fatalism. When he opens the bathroom door and finds his fallen wife, he thinks that she's sick, dizzy. He looks for blood, vomit, but all he sees is the white of the bathtub and her glazed, naked skin.

Without exchanging a word, in a strange silence, Leandro prepares to pick her up. He takes her old whitish body in his arms. The flaccid flesh, the melted breasts, the inert arms and thighs, the veins that show through in violet lines.

No, don't move me. I think I broke something. Did you slip? No, all of a sudden . . . Where does it hurt? I don't know. Don't worry. In a gesture he can't quite explain, Leandro, who has been married to Aurora for forty-seven years, grabs a nearby towel and covers his wife's body modestly.

Leandro notices the bottom of the bathtub. It's worn down by the water's chafing and repainted in some stretches with white enamel that doesn't match the rest. Leandro is seventy-three years old. His wife, Aurora, is two years younger. The bathtub will soon have served them for forty-one years, and Leandro now recalls that two or three years ago Aurora had asked him to replace it. Look for one you like and if it's not too much of a hassle we'll have it put in, he said to her without much enthusiasm. But why had he stopped in that moment to think about the bathtub?

What am I doing? he asks, lost, unable to react. Call an ambulance. Leandro is overcome by an irrepressible shame. He thinks of the commotion it will cause in the neighborhood, the explanations. Really? Yes, come on, make the call. And get me dressed, bring me my robe.

Leandro calls the emergency number. They connect him with a doctor who recommends that he not move her and asks for information about the fall, the pain symptoms, her age, general health. For a moment, he thinks the only attention they are going to get is over the phone, like any other kind of customer service, and then, terrified, he insists, send someone, please. Don't worry, an ambulance is on the way. The wait is more than twenty minutes. Aurora tries to dress herself, she's managed to stick her arms into the sleeves of her robe, but every movement is painful. Put a nightgown in a bag, and a change of clothes, Aurora asks him.

The EMTs bring noise, activity, which is somehow comforting after the tense stillness of the wait. They take Aurora downstairs on a stretcher to the ambulance. Leandro, disoriented and out of place, is invited to accompany her. His gaze searches through the ring of neighbors for a familiar face. The widow from the first-floor-right apartment is there, the one they locked horns with over her no vote on the installation of a communally funded elevator in the old building. She looks at him with curiosity in her miserable little eyes. He asks Mrs. Carmen, who lives on their floor, to go up and close the door that he left open. On the way to the hospital, beneath the high-pitched blasts of the siren, Aurora takes Leandro's hand. Don't worry, she tells him. The nurse, in his ridiculous phosphorescent jacket, looks at them with a smile. You'll see, it's nothing.

Call Lorenzo from the hospital, keep trying, he usually carries his cell phone. Sylvia will be in class, but don't frighten them, okay, don't frighten them, warns Aurora. Lorenzo is their only child and Sylvia is their granddaughter. Leandro nods, holding Aurora's hand, uncomfortable. I love her, he thinks. I've always loved her. He doesn't say anything because at that moment he's afraid. It is a paralyzing and menacing fear. From inside the windowless box, he senses the speed at which they are moving through the city. What hospital are we going to? asks Aurora. And Leandro thinks, of course, why didn't I think to ask, I should be taking care of these things, but his head is a confused static of a thousand jumbled feelings.

3

Lorenzo listened to the morning arrive, as if on tiptoe. The rhythm of the cars increasing. The garbage truck. The first hums of the elevator. The metal gate of a storefront opening on the street. His daughter's alarm clock, with those three minutes of respite it grants her before ringing again. He listened to her shower quickly. Eat breakfast standing up and leave the house. The police helicopter that crosses over the city at that time of day. Some horn, a car that's having trouble starting. His hands tensely grip the top of the sheets. As he releases them, he notices his fingers are stiff; they've been clenched for hours, grabbing the bedspread like a mountain climber would his rope. The autumn sun has started to beat against the blinds and warm the room.

He runs his hand over his head. He's lost so much hair in the last few months . . . When he was younger, he'd had a receding hairline, but now it was devastating. He took Propecia and bought an anti-hair-loss shampoo, after less conventional methods failed. At first Pilar laughed when she saw him counting the hairs left in the comb or meticulously placing a lock. Then she realized what a big deal it was for him and avoided the subject. Fuck, I'm going bald, Lorenzo said once, and she had tried to ease his mind, don't exaggerate. But he wasn't exaggerating.

His hair was the first of a long list of lost things, thought Lorenzo. His hands gripped the sheets in a protective gesture, trying to hold on. As if losing everything wasn't an abstract fear but rather something that was happening to him right here and now.

What have you done, Lorenzo? What have you done?

It's almost ten a.m. when the phone begins to ring insistently. He had turned off his cell phone and put it away in the bedside table. But the landline kept ringing and ringing. In the living room and in the kitchen. Each with its own ring. The cordless in the living room, more high-pitched, more electrical. He wasn't going to pick it up, he wasn't going to answer. He wasn't home. He heard it ring for a while and then stop. A short pause and it rang again. It was obvious that it was the same tenacious person calling repeatedly. Weren't they ever going to get tired? Lorenzo was afraid.

What have you done, Lorenzo? What the hell have you done?

The night before Lorenzo had killed a man. A man he knew. A man who had been, for several years, his best friend. Seeing him again, in spite of the unusual circumstances of their meeting, in spite of the violence that was unleashed, Lorenzo couldn't help remembering the last time they had seen each other, almost a year ago. Paco had changed, a bit fatter. He still had his hair, with the same pale wave as always, but he seemed slower, heavier in his movements. We've both changed, thought Lorenzo, crouching in the dark. Paco had a placid face. Was he happy? wondered Lorenzo, and the mere suspicion that he was could extenuate what would later happen. No, he couldn't be happy; it would be too unfair.

Lorenzo had fled with Paco's gray eyes still fixed on his. It isn't easy to kill a man you know, to fight with him. It's dirty. It has something of suicide to it: you are killing a part of yourself, everything you shared. It has something of your own death in it. It's not easy to remain motionless in front of a dying body, either, trying to tell if it has stopped breathing or just fainted.

Then go over every mistake, every movement, thinking of the person who will later arrive to figure out what happened. Prick up your ears to make sure no one is listening, prepare your cowardly getaway. Is there such a thing as a brave getaway?

Lorenzo went out the same way he had come in. Over the rear fence, after running his hand along the back of the dog, who had licked his boots. He had left the hose in the garage running, to flood the place. Turning it into a fish tank would help to eliminate prints, make reconstructing the scene more difficult. He raised himself up, looked both ways, and jumped over the fence. He could be seen by a neighbor, recorded by a security camera. He walked to his car, taking his time. Someone could be watching him, jotting down his license plate, remembering his face. It wasn't an exclusive neighborhood, but in that area of Mirasierra, filled with single-family homes and buildings with few apartments, strangers attract attention. It wasn't dawn. It was eleven-fifteen on a Thursday. A normal, workaday hour, not a criminal time of day in the slightest. He had killed a man in the garage, a man he knew. It had all been an accident, a mistake fueled by the grudge Lorenzo held against Paco. Men shouldn't listen to their resentment; it gives them bad advice.

Lorenzo didn't consider his crime something cold, something calculated. It wasn't what he intended to do. But when he was taken by surprise by the car's headlights, when he raised the garage door and hid behind the barbecue grill wrapped in its green cover, he already knew what was going to happen. He didn't hesitate.

Lorenzo had brought a machete. When he bought it, just in case, he was thinking more about the dog than about Paco. Even though he knew it was a friendly dog, who barked at first but then was thrilled to have visitors. But that dog could have since died and been replaced by a different one, a really violent one. So the dog had justified the machete. But when Lorenzo extended his hand and grabbed the handle at the bottom of the sports bag, he knew the machete had always been meant for Paco. He remembered being in the mountaineering store, feeling the sharpened blade. What had he been thinking of then?

Afterward, Lorenzo followed his established plan. After changing in his car, he sprinkled gasoline over his clothes and the boots two sizes too big. He left them burning in the dumpster at an out-of-the-way construction site, but anyone could have seen the flames, even though it was on the other side of the city, and made a connection between the man who started the fire and the murder. They would describe Lorenzo as a stocky man in his forties, bald, yes, they'd say bald, who drives an old red car, and if they were someone who knew about makes, they could even specify it, an Opel Astra. The time that it would take for them to put the evidence together is the time that Lorenzo took cover between the sheets, with an aching forearm from the night before. He still hadn't seen the intense bruises that his friend Paco's fingers had left on his forearms, a sign of the struggle. When he sees the oval-shaped marks as big as coins, he'll recognize the physical stamp a man leaves as he's trying to cling to the life slipping away from him. The telephone rings again. Like a threat hanging in the air.

4

Ariel is the kind of person who never could've imagined himself crying in an airport. As moving as he finds other people's tears in those bastions of farewells and reunions, he had been convinced that embarrassment would keep him from ever shedding them himself. Now he's glad that he's wearing sunglasses, since his eyes are flooded.

The head of security for the soccer club, Ormazábal, told him to ask for Ángel Rubio, the airport commissioner. The officer at passport control heard his boss's name spoken and looked up. He recognized Ariel behind his sunglasses and let him pass with a complicit smile. So Ariel was able to accompany his brother to the boarding gate. At that time of night, on a Saturday, the airport was quiet. At check-in, he had been struck by the sight of his brother's suitcase, metal, enormous, covered with stickers, dragged along by the conveyer belt. The suitcase, the same suitcase that had arrived with them a month and a half earlier. It was leaving. And Ariel was being left behind in this city he still hasn't conquered, in an enormous house where he would only be greeted by the echo of his older brother Charlie.

Charlie was the noise and the euphoria, the ruckus, the decisions, the temperament, the voice. In Buenos Aires, when the murmuring about some Spanish team's interest in him went from rumor to reality, Ariel didn't hesitate for a second. You'll come with me, Charlie. His brother was evasive. I've got my life here. My wife, two kids, I'm not a guardian, a babysitter, a chaperone. He never said yes, but during the negotiations there was talk of plane tickets for both of them, three trips for two per season, the house where they would live, the day they would arrive, their best interests.

At the Ezeiza airport, when Charlie's two children hugged him good-bye, Ariel felt selfish. He needed his brother to go with him, to have him close, someone who could solve everyday matters. But he also knew he was doing Charlie a favor. He was suffocating in Buenos Aires, work and family life were crushing him, as he used to say. Although he heard him comforting the boys, don't worry, it's Uncle Ariel who's leaving, I'll be back real soon, he knew that Charlie was glad to escape, that he longed for Madrid. He was dragging his older brother along because he knew that he was enjoying the adventure. Ariel's soccer career had always been an experience Charlie lived vicariously, even more so since his brother had become a professional player.

They left their parents behind, he with his job as a municipal engineer and she acting tough, although she quit the act the day they left and warned, I'm not going to the airport, I've got to protect this heart. Their father did come, remaining on the other side of security, holding tight to his two grandsons' chests and with Charlie's wife at his back. She was crying. She might be losing a husband, thought Ariel then. But their old man wasn't crying. He was witnessing, with a mix of pride and tension, his son Ariel leap into adult life.

They knew other players who left Argentina to try their luck in Europe traveled with an entourage. Family members, nannies, and friends became professionals in the business of creating an intimate circle. Fair-weather friends, as "Dragon" Colosio would say, the kind who disappear when a storm blows in. Club and cabaret friends who manage to make closing hour less abysmal. One had to protect oneself from the void, from the unknown. When Ariel suggested he come to Madrid, his father had answered him, don't be like those morons who let the people around them burn up their cash and their life. Take this chance to get to know another country and face up to it like you should, for yourself. When he found out Charlie was going with Ariel, he just shrugged his shoulders.

With Charlie by his side, Ariel could close his eyes on the plane and sleep for most of the flight, his brother restlessly nearby, watching all the movies at once on the channels of his screen, asking for another beer when he still had half of one left, speaking loudly, flirting with the flight attendant, So are all the chicks in Spain as pretty as you? He radiated the confidence of an older brother, the same confidence he'd had when he had taken four-year-old Ariel by the hand and walked him to the Admiral Curiel Preschool on the first day. When they stepped onto the run-down playground, Charlie said, if anyone touches you or gives you any shit, get their name and tell me later. Don't you get into it with anyone, okay?

Ariel felt like that same kid on the first day of school when he landed at Barajas Airport on a soupy summer day in July and found himself cornered by a troupe of photographers and television cameras shooting questions at him about his expectations, his favorite position to play, what he knew about Spanish fans, and the supposed controversy surrounding his jersey, that Dani Vilar didn't want to give him the number seven. Charlie guided him toward the exit with a lopsided smile, repeating, there'll be plenty of chances for questions, gentlemen, plenty of chances. Then he met up with the club's representative, the first time he had seen Ormazábal, and said authoritatively, where the hell is the car? He was the same brother who, at ten years old, had convinced Ariel on his fifth birthday that he would always be twice his age, just as he was then. When you're ten, I'll be twenty, and when you're fifty, I'll be a hundred. And even when math denied that forced logic, Ariel had never doubted his brother was always twice what he was, in everything.

But now Charlie was leaving. That's why Ariel hadn't taken off his sunglasses, even in the VIP room where they waited for boarding to start. He didn't want anyone bothering him for an autograph, but he also wasn't sure he'd be able to hold back his tears, even though his brother was downplaying the separation. It's time for me to be getting back. It's a bit sooner than I had thought, sure, but these things happen.

Charlie reviewed with Ariel all the things that were organized and in order. The house rented by the club, on the outskirts of town, in an exclusive housing development where there were retired politicians, successful entrepreneurs, a couple of television stars, a place where a soccer player didn't turn anyone's head. Emilia and Luciano were the couple who took care of the house. He did the gardening and repaired anything that needed fixing; she cleaned and cooked. They both disappeared at three in the afternoon. When Ariel apologized one morning for the living room table filled with empty beer bottles, ashes, and butts left by Charlie, Emilia told him not to worry. These past two years we had a British executive and, honestly, I've never met anyone so disgusting. Suffice to say that Luciano had to repaint the walls and even change the toilet bowl lids. And this guy was the head of a multinational company that makes cleaning products. But then, the shoemaker's children often run barefoot.

Emilia, Charlie told him, will treat you like a son. You've already seen how she cooks. The car issue was solved twelve hours after their arrival in Madrid. The club had offers from all the manufacturers, and Charlie chose a platinum Porsche Carrera after visiting the dealership with the publicity manager's assistant. Charlie's response to Ariel's hesitations was categorical: it's a bold car, to make it clear to everyone that you've come to be seen. On this team, you have to earn your spot even in the stadium parking lot. And if you get tired of it, you'll just switch, the brands are all dying to have soccer players drive their cars. At the airport, Charlie warns him, now don't go changing your car for a SUV, I know how you can be. Only moms drive that kind of car here, to feel more protected in their little tanks.

In the club, there were no more mysteries to be revealed. Ariel knows the staffers who are useful to him. The president was a man who had earned his stripes in the construction business, but he now presided over a true empire of private protection, with more than a hundred thousand employees: a manufacturer of armored cars, trucks for transporting money, alarms, reinforced steel doors. He wasn't interested in soccer unless he was getting insulted in the stands; then he was irascible, unpredictable, and childish in his reactions. He was unappealing, slightly hunchbacked, with graying hair; the players called him "the mother from *Psycho*." In the first training sessions, he had come down to the field to greet the players, and when he shook the hand of the captain, Amílcar, a veteran Brazilian player who had become a nationalized Spaniard, the president said, are you still here? I thought you'd retired by now. Even though he was serious, everyone laughed at the joke. He compared his business success with game philosophy. I want my team to have the best defense in the league, no one should steal the ball from us. During Ariel's official presentation, before the ridiculous tradition of showing him to the television cameras kicking around the ball alone on the field in his jersey, the president spoke to the journalists. I'm still determined to sign defenders, to have a team as safe as a fort, and they told me the Argentinians are good kickers and they work their tails off on the field. Ariel found himself forced to laugh and joke around with the journalists. They always told me that the best defense is a good offense, without knowing for sure if the club owner was aware that he'd just signed a left winger.

It was the sports director who was really in charge, a former player for the team, a center back whose mantelpiece, they said, boasted several tibias, quite a few fibulas, and even the femur of some opponents hunted on the playing field. His career in the team's offices was based on opposite tactics: he was a devious and inscrutable negotiator. They still called him by his nickname as a player, Pujalte, and when Ariel asked what his real name was, he answered, forget about it, everybody calls me Pujalte, it's simpler.

The coach, on the other hand, had never been a great player. He had made a name for himself on a modest team that had been promoted to the Second Division. He lowered his head almost imperceptibly around Pujalte, who spoke to him with an almost physical authority, challenging him with his experienced past as a player. His name was José Luis Requero and he practiced laboratory soccer, preferring the chalkboard to the grass. His laptop was filled with statistics, and he always had a delicate, shy young man nearby, some relative of the president, who spent his time recording and editing games in order to correct the team's errors or prepare for confrontations with rivals. Requero claimed to use group psychology. He gave long tactical talks based on jottings from the notebook he always carried with him, and when some journalist suggested he was starting to be known as "the professor," he smiled with open pleasure. It was his second season with the club, after a discreet year without titles. The first day of training, he introduced them to his associates, including a physical trainer with two assistants who looked almost exactly like him; the masseurs; the head equipment man with his small troupe; and the goalkeeper coach, a former goalie born in Eibar with pre-Neanderthal features. Then he gave every staff member a copy of the book *Shared Success*, written by two young American entrepreneurs, which opened with a maxim: "When you celebrate a triumph, don't forget that you would have never achieved anything without the help of those around you." Just a few days into the preseason, the book was already the object of widespread mockery in the locker room, particularly because of a sentence pulled from page twenty-six that they claimed was charged with hidden homosexual content: "a man and another man by his side are much more than two men." Yeah, sure, two big faggots, summed up the fullback Luis Lastra to the delight of his audience.

Ariel had worked with different coaches since he had been signed, at seventeen, to San Lorenzo. Up until that point, he had been a player with just one teacher, Sinbad Colosio, who ran a soccer school near the old Gasómetro where hundreds of players had trained for a small team that played in the Fifth Division. He had invited Ariel to join them at twelve years old, after seeing him play in a city championship. He always said to Charlie, the only way to get anything out of your brother's left leg is to keep him away from the professional teams for a while. Save him from this country's sick obsession with finding a new Maradona. Ariel had him as technical director for five years, and it was with him that he became a soccer player. In Buenos Aires you have to get to the big leagues in a submarine, because here the expectations kill you as fast as a dagger, Ariel heard him say on one occasion.

Sinbad Colosio had been a second father to Ariel. His own father's lack of interest in soccer, which he labeled our "home-grown opiate" or "national disgrace" depending on the degree of irritation its ubiquitous presence provoked in him, had handed over young Ariel to the old coach. Colosio was a sad-looking man in a worn sweatsuit, with graying hair, who spoke slowly as he took you by the shoulder. Ariel's father didn't want to repeat with his younger son the mistakes he felt he had made with Charlie. His determination to keep him out of sports and off the streets had only meant his older son ended up an unskilled worker in the business of some friends who owed him favors. Charlie married young and at twenty-two already had two kids. During Charlie's teenage years, their relationship was more like that of two rabid dogs than father and son, so when Ariel's turn came, his father opted for calm and relaxed, which allowed Ariel to devote most of his time and energy to soccer and not worry too much about his grades.

They called Colosio "Dragon." The nickname had stuck from his days as a player. Now sometimes they called him Sleeping Dragon, because he seemed to have mellowed, that is until he exploded with a fierce lash like the irascible dragon he must have been back when, they said, just the sound of his breath made the forwards lose the ball. He came to pick up Ariel in

Floresta three times a week, in his white 1980 Torino. By then he had already picked up Macero and Alameda, who lived in Quilmes and Villa Esmeralda, at the bus stop. The three boys sat in the backseat, Ariel gave them his extra trading cards from the championship collection, and they waited for Dragon to tire of his own silence and offer them some soccer anecdote. About soccer from the fifties and sixties, when the young players had to shine the veterans' shoes, when the balls were sewn, when the only drugs in the locker room were a thermos of strong black coffee and the first amphetamines, when the goalie called you "sir" when asking for the ball, when there was no television and you had to store the crackerjack plays in your own memory and recount them like Fioravanti, when making a living playing soccer was a luxury for only the best. He spoke without nostalgia, without mythologizing the past, and always ended by grumbling, what crappy years, kids, what crappy years.

Dragon Colosio had taught him to play angry, to not go onto the field looking to make friends, to curse at the fullbacks, to practice for fifteen minutes at the end of each game because if you're not thinking about the next one you're not a soccer player, to step on the lime sideline when you forget that you play left wing, to not cry over losses because crying is for tangos. And when Ariel wanted to sign with a pro club at fifteen and Charlie insisted he accept, Colosio told him something that perhaps today, in the Madrid airport, was still valid: Ariel, your brother is your brother and you are you. Then Ariel stayed, as much as Charlie tried to convince him, Dragon is a loser and you can't let a loser run your career. Now he was alone again and thinking, Charlie is Charlie and I'm me. But who am I?

Your routine will keep you busy, Charlie was saying to him, you won't have time to be lonely. Charlie is the last one to board, almost defiant toward the airline employees. He hugs Ariel and whispers into his ear, in a very soft voice, finally referring to the reason for his hasty departure. I fucked up, Ariel, that's why I don't deserve to stay by your side. I don't want to tarnish you. Now you have to fly solo. I hope you'll make us proud. Deal? Deal.

He squeezes Ariel's back hard, pulling him toward him. Don't cry, you dope, someone who earns two and half million dollars a year can't cry. And he disappears into the breezeway that leads to the plane.

Ariel retraces his steps until he gets to the car parked in front of the terminal. He goes back to the hotel where the team is spending the night before the next day's game. Pujalte had given him permission to leave the pregame preparation and take his brother to the airport; of course, family comes first.

When he enters the hotel, he sees some of his teammates chatting in small groups before going up to their rooms. Amílcar waves to him. He is the team's most veteran player. Beside him is Poggio, the reserve goalie who has been warming the bench for five years straight, which makes me the highest-paid ass in the world after Jennifer Lopez, he declares. There's also Luis Lastra, a guy from Santander who joined the team the previous season and has a contagious laugh with which he loudly celebrates his own jokes. Standing, resting an immaculate sneaker on a chair, is young Jorge Blai, who readjusts his straight bangs again and again. At the bar, the Ghanaian Matuoko, a compact human refrigerator, surreptitiously drinks a gin and tonic, moving it away from him after every sip as if he wants to make believe the drink isn't his. There are two or three more players nearby, the group of Brazilians, and the goalie coach who eats olives in bunches and shoots the pits into a distant trash can like a machine gun.

Ariel returns their greetings, but doesn't join the group. He walks toward the elevators and someone speaks to him by the reception desk. Did your brother leave already? I would have liked to say good-bye. Ariel turns. He recognizes the sweaty face beneath the red curls and the thick black plastic-framed glasses. He's a journalist. His name is Raúl, but everybody calls him Husky because he sounds as if he has barbed branches in place of his vocal cords. A regular at practice and press conferences, in his newspaper columns he always wrote favorably about Ariel. They have had dealings on a few different occasions, but Ariel avoids creating any fake intimacy, doesn't trust journalists. They write about fishing, Dragon used to say about them, when the only fish they've ever seen in their life is the one served to them in restaurants. Husky has jotted down his phone number on a hotel business card and holds it out with two fingers. Call me if you need anything.

Ariel shoots him an appreciative expression. In the elevator mirror, he will check if his eyes are red, if they give away that he's been crying. Before he heads off, he hears the journalist saying to him, with his raspy, weak voice, good luck tomorrow.

5

Sylvia listens to her father go out; he had plans with some friends to go to the soccer stadium. She saw him wrap up a cured pork loin sandwich in tinfoil and take his team scarf off the coatrack in the entryway. Like a kid, she thought. They had eaten in the hospital cafeteria earlier, with her grandfather. Leandro seemed tired after two nights without sleep. They had managed to convince him to let Aunt Esther spend that night in Grandma's room instead. There couldn't possibly be two more different women, in Sylvia's opinion. Grandma Aurora is nimble, with light eyes, gentle, often putting her hand over her mouth, as if she were secretly laughing or yawning or keeping something to herself. Aunt Esther is conventional, expansive. She speaks loudly and when she laughs she shows her pink gums, larger than the enormous teeth that make her mouth look like a front-end loader. She's married and has five children and seven grandchildren, whose photos she proudly displays when someone shows any interest, and even when they don't. Sylvia barely sees her cousins, but Aunt Esther shows her their pictures every time they see each other, as if displaying a catalog of products for sale. She remembers one of them well, Miguel; he's her same age. He broke one of Sylvia's baby teeth years ago with a racquet slam. Apparently as a sign of love.

The kitchen clock marks four-thirty. Her father left the radio on, and it floods the late Sunday afternoon with the pregame report, and ads for liquor and cigarettes. Sylvia trembles nervously. She puts on music in her room and turns up the volume. Her right foot swings as if it had its own motor. She sings over the music and tries not to think. Cold chills desire; we light the fire. She'd rather not hear the ring of the intercom that sounds with a short pulse, but she does hear it. She slowly goes toward the door to let Dani in.

Over the course of the weekend, Sylvia had been tempted several times to cancel. That very morning, she wrote a text message on her cell phone in the hospital hallway—"There's no birthday party after all, we'll talk later"—but she hadn't sent it to Dani. Ever since she had invited him to her fake party, she felt ridiculous. The same childish, almost hysterical, nervousness she had felt last summer when she hung around the beachfront bar or played the video game machine to suss out whether one of the waiters was into her or if, on the other hand, his being twenty-something was an insurmountable gap. The gap between what one desires and what one can get, between what one is and what one wants to be. Just like when she invited Dani to her birthday party even though there was no birthday party.

That Friday she had walked home peeling apart the cardboard corner of her school folder. She arrived convinced she should call him to cancel the invitation she had made just minutes before. But she found a note from her father next to some toast crumbs. Grandma Aurora was in the hospital. She went there right away and so avoided the temptation of regret.

Don't be frightened, was the first thing her grandmother told her. In two hours, they were going to put in a corrective prosthesis, a plastic solution to the aging of her bones, but she seemed calm and in good spirits. Some women put in plastic lips or breasts, well, I'm getting a hip.

It's routine, the operation is just routine, repeated her grandfather. Right, Lorenzo? Isn't that what the doctor told us? But

Sylvia's father didn't answer; he was pacing around the room, as if in a cage. Lorenzo was sweating and complained about the heat. I found out late this morning, because I've been on job interviews and had my cell phone turned off, he justified.

The doctor was tall and had a face lined with red veins. He spoke to himself, as if he were going over his to-do list instead of discussing her condition with the family. Sylvia noticed a reddish stain on his white coat, but it wasn't blood; it looked more like chorizo. After the operation, when they brought her back up to the room, Grandma looked weak as a wounded bird. Grandpa insisted that Sylvia and Lorenzo leave, go home. She's still under the anesthesia, there's no point in you being here, he told them.

Sylvia and her father went home. She made some dinner. Lorenzo combed through the news, channel after channel. Call your mother and tell her about it, he said to Sylvia. She called her later, on her cell. She could hear the sound of conversations in the background; she was in a restaurant. Pilar asked for the number of the hospital room and then they talked about spending a weekend together soon. They said good-bye affectionately. Are you okay? her mother asked her. Sylvia said she was.

Her mother had left her father five months earlier. Sylvia never imagined that would happen. For her, her parents were a unit, two pieces fitted forever. When it all fell apart, she understood that they had shared the remnants, just the remnants, of a marriage, that they only spoke about insignificant day-to-day stuff, that they were barely intimate even though they shared a home. Pilar made the decision one day in March. It was raining in gusts and she confided in her daughter before telling her husband. I'm going to leave your father, Sylvia. They hugged and talked for a long time. Love fades without you even realizing it's happening, Pilar told her. She explained that she had been able to tolerate the slow desolation, she had gotten used to surviving among the ruins of what was once love, but it became an unbearable weight the day she discovered passion again, for another person. Life becomes unlivable and the lie starts to hurt. I'm forty-two years old, don't you think I deserve another chance?

Sylvia didn't have to struggle to understand her mother, in spite of the unexpectedness of the situation. But instead of conveying that to her mother, without really knowing why, the first thing she said was, poor Papá. Pilar started crying, very slowly, with her lips clenched. She had fallen in love with the head of her office in Madrid, Santiago. She said his name the way you only say the name of someone you love. Her mother worked in a company devoted to the planning of trade fairs and cultural and social events. In the last couple of months, Pilar's traveling and after-hours work obligations had increased; now Sylvia understood why. Pilar and Santiago had been having a prudent affair before deciding to take a chance on the new relationship. Then he had been offered a job running the branch office in his city, Saragossa. Long before that happened, your father and I only shared the comfortable habit of living together, of raising a daughter together, of getting together with friends, and that's about it; we let time slip away, she explained. Mothers don't leave fathers and much less daughters, thought Sylvia. On this occasion, traumatic but illuminating, Sylvia looked at her mother as a woman, not just a mother, that sort of sentimental household appliance, and she told her, you have to be happy.

Sylvia's father had latched on to the television, to music, to Sunday soccer games, to his work, to balancing the accounts, to getting back in touch with some half-forgotten friend, to his daughter, anything to avoid letting his defeat show. Sylvia observed him. She tried to spend more time at home, to cook for him when she noticed he had no energy for anything, to go with him on Sunday afternoons to her grandparents' house. He always said "your mother" and never "Pilar." Little by little, the photos and mementos disappeared, the details accumulated over twenty years of marriage. In two quick visits, she had finished taking her clothes and her work stuff, which filled the most frequently used shelves of the small office. Her bathroom things and other various belongings faded like afternoon light. In front of Sylvia, her parents hadn't argued or displayed any more awkwardness than a thick silence that covered those scenes of separation. Mai always told Sylvia that the worst period of her life was her parents' divorce, when a fucking psychologist told them that for her sake, for their daughter's good, and I was seven years old, instead of separating cleanly they should do it bit by bit: they spent eight months insulting and beating each other up, so in order to save me the trauma of the separation I had to put up with the horror of their forced coexistence.

She met her mother's new love in an icy scene at a restaurant in Madrid. Later Sylvia was embarrassed about her stingy, ungenerous behavior. She saw him again when she traveled to Saragossa to help her mother settle into another city, another apartment, another life. But Sylvia maintained an unshakable loyalty to her father. He needs me more, she would say.

One day, suddenly, the objects in the kitchen were organized differently and the various elements of the house seemed to be rearranged. The remote control for the television slept on the sofa, and no one put it back on the little side table. The cordless phone never awoke on its charger, the washing machine didn't sound with the same noise as its drum turned, the fruit bowl on the counter wasn't always full. Her mother's shadow hadn't completely disappeared, but her hand was no longer felt in every detail of the house.

Sylvia spoke with Mai on Saturday afternoon. She was with her boyfriend, far away. The conversation was short. Sylvia didn't say anything about inviting Dani to her fake birthday party. She locked herself in her room to listen to music and her father asked if she was going out that night. I'm going to take a walk, he announced. Sylvia imagined him as one of those middle-aged men she sometimes sees in a club or a bar who seem to be flying low, like sad predators, out for the night without a partner, exposed. In bed Sylvia strokes herself with hands she imagines are someone else's. Mai's advice had been that she should sit on her hand for a good long time. Until it goes numb—then it seems like they're someone else's fingers and it feels better when you touch yourself. She had fallen asleep having decided to cancel her plans for the following day, feeling guilty and ridiculous.

Dani brings two wrapped packages, which he hands to Sylvia as they exchange a kiss on the cheek. Am I the first one here?

Didn't I tell you? feigned Sylvia. In the end I canceled the party because Mai was going to León and it wasn't a good day for people. No shit, should I leave? he asks, somewhat uncomfortable. No, no, how stupid of me. Dani hesitates before entering, how embarrassing, me here by myself. Well, we can celebrate it just you and me. It's not like we need a lot of people to have a party, right?

Sylvia leads him to her room where the music is still playing. She closes the door behind her. My father went to the soccer game. Sylvia opens the smaller package. It is a Pulp CD, with an almost plastic blonde on the cover, naked and upside down on velvet as red as her painted lips. A reduced price sticker. She can't manage to open the plastic wrapping, absorbed in her effort as she notices her face reddening. Someone calculated that on average each person wastes two weeks of their life just getting the fucking plastic off CDs, says Dani. While he talks, he unwraps the second present, a bottle of Cuervo tequila. I thought there would be more of us, but now we're going to have to drink it ourselves, he says.

Sylvia gets two small glasses and sits on the bed. Dani looks over the walls of her room while the new CD plays and they nod their heads to the beat. Sylvia reviews the decorations in her room in search of inexcusable mistakes, something she should be embarrassed about. There are photos of her with Mai, some posters, and it's pretty messy. They each drink the first shot in one gulp and then toast with the second one. Sylvia opens a bag of potato chips and puts some pistachios in a bowl. They start unshelling them and every once in a while one of them comments on the music. "Why do we have to half-kill ourselves just to prove we're alive?" It's good, right? Yeah. The shots burn in Sylvia's throat and then lodge themselves in her stomach like a bubble of fire.

Can I mix it with Coca-Cola or is that a sin? No, it's a good idea, says Dani. And then his eyes land on the photo of a singer on her wall. You think that guy is good-looking? Depends on who you compare him to. Yeah, of course, if you compare him to Lelo, says Dani, referring to Don Emilio, the physics teacher. Did you have him as a teacher, too? As a teacher is overstating it. He spent a semester taking hikes around our desks while we stuck our pens out on the edge so his lab coat would get ink lines all over it. The guy was a real mess.

Later he translates for Sylvia while the singer drags out each syllable: "It's the eye of the storm. This is what men in stained raincoats pay for but in here it is pure." Fuck, it's strange, right? says Sylvia. And then she feels ridiculous about her comment. She moves a step forward and Dani brings a hand to the nape of her neck, beneath her curls. Sylvia feels like he takes forever to bring his mouth close to hers and kiss her delicately. The first thing she notices is the thin frames of Dani's glasses brushing her cheek. His mouth tastes of tequila and when their lips separate they both take another drink.

They lose all sense of time, but they spend forty-five minutes kissing, caressing each other's backs, drawing themselves toward each other. When Dani brings his hand to her ass, on top of her pants, and then scrabbles under the waist to plunge onto her bare skin, Sylvia sucks in her stomach because she feels fat and then she leans against the wall. She unbuttons his plaid shirt slowly and strokes the line of his ribs with the tip of her finger. I'm really drunk, she announces, and his only response is to fill up their glasses. They kiss with their mouths flooded with tequila. It spills down their chins and they laugh. He unbuttons her pants, she feels Dani's excitement when she places her hand over his pants. She stops him from releasing the clasp of her bra. She fears that her breasts will spill everywhere, taking over. Aren't you going to let me take off your clothes? asks Dani. No, it's my birthday, says Sylvia.

She is aware that her fear will ruin the moment. It will come to nothing and she shivers. She's going to waste it all. She seizes the initiative as her only means of escape. She pulls down

Dani's pants. They are standing close to each other. She pushes his hands away when he brings them to her breasts. She feels him beneath his underwear and for a second she avoids thinking that this is the first time in her entire life that she's touched a dick. She lowers his waistband so he's naked, but she doesn't look down. They continue locked in a kiss that seems to fill the moment, a kiss they focus on so as not to notice all the rest. Sylvia runs her fingertips over his naked body. On the table, she reaches for the wrapping paper that had covered the bottle and, amused, she wraps Dani's penis in it. This is another present, isn't it? Dani laughs. She starts to jerk him off with her hand underneath the gift wrap. Will this distract him or will he know it's just me running away, a display of panic?

Dani comes with a spasm and the wrapping paper dampens and two drops slide to the floor. Sylvia stops and the moment is filled with a cold stiffness. They separate cautiously after a kiss in which she gives more of herself than he does. Their salivas, suddenly, start to taste different. Sylvia lets the wrapping paper fall into the metal wastebasket. Dani pulls up his pants.

They drink a couple of shots without knowing what to say. The sexual nature of the moment appears to have passed. Sylvia feels small, even though she smiles. She doesn't want Dani to come near her or touch her, she would understand if he just left right then. I wrapped his dick in gift paper and jerked him off, she says to herself, as if she needed to enunciate her actions in order to realize the embarrassing spectacle she staged. If the floor sunk into the apartment downstairs, it would be doing her a favor.

The conversation dies out, even though she changes the music and goes to sit on the bed. He makes himself comfortable, straddling Sylvia's swivel chair. They avoid looking at each other.

Maybe I should go, huh? says Dani once enough time has passed. Sylvia checks her alarm clock and she brings it to her eyes as if she were nearsighted. My father's probably coming back pretty soon. They say good-bye at the door to the apartment, with a kiss on each cheek, avoiding their lips, irritated by the friction of their exchange. Sylvia sees him go down the stairs without waiting for the elevator. She lies down on her bed, grabbing a cushion, her back against the wall. She feels like crying or screaming, but all she does is write a text message on her phone to Mai asking what time her bus gets into South Station. "11:45," she answers.

Sylvia needs to talk to her, tell her everything, find out if what she did was the lowest expression of stupid immaturity or if there is any way to salvage it. She needs to tell her how suddenly she knew she didn't want to make love to Dani, that she felt like she couldn't take off her clothes for him. She suspects that if he had insisted or if he had taken control of the situation she wouldn't have been able to refuse him. Her fear of looking ridiculous would have won out over her modesty. She wanted to laugh with Mai, for her to say it had been a "pathetic sexy" moment, as she sometimes says, for her to repeat her motto of how the pitiful and the glorious are only separated by a fraction of an inch. She wants to hear Mai downplay what happened with her usual bluntness, like when she shouts, wipe those cobwebs off your pussy! Or, stop being so chickenshit, what do you think, that dicks are like those drills they use to bore out metro tunnels? She wants to share with Mai her fear that Dani will talk about it at school or that from now on he'll think they're a couple or the opposite, that they'll never speak again. She's confused and she needs her friend's advice.

But Mai gets off the bus with a tired expression. The fucking shoot-'em-up movies didn't let me get a wink of sleep, she says. She hadn't slept the previous nights, either. She tells Sylvia that she spent the four-hour ride sending messages to her boyfriend's cell phone because she missed him from the moment she got on the bus. Sylvia decides not to take the metro with her and watches her descend the stairs. Mai turns before disappearing. Happy birthday, girl, I owe you a present, she says.

Sylvia, alone on the street, walks quickly to release her rage. Mai's happiness is a betrayal, her tiredness a personal affront. She steps down onto the street to avoid any unpleasant encounters on the sidewalk, some pimp or pervert pushing her into a doorway. It is Sunday night and the city empties as she walks. People gather in their homes to shield themselves from the end of the weekend. The ground is dry and the streetlights barely reverberate on the asphalt. The lace on one of her black-rubber-soled boots has come untied, but Sylvia doesn't want to stop to retie it. She takes aggressive strides, as if kicking the air. She is oblivious to the fact that, crossing the street she now walks along, she will be hit by an oncoming car. And that while she is feeling the pain of just having turned sixteen, she will soon be feeling a different pain, in some ways a more accessible one: that of her right leg breaking in three places.

6

Leandro walks at that vague hour between day and night, on Sunday, when some are returning from Mass or the theater, when couples are headed home, when the streetlights are beginning to warm up and slowly gain intensity, when young people share the last kisses of the weekend, kisses that taste of farewell, tedium, or passion. Relatives are leaving hospitals and old folks' homes, and the droning results of a soccer lottery, which no one's won, are heard from distant car radios or some apartment with its windows open. Leandro continues along a residential street, among yellowing trees, a street with barely any traffic, with no people except some neighbor being walked by his dog. In a few hours, it will be Monday, and an early gray mist spreads.

Leandro looks for number forty, but from the odd side of the street, to keep a certain distance. The houses are low, with small backyards and narrow entrances. There are apartment buildings with four or five stories that defy the old buildings with their new bricks, their aluminum terraces, and their uniform ugliness. Number forty is a two-story chalet, the high fence obscuring everything but the tops of the trees and the walls of the upper floor, cream-colored but so worn they look gray. The roof is made of slate slabs and the façade is the victim of a renovation that robbed the chalet of what little charm it had. All the blinds are lowered. Beside the plaque with the house number is a light illuminating the doorbell.

Leandro passes without stopping.

He gets a few feet away and waits on the other side of the street. He doesn't dare look at the chalet for too long, as if it were human and he wants to avoid locking eyes. He lowers his gaze. He looks up again. There is nothing threatening. Why is he being so careful? No one ever suspects anything from a seventy-three-year-old man. Everyone knows that his steps lead nowhere.

He chooses not to prolong his prowling. He decides to cross the street and walk up to the door. He feels a coldness that sets him on edge, that tempts him to abandon his pursuit. He makes sure no one is watching him from the sidewalk or some nearby window, waits for a car to quickly pass, and hides his face so he can't be recognized. He rings the bell and the only response he hears is a lengthy electrical buzzing that invites him to push the fence door open. There is a path through the grass of flat stones that ends at a small porch and a white door beneath a yellow fluorescent light. The walk is barely fifteen paces, but it leaves Leandro exhausted.

The two previous nights, he had slept intermittently. The extra bed he set up in the hospital room with cushions from the armchair is hard, short, and uncomfortable. It gives him a sharp pain in the kidneys. At midnight a nurse comes in to change Aurora's catheter and the bustle of cleaning starts before seven. Leandro is worn out from the last few days. The emergency admittance on Friday, Aurora's operation, the anguish of getting her back from the operating room asleep and fragile. The visits the next day, Aurora's draining sister with her senseless cheerfulness, and two pairs of friends who had heard about the accident, including Manolo Almendros and his wife, who spent Saturday afternoon in the hospital. Leandro had a lively conversation with him, but his friend's energy was more than he could match. He walked through the hall with such intensity that he could have left grooves in the terrazzo. Almendros thinks aloud, he is witty, tireless. Ever since he retired from his job as a pharmaceutical sales representative, he reads huge tomes of philosophical theory that he later feels obliged to share with Leandro and with the world. He writes letters to the newspapers and once in a while he tracks down old college classmates.

Manolo, did you come to see my wife or to give me a lecture? said Leandro in an attempt to shut him up.

Yet he could see how Aurora was cheered up by the visits. She got some of the color back in her face, and although she didn't take part in the conversations, she looked around her gratefully. Leandro went by the house to change his clothes and let Luis, his Saturday morning piano student, know that they'd have to postpone class. His wife had had a mishap. The walk through the hospital floor, the snippets of other patients' and relatives' conversations, curiosity about other people's pain, the bustling of the medical staff, that was how he whiled away the day.

On Sunday he ate lunch with his son, Lorenzo, and his granddaughter, Sylvia. Leandro envied the caress of the girl's hands over Aurora's face, running over her forehead and cheeks. Those spotless hands, with barely any signs of wear, with everything ahead of them. It was Sylvia's birthday and she toasted during the meal with her can of Coca-Cola. Leandro remembered her birth, the joy at the arrival of a baby, Aurora's willingness to take care of the girl often. The dizzying speed at which time had passed, sixteen years already. The fruitless piano lessons he had given her, which were ended in silent agreement. She inherited her father's bad ear, not much musical talent, Leandro said to himself. On the other hand, she showed her mother's sensitivity in everything else. Through all those years, they watched Lorenzo's marriage to Pilar wither, once so full of life and complicity. Leandro witnessed his son's loss of status, his hair, his work, his wife, and even his daughter, the way one always loses kids in the teenage years. As a father he, too, had felt that irremediable distance, the displeasure at seeing Lorenzo quit school and devote himself to a job that gave him stability for a long time, but was now gone. He had seen him become an adult, husband, father, build a normal life for himself. He couldn't deny that that normality was a few notches below Aurora and Leandro's expectations. But all parents expect too much of their children. With time they come to believe that normality may be the recipe for happiness. But that wasn't the case. Or it was for a while, until everything started to fall apart. Their son doesn't like to talk about his problems, so they maintain a loose relationship, not seeking out what's missing. They ate together on Sundays and at the table they talked about everything that wasn't painful.

Esther, Aurora's sister, showed up with a small bag of clothes at seven p.m., ready to spend the night at the hospital. Go home already, don't wait until the last minute, Aurora told Leandro. She felt uneasy about keeping him occupied, away from the house, distracted by the visits; she knew how allergic her husband was to the unexpected and the unplanned, how much he adored routine. Esther's husband offered to give him a ride in his Mercedes. There was no love lost between them. His brother-in-law worked as a facilitator of official administrative matters and made big bucks smoothing the progress of licenses, speeding up or conquering bureaucracy through his contacts and bribes. He was trained in the art of fake cordiality. I'd rather walk, declined Leandro.

Something that happened early that morning had awakened a dampened instinct in him.

He had been awakened by the commotion in the hallway, the metallic squeaking of carts, some voices, but he was still lying down in bed when the nurse on the morning shift came in like a gale. She was in her late thirties, with her chestnut-brown hair pulled back in a ponytail. Her face was cheerful, well laid out, moisturized, and friendly. She placed herself between Aurora's bed and Leandro's and she leaned over to change Aurora's catheter and check her dressings. As she bent forward, Leandro's eyes crept up her bare legs beneath her white coat and managed to see her thighs rubbing together as she moved. Tanned during her recent vacations, they rose powerfully from her knees' back fold. Beneath the nurse's uniform, he could make out the lines of those teensy panties that made Leandro think of the old pinup girls and that girls today showed above the waist of their pants. In that furtive instant, Leandro felt the excitement of desirable flesh close by and looked on from a privileged position.

That morning, when Aurora complained of a dull pain in her side, Leandro hastened to tell the nurse just for the simple pleasure of seeing her again. The unexpected erotic awakening had led Leandro to the jam-packed section of the newspaper devoted to sexual business. He had found a series of boxed advertisements, some accompanied by a drawing of women with bared breasts, in suggestive postures. One of them caught his eye: "Luxury chalet uptown with a selection of young, elegant ladies. 24 hours, including Sundays. Absolute discretion." Leandro memorized the phone number. It was easy for him to do; it was the sort of mental exercise he had practiced since he was young. Even Aurora used to joke about it, calling him "my walking phone book" before asking him for some friend's number.

He made the call from the hallway.

We're here any time of the day, said a woman's voice, why don't you come and see us? I will, I will. Leandro said goodbye after memorizing the exact address. The very address where now the solid white door with molding was opening in front of him.

The woman who receives him has dyed blond hair, and to find her features he would have to scrape off her makeup with a trowel. She leads him to a small reception room with a sofa placed in front of a low table. Leandro accepts a can of beer she brings him with a short glass and a plate of almonds. He hates the almond pieces that lodge between his teeth and he smiles to see himself sitting there like on any old friendly Sunday visit to a relative's house.

The woman explains the rules. Drinks are courtesy of the house, and in a moment the girls will come through one by one so he can pick the one he likes. Payment is in advance, in cash or with a card, and the rates are the same for every girl: 250 euros for a full hour. Finally, she informs him that if he needs a receipt, he will be given the name of a business that, of course, does not specify the nature of its activity.

When Leandro is left alone, he remembers the last time he paid for sex. It was in a dirty, sordid bar in the sticks, with a friend who was traveling with him for some school concerts. It had been almost twenty years ago, and the woman he had gone to bed with after a few drinks didn't manage to excite him. She was a young Galician who, worn out, had told him, there's nothing more I can do, I'm gonna get a cramp from so much pumping, so it's up to you but I think we should just leave it 'cause as they say where I'm from: don't milk a dry cow. That day confirmed that he couldn't find satisfaction in prostitutes. Manolo Almendros, his friend, said to him, pointing at the section of the newspaper devoted to the business, look how the sex trade grows, it's incredibly strong, a business that works. He reminded him, with that habit he has of pulling up his pants almost to the height of his tie, stating, with reliable statistics, that in

Spain there were more than 400,000 active whores. One percent of the population. Supply and demand. What people spend their money on. But not Leandro, who had left the bar that smelled of disinfectant on the outskirts of Pamplona swearing to never go back to a place like that.

He didn't really know what had drawn him, now, to this place that was as conventional and well taken care of as a relative's house. With Aurora he still found dependable satisfaction when he needed it. The girls begin to appear, affable and approachable; they stop for a second in front of him, and then they give him a kiss on each cheek and depart, leaving the door ajar for the next one to come in. Up to a dozen clean, scantily clad girls, who seem more like coeds in their dorm on a day off from school than brothel employees. They ask him his name and whether it's the first time he's visiting the chalet. A French girl passes by, two Russians, three Latin Americans, and two Spaniards with big fake breasts and more authority, perhaps because they were playing for the home team. A tall Ukrainian comes through and then a young black girl with a spectacularly laid out body. How old are you? Twenty-two. She's from Nigeria. What's your name? Valentina. The girl wears a plunging neckline and short little elastic pants and she touches Leandro's hand with damp fingers. He feels like a character in a novel who has no other choice but to proceed to the next chapter. Should we go upstairs? asks Leandro. Wait here for a second, she says.

She leaves and the woman in charge comes back instantly. I think you've made up your mind, isn't that right? Leandro stands up and pulls out the bills from his wallet. It's not easy to find an African girl in these places, but don't worry, she wouldn't be here if she wasn't completely clean. Still speaking, she leaves the door slightly open. Leandro is left alone, and nervously eats one more almond, then another. Valentina reappears to lead Leandro upstairs. She goes ahead of him, holding tightly to the braided banister. Leandro starts to cough. A little piece of almond is stuck in his throat.

You have a cold? she asks. She speaks with an accent, and hasn't quite mastered the language.

Leandro can't stop coughing, unable to speak. She takes him to a room at the end of the hallway. A bedroom that looks like a teenager's, with a bed and a built-in shelf, a television and a brown bedspread. The blinds down and a light-green curtain drawn. Leandro coughs again and can't seem to get the piece of almond out. He feels ridiculous when the girl gives him a couple of pats on the back. He sits on the bed and pounds on his chest.

Sorry, he says, but I can't stop coughing. The girl brings him a glass of water from the adjoining room. She holds it out to him with a smile. The edge is covered with lipstick. Leandro drinks but doesn't manage to calm the cough.

Don't die on me, all right? she says. Leandro, in a weak voice, asks if there is a bathroom. The girl points to the door. Leandro, without taking the time to look around the place, drinks from the faucet, tries to gargle, and finally manages to get over his coughing fit. How absurd. How incredibly stupid, to be here coughing, choking on an almond. He wants to leave. He peeks into the room and finds the girl sitting on the bed, looking at her foot lifted into the air. All better? Yes, forgive me, I had something stuck in my throat, it must be the nerves, I'm not used to this. Leandro stops. Suddenly it seems ridiculous that he should, at his age, pretend to be a novice at something.

The girl holds out a large, worn towel and tells him he has to shower. He undresses quickly, leaving his clothes on a chair, and she places a blanket on the mattress. She leads him to the adjoining bathroom and helps him into the pink bathtub. She checks the water temperature as if she were a mother showering her son and wets Leandro from the waist down. She puts a little gel in her palm and soaps up his inner thigh. Aren't you going to shower? he asks. If you want? Leandro nods and she hands him the showerhead. She has her hair pulled back in thin, intricate braids, and when she moves they shake like beaded curtains. When Leandro lifts the showerhead, she says, no, wet hair, no.

She washes without really washing, more as a show than anything else. You lather me up. Now it is Leandro who pushes down the pump on the bath gel bottle and runs his hands over her body. White foam accumulates at their feet. The action lasts for a while. Then she turns off the faucet and gets out to dry herself. Leandro reaches for his towel.

In the bedroom, she lays him on the bed. She has put her bra back on. She opens a condom wrapper with her fingers, in spite of the long fake nails. She tries to get him excited before putting it on him. Leandro observes what she does, her professional manner like a supermarket checkout girl putting merchandise in a plastic bag.

Valentina's youthfulness falls onto Leandro's old skin. She places her breasts, her mouth, the opening of her legs, and her hands onto different parts of his body. Leandro continues his exploration of something so foreign it seems unreal, letting his excitement grow. The contact is strange. The brushing together of such dissimilar skins makes the different textures more obvious. Leandro, with the shame of a slave owner, feels like a sinning missionary. A lot has happened in the world while he was busy reading the newspaper at home or giving piano lessons, while he was making himself soft-boiled eggs for dinner or listening to the news on the radio. He contemplates the strange, young body that fakes moans of pleasure by his ear to satisfy him. If he forgets himself and the situation, he is able to work with her in constructing his arousal.

Afterward they talk, lying down. He asks her what her real name is. She hesitates before telling him. My name is Osembe, but Valentina more pretty in Spanish. I like Osembe better, says Leandro. What does it mean? Nothing, in Yoruba, nothing. My mother used to say that in the dialect of her parents it was Something Found. And Leandro? What means? Leandro smiles for a moment. No, they gave me that name because of the day I was born on the calendar of saints. Osembe asks how old he is and Leandro answers, seventy-three. You don't look that old, she says. What would you have guessed, just seventy? But she doesn't get the sarcasm and doesn't laugh. Leandro touches, with his fingertips, the nipple beneath Osembe's bra, which is like a dark chickpea.

You are very pretty.

Breasts not pretty. And she squeezes them at the top of her bra and adjusts them so they're higher. Surgery to put here.

Is Nigeria pretty? Osembe shrugs her shoulders. A voice is heard in the hallway. A voice that Osembe seems to obey. She sits up on the bed and starts to get dressed. It's time, shower, and she gathers the condom and the damp towels with her fingertips and tosses them into a wastebasket lined with a plastic bag.

They kiss on the cheeks at the door to the room. She smiles, showing her teeth. Leandro goes down the stairs. The manager takes him to the exit door. The night is unpleasant, a bit cruel. Leandro takes a taxi. He goes into his house, avoiding the living room. He takes refuge in his study. He sits in the armchair where he usually listens to his students playing the upright piano, an old Pleyel with a somewhat scratched wooden body. He breathes heavily and is cold. He takes a record off his shelf and places it on the record player. Bach would do me good. After the initial frying sound, the music plays and Leandro turns up the volume. He feels a bit older and a bit more alone. The Choral Prelude in F Minor begins. It's that firmness Leandro appreciates, that robust harmony building an emotional architecture that gives him a shiver of feelings.

He thinks about his life, in the days when he knew for certain that he would never be a great pianist, that he would always remain on this side of the beauty, among those that observe it, admire it, enjoy it, but who never create it, never possess it, never master it. Although he feels rage, the music imposes its purity, distancing him from himself. Perhaps he is traveling far away from himself, neither happy nor miserable. Strange.

7

Lorenzo is sitting with his friends Lalo and Óscar. They follow their team's fullback with their eyes as he races to the goal line. The center isn't very good and the stadium responds to the missed opportunity with a general sigh. Lalo whistles, sticking two fingers under his tongue. Don't whistle at Lastra, at least he gets his jersey sweaty, says Óscar. Lorenzo nods vaguely.

The game finally opens up toward the end, escaping the useless combat that dominated the rest of the match, the ball dizzy from being kicked from one side to the other. Lorenzo has sat for years in the northern area of the stands, near the goal that his team attacks in the first half. So he is used to spending the end of the game in the distance, with his players like ants trying to break the lock on the rival's goal. The crowd is impatient, scoreless games create a shared frustration, they exaggerate the subsequent void. They follow the final plays with greater concentration, as if that would help their team. But not Lorenzo.

Lorenzo turns back; he has been unable to get into the game. When his eyes meet someone's gaze, he looks away. He tries to recognize the fans who usually sit in the seats around him. Later he regrets his fits of anxiety, his worries that keep him from relaxing and enjoying. Like when on Friday he finally listened to his father's phone messages and realized his mother had had an accident, he felt ridiculous for having hidden all morning. When he leaves the stadium, he will also be sorry he didn't take better advantage of the opportunity for distraction.

On Saturday the newspaper announced the news. The television news programs did, too, announcing it along with two other crimes. A businessman, they said, had been stabbed to death in the garage of his own home, the only motive apparently robbery. An image of the entrance to the house, the fence, the number, the street sign. Filler tactics for a news item that may end up in the limbo of unsolved cases. Lorenzo could have filled in the details. He could write that the killer and the victim had met seven years earlier, when they worked together as middle management in a large multinational company devoted to cellular phones. They had both profited from the opportunities offered by an expanding market. The division where Lorenzo worked had been absorbed and Paco was a proficient and decisive executive, the kind who needed to get the best yield from a flourishing business.

It was a fast friendship that grew quickly. They ate together beside their desks. One day they both bought the same car thanks to the special offer they got from someone Paco knew at Opel. Both red, both turbocharged. Paco was married to a quiet, very thin woman. They didn't have kids. Teresa was the daughter of a building contractor who had created a great company from nothing. The shadiness of his beginnings had long since been smoothed over by the expensive ties that affluence allowed him to wear. When my father-in-law dies, joked Paco, I'll cry with one eye and with the other I'll start shopping for a yacht. Paco taught Lorenzo how to live. Meat is eaten rare, Paco told him; ham must be painstakingly cured so that the fat melts into the meat; disregard bread; you have to squeeze your Cuban cigar with your fingertips and feel the texture of the tobacco leaf, and when you flick the ash the tip of the cigar should maintain the shape of a cunt; your tie should match your ambitions, not your suit; it's better to have just one pair of super-expensive shoes than six cheap ones. With Paco he subscribed to a wine club and each month they sent him a box of bottles and a pamphlet to get him started in gourmet wine tasting. When, by then partners, they were working late, Paco would uncork a nice wine and while they resolved the paperwork they discussed the flavor of a Burgundy or a Rioja and they ordered in Japanese food. And on the way out Paco would insist on showing him an apartment where erotic massages were given by Asian women who were the height of submissiveness, but the only time Lorenzo agreed to accompany him he was attended to by a retarded little Chinese woman who laughed too much, so he paid quickly and went home without even waiting for his friend.

Every Thursday night, since he married Teresa in the Jeróni-mos Church, in the official celebration of definitive pussywhip-ping, Paco went to his father-in-law's house and played poker with him and two old friends. When we're bluffing, when we up the ante to trick the other team, Paco explained to Lorenzo, when we pretend to have a hand we don't have, I think that's the only moment since we met when we tell each other the truth.

Pilar never liked Paco. She didn't appreciate his influence on Lorenzo. He smacked of nouveau riche, of tacky, of arrogant. You don't understand him, Lorenzo corrected, all that attitude is a joke, he has a great sense of humor about it. Pilar didn't become close with Teresa either. She doesn't talk, and I don't know if it's because she doesn't have anything to say or because if she spoke she'd say too much, concluded Pilar after six or seven uncomfortable dinners between the two couples. Pilar never confessed to Lorenzo that one of the things that distanced her from Paco was the way he looked at her. It was challeng-ing. He not only aspired to seduce her, as was his natural way, but he also considered Pilar a rival. Lorenzo was the prey, the object in dispute.

When the business stopped growing, the time came for cut-backs, for firings, restructurings. These companies are like an orange: once the juice is squeezed out, what do you want the peel for? Paco convinced Lorenzo to negotiate a reasonable lay-off settlement with the company, with severance pay that would allow him to strike out on his own. There is nothing sadder than a labor claim, Paco told him, it's like crying to the woman who just left you. Paco had his own ideas: the pie had been divvied up, it was better to eat the piece they give us than get stuck with the empty tray. Around that time, the workers were protesting every day in front of the multinational company's imposing building and had been recognized by the general population. Solidarity is only the first step toward guiltless indifference, warned Paco. He pointed to a vociferous colleague. Admit that it's pathetic to shout at a building, at an acronym, throw eggs or paint, I prefer to put all my energy into being the one who lines their pockets next time.

Lorenzo let himself be convinced. He knew that he wasn't made of the same stuff as Paco. Lorenzo came from a family that never valued money. He noticed how his parents grew bored when he went into details about the company he founded with Paco. After having their daughter, Sylvia, Pilar had been slow to find work, but when she did she always had Grandma Aurora available to take care of the girl. Pilar's parents had died years before in a car accident and Lorenzo's mother did everything she could in her role as sole grandmother. Although he never heard a complaint, Lorenzo hated depending on his parents. If he managed to get ahead, if things went well for him, Lorenzo would finally be able to show them his success.

Lorenzo and Paco bought two buildings and set up a store that sold cell phone accessories. Paco had a magic touch that gave everything the illusion of profitability. He might be late with payment to a supplier, but they never refused him a few beers, a couple of jokes, or a new shipment on account. He never went over the numbers; for him a diagram drawn on a sheet of paper was enough to justify a new investment. He was decisive, brave; he bet big and he landed on his feet. We'll balance the books tomorrow, today just tell me I can order a Ribera with dinner and a Partagás with coffee—this was one of his lines. Lorenzo let himself get swept up. He didn't go to all the dinners and parties, he took refuge in Pilar, at home with Sylvia, he kept his old friends, Lalo, Óscar, but then he had to listen to Paco tell him friends are only good for filling the time one doesn't know how to fill alone. Paco recited the catechism of an individualist and a winner. And if something sounded bad to Lorenzo's ears, it was always burnished with just enough irony to be taken as a joke. No one could lose by his side. But Lorenzo lost everything.

Something that bothered him about Pilar was the silent accusation, the "I told you so." That part of the defeat felt even worse than the defeat itself. It was so easy to come to the superficial idea that Paco was an illusion, a fraud, a player who laid waste to those around him. Lorenzo resisted it for months. In fact, during the collapse, the losses, the disastrous debacle of the business, their friendship seemed closer than ever. Paco talked about projects. Sure, Gruyère has holes, but doesn't it taste good? he used to say. But the hole grew until it ate the cheese. The creditors were endless and Lorenzo lacked Paco's ability to evade them, to trick them, to put off their indignation for four more days. The buildings were sold at a loss, the payout of the business was piddling, and the two years of work and the severance money had gone up in smoke. When Pilar forced him to see the company's end, Lorenzo went through the bitter experience of asking his parents for money to settle the accounts.

Paco embarked on another adventure and Lorenzo didn't want to get involved. That was where the distance was forged.

They barely saw each other. Lorenzo took refuge in his lair. He came up with a theory. Paco was a vulture, some kind of parasite, someone who sucks other people's energy. He remembered how Paco used to arrive mid-morning with coffee the way Lorenzo took it, with just the right amount of sugar. How he always had some witticism, how he made fun of their co-workers and sowed temptation like music in Hamelin. He stole my luck, Lorenzo would tell himself. He came into my life and stole my luck. Because Lorenzo without Paco was a man forced to start from zero but now without luck, the doors didn't open for him like before. All the good cards had already been dealt. Pilar had gotten established at her job; she liked it, she felt useful, and she advanced rapidly. That's where Santiago came in, of course, Lorenzo said to himself. He came through the cracks of Lorenzo's stability, smelling of power. Lorenzo barely lasted months in three new jobs. Sometimes the most exciting part of his day was picking Sylvia up after school, helping her with her homework. It was obvious Paco had shown him a much more attractive, fun, and passionate way of living than the one that now seemed to be his destiny.

Pilar came home from her office one day with wounding news. It was Lorenzo's final, devastating humiliation. If only she had kept it to herself. The name of one of the creditors of Lorenzo's business had rung a bell with Pilar. It was a name she had heard Lorenzo repeating in his nightmares every night. We owe Sonor more than three million. The sale of their last building went entirely to paying that debt. This afternoon I looked into Sonor's business registration, Pilar told him suddenly one night, after putting the girl to bed. Lorenzo didn't really understand, but he raised his eyes and listened carefully. The only partners of Sonor are Paco and Teresa. She showed him the photocopies, the signatures on the company documentation. If Paco had ripped Lorenzo off, that changed things. If he had been capable of setting up the vague engineering to sink one company to the profit of another one, which he owned, then Lorenzo was a victim, not an unwitting accomplice. There must be some explanation, he said to Pilar, and he pretended in front of her that the news, so many months later, didn't affect him very much. Pilar didn't insist, she just left it at that; she regained her silence, a silence that Lorenzo sometimes considered insulting. He didn't yet know that it was the civilized start of her demolition plan for their marriage. Termites work in silence, too.

Lorenzo let the days pass, but that information was the catalyst for him seeing Paco once again. For the last time before the time he killed him. He went to see him at his house. My wife's house, don't you think it humiliates me to know that the only reason I'm not broke is because I'm married to her? Paco had shouted at him once when Lorenzo was blaming him for his misfortune. Lorenzo heard the dog bark, but when the gate opened the animal searched out his hand with his back for a pat. He's trained just the opposite of how he should be, he barks and then is affectionate, instead of being affectionate and biting when you least expect it, said Paco.

Lorenzo knew the house well. He had been there many times. When everything was running smoothly and then also when they were looking for solutions, ways to stop the final collapse. He had seen Paco take out a locked toolbox, hidden behind the shelves of brushes, rags, and cans of paint in the garage, and extract a wad of bills for emergencies. When my father-in-law has too much undeclared cash, I store a little bit of it here for him.

That last time they didn't get further than the yard. Paco came out to meet him, smiling, offering him a hug, but Lorenzo stopped him. You ripped me off, you cheated me. Paco didn't change his expression; he waited for Lorenzo to continue. Sonor was yours, we owed you money. It was all a trap. Paco tried to curb his suspicions, told him it was a different company, one Paco had set up with Teresa using his father-in-law's money and that the debt was real. I hid the fact it was mine from you, but the debt existed, I can prove it. You were in charge of the accounting, he then added, you know it's true, I never took care of the books, I lost as much as you. Lorenzo felt like laughing, but he just answered, not as much.

Not as much.

It was painful to say. At that point perhaps he sensed everything he had lost. More than the money from the severance claim, his savings, and two years' worth of work. Much more. He had lost his family's respect, his position. He had lost his luck. Lorenzo looked at the two-story house, the cropped lawn, Paco's suit, his blond wave, his relaxed appearance. All nourished by betrayal. He felt rage and an irrepressible desire to punch his old friend. Paco tried to calm him down, he invited him in, he offered to go over the books. We fucked up, Lorenzo, we fucked up together, don't blame yourself, but don't blame me either, said Paco. We're equal in this. It sounded fake. Lorenzo would never be like Paco. Paco never lost.

Perhaps in that instant, stopped in the middle of the yard, on a cold November morning, months before Pilar left Lorenzo, in that silence of spent explanations, the crime was forged. Paco ran a hand along Lorenzo's shoulders, paternal, pacifying. If you need money, I can lend you some . . . But Lorenzo didn't let him finish; he pushed Paco's arm away roughly and lifted a fist to hit him in the face. He didn't do it. He froze his rage in the air. And he felt that he had won for a second. He looked up toward the house and saw Teresa peering out a window in one of the rooms, amid the lace curtains. He relaxed his fist and turned around very slowly. They didn't say anything more to each other. Lorenzo walked toward the gate. His bitterness needed time to grow, until the obsessive certainty that Paco had stolen his luck would drive him once again to that residential neighborhood and lead him to commit a crime.

Now a killer, he watches the soccer game. There are fans who leave the stadium before the match is over to avoid the traffic, the crowded mass of people. Some of them are lucky to miss how their team is served with a definitive, last-minute goal. The Czech goalkeeper picks the ball out of the net and rapidly hands it over to a teammate. The coach orders a quick subsitution of the left winger. A recently signed Argentinian whom the crowd whistles at and heckles. Lorenzo gets up to whistle at him, too. Go home, Indian, go home, a group of kids chant. The player doesn't run toward the touchline, and that makes the stands even madder. Run, you shitty spic, someone shouts at him. And Lalo and Óscar laugh. He's got some nerve, why doesn't he run off? We're losing. The crowd's protests relax Lorenzo, reconciling him with himself. Taking part in the general indignation is a way of escaping. And those five minutes in which the stadium pushes the local team to pull off a tie that never comes are the only five minutes he has enjoyed in the last few days.

8

Getting drunk is never the same twice. The last time, before he left Buenos Aires, had nothing to do with this one now. He wasn't by himself. He's just left Asador Tomás, where he had dinner with two teammates. They're young like him, but they seem less affected by the defeat. We'll win next time, Osorio told him. But Ariel's twisted expression wasn't about the loss, or not just about that. He was hurt by the whistles, the substitution, even though it was the third time in a row the coach pulled him out at the end of a game. During the match, he kept repeating to himself, I got it, it's not so hard, gotta play one touch. When he received the ball with his back to the goal, he couldn't find a teammate. A forward has to create the space and then run into it, Dragon used to tell him. During the whole game, Ariel couldn't shake the fullback's breath on his neck as he kneed him in the tailbone. Every once in a while, Ariel stuck him with his cleats and cursed his mother. The ball came to him imprecisely, it burned at his feet. Again the whistles, trying to create a play that never went well.

Tired of waiting for the ball, Ariel dropped toward the center of the field, and the traffic jam was worthy of rush hour. If no one is where they're supposed to be, Dragon used to say, then there's no soccer. Legs and bodies are glued together and the ball just gets battered. What I don't understand is why the ball doesn't sue you, shouted Dragon in irritation when they played like that. Ariel heard the stands, felt the pressure like a physical presence. He asked for the ball even though he didn't know what to do with it. They weren't passes, they were teammates passing the buck. Let somebody else lose it. And Ariel lost it.

The restaurant didn't charge them. Its wall was filled with portraits of famous customers, most of them soccer players, some politicians, and the king with a group of hunters. There was also a photo of the owner on his knees before the Pope in an audience at the Vatican. From one of the nearby tables come persistent glances from two girls with high breasts in tight sweaters. They're whores, Poggio said. You're crazy, man, responds Osorio. They ask the owner to introduce them and they strike up a lively conversation. Should we call a friend? asks one when she sees Ariel's serious expression, as he downs his wine. Ariel shakes his head. He stands up. I'm going home.

He leaves a generous tip for the maître d', who sends for his car keys. Do you like *orujo*? he asks, extending a thick glass bottle with a cork. The owner makes it himself. It's dry and has no aftertaste. Ariel takes the bottle and picks up his car at the front door. He's in the mood to drive. He puts on music and flees toward any highway. The last time he got sloshed was definitely nothing like this.

It was in Buenos Aires. In a restaurant owned by the sister of his teammate Walter, to whom he had rented his little apartment in Belgrano when he left. The night before his flight, Ariel had gotten together for dinner with some friends from the neighborhood, players from his team, and the physical trainer, Professor Matías Manna, who swore that the great opera singers had a gin and tonic before going onstage, thus justifying his fourth of the night. Macero was there, too, still a close friend, even though he now plays for Newell's and holds the championship record for red cards. Charlie didn't come. You go out with your friends, it's your night. But Agustina did, his girlfriend up until a few months earlier. They joked with Ariel, saying he should remember them when he's a millionaire. Several of them brought gifts that Ariel had to unwrap. An Argentinian flag, for you to put up in the locker room. Alberto Alegro, grandson of Aragonese exiled after the Spanish civil war, who studied with him during the last few years of high school, got up to sing him the schottische "Madrid," and the others crooned trombone chords. By then most of them were drunk and some proposed going to Open Bay for drinks and others suggested dancing at Ink. Agustina was one of the first to say she was headed home, using the confusion at the restaurant door to say her parting words. I guess your trip will help me get over you, she said, and then kissed him on the lips. The breakup had happened without much explanation. I didn't know how to do it, Ariel reproached himself. She was still in love with him and he felt nothing more than vague affection leftover from his initial enthusiasm in their relationship, one that was calm and sweet, but never completely fulfilling. He said good-bye more noisily to the others who were leaving, but with her he drew a strange, cruel curtain on their love. All the good-byes were bitter, as if he were closing a chapter. But the alcohol helped. He refused to stand up and say a few words, even though they demanded it, shouting, speech, speech. It was the sunrise that finally sent them home to bed.

Now in the car, miles away on the almost empty highway, Ariel remembered the months he played in the "Cenicero," which held only a third of what this potbellied Madrid stadium could pack, luxurious in its vertical expansion, with glassed-in box seats for special guests. Yet on the field the space seemed to be reversed. There he had enjoyed playing, he didn't feel pressure, and it was easy to find open spots. He escaped the fullback's brusqueness. When he played at home, the crowd chanted his name or sang to the team like familiar background music, show some balls, show some balls, let's see some real balls. The fans over there insulted them when they lowered their guard or didn't perform, but that was the price of passionate, sometimes brutal, love. Yet they were never cold and expectant like the fans in Madrid. His legs weren't heavy there like they were now. There he was still just the kid who one day, after practice, was told that a Spaniard was waiting to talk to him.

The agent was named Solórzano and he wanted exclusive rights to negotiate on his behalf. Let's not lose our heads, Charlie said to him, but he was the one who most wanted to lose his head. The Spaniards come loaded with money, soccer over there pays anything you want, anything you want, repeated Charlie. That same night he took them out for dinner at Piégari. If you're not playing on a Spanish team next season, I'll cut off my ponytail, Solórzano told them, and Charlie cracked up laughing. The guy is bald, we've got nothing to lose. I don't work alone, Solórzano explained. Ariel's team preferred quick money, they were already in talks to sell his player rights to a company owned by two well-known middlemen who moved Iranian capital and had bought a club in Brazil and were in negotiations with another in London. They had to act fast. It seemed that Boca was offering a million and a half dollars for 50 percent ownership of the player. I don't want to end up where they tell me to go, I want to choose my team, Ariel insisted to Charlie.

After signing the exclusive with Solórzano, they realized what he meant when he said that he didn't work alone. An article appeared about him in the Spanish soccer press. "Everyone wants to sign the player of the moment, the winger from San Lorenzo, Ariel Burano Costa." In the next match against Rosario Central, Ariel made the second goal and the wife of Puma Sosa, the Uruguayan center midfielder, told him that he had also been on the international Spanish news channel. Solórzano called from Madrid, you're all set up perfectly, next week I'll tell you about the offers.

Days later he had a live telephone interview with a Spanish radio host who asked him things like, is it true what they say, that you can make so many feints on a patch of field that the defenders stop to watch and then applaud? Ariel started to understand Solórzano's domino game. How he set up the pieces so that they all worked in the same direction: Madrid.

By fax Solórzano sent them another clipping from a Spanish newspaper, the peninsular equivalent to *Clarín*. They profiled Ariel as one more player who had sprung from hardship, a born competitor, quick, intuitive, an artist. "In the streets of a poor section of Buenos Aires, Ariel 'the Feather' Burano learned to keep the ball at his left foot at all times. They call him 'Feather' because he moves with the weightlessness of a dancer." Ariel smiled at the clichéd image. It must not sell as many papers to say he was the son of a middle-class family from Floresta and that he had learned his mastery of the ball during endless classes at the Lincoln School, where they scuttled the ball from left to right, beneath the desks, as a distraction from the tedium of the lectures. They really called him Feather because they said he could be sent down to the ground just by blowing on him. In rival stadiums, every time he fell to the grass, they chanted: fall, fall.

Ariel later learned that a scout had written to the Spanish club recommending they sign him: "In two years he'll be playing for

Boca or River and he'll cost twice as much." Someone from the board of directors leaked to Solórzano the names of the players they were going to try to sign and then Solórzano would work his way in. The first thing he would do was raise the price, don't worry, the more expensive a player the more interest, because a lot of people live off the money that falls by the side of the road in the process. Solórzano shared commission with the deep throat inside the board of directors and then stirred up a media storm, greasing palms with privileged information and the occasional banknote. The idea was to multiply the price, get other buyers interested, and force the signing with expectations created by the media. If the public starts pushing, you get the president on the ropes and he'll pay whatever, as long as you always let him make a little, send a pinch of dough to his account in the Caymans and everybody's happy. The important thing is that everybody's happy, right? Isn't soccer all about making people happy? lectured Solórzano.

For Ariel Spanish soccer was familiar. He knew players who had gone over there, and on satellite TV they showed live games on Sundays. Even though many players return from abroad without having succeeded, going over there was still the dream that year for Martín Palermo and Burrito Ortega and, on his own team, Loeschbor and Matías Urbano. But on Solórzano's next trip, things seemed less close. It's gotten complicated, but we're working on fixing it. The club filled all its spots for non-European foreigners. They're leaving us with our pants down. They don't want to bring over an Argentinian and this is after it was all sewn up and the press already said you're the next Maradona. He showed him the cover of a sports newspaper with his photo and a huge headline: "Bring over this kid."

Burano is an Italian last name, right? Solórzano asked them one day. Charlie nodded unconvincingly, they say my father's grandfather comes from over there. Two weeks later, Solórzano showed them the birth certificate of a Burano great-grandfather expedited by an Italian parish. For a modest sum, I'll make you a family tree where your mother's the Mona Lisa. Carlo Burano was the name of the forebear, their made-up great-grandfather. With his Italian roots, Ariel would take a European spot, he wouldn't have to fight for his place with Brazilians, Africans, Mexicans. With that cocky face and that gangster hair, you could only be Italian, Solórzano said to Ariel. We aren't doing anything wrong, just finding some lost family papers. There's no stopping the machine.

Solórzano didn't inspire trust in either Ariel or Charlie. He drank red wine and smoked cheap cigars. His teeth were like an unmopped floor that ended in two gold molars. Even though he assured them that the only flag he bowed before was a waving banknote, several times, egged on by alcohol, he would confess that what Spain needed was another Franco and Argentina another Perón. He was sarcastically nostalgic, and a veteran barhound. He traveled with a young lawyer, a representative of the club, to close deals, and they all met in the offices of Ariel's financial advisers. Charlie acted as a security guard, but Solórzano, his laughter breaking into a cackle, relaxed the atmosphere with his endless anecdotes. He told them where the team's president—the one they called "the mother from *Psycho*"—found his love for soccer. He bought a team in the north, which shared ownership of the stadium with the city hall; he managed to get the team knocked down to Second Division and then lower than Second, and then bankrupt it. It was absurd. Instead of trying to get the team to win, he did everything possible to make them lose. It looked like the world turned upside down. But the whole business brought about the demolition of the stadium, which was near the beach, and on the site they built fourteen hundred luxury apartments, splitting it with the municipal government, of course, so there were no legal qualms. The season ticket holders wanted to kill him and, in a gesture he carried off with the utmost dignity, he sold the team. At that point, the team's legacy was all in its name and its coat of arms, that's it. A few years later, he was so solvent they practically sought him out to preside over the Madrid team. Now it gives him social prestige; a box seat in Madrid is tantamount to the king's court. You can do business with those kinds of people, concluded Solórzano, because they're like me: there's only one thing they respect more than money . . . and that's a lot of money. This chatty, obnoxious guy, with his bad breath, his rust-colored hair, golden tie clip, and woven leather shoes, took him to Spain, and judging by his shifty charm Ariel should have suspected that nothing was going to be easy.

In early July, Ariel went to visit Dragon. He followed the kids' practice from the sidelines with his sad, bespectacled eyes and his old whistle with the tiny wooden ball in it. I'm going to Spain, Ariel told him. I heard. Dragon's eyeglasses were old, from twenty years ago. I came to say good-bye. The coach nodded his head without taking his eyes off the kids. Ariel stood by his side for a long time, waiting for him to say something. Once, after watching a Korean World Cup game at his house, during which his wife laughed at him for getting up to urinate every five minutes, Dragon had told him that soccer is for the humble, because it is the only line of work where you can do everything wrong in a game and win and you can do everything right and lose. Ariel hadn't forgotten that and he feared his old coach would now think that with his million-dollar signing and his move to Spain he had lost humility. He wanted to tell him, I'm the same kid you used to pick up in the afternoons to take to practice, with Macero and Alameda. They remained in silence for a while longer, until Dragon pointed out a boy that was playing. He has the same name as you. Send him an autographed T-shirt, he'll flip. Sure, said Ariel. It's rare for good players to come out of here; the only promising kids come from the countryside. Dragon turned toward him and grabbed him hard by the shoulder. He gave him a talking-to. In this game, the worst thing that can happen to you is thinking you're a little better than you really are. That was his way of saying good-bye. He crossed the field to correct some player's move. Ariel watched him from a distance and left.

For a while, he thought that good-byes were harder than arrivals, but he was wrong. Now he saw himself, alone, his only companion the line down the middle of the highway, not caring about where he was going, the bottle of *orujo* between his thighs and the same song over and over again, "Four roads ahead, all four lead nowhere." He was afraid of failing in this country, a country that was sometimes welcoming, sometimes hostile. After his first game, in a friendly tournament, he returned to the locker room feeling ripped off. Now they'll come in and tell me it was all a joke. We know that you're totally mediocre, you can go back to Buenos Aires now. Perhaps it was all just a terrible misunderstanding. But then Charlie was still nearby, he showed him the details of the plays that worked, the good vibes, he calmed him down. They called home and Charlie told his kids about the game as if he had witnessed a different one in which Ariel pulled off his feints, and Charlie said that he's the fullback everyone was waiting for.

He takes an exit off the highway and follows the signs back to the city. From there he can get his bearings. He only really knows the route home from the stadium and he has to go back there. It's his starting point in Madrid. The center of his world. The stadium is hidden and then suddenly appears all at once. He chooses a wide, deserted avenue, but the traffic lights seem to be against him. Once he passes a green light, the next one turns to red again, as if they were holding the car prisoner. Finally it changes and he floors it to catch the next one, but from the nearby darkness a shadow emerges, he twists the steering wheel but can't dodge it, the bottle falls between his legs, and he brakes hard. He hears a loud knock against the hood and the car stops. Ariel remains motionless in an instant of panic. He has hit someone. The song keeps playing, but now out of sync with the moment. He is afraid to get out, to open the door, to face reality. He feels like his drunkenness has disappeared suddenly; only terror remains. His sock is soaked with *orujo*. He gathers his forces. It all lasts no more than three seconds.

9

A memory of Grandma Aurora comes back to Sylvia. As a little girl, she spent a lot of time at her grandmother's house; they played together on the double bed. They made up vacations for Sylvia's favorite doll. First they had her scale the pillows as if they were snow-capped mountains. Then they lowered the bed-spread and pretended she was frolicking in the sea. The folds were the waves the doll swam over. As their game progressed, the waves grew, the sea got choppy, and eventually, in a fit of inspiration, they created a big wave that covered Grandma, the doll, and Sylvia, who cracked up laughing. Sometimes, when they came out from underneath to catch their breath, Grandpa Leandro was watching them from the doorway, taken aback by the commotion. He smiled, but said nothing. Then Grandma Aurora always turned to Sylvia and said, now you're going to have to help me make the bed again.

Her father had just left the room. He had taken note of all the room's details, the venetian blinds, the television that hung in the corner, the new wall lights, comparing them to the hospital her grandmother is in, where everything is old, and used. The worn walls don't give you the feeling you get here, that you're the first patient to occupy the room. What a difference, you're like a queen, Lorenzo had said to Sylvia, Grandma has to share her room with a patient who snores like a buzz saw.

That morning she woke up with her mouth dry, her father sitting on the sofa reading the sports pages. After the operation, Sylvia had her leg in a cast, lifted up into the air. Mai had signed it with a marker. Her friend hadn't stayed long, just long enough for Lorenzo to get a bite to eat. Does it hurt? A little. Mai told her about her weekend. Sylvia didn't say anything about her time with Dani, about her absurd birthday party. When his name came up in conversation, Sylvia got nervous. He asked about you this morning, Mai told her. I told him what happened to you, but I thought it was better if he didn't come, right?

Yeah, that's better.

She was sitting at the foot of the bed when the door opened and Pilar came in. Sylvia's mother and Mai greeted each other and then Pilar hugged her daughter. How did it happen? Mai said, good-bye, I'm outta here, I'll come see you tomorrow, okay?

Sylvia felt her mother's tears on her face. I'm okay, it's nothing serious. Pilar sat up and put her hand on the cast. The national soccer team's doctor operated on me, Sylvia explained to her. He says that in two months I can compete again, of course the coach will have to give his say-so first. Pilar smiled. You're coming to my house until you can move around on your own. We'll see, answered Sylvia. And your father? He went out for lunch. He can't take care of you now, said Pilar, he has his things. Mamá, I can take care of myself, I'll have some crutches, I'm not an invalid. Sylvia pulled her arm out from under the sheet and Pilar saw the bruises. The son of a bitch really hit me hard. Sylvia, don't talk like that. Well, then that very lovely man struck me harshly.

Sylvia wasn't trying to hurt her mother, but she didn't have the patience for talking to her. Often she used sarcasm to shorten the distance between what her mother wanted to hear and what she felt like telling. When they lived together, Sylvia was unaware of how lonely that made her mother feel, how frustrated she was by being denied access to her daughter's worries. What do you feel like eating? I don't care. Are you going out? Yes. Where? Just around. With who? With Mai. Just you two? No, with a couple of Civil Guard officers. Sylvia's caginess was hard for Pilar to accept. She's starting to have a private life, she told herself.

If you are going to see Grandma, don't tell her anything, she's got enough on her plate . . . , Sylvia told her. The door opened and Lorenzo came in. He and Pilar looked at each other and after a moment's hesitation he approached her and they kissed on both cheeks. It was more a mechanical gesture than a kiss, their cheeks brushing strangely after twenty years of kisses on the lips.

I told her I think she should come stay with me for now, until she can walk well. I don't know, whatever she wants. A little bit later, they argued again, without really arguing, both of them offering to spend the night. Sylvia insisted they leave. She didn't like to witness those parental competitions, the hundred-meter sprint to prove their filial love. She had gained independence thanks to their separation, maybe out of negligence, but she was happy, less protected, less scrutinized. Living with her father was the closest thing to living alone. With her mother gone, Sylvia had matured at a spectacular rate. She had realized what it means to not have someone around to take care of all her daily needs.

Doctor Carretero visited her late that evening. He greeted Pilar and explained Sylvia's recuperation process to her, with the same patience he'd had with Lorenzo that morning. She'll be in a cast for five weeks and then she'll have very minor rehabilitation. He was a man in his fifties, his gray hair combed with a part and his hands delicate. In two months, she'll be skipping rope again. Sylvia's expression twisted. I think it's best if she spends the night here and I'll release her tomorrow, okay? She has several contusions and I'd rather not take any chances. He left the room and Lorenzo explained to Pilar that all the expenses were being taken care of by the driver of the car. He had brought her here and asked to be kept informed. We're lucky, because she was hit by good guy, these days most of them hit and run.

Yeah, incredibly fucking lucky.

Don't talk like that, Pilar corrected her daughter. Then Sylvia said, I was totally out of it. This morning the guy came in to talk to Papá and I didn't even remember his face. I think there were two people in the car and I saw the other one. Did you black out? asked Pilar. I don't know, maybe . . . It was all really strange. After I got hit, I tried to get up and it felt like my leg was made of rubber, so I got scared. That's when he put me in the backseat.

She was pretty lucky. Crossing illegally without looking, in the middle of the night, interjected Lorenzo.

Peace. That was what she felt when they left her alone. First her mother. I'll call you later, she said. Do you want me to bring you some clothes? But the question died on the vine. It only took Lorenzo's proud expression to remind her that the clothes were at his house and not within Pilar's reach. Lorenzo stayed a bit longer, as if he didn't want to leave with her.

Sylvia flips through the television channels with the remote control. There's news at that hour. She finds a music video station. She leaves it on in the background, not paying much attention. A lead singer deliberates between a dozen women who stroke and caress him, begging longingly for the chance to be with him. Lorenzo had left newspapers piled up on the sofa, but she's not tempted to look at them. A nurse brings her dinner. Sylvia eats with a good appetite. She gets a message from Dani on her cell. "Take care of that leg." Sylvia replies with concise coldness. "I'll try."

A while later, they take away her dinner tray. The nurse wishes her good night, shows her the call button. On the television, a woman sings in a bathing suit, slithering along the ground near a pool like a snake in heat. When she hears a short tapping of knuckles on the door, Sylvia puts the remote control down on the bedside table. Mamá? The door opens very slowly and a coppery face, surrounded by a messy, longish mane of hair, peeks in. A small but stocky body. He has a box of chocolates in one hand.

You're not my mother, I don't think.

No, I don't think so, answers the young man. You're Sylvia, right?

It's his accent, the sweet cadence of his speech, that attracts Sylvia's attention. She watches him as he turns to close the door behind him. He holds the chocolates out to her. I brought you this, it's the least I could do. Thank you. Sylvia grabs the box, and lifts the sheet to cover her breasts. She isn't wearing a bra under her T-shirt. She doesn't want his gaze, those honey-colored eyes protected by incredibly long lashes, to be distracted. He has pointy eyebrows, the left one interrupted by a small scar. His slightly deviated septum gives him a tough look that contradicts a delicate mole halfway between the corner of his mouth and his left eye. Tough and sweet.

You're the one who ran me over, right? asked Sylvia.

10

On Tuesday he goes back.

Leandro is received by the same madam. She leads him to a different room, smaller, narrower. Leandro realizes this is all set up so the customers never meet. Call me Mari Luz, please, says the woman. Leandro prefers the cold, professional treatment he got the first day. He finds the warmth disquieting; it makes him feel worse. A moment earlier, still on the street, while schools were letting out, he had considered turning around. The bustle on the street was threatening. A school bus passed, more cars. It was impossible that the neighbors on a residential street like that one didn't know what went on at number forty, where the blinds were always drawn. Clients, like him, would be scrutinized indignantly. There goes another one.

Leandro doesn't want anything to drink. I would like the same girl, he says. Valentina, right? asks Mari Luz without waiting for a reply. Let me see, you're going to have to wait a little bit, not long, ten minutes, if you want I can show you some other girls. No, no, Leandro cuts her off, I'd rather wait.

Leandro sits down. In front of him there is a window through which he sees a gust of wind blow leaves off a plane tree. There is a sound of footsteps. A woman's voice. But nothing that betrays what is going on in the rooms. He supposes Osembe is with another client. He left Aurora in the hospital, sleeping. Esther had come to spend some time with her in the afternoon. I'm going to go out and stretch my legs, Leandro had said to them.

He had spent Monday wracked with guilt. Less for what had happened the evening before than for his irrepressible desire to do it again. He had arrived early to the hospital to relieve Esther. He soon learned about Sylvia's accident. At first he was scared. She got run over last night, he heard from his son, and he connected what happened to Sylvia to his meeting with Osembe. It was the punishment. His granddaughter run over at the same time he was . . . She's fine, there's nothing to worry about, Lorenzo told him. They agreed not to mention it to Aurora.

He slept horribly on the sofa bed. Arousal and shame. He heard Aurora's breathing, very close by, like he had so many nights. He thought of the few occasions he had looked for sex in someone else. In his room, he kept a book of nude female photographs. They were artistic nudes, most of them in black and white. Masturbating brought him back, with cruel irony, to his teenage years. He never imagined himself sitting alone in the little reception room of a chalet like that one.

Some nights he and Aurora still had something similar to an erotic encounter. It would happen on those strange nights when she could tell he was having trouble sleeping. She would feel between his legs and find him aroused. She relieved him with her hand. Sometimes Leandro would sit on top of her and they would make love without penetration, which hurt her, so they just rubbed their genitals together, caressed each other. They never spoke about it. When they finished they turned over and went to sleep. No one teaches us how to be old, do they? she said to him one night. Desire should have died out long ago and should rest buried unceremoniously beneath the springs of their bed.

Tuesday morning when the doctor came by the room, he was calmer, but still had the same chorizo stain on his white coat. He took Leandro to a nearby room and showed him some X-rays. The cleaning ladies had just left and it smelled of disinfectant. The doctor opened the windows as wide as possible. He spoke while he moved the pen like a pointer. Let's see, a broken hip isn't anything serious, as I told you. It's a common thing, we consider it an epidemic of old age. Every year in Spain we treat forty thousand broken hips in the elderly, particularly women. So that's incidental.

Leandro felt fear. He feared the moment the doctor would start to talk about what wasn't incidental. The problem is that with these type of fractures sometimes they're the first clue to a general debilitation. We are going to send your wife home, but we are going to do some serious tests on her, aside from the fact that she has advanced osteoporosis she was already being treated for . . . Leandro stuck his hands into the pockets of his jacket. He was cold. I had no idea, he said. The doctor smiled, opened the folder with Aurora's information. You know how women are, they keep their problems to themselves.

Yeah, replied Leandro. The doctor talked to him about densitometry and degrees of mobility, he named other tests that he was going to perform, but he never seemed to get to the point. Leandro asked him about rehabilitation after leaving the hospital. The important thing is to not let her get too frustrated, was all the doctor said. It's just part of old age.

The conversation languished. Confused, Leandro walked through the hall on the way back to Aurora's room. His ineptitude for domestic tasks infuriated him. Up until that point, Aurora had taken care of the house. For Leandro the washing machine may as well have been a refrigerator that washed the clothes. He took care of the financial stuff, the bank's itemizations, paying the bills, buying the wine, attending the miserable building meetings, but he didn't attend to the inner workings of the house. He knows that on Sundays Lorenzo and Sylvia come for lunch and there is almost always rice soup and batter-fried hake. And that on Thursdays when Manolo Almendros shows up at midday Aurora always invites him to stay and offers him his favorite chocolates for dessert. But he doesn't know how she manages to have them on hand. It upsets him to think of his wife disabled in a house that isn't prepared.

In three days, we'll be at home, he announced to Aurora, who was reading in bed. Then he sat close by her and opened the newspaper. They were both silent, reading almost in unison. Perhaps they were asking themselves similar questions, but they didn't say anything to each other. Mugshots of Islamic fundamentalist terrorists. The death of Yasser Arafat. The recent elections in America.

Osembe had come down to find him. Leandro sees her through the glass. She smiles and they kiss on both cheeks, yet she conveys the same absent air of their previous encounter. She brings him upstairs to a different room, somewhat larger. The window opens onto the backyard and the blinds are not completely lowered. The afternoon light streams in. Different room, he says. It's better, she says. The bathroom is bigger, with pale yellow tiles. Above the sink is a fixture with three oval mirrors. Leandro notices that it is almost identical to the one in his apartment, which unnerves him. She sits over a bidet and soaps up. Leandro feels a stab of disgust at the idea that she was underneath another client just a minute ago. He runs his fingers through his hair and looks in the mirror at the blotches on the skin of his forehead and cheeks. His is the face of an old guy. There's a Jacuzzi, you want to go in? asks Osembe. Maybe later, replies Leandro.

When he sits down to undress, he looks out into the back garden. He sees a half-filled pool and a white seesaw with rusty axles. Take off your clothes, Leandro tells Osembe. She places herself in front of him and undresses, without adding any intention to the purely mechanical act. She is slow to take off her last pieces of underwear, as if she wants to seem modest. She looks at herself and tenses the muscles in her thighs and buttocks. For a moment, she seems to forget that Leandro is in front of her. She chews gum. Leandro gets up to kiss her and gets a strong waft of strawberry breath. She doesn't move her mouth away, but she kisses him without passion, hiding the gum between her teeth.

Leandro hugs her and finishes undressing her. She laughs, without arousal, distant. I'll do it, lie down. Leandro obeys, going over to the bed. She is in control of the situation. Leandro tries to defy her authority because he finds no pleasure in her series of mechanical caresses. Do you want to fuck? she asks. Leandro feels ridiculous. He wants to make the encounter intimate, but he realizes that she refuses to break with her routine. She would rather everything be predictable, flat, professional. Leandro senses there could be a more distant, hidden pleasure, but he is forbidden access to that place. She chews gum, her thoughts far from there. It is obvious Leandro isn't managing to excite her as he rubs her sex, more like industrial than erotic manipulation. Come on, grandpa, she says. As if that's going to encourage him. A bad mood overtakes Leandro. That's okay, forget about that, she says and sits on the bed.

He wants to leave. What am I doing here? he asks himself. Her eyes look empty, as if nothing matters much to her.

The situation is then uncomfortable for them both. I suck, she says. No, says Leandro. He sits behind her and hugs her tightly to his chest. He caresses her arms and stomach. She tries to move, to change position and get back to the routine, but Leandro doesn't let her. She only wants the client to come. It is the only way she has of understanding her job. Like a craft. She doesn't aspire to get into his head. In fact it makes her uncomfortable to know Leandro is after something more than just an orgasm.

Leandro buries his face among Osembe's bands of hair. She laughs as if he were tickling her. She doesn't understand how he can find pleasure in running his hands over her back, her shoulders, in traveling the entire length of her body with his fingertips and resisting penetration. He, on the other hand, knows that that is what brought him back.

Early that afternoon, he had accompanied Luis, his student, to a store that sells used pianos where he knew the owners. It was an appointment they had scheduled a while ago. The owner was very friendly and the boy didn't dare try out the pianos. Leandro did it for him. They had a price limit. My parents won't let me spend more. Don't worry, Leandro told him, we'll find something good for that amount. They went to another store and there Leandro noticed a perfectly restored black upright piano that was less than thirteen hundred euros. He played it for a moment. It sounds wonderful, he said. As he ran his finger over its smooth black wood, Leandro knew that, as hard as he fought his desire to meet Osembe again at the chalet, that very afternoon he would go there again. And then he was overcome with an enthusiasm that his student and the salesman misinterpreted. Ah, Don Leandro still has the same passion for music as he did when we met. And it's been almost thirty years now, hasn't it?

Leandro had lost some of the enthusiasm he'd had earlier, even though now he was touching the skin he craved. He noticed a long scar beside the crease in Osembe's elbow. The wound intrigued him. Perhaps an accident in the village, a wild animal. Her dangerous childhood in Africa.

I got caught in an elevator when I was a little girl, she explained. In a department store.

And he busies himself with the rough skin on her elbow for a long while. Then he puts his fingers on her shaven sex. He feels the sandpaper of her pubic hair and how she tightens her strong muscles to impede his access. You want to fuck? Time's running out, says Osembe. Leandro notices she's uncomfortable with being touched. And he doesn't want to do anything but touch her. He discovers her ugly feet, with twisted toes and deformed toenails badly painted with white polish. He strokes her legs and arms, touches her nose, which flares when she breathes. I just want to get to know you, he explains, but she can't understand. Osembe gets up and shakes her ass comically up to Leandro's face. She moves her gluteal muscles up and down just by changing the muscle tension, happy as a girl who's proud of being able to wiggle her ears. You like my ass? Leandro studies it in front of his face, high, weightless, muscular.

No. I like you. And then he kisses it and she laughs and pulls away.

You want to pay more? asks Osembe when the time is up. You can pay for another hour. Osembe fondles her breasts, sticking her hands under the bra she hasn't taken off. Whitish stretch marks peek out.

Okay, says Leandro.

11

Lorenzo had painted the kitchen when Sylvia was seven years old. He remembers this now, sitting in front of the cordless phone. The wall is tiled halfway up and crowned by a blue braided stencil. The rest is painted by him. Salmon, said Pilar. But as Lorenzo made the first brushstrokes, she said, that isn't salmon, it's orange. They argued about the tones and the true color of some salmon slices they had eaten days before. They were like this, said Lorenzo pointing to the wall. No, salmon is salmon, she said. Then Pilar went to pick Sylvia up from school. The little girl went into the kitchen and saw her father up on a ladder, brushing a second coat into a corner. The kitchen looks so pretty painted orange, Sylvia said to him. Pilar smiled. I swear I didn't tell her anything. He never knew if Pilar had mentioned something about it to her on the way home. He does remember that they laughed. Those were other times.

The orange color had faded somewhat, as had the kitchen. A tile was still chipped from the day he had tried to screw in a hook to hold a rack for pots and pans. On the floor, a piece of the terrazzo was broken where Sylvia had dropped the flour tin while helping her mother make a cake. The door to one of the cabinets had been replaced, and the new one wasn't the exact same shade of white as the others.

Scars.

In the phone book where they kept frequently called numbers, many had accumulated that they had long since stopped calling frequently. Sylvia's pediatrician, various offices, the home phone number of a secretary, the babysitter they used to call when they went out for the night, three or four deceased relatives who remained in the limbo of the phone book, someone completely forgotten, some friend of Pilar's whom they didn't see anymore, the number of the school Sylvia used to go to, and there, under the letter *p*, were Paco's numbers. Home, cell, in-laws, and the summer place in Altea. Lorenzo inhaled before dialing the digits into the telephone.

The previous days had been intense. His mother in the hospital, his father fearing she'd never walk again, Sylvia's accident, Pilar's arrival. He spent two days in a row with her at the clinic. He offered to let her stay at the house. No, I can stay with a friend, she told him. Pilar asked how everything was going for him, if he was still looking for work, if he needed money. No, no, I'm fine, he lied. And then he said, did you hear about what happened to Paco? He was killed at home, it was in the newspapers. Pilar was silent. The news seemed to affect her. Lorenzo had decided that he could talk about it, that he should. He mentioned it to his father, to his friend Lalo; he told Sylvia about it.

Tuesday around noon, he had found a message on the answering machine. A detective named Baldasano identified himself as a part of the homicide team and left a phone number. When Lorenzo called, the man was very brief. I just want to ask you a few questions, he said. We know that you were Mr. Garrido's partner. Yes, of course, I found out from the newspapers, said Lorenzo. You understand that we want to have a little consultation with you. The word sounded ambiguous, worrying. Lorenzo explained that that afternoon he had to pick up his daughter from the hospital, he told him about the accident, asked if it would be possible to postpone the appointment until tomorrow. Everyday life, normality, was the best evidence in his defense.

A policeman led him into an office where he was received by Detective Baldasano, who was drinking coffee from a short brown plastic cup. He offered Lorenzo a coffee as he opened a file. No, I just had breakfast, thanks. Lorenzo was nervous and thought that the best thing would be to admit it. I'm kind of nervous, to be honest. There's no reason for you to be, the policeman reassured him. Look, it's very simple. Everything points toward a robbery by one of the regular gangs that operate in the city, the violent ones, Colombians, Albanians, Bulgarians. But there are some things still up in the air. We asked Mr. Garrido's wife to give us an update on her husband's business dealings, to tell us about people he might still have unresolved conflicts with, and I'm gonna be honest with you . . . your name came up.

Lorenzo nodded, without allowing himself to be surprised. Paco and I had a relationship, well, we were friends and partners and the whole thing ended terribly, that's true, said Lorenzo. We know, the detective reassured him, but his tone wasn't reassuring at all. It happened a while ago and we hadn't seen each other in a long time. We stopped being friends, but that doesn't mean we were enemies. I don't hold any . . . Well, I don't know, Paco was a slick operator, the term had slipped out casually, lightly. Lorenzo was glad he had said it. It was effective. The detective chewed out a yeah.

Paco cheated me. We set up a small business together, I lost my money and, well, he didn't lose as much as I did, and, I don't know, that made me feel ripped off. We're talking about two or three million of the old pesetas, we're not talking about amounts that . . . Lorenzo stopped himself. He didn't want to talk about the murder. Paco had his wife's family money and, well, for him the business going under wasn't such a big deal.

I've tried to remake my life elsewhere and I've never made any claims on him. The detective didn't speak; he was waiting for Lorenzo to add something more. He did. When I read the news I felt sad, I wasn't pleased at all. I felt sad for her, Teresa, more than anything.

Lorenzo thought he shouldn't talk too much, but maintaining the flow of words calmed him. Lying so naturally surprised him as much as it soothed him. It gave him the strength to confront the detective's silences. Did he have many enemies? asked Baldasano. As the detective lifted his face, Lorenzo saw that he had a wound on his neck, covered by his shirt, a pink scar, not very long. It looked more like a burn than a cut. *Enemies* is a strong word, said Lorenzo. He didn't make a good impression on people, that's for sure. The detective asked him about Thursday night. Do you have anyone who can testify they were with you? Lorenzo thought for an instant. My daughter. I live with my daughter. I'm separated.

The detective nodded his head, as if he already knew those details. He lifted his eyes toward Lorenzo. I'm going to ask you a question that you have every right not to answer. This is just a consultation, though.

There it was, that word again. Outside the door was such a wide variety of telephone rings that you could mistake them for carousel music. Above the detective's head, on the ceiling, was a gray, moldy, damp leak.

Do you know anyone, from your professional relationship, who might have enough motive to murder Mr. Garrido? Lorenzo pretended to be thinking, going over the list of Paco's acquaintances. For a moment, he tried to find someone and the exercise calmed him, transporting him to a distant idea, making him innocent in the simplest way. No, he said. And, without really knowing why, he felt the need to add that Paco was a person you couldn't hate.

Lorenzo didn't say anything more. He looked up at the leak on the ceiling again. The detective also looked up toward the stain. Can you believe it? It's been like that for six days. It's the bathroom upstairs, in the passport department. I can assure you it's quite unpleasant to sit here all morning knowing you have a puddle of piss over your head. Well, I won't take up any more of your time. I will ask you to jot down all your contact numbers. I'd like to have you always on hand, in case I need to consult you on anything.

He was in love with that word. *Question* must have sounded too threatening to him. Tricks of the trade. He held out a sheet of paper to Lorenzo, for him to write down his phone numbers. The last one is my parents' house, just in case. Then he thought maybe that was being too solicitous. He left the office and was grateful that one of the policemen came up the stairs right then, shouting because someone had vomited on his shoes. Goddamn it, even my socks are soaked, fuck. Amid the laughter and joking of the other cops, Lorenzo looked for the door.

He left the station calmer. Lying had given him the same feeling of freedom as telling the truth. A false confession is still a confession. Talking about it, putting himself in a different place, had helped him get distance. Sometimes a lie fits perfectly over the truth. When he said Paco was someone you couldn't hate, he said it because it was true. He thought that that's where his mistake lay, from having crossed the line. Actually hating him. Paco was the one to blame for his work situation, for his inability to give Pilar what she needed, for his parents' commiserating look when they lent him money, for his fall from grace. Paco was the one to blame for his daughter no longer falling asleep on the living room sofa so he could carry her to her bed. To blame for his having blanked out in a job interview, there in front of some young slick-haired executive who had just asked him, why do you think a professional like you hasn't achieved job stability in all these years? To blame for the fact that he shares the streets at midmorning with housewives and old folks. To blame for pushing him off the path, a path he now has to find again without anyone's help.

In the kitchen, Lorenzo dials Paco's home number. The same number he called so many times to hear his friend's voice, the voice that arranged to meet him at a restaurant or said, see you tomorrow at the office. The same voice that one day told him, Loren, I think we've lost it all, and he was lying because only one of them had. The phone rang once, twice, three times, before Teresa answered in a whisper. That lifeless, silent presence, that woman whose reserve compensated for her husband's expansiveness. The same one who had pointed Lorenzo out as a suspect. The police often work like that, they have no leads, they have no clues, they have no indications, but they pressure a suspect, they pressure him until he crumbles, and then they work the investigation back from the conclusion, they solve the crime with the criminal. But it wasn't going to be so easy to defeat him.

Hello, Teresa, it's Lorenzo. Hello. Her voice sounds distant, as if rising from the depths. I heard about what happened to Paco and I've been debating whether or not to call, I don't know, I wanted to tell you that I'm really sorry, if you need . . . Lorenzo pauses. He doesn't want to be cruel to himself, to the last grain of sincerity rising up inside him. Thank you for calling, she says. No, I . . . I know it isn't easy, but I wanted . . . It's okay, thank you, she says, cutting him off. A second later she hangs up the phone.

Lorenzo gets up from the chair and drinks water straight from the kitchen faucet, like a kid at a fountain. It bugged Pilar when he did that. Why dirty a glass? he used to say. He leans on the counter and the world seems to stop. She suspects me, thinks Lorenzo. She has a right. It's not going to be easy. It's not going to be easy.

12

Ariel drives into the house's attached garage. The living room is cold. When the sun goes down, the weather changes. There are newspapers piled up beneath the table, towers of CDs on the floor, a flat-screen television stuck to the wall. Emilia's hand organizes it all, imposing an impersonal air that rules over the house. Charlie is no longer with him and the only sound is the refrigerator engine and the sprinkler that spits in the yard.

When he overcame his paralysis after running over the girl, he was able to get out of the car and pick her up off the ground. He helped her to stand, but then she collapsed. He got her settled into the backseat. She was almost a little girl, her curly hair messy, covering her face. She didn't say anything, she didn't complain about the pain. Through the rearview mirror, Ariel saw the girl's torn pants, her chest heaving as she breathed. He couldn't get his bearings, he didn't know where the closest hospital was, he feared he had made a mistake in lifting her, moving her. He dialed Pujalte's number on his cell phone, thinking that it was the most sensible thing to do. I just ran over a girl on the street, he said, I don't know what to do. Pujalte calmed him down, didn't ask him for any more explanations. Where are you? Ariel referenced the places he knew. You're very close to the stadium, can you get there? Of course, he said. Wait for me at door fourteen.

It didn't take him long to drive there. He stopped in front of the designated door after going around the building. He got out of the car. Through the window he saw the girl lying down. She was breathing, she seemed calm, as if she had fainted. The waiting seemed eternal. The stadium grounds were still littered with trash from the game. Papers, cans sprinkled around the sidewalk. Finally a car arrived quickly, running a red light. It stopped beside him. It wasn't driven by Pujalte, as he was expecting, but by Ormazábal, the head of security. Did she recognize you? Did you talk to her? No, hardly at all, said Ariel, I just whispered don't worry, we're on our way to the hospital.

From the front passenger seat emerged a man about forty years old, with short black hair. He took the keys out of Ariel's hand and sat at the wheel of the Porsche. He'll take care of it. Come on, get in, I'll take you home, relax. Ariel saw his car head off, driven by the man. It took him a little while to get into Ormazábal's car. They barely spoke. He seemed to know the way to Ariel's house without any directions. His cell phone rang. Ormazábal nodded, two, three times. Uh-huh, he said. Then he turned toward Ariel. Everything's under control, the girl is fine. Ariel wasn't able to ask him anything. A bit later, the phone rang again. Ormazábal passed it to Ariel. It was Pujalte. Well, she's at the hospital, with reliable people. Ormazábal's guy took care of everything, he said that he was driving. You don't need to worry about anything. Is it serious? asked Ariel. It was an accident, nothing special, she has a fracture, but she's in the best hands. Ariel was silent. You were drinking, it looks like. A little bit. Well, tomorrow I'll see you at practice, okay? Go home and get a good night's sleep. Everything's fine. Thank you so much, said Ariel. It's my job.

Pujalte's reply stuck in him like a dagger. That was his farewell. Then he hung up. Ariel felt like the smallest man in the world, paralyzed there beside the stadium. The place where he had supposedly come to make it big. The loudspeaker that would make his name known throughout the world now was merely witness to his cowardice. Up until that point, he had been an exemplary player, never argumentative or aggressive, and now at this new post everything was a problem, unanticipated difficulties. Ormazábal left him at the fence that surrounded his house. These things happen, he said as he drove off. He was a cold, creepy person and he went to great pains to seem friendly, but he didn't pull it off.

Ariel had trouble sleeping. He didn't call his family, even though he promised he would after the game. He didn't want to share bad news. Charlie had left him a message. He was already in Buenos Aires.

In the morning at practice, he waited for Pujalte's arrival on the edge of the field. He lay down on the ground for the first stretches and he liked feeling the dampness, the smell of fresh-cut grass. That was the same in every field. Caressing the green, feeling your cleats sink in like an affectionate bite.

There wasn't a lot of press, just the usual. The cameras would arrive later in the morning. The group of kids who had skipped class to collect autographs and the retirees gathered in the stands. Pujalte appeared and stopped to chat with the physical trainer. Then he gestured for him to come over. Ariel ran toward him. That was power. That and his street shoes on the damp grass, something that always bothered the players.

Pujalte put an arm over his shoulders and walked with him along the sideline. He explained that Doctor Carretero had taken care of the girl, there was total discretion. They had talked to the father, everything was worked out. Your car is in the parking lot. For all intents and purposes, someone else was driving, you got that? Ariel nodded. The girl is sixteen, she'll heal fast.

Ariel was quiet. So much so that the sports director gave him an encouraging slap. Come on, what you should be worrying about now is the game. Ariel thanked him for his words with a nod. Last year the vice president died on us in a hotel in Bilbao, fucking a conference hostess. We had to be quick on that one, fuck. That thing with your brother, too, he added, these things happen. It's better if they don't, okay, but we're here to solve problems, keep the ball out of the goal box. That's what I've spent all my life doing. Pujalte smiled with his whitened teeth. I was never an elegant player, but I was effective.

Ariel went back to practice. He joined in the one-touch passing exercise. When it landed in the center, he was slow to recover the ball. Sixteen years old? He thought, poor girl. Had Pujalte lied to him? Was it worse than he had said? He tried to remember the impact, if something more than her leg had been hurting her. She was passed out for a while. The coach handed out the bicolored training bibs for the final practice game. Ariel couldn't focus; he just killed time.

In the parking lot, he looked for his car. The keys were in it. There was no trace of blood or the girl or the bottle. Someone had gone to the trouble of cleaning up after him. Knuckles knocked on the window and Ariel jumped. It was a journalist, young, with blond bangs. Ariel lowered the window and she approached with a tape recorder. She introduced herself and asked him some questions, the last one: when do you think the Spanish fans will see you in full form? Ariel hesitated. The young woman made an effort to have her body language mimic the gestures of a man. Looking him straight in the eye.

Soon, I hope.

When he got home, Emilia was almost finished making *cocido*, a traditional stew in Madrid. Have you ever tried it? Yes, well, something similar, it's like *puchero*, said Ariel, looking at the mess of chickpeas, vegetables, meat, chorizo, bacon, and black sausage. I'm leaving you a pot of soup. He tried to nap, but he ended up in the yard knocking the ball around. When he was thirteen, he once spent an entire afternoon kicking the ball without it touching the ground. He got up to five thousand kicks without it dropping. It was a useless exercise, exhausting, but at that moment it helped him to clear his head, to bring him back to a state of comfortable oblivion. Suddenly, he decided the exercise was over. He stepped hard on the ball.

He had made a decision.

Being recognized was the most absurd part of his job. He liked when some kid asked for his autograph, when they looked at him on the street, when he was recognized in restaurants, but it was a pain in the neck when you were trying to lead a normal life. The accident would have been completely different if he wasn't a celebrity. He had been drinking, he was driving fast, it would be easy for the press to vent their anger on him, for it to get him into real trouble. He understood the club's cover-up, the favor they'd done for him, erasing his trail. But he wasn't like that. He arrived at the hospital when it was already night. When he could be sure visiting hours were over.

He knew the place. He had had his physical examination there the day after he arrived in Madrid. And when he left, he posed for the reporters. Do you know how much they pay us to photograph you here? Pujalte whispered to him. Twenty thousand euros. It was his way of explaining how the advertising business around soccer worked.

The receptionist recognized him. I'm here to see a friend, she was run over yesterday, a young girl. Three twelve, she said. Sylvia Roque. Then she pointed to the elevator with a huge smile.

Ariel was slow to approach the door. He knocked cautiously. He was surprised at how the girl received him. You're the one who ran me over, right? She had beautiful curly black hair that fell onto the pillow. The bedspread covered her, pulled up over her breasts. She smiled with one leg in a cast that hung in the air. And that accent? Where are you from?

From Buenos Aires.

Buenos Aires, never been there. Is it pretty? The girl seemed comfortable. Ariel had suspected it would be tense. But she showed him a crooked, self-assured smile. She opened the chocolates. Ariel looked around the room. You want one? Ariel refused with a gesture of his hand. He watched her eat a chocolate. She had a pretty mouth. The television spat out music in English.

I really came to apologize, for not bringing you to the hospital myself. It would have gotten me into a bad fix and, well, I was with a friend. He started to lie again. He decided to stop suddenly, not do it again.

You're a soccer player, right? Ariel nodded. What's your name? Ariel approached the bed, at thigh height, where her cast began. Ariel. Ariel Burano. Ariel, that's nice. It's the name of a detergent brand here, she said. I know. Ariel reached for one of the sports newspapers and showed her his photo on one page, with the headline MISSING IN ACTION above it. As you can see, I'm wildly successful, he added.

Sylvia looked into his eyes. And why did you come now? I felt morally obligated. I don't know, I felt awful about not telling the truth. I wanted to make sure you were being well taken care of, all that. My father is a fan of your team, he loves soccer, Sylvia told him. But you don't? People here are batshit over soccer. It's the same in Argentina, isn't it? The same or worse.

Sylvia thought for a second and smiled again. So you mean I could go to the press with this story and get some serious dough. Yeah. Relax, I'm not going to. My father says your friend was very good to me. He works for the club. As a scapegoat? I don't know the city, I didn't know where to take you or how to get to a hospital, Ariel justified.

Sylvia shook her head. It was an accident. I'm glad you came and we met. Will you invite me to a game when I get out? Ariel appreciated the opportunity to be gracious. If you want. Sylvia's smile didn't fade. The doctor says I'll be better pretty soon and then I could steal your job. I wouldn't be surprised.

Ariel pulls his cell phone out of his jacket pocket. Do you have a cell phone? Sylvia gives him her number. Ariel gives her his and as they exchange numbers it seems that their hands intertwine, without actually touching. If there's anything you need, call me.

Stop feeling guilty. How do you know I didn't throw myself under your car because I wanted to kill myself? Ariel smiled. Why would a girl like you want to kill herself?

Should I make you a list?

When they said good-bye, Ariel said, it was a pleasure to meet you. Well, the next time you want to meet a girl, you don't have to run her over.

Ariel still hadn't figured out how to turn on the heat. He puts on a sweatshirt. He has leftovers from lunch for dinner. He calls Charlie. He doesn't tell him anything about the accident. I played like shit. Don't say that, reprimands his brother. You have to see our folks, they got fat, they think they're Maradona's parents. Ariel tells him that the first critical comments are starting to appear in the papers. Do they think you're gonna be the first bad Argentinian player they ever sign, you're not even original in that, goaded Charlie. Why don't you invite someone to spend a week there with you? Ariel thinks about his brother's suggestion. It's not a bad idea. Maybe he's thinking about Agustina. They say good-bye and Ariel is soon asleep. He rests for the first time in days, with the help of Sylvia's gaze from her hospital bed, infected by the peacefulness of her smiling eyes.

13

The room is covered in pine shelves that sag from the weight of the books. There are books on their spines, on their fronts, stacked on top of other books, books two and three rows deep, books on the floor, beneath the bottom shelf. Some of them have wrinkled, gnawed papers sticking out between the pages; they look like notes, photocopies. Sylvia looks at them as if they formed a whole, nearly a sculpture. The room has nothing else, except for the lamp, her bed, and a small round table. She had come to her mother's new house a few days after leaving the hospital. She should say Santiago's house. Light filters in through the blinds. She isn't sleepy.

At first her mother's job was an awkward obligation. What's the point of suffering? Lorenzo used to say. She worked producing cultural events, but her job was more bureaucratic and less creative: permits, organizing trips, hotel stays, filing invoices. Now it turns out she's discovered that being a secretary was her lifelong dream, Sylvia heard her father say one day. Lorenzo never liked his wife's job, which often required overtime that slipped like lava into the weekends, into her time at home. Pilar was about to quit. That was when Santiago came to take over the Madrid office.

Sylvia witnessed the change. Suddenly her mother's job was interesting, it was what supported them, an activity that generated conversation over family dinners. She seemed happy, busy, with an overflowing engagement calendar always in her hand. At that same time, her father's job began to be a source of problems, of tensions, of uncertainty, of bad feelings. Paco,

Papá's partner, the fun guy who always brought her presents, stopped coming by, became someone whose name couldn't be mentioned, who no longer called. A ghost.

You hooked up with your boss? thought Sylvia when her mother told her who her new boyfriend was. Santiago was planning to go back to Saragossa, his hometown. She was moving there with him. What are you going to do there? Sylvia asked. The same thing I do now, the work is the same.

Her mother often told her about the new city. It is smaller, more accessible, friendlier than Madrid. You don't waste your life in traffic jams or getting from one place to another. Getting away from Madrid has done me good. For me that city will always be linked to Lorenzo.

Santiago's house in Saragossa is big. It's filled with papers, books. There are two abstract paintings, one in the living room and another in his study. There is also a poster from a 1948 Picasso exhibition and in the kitchen there's a huge drawing of a table filled with fruit, vases, flowers. Through the living room windows you can see the iron bridge, painted green, over the river. It's a beautiful, relaxing view that Sylvia has spent hours looking at when she's alone in the house. The water flows forcefully and is the color of mud.

Her father had driven her home from the hospital. He left her at the door while he looked for a parking spot. Sylvia held the manila envelope with her X-rays between her fingers. She still hadn't mastered the crutches. She waited. Finding a spot at that hour could take a while. Her father had been complaining ever since they left the hospital. And now, parking, you'll see . . . he said. The Ecuadorian woman who takes care of the boy on the fifth floor came in from the street. The boy had fallen asleep in his stroller with his legs dangling like a marionette at rest. The young woman had a pretty face. She was stocky and as she turned Sylvia got a glimpse of her round thighs. They greeted each other without a word. She called the elevator and noticed Sylvia's cast. What happened? I got hit by a car, Sylvia told her. Damn cars. Sylvia nodded and watched her skillfully fit the stroller into the elevator. The boy's little legs swung with her maneuvering.

Lorenzo came back after some time. It's incredible. What, are we supposed to just swallow the car? Sylvia found her father's constant complaining amusing. That night they sat together in the living room to watch a soccer game. Ariel was playing and Sylvia followed him with her gaze, as her father criticized him harshly. That kid is no good, he's got no blood in his veins. Why do they call him Feather? Is he gay? asked Sylvia. Her father looked at her insolently. There are no gay soccer players, are you crazy? They call him that because he's little. Well, he's not that small.

Lorenzo's harsh criticism of Ariel eventually started to irritate Sylvia. I don't think he plays so bad. The other ones aren't exactly doing much either. What do you know about soccer? The cameras showed Ariel's annoyed expression when he was taken out of the game. They were beating a Polish team, one nothing, one of those teams that the sportscasters claim have no competitive pedigree. Sylvia saw how Ariel's sweaty hair stuck to his forehead, how the television darkened his face and made him seem more hefty. When they substituted him, he went to sit on the bench and loosened the laces on his sneakers, lowered his knee socks, and tossed his blue ankle supports to the ground. He put on a zippered sweatshirt and lifted his legs, pulling his knees to his chest. For the last fifteen minutes, Sylvia hadn't really been following the game. Her father had put a cushion beneath her cast so she could rest it on the table. He offered her something to drink and fried some eggs for dinner.

Mom says I should go stay with her until Monday, said Sylvia. Lorenzo shrugged his shoulders. Whatever you want.

Pilar comes into Sylvia's bedroom after knocking lightly on the door. She helps her sit up. You want to shower? Later, says Sylvia. Her hair is tangled and her eyes swollen after sleeping almost twelve hours. Pilar thinks she looks gorgeous and tells her so. Santiago went to Paris and won't be back until tonight. Sylvia puts a sweater on over her T-shirt and her mother puts a winter sock on her other foot. They go to the kitchen, Sylvia hopping. Pilar makes breakfast for her. Drink your juice first, otherwise it loses its vitamins. Are you cold? Do you want me to bring you some pants?

Her mother usually dressed down at home. Sometimes she would share a worn bathrobe with Lorenzo. So Sylvia was surprised by the skirt and shoes. They were new. They looked good on her. The thick weave of the sweater hid her extreme skinniness. Her hair was better taken care of, tastefully cut and dyed a mahogany shade that brought out her eyes.

The night before, Sylvia called Mai. She had gone to León again this weekend. Mateo is treating me horribly, I'll tell you about it later, she told Sylvia. It's that I'm super-clingy. It was hard to talk to Mai about anything but her new relationship. She had talked to Alba and Nadia, too. No news at school. She'd missed a week, but, according to them, nothing happened. She hasn't spoken to Dani since the chilly text message exchange. She checks her cell phone every once in a while, carrying it in her hand when she moves around on her crutches. It's strange, but she often has the feeling that Ariel is going to call her. When it rings or a message comes in she's surprised to notice that she gets a little worked up imagining it might be him.

But it never is.

Pilar sits in front of her and brushes a lock of hair out of her face. Do you want me to pull it back for you? Sylvia shakes her head, making her curls quiver. How does Lorenzo seem to you? Pilar asks her. All her life, he's been Papá and now hearing her mother call him Lorenzo surprises her; she finds it strange, as if Pilar were talking about someone else. Maybe she is. Does he see his friends much? Sylvia shrugs her shoulders. I don't know, the usual, they go to games. They talk about Grandma Aurora, the string of hospital stays. Pilar gets serious. I'm going to give you some money, I don't want you to have to ask Papá for money during all this. Sylvia smiles and holds the glass of warm milk with both hands. I should warn you that I'm going to spend it all on drugs and men. I have no doubt about that, replies Pilar. Better to spend it on men, and on quality ones, at least. Sylvia looks up. My problem isn't quality, it's quantity. Pilar gathers up the glasses and brings them to the sink. Do you have a boyfriend now? Sylvia is taken by surprise. *Now?* As if I ever had a boyfriend *before*. Sylvia shakes her head, takes a bite of her toast. There's no rush, says her mother. Well, I hope it's before I'm an old crone. Pilar turns, amused, I notice a certain hint of desperation. A certain hint? I'm totally desperate.

A second later Sylvia asks, Mamá, how old were you when you first had sex? With a man? No, with your teddy bear, responds Sylvia. Pilar pauses. Twenty years old. Sylvia lets out a whistle. I hope it's not hereditary. She observes her mother's shy smile and makes a mental calculation. But, then, that was with Papá, right? Pilar nods. Papá was your first? Sylvia's gaze wanders before settling on the table. She makes the plate dance on the tabletop with her fingertip. She doesn't look at her mother as she asks, and Santiago was the second? Pilar nods.

For a moment, she only hears the sound of a bus opening its door at the stop. Sylvia thinks about her mother, reviews her life in fast-forward. Without really knowing why, she says, what a life, huh? Kind of . . . Pilar looks at her, and her eyes dampen. There was a time when I was very happy with your father. I may never be that happy again with anybody. I haven't missed . . . but she stops, she doesn't finish the sentence. Sylvia plays with a lock of hair and brings it to her mouth. Pilar sits back down in front of her and pulls the lock out. They don't say anything. Sylvia reaches for the radio on the corner of the table. She searches for a station with music that's not too cheesy. Heavy guitars. Do you really like that noise? asks Pilar. Who would have guessed it.

14

He goes back on Thursday.

Leandro is in the Jacuzzi. His back rests against Osembe's chest and his hands are on her thighs. She caresses him with a sponge and for a moment it looks like he is going to fall asleep in her arms. The bathroom is not very large and has a shower with a murky glass door splattered with drops. The Jacuzzi is blue, oval. Every once in a while, it shoots out jets and Osembe laughs at the underwater massage. A thin layer of foam has formed. Leandro's gray hair is damp and hangs limp. I've been reading about your country, says Leandro. It's very big. It has more than a hundred million inhabitants and they say that soon it will be the third most populated country on the planet. I'm from the Delta, she says, Itsekiri. And she pronounces the word in a very different tone from the one she uses in Spanish, less tentative. You're in good spirits today. Happier, Leandro says to her. Osembe squeezes up against him. You come, I happy.

Leandro had sat among the students at the outsize tables of the Cuatro Caminos public library, with the encyclopedia open, to learn something more about Osembe's country, as if he, too, were preparing for an upcoming exam. He read about its history, its legendary founding, the religious divisions, the poverty, independence, corruption. You know more than I do, says Osembe now when she listens to him. My country is very rich, the people very poor. Someone knocked on the door. It's Pina, an Italian girl with very short hair, dyed blond. She comes in wrapped in a towel, as if she just finished a session. This is the life, she says with a chipper accent. Leandro remembers her from the parade of girls the first day. Do you mind? Leandro feels them both watching him, waiting for his response. Okay, he says.

Pina takes off the green towel. Her body is thin, with scant breasts, her ribs showing. She gets into the tub and sits in front of them. She extends her arms, approaches, and the three bodies touch. Very lucky grandpa, two girls for him, she says, and Leandro regrets having let her get in, though he is still smiling. She seems too cheerful; maybe she's on drugs. She kisses Leandro on the mouth, but a second later caresses Osembe's breasts and kisses her on the shoulder. You like to watch? Pina strokes Osembe and they mock him with a very coarse, obvious lesbian game.

That afternoon Leandro was reading the newspaper beside Aurora's bed. She seemed to envy his concentration. Read me the news. Leandro looked up. At that precise moment he had been immersed in the international pages. In Nigeria, which had attracted his attention because it is Osembe's homeland, there was a strike of workers at the oil refineries. More than fifty dead during the protests. It was a devastated, polluted territory, where the large oil company controlled all the resources. Yet the violence had been sparked by religious conflicts between Muslims and Christians. What do you want me to read to you? asked Leandro. Whatever. He skipped over the international pages. It was also best not to read about domestic politics. Endless electoral campaigns. He read her the crime section. A man had killed his wife by throwing her off the balcony of their house. The young woman was four months pregnant. Two men had stabbed each other in an argument over soccer. It seems they were brothers and had gone to the game together. What is the world coming to, my God, said Aurora, and Leandro took that to mean he should skip that section, too.

He read her an interview with a British writer who had fictionalized the life of Queen Isabella "the Catholic." Today, in his opinion, she would have been locked up in a psychiatric institution as a hopeless paranoid with hysterical delusions. Leandro looked up. Aurora seemed interested. He continued. The decision to expel the Jews was actually made by her mediocre advisers, who were afraid of the economic and social power the Jews were beginning to enjoy. The advisers feared losing their positions of influence, choosing instead to go against the best interests of the country. He had heard his friend Manolo Almendros talking authoritatively on the subject at some point. With the expulsion of the Jews, Spain makes its first formal declaration of mediocrity, officially becoming a despicable nation filled with complexes. And on the second of May, he added, territorialism won out, each region making up for the national powerlessness. Leandro continued reading, but an ad on the bottom of the opposite page drew his eye. As part of a classical music series, sponsored by a bank, it advertised a piano concert by Joaquín Satrústegui Bausán. On February 22. He mentioned it to Aurora. Look, Joaquín is going to play the Auditorio. Are you going to get tickets? How long has it been since we've seen him? she asks. Almost eight years. It would be nice to see him play again. Leandro hesitates. I don't know, if you want to.

Leandro and Joaquín Satrústegui had known each other since childhood. They grew up on the same street in Madrid. They played together among the ruins of the bombings during the war. They collected bullets, remains of the bombs launched by Franco's planes. With Joaquín he had found a corpse amid the rubble on an embankment that is now part of the Avenida de la Castellana. A swarm of flies had clustered on the man's swollen belly and Leandro threw a big rock onto him to scare them off. The rock, when it sunk into the chest, made a dull sound, like a parade bass drum breaking. The two boys ran off, but the scene gave Leandro recurring nightmares throughout his childhood. He still can't eat raw meat. That morning Leandro told his mother what they had seen. Beasts, was all she said. Nothing more. But he never forgot the desolate tone of her response.

He had vague memories of the war, that boundless time

when kids lived in the streets. The victory meant the return of men, the return of the absent authority figure, the end of freedom. Leandro's father purged his Republican affiliation with two years of military service, but his destiny was helped along by Joaquín's father. During the war, that man, a career soldier, had been given up for lost near Santander and, in the neighborhood, everyone treated Joaquín like an orphan and helped his mother survive and raise him and his older sister. But his father came back with an important military post and a tidy situation once the war was over. They said he was a hero, that he had been in Burgos, close to command. He was a large man, with a heavy gait, his face run through with tiny red veins and an enormous double chin that spilled over his chest like a fleshy bib. Joaquín's piano lessons took place at the house and Leandro, by then known to everyone as the seamstress's son, particularly after his father's death from gangrene, was allowed to join in. Don Joaquín also paid for both of them to study at the conservatory. He told them, work hard, because art is what distinguishes men from beasts. Any animal knows how to bite, how to procreate, how to survive, but can it play the piano? Joaquín and Leandro secretly made fun of him and forced Inky, Joaquín's mother's ugly, bad-tempered dachshund, to play the piano with his paws. Boy, will my father be surprised when he sees you play Chopin's nocturnes.

As a teenager Joaquín's relationship with his father grew more tentative. At seventeen he moved to Paris to continue his piano studies. He and Leandro kept in touch, at first by writing, then sending greetings to each other through mutual friends, and finally they only saw each other when Joaquín came back to Spain for some concert, after he had become a celebrated pianist. Losing friends is a slow process, in which two people who are close move in separate directions until the distance is irreparably great. Leandro saw Don Joaquín die, old, sad, longing for news of a son he admired, but barely spoke to. Leandro understood the man's bitterness. He, too, had become something remote to Joaquín, a memory of another time. He might not even remember us, he said to Aurora. Come on, she replied, don't be silly.

Aurora urged him to order tickets for the concert; Leandro gave in. It moved him that Aurora was more enthusiastic about it than he was. He's your friend, he'll be glad to see us. Shortly after, he stopped reading because of the aggravating presence of Benita, the cleaning lady, who, at that point in the morning, was more focused on conversation than on physical labor.

When they left the hospital, the doctor recommended that Leandro get a wheelchair for the first few days, for trips outside. That afternoon Leandro went to a specialized store on Calle Cea Bermúdez. The wheelchair was heavier than he thought it was going to be. He doubted his ability to maneuver it and decided to rent it. With any luck, Aurora would walk again without any difficulty; at least the doctor was optimistic. His relief at leaving the hospital was overshadowed by his panic at the new situation. Buy the nurses some chocolates, they've been good to me, said Aurora.

Now Pina was laughing hysterically, showing two large incisors, one on top of the other, an ugly mouth with thin lips, and a gaze that made Leandro uncomfortable. It is the first time he has been in one of those enormous bathtubs, filled with orifices. Osembe pushes Pina away from them twice, both times when the Italian woman is being too bold. Leandro lets her masturbate him for a while with her bony hands, the nails painted dark purple, but he moves closer to Osembe to make his preference clear. The afternoon ends without ecstasy or even real moments of shared pleasure.

The madam, Mari Luz, accepts Leandro's credit card. He explains that he doesn't have enough cash on him when she informs him that he has to pay for both girls. Leandro doesn't want to argue, but while the card receipt is printing he adds up the amounts. Today he's paying five hundred euros, plus the ten euro tip he slips into Osembe's hand every time he says goodbye. In two visits, he's used up his entire retirement check. I don't want the Italian girl to join us again, okay? Mari Luz nods, you're the boss, and Leandro feels he has regained control over the situation with that show of authority.

Leandro heads out into the street. His damp hair traps the cold afternoon breeze. He had combed his hair in front of the bathroom mirror. The little cabinet was empty and dirty. It had a comb and a worn toothbrush in it, a tube of toothpaste without a cap, crusty and clogged. The dirtiness of the place seemed to be tucked into corners, just hidden; you had to work to find it. On the street, he looks back at the chalet with the lowered blinds. I'm totally irresponsible, insane. He calms himself by thinking that maybe it is the last time he'll see that place. This has to end. It doesn't make sense.

It doesn't make sense.

15

Lorenzo waits at the door to his parents' house. He paces ten yards up the sidewalk, and then back down. The entryway is exactly as it was in his childhood, only the solid door was changed to a lighter, uglier, and more fragile one when they installed the intercom phone. After school he used to wait in that hallway for his mother if she hadn't yet arrived from shopping or some errand. He had spent many hours of his life sitting on that step. His childhood street was no longer how he remembered it. There used to be low houses with whitewashed walls and red roofs. Now the number of apartment buildings with aluminum windows has multiplied. The old couples that founded the neighborhood in the forties and fifties had almost all died. When they go out for a walk, they look more like shipwrecked sailors than neighbors.

Lorenzo responded to his father's call. His mother wants to go for a stroll and he can't get her downstairs alone. After two days of almost nonstop rain, weak sunlight illuminated the street. Lorenzo helped his father carry the wheelchair the two flights with no elevator. On the first landing, Leandro rubbed his hurting hands on his jacket. At home, his father's hands had always been protected. He never cooked or used knives, he didn't open cans or jam jars or carry dangerous things. He never did odd jobs around the house like other fathers. See if you can do it, you know Papá shouldn't touch it, Lorenzo's mother would say to him when it came time to hang a painting or check an outlet. His father's hands were what supported the family, and once when he hurt his finger by pinching it in a chair, he wore a leather fingerstall for days to protect it. That morning he carried the wheelchair to the street and it made him think, I'm too old and weak to take care of a sick woman. They live in a building without an elevator, with a wide, old staircase. They are banking on Aurora recovering her mobility, but if that doesn't happen, they'll both have to get used to a new way of living.

We'll take a stroll through the neighborhood, but we'll be back soon. Lorenzo had lied to them when he said he had a job interview. It wasn't hard to find a bar; that was one thing that hadn't changed. There's practically one for every two doorways. They survive over time, just bare bones. They're small, dirty, completely unsophisticated, but people use them as offices, meeting places, lunchrooms, confessionals, living rooms. There was a woman at the back sticking coins into a slot machine with her empty shopping cart parked beside her. The bar's aluminum countertop was so scratched it looked white. In the newspaper, he found a feature article on Madrid's lack of safety that mentioned Paco's murder. It was written in an alarmist tone, describing "the violated tranquillity of a man returning home at night." They called it a "brutal murder." Lorenzo continued on to the classifieds. He circled two. Maybe he'd call later.

He missed Sylvia. The rainy days without her at home had become heavy and sad. Lorenzo was comforted by the constant stream of music that came from her room. He liked to hear her going in and out in a rush, listen to the murmur of her talking on the phone with her friends. Without her the house was quiet. It didn't matter if he put on the TV or the radio, sat down to balance his checkbook in the kitchen, whistled in the living room. If she wasn't there, the echo turned the house into the den of a wounded wolf.

The day she left, Pilar came for her and Lorenzo offered to drive them to Atocha Station. He brought the car up to the doorway and as he was helping Sylvia get comfortable in her seat, another car appeared, honking and demanding to pass. Lorenzo turned violently and confronted the driver. It was a woman. What's the problem? Are you blind? The woman shot him a disdainful look and Lorenzo was about to walk over. Papá, leave it alone. That bitch saw your cast and still honked, what a joker. Lorenzo contained himself, seeing Pilar's nervous gesture in the backseat. He took his time sitting down behind the wheel. He stretched out the process of turning on the ignition. The city sometimes produced these car duels. The woman behind honked again. Lorenzo lifted his middle finger and showed it to her in the rearview mirror. Fuck you, moron.

Lorenzo sees his parents reappear on the corner, moving slowly, the wheelchair advancing in fits and starts. They pass a Filipino family and there is a car parked on the sidewalk that forces his father to maneuver the wheelchair pathetically down the curb. Have you been waiting long? No, no. They go upstairs. Aurora seems tired. What a nice day, don't you think? And she says it with a melancholy that tries to encompass more than the good weather. His parents' apartment now seems smaller to him, the hallway narrower, the living room inadequate; even the upright piano in his father's studio seems tiny. The cleaning lady bustles about. You still have her? asks Lorenzo. His father shrugs his shoulders. Months earlier Lorenzo had heard them argue over Benita. Poor woman, said Aurora. It seemed the problem was that her obesity only allowed her to do a rather superficial job. Also, given her short stature she would need stilts to dust the tops of the furniture. Your mother keeps her on out of pity, Leandro explained. No one has a cleaning lady out of pity, said Lorenzo, you hired her to work. She needs the money, she'd be so upset if I told her not to come anymore, I can't do that, concluded Aurora.

Lorenzo takes the bus back to his neighborhood. It's not far. He rides the 43 and then walks from the stop toward his house. In the market he buys a chicken breast cut into fillets. He heads home with the little bag. His friend Óscar had called him to go have a bite somewhere that night. He'll go out with him and his wife, maybe Lalo will join them. They'll chat about politics, soccer, someone will talk about some TV program or an incident at work. It's always better than staying home, watching television. The night before, Lorenzo went to bed early, but when he got under the sheets his sleepiness disappeared. He pulled out a Barbie doll he had been hiding in the back of the closet where his clothes piled up, sad that they no longer hung alongside Pilar's clothes. The Barbie was one of Sylvia's childhood toys, now forgotten, abandoned, too. She was blond, although her hair had lost its shine. She wore a short little dress that closed with Velcro. Lorenzo got into bed with her, took off her dress, and masturbated as he caressed her protruding, dynamic, streamlined breasts. His hands traveled over her shape, her perfect thighs and her almost tiptoed feet. He fantasized about the doll's ass, imagined it was real. Sometimes he made love to her in bed, other times in the bathtub. He had found her at the bottom of a box of toys that was lying around. When Pilar left, closets were gone through and the house got reorganized. It was like a partial move. The doll had taken him by surprise, as if she'd come back from the past. He was about to throw her into the garbage, but something stopped him. The doll spoke to him, her plastic touch aroused him, her studied form, the perverse design of her curves, her body language, her haughty, somewhat disdainful, cold, elitist nose. She became an absurd partner in his erotic games, a lonely comfort. After he came, Lorenzo dressed her again and hid her at the back of the closet, beneath the thick socks and the T-shirts he no longer wore.

Lorenzo arrives at the entrance to his building and calls the elevator, until he notices the little sign that says it's broken again. He sighs with annoyance. It happens too often. It's slow, small, and its motor breaks down every two or three weeks. When Lorenzo starts to climb the stairs, he hears the door to the street open. The Ecuadorian girl who works for the young couple on the fifth floor comes in. She's pushing a stroller and from the handles hang two full shopping bags. He sees her stop in front of the elevator and then head toward the stairs. He is about to ignore her, but thinks better of it. Let me help you. She thanks him, unsure if she should give him the bags or the stroller to carry.

Lorenzo puts his little white bag on the sleeping boy's lap and grabs the stroller by the front wheels. He lifts it up in the air. She does the same from the other end and they carry it up the stairs. The effort is somewhat repetitive: an hour earlier he carried his mother up in a similar way. The boy is sleeping, unaware of the clatter. Were you planning on carrying it up yourself, five flights? Lorenzo asks her. She shrugs. They have never exchanged more than hello; sometimes Lorenzo sticks out his tongue or winks at the boy, but with her there's never been more than a smile and a brief greeting. Now he watches her. She isn't very tall, she has straight brown hair that falls over her shoulders. Her body seems to widen as it goes down, but her face has lovely indigenous features. Her sharp, almond-shaped eyes, her thin but pretty mouth, her nose with personality, rounded but pleasant. Where are you from? Ecuador, she says. And your daughter? Lorenzo doesn't really understand the question. How's her leg? Oh, fine, fine. She went to spend some time with her mother. He's starting to feel tired but he'd rather not stop if she doesn't. Are you separated? Yes, but my daughter lives with me. Lorenzo can't help a burst of pride. Now I'm the father and the mother. Your daughter is great, really nice, she says. Sylvia? Yes . . . and Lorenzo thinks that maybe that's her way of criticizing him for not being very friendly. What's your name? Daniela, and you, sir? Sir? No, please, just Lorenzo.

A straight lock of hair has fallen in front of her face and Lorenzo has a desire to brush it aside; she blows it out of the way. In Loja we had a Spanish priest named Lorenzo. He told us about the martyrdom of Saint Lorenzo, it was very frightening. Lorenzo lifted his eyebrows. Yes, well, of course. On the grill and all that. They cross the third-floor landing. I'm named after San Lorenzo de El Escorial. It seems I was conceived there, on one of my father's jobs or something, they must have liked the name, because there are no other Lorenzos in my family. That's what they always told me. Daniela smiles shyly. Is El Escorial pretty? I've never been there. Lorenzo thinks for a second. Pretty? Well, it's . . . interesting. I can take you there someday if you'd like, I haven't been in ages. No, never mind, Daniela says, excusing herself as if she feared there had been a misunderstanding. Lorenzo becomes uncomfortable. She puts the stroller down. They have gotten to the fourth floor. This is your apartment, isn't it? Lorenzo objects. No, no, I'll take you up to yours, please. Daniela resists, but they go up the last flight quickly, barely speaking. Their breathing sounds heavier. They say good-bye once Daniela opens the door. And any time you want to go to El Escorial, I'll take you, okay? I'd love to, really. Daniela laughs and thanks him two more times.

Lorenzo tosses his jacket onto the sofa. He has broken out in a sweat from the exertion. He goes into the kitchen and drinks straight from the tap. Pilar didn't like it when he did that. Now it didn't matter anymore. She didn't like it when he shaved in the kitchen either, as he sometimes used to do. The light is better. And she laughed when she heard him urinating and flushing before he was finished. Are you in that much of a hurry? Now there was no one to call him on his little vices.

The doorbell rings. Lorenzo turns around. He lets it ring again. When he opens the door, he's surprised to see Daniela standing in the threshold. She lifts up Lorenzo's little bag with his groceries from the market and smiles. This is yours, right? Lorenzo grabs the little bag. Thanks, it's my food for today. That's all you're going to eat? Lorenzo shrugs his shoulders. I'm by myself. Suddenly he realizes that Daniela feels pity, almost sorry for a man over forty coming home alone with a ridiculous little bag of food. They don't say anything, but Daniela points to the apartment upstairs and reminds him that she has left the boy alone. Lorenzo watches her head up the stairs. She is wearing skin-tight pants, black jeans. He thinks of Pilar: she would never have dared to wear such snug clothes, no matter how thin she was. But these girls are that daring. They play up their breasts, butt, thighs, curves, they use bright colors, sometimes plunging necklines, they walk around with their bellies exposed, they show off without hang-ups no matter what their size. Sylvia inherited her mother's modesty about her body. She wears black, baggy clothes, she pulls at the sleeves of her sweaters until they are stretched out and cover her hands. If she is going out with friends, she ties a jacket around her waist to hide her ass.

Lorenzo leaves the living room television on, with the news, as he fries the chicken breast in a pan. He arrives in time to sit down and watch the fifteen minutes of sports devoted to soccer. In the fruit bowl, all that's left is a bruised pear, which shows a mushy, dark side.

16

Ariel flies at night, tired, on the charter plane that brings the team and reporters back from Oslo. That evening they played against a tough, rugged team, on a frozen field, beneath a blanket of cold. They had lost two nothing and he had played one of the worst games of his professional career. He could argue that the ball wasn't really circulating, that all his team's midfielders had done was return the Norwegians' fast clearances and that in every tackle and rebound the opponents' size weighed in heavily. He could argue that the touchlines were two degrees colder than the rest of the field, that he had chosen the wrong cleats, or that the fullback defending him was a super-fast blond who used his arms like windmill blades. He could also point to their fourteen fouls, but he knows full well that when you lose there are always too many excuses.

His teammates doze on the plane. The coach looks over the notes in his work. Matuoko snores with his mouth open. Jorge

Blai, confident that no one is watching, sticks boogers underneath the foldout tray in front of him. Seated in impossible positions, four or five players play a card game called *pocha* without the shouting that usually accompanies it. They lost and have to keep up appearances.

Osorio, seated beside Ariel, is playing video games. Ariel has his headphones on and is listening to Argentinian music. He finds it somewhat absurd to be hearing, on his way back from Norway, the verses of an old Marcelo Polti song that complain about the heat: "*hace calor, tanto calor que tus piernas esconden el centro de la tierra.*" He had met Marcelo, a huge San Lorenzo fan, two years ago. On the day he was made an honorary member of the club, Marcelo got down on his knees in the circle in the middle of the field and ate a fistful of grass to the euphoric applause of the stands. Then he invited the entire team to one of his concerts at the Obrero. I think I have all your albums, Ariel told him when they met backstage. You'll be able to say that tomorrow, Marcelo whispered to him, and the next morning he received two CDs with eighty songs that had never been released. They became good friends. He came to the Nuevo Gasómetro for every match and Ariel had twice been to Marcelo's house in Colegiales, with its basement turned into a recording studio, from where, he said, I only leave to steal moments and stick them into songs, like a vampire. He was pedantic, excessive, a wannabe genius, chaotic, an inveterate smoker and yerba maté drinker, allergic to drugs after having tried them all; Ariel fell in love for the first time with one of his songs, with a girl who only existed in lyrics from 1995, named Milena. "Milena, those kisses into the air, my arms around nothing, I'm saving them for you, baby . . ." Every week he got a protracted e-mail, encouraging him if his morale seemed low, remember that I ate the grass you walk on. Marcelo tells him the latest news and congratulates him on the distance, an ocean away from this country seems perfect. He was going on about Mr. Blumberg, practically a national leader, whose teenage son Axel was murdered by kidnappers with a bullet to the temple in a dump in La Reja. Ariel was in the massive march on April 1 in front of Congress. There the boy's father led the citizens' rebellion against violence and lack of safety. Marcelo ridiculed the political weight he was starting to throw around. This is a country of crazies, they've turned around what being a victim has always meant, now they use pain to beat down those on the margins of society, as an alibi to punish the poor, and he went on like that for paragraphs and paragraphs, venting on current events in Argentina, the only country in the world where two things and their opposites happen every fifteen minutes, according to Marcelo's definition of it.

The reporters' laughter is heard from the rear seats. The vodka they bought at the airport helps them fight off fatigue. They are listening to Velasco, a radio announcer with an unmistakable voice, telling off-color jokes and impersonating celebrities whom Ariel doesn't know. Husky comes up from the back of the plane and leans over his seat. Seeing Osorio wrapped up in his video game, he warns him, with a smile, take care of your brain cells, you. Ariel takes off his headphones. Tomorrow they're going to give you a thrashing in the press. I played badly. Badly? You sucked. Are you sure the Norwegians didn't put a square ball in the game? Ariel smiles. Husky continues, I'll take you out to dinner tomorrow night. They assigned me to interview you. That way you'll get out a bit, okay? Ariel concedes. Husky goes back to his seat after saying, I'm outta here, this is like a wake. He shakes the team delegate's hand, a man who's spent his entire life in a trench coat, handling minor matters for the team in his old-fashioned way.

Ariel had met Husky during the preseason. He was a journalist who attracted attention in the press room because of his hair, red like an Irishman's, and his voice, which sounded like a guitar being played with hammer swings. The club confined the team to a hotel in Santander for the month of August. Physical training, getting up to snuff with the coach's statistics, the first tactical conversations. Ariel shared a room with Osorio, a young guy his age, who had grown up in the club's reserve teams, and who had little chance of being a first-string player during the season. He spent his free time playing with the PlayStation. Sometimes after dinner Ariel would join in on a pool game with one of the veterans: Amílcar or the substitute goalie, Poggio, who suffered from insomnia. By the third day, the monotony was unbearable: living with his teammates, the strict schedule, the boredom of repetitive meals, pasta and chicken or chicken and pasta. At noon it was time to go to their rooms; sometimes they got together to chat or watch TV and listen to the comments of what a babe, did you see those tits? that marked the appearance of a woman on screen. Charlie came to Santander in the Porsche. Tonight I'm taking you out on the town. The way he said it was "*te saco de marcha.*" He'd been talking like that ever since they first arrived, borrowing expressions he heard the Spaniards use. Ariel slipped out secretly to meet up with him in the parking lot. He lay down in the back of the car, covered himself with two towels to get off the premises without being seen. When he left the room, Osorio said bye, get laid for me.

All the bars are packed, mostly with people summering. They go into a club with deafening music and scope out a corner.

At the end of the bar, Ariel recognizes Husky. We fucked up, there's a journalist, he told Charlie. Journalists always end up using every player indiscretion, sometimes not even to hurt them, just to show off how well-informed they are. But Husky came over to say hi. I haven't seen a thing. Do you want me to ask the owner to give us a private area? It's better if not too many people see you. They agreed.

They were put in a room where the music was muffled. In spite of being private it was crammed with people, but the owner prepared a table for them off to one side. Husky, accompanied by a photographer who played the role of a mute whisky and Coke drinker, told them stories about the coach, the team, some of the players. He was sweating. He took off his glasses to wipe his face with paper napkins, which he then balled up and threw. He asked Ariel whom he was sharing a room with. Osorio? His last brain cell committed suicide, out of boredom. They talked about Solórzano and Husky told them that in the club they called him Mr. Commission. If you said good morning to him, he kept the good. Husky drank beers at a feverish rate. He was as tall and slim as a basketball player. Solórzano is protected by some club executives, remember this is a snarled nest of social climbers, businessmen wanting to impress and be famous. The president's box is their trampoline to get their illegal rezoning, unearned favors from the city councilmen, social prestige, certain notoriety, and, in the best-case scenario, they can hook up with some beauty queen who will suck their dick in exchange for a taste of luxury. Maybe Argentina is an incredibly fucking corrupt country, but here they've managed to make corruption photogenic and legal, and that's that.

He told them that Coach Requero was called "clean hands": he never made a mistake. Husky inspired trust. He smoked black tobacco and held the cigarette inside his palm, protected. He talked about some of the players, about Dani Vilar, who had been the most critical of signing Ariel. He's a good guy, but he's lost the physical edge needed in your position, it's kind of sad to watch a guy who's a millionaire drag himself around the playing field. But, of course, retiring is traumatic, and even more so if you have five kids and a wife like his, who they say is a Legionary of Christ. I promise I won't say a word about your sneaking out, last night Matuoko took three whores up to his room.

In the third bar they visited, Charlie and Ariel met two Argentinian women signed up for a summer course on "emotiveness" at the Palacio de la Magdalena. Inside the car, parked near the team's hotel, the women were able to put some of what they had learned into practice. One of them talked even when she had nothing intelligent to say, but Charlie considered that a virtue, as if she had piped-in music. Flying the flag, brother, flying the flag, he shouted as the four of them fucked uncomfortably in the car. It looked like nothing could go wrong. The next day there were no repercussions for his escape. It helped that early that same morning Wlasavsky had totaled his car against a fence, to avoid hitting a cow crossing the highway near Torrelavega according to him, and on his way back from a whorehouse called Borgia IV according to everyone else. Two days later six of the team members, including the goalie coach, got food poisoning, probably from some shellfish. Ariel was spared; he never could stand seafood.

Things had been like that from the beginning. Charlie made it all crazier, but more fun, too. On his first trip, before he was signed, they stayed in rooms next door to each other in a luxury hotel near the stadium. The club had been in a stir; they had just canceled the signing of a Brazilian striker because there were traces of tetrahydrogestrinone, a banned anabolic steroid, in his blood. It was leaked to the press that the guy had a bad knee, but since Solórzano was handling both signings, the negotiating got tense at the last minute. Someone had the nerve to suggest that either they sign them both, or didn't sign either. Charlie turned serious. My brother is clean; it was the other guy who took THG. But for two days the signing was on hold. In the end, the Brazilian was admitted into a dialysis center, had his blood cleaned, and got signed by a French team. Ariel could pose for the contract signing, he passed the medical exam, and they waited a few days to find a house in the city.

The club and Charlie took care of finding it. You have to live like a rich guy, his brother warned him. The third day in the hotel, they put a journalist's phone call through to his room. Charlie refused to give exclusive interviews, no matter how much they insisted. Ariel listened to him arguing authoritatively. Suddenly Charlie cracked up laughing and handed the phone to Ariel. Listen to this. Hello? Said Ariel. And a woman's voice, nervous but chipper, spoke. Are you Ariel? Well, I'm not really a journalist, I'm here in the lobby, and, well, I'm here to give you a welcome fuck. Ariel didn't even have time to be shocked; his brother grabbed the receiver from him and invited her up.

Two minutes later a woman in her thirties came in, with enormous breasts and dyed blond hair with laborious curls. Smiling, fun, uninhibited. They drank three beers and Charlie was the first to cuddle her. They got naked and entangled on the bed. Seeing Ariel's passivity, she insisted, hey, I came here to fuck your brother. Ariel, half amused and half astonished, took off his clothes. While Charlie penetrated her doggy-style on the bed, she took Ariel's penis into her mouth. She had a bright red piercing on the tip of her tongue. She was from Alcázar de San Juan but she lived in Madrid, well, in Alcorcón, and before she left she told them that she had fucked seven First Division players. I haven't done this really cute one on the Betis, but everyone says he's gay.

A reception like that still surprised Charlie and Ariel, even though they were used to the Argentinian *botineras*, the girls who milled around the players like groupies around rock stars. Ariel had trouble holding back a chuckle when the next morning a public television journalist asked him if he had been well received by the Spaniards. Well, I feel loved; I just hope I can please them on the field, replied Ariel. At the back of the pressroom, by the door, Charlie laughed uncontrollably, attracting the gaze of reporters, who by then were aware that Ariel was traveling with his older brother.

But now the situation wasn't so relaxed. The team wasn't working. They were sixth in the division and the only thing that mattered was winning. The European tournament had gotten off to a bad start. Ariel was coming back from training one morning and heard two commentators talking about him on the car radio: he's no ace, that's obvious, he's just another of those dime-a-dozen players from Argentina. Even when you're used to the categorical tone of the sports press, the criticism always hurts. The day after his debut game, a prestigious reporter at one of the soccer dailies wrote: "Ariel Burano has said that he doesn't think he's the next Maradona. Well, there was no need for that declaration, it's painfully clear. You just have to see him play. He dribbles his way to the corner flag, but will his flourishes satisfy the demanding Madrid fans?"

Charlie downplayed those comments. He's just an asshole, I asked in the club and turns out he's a jerk who was trying to get them to bring that Mexican Cáceres in for your position, his brother-in-law is an agent. How is that your fault? Many times he had heard Dragon say that the press had to be taken with a grain of salt, or better yet not taken at all.

In the account of his first official game, another reporter described him with just one adjective: autistic. "Ariel Burano was autistic. Three teams played. The home team, the visiting team, and him. It remains to be seen if it's just an adaptation problem or if it's a symptom of an incurable disease." Patience, pleaded Charlie. If you take the time to read everything they write about you every day, you won't even have time left to piss.

Ariel counted on being able to slowly convince people he was a quality player, but he wasn't counting on his brother's hasty exit. Charlie was his point of reference, his first line of defense against reality. Far from his native soil, any place shared with his brother smelled like home. Charlie's mishap happened on the night of the second league game, in Santiago de Compostela. The team played late that Saturday. The match was televised throughout the whole country. They spent the night there. Ariel and Charlie went out for dinner with two Argentinian players on the opposing team. There were thirty-two Argentinians playing across the Spanish First Division. Ariel didn't know Sartor and Bassi. He met them on the field. "Mastiff" Sartor earned the nickname for his resemblance to those Argentinian mastiffs that, once they sink their teeth into something, never let go. He marked Ariel on every corner kick and he brought his flat-nosed face a palm's distance from Ariel's. He shouted dirty spic at him, faggot, whore, pack your bags and take them back to your piece of shit country, asshole. He told him he was going to fuck his mother, that his sister was a lesbian, that his girlfriend in Buenos Aires was fucking the River center forward, anything he could think of to provoke him. In a play where Ariel threw himself to the ground pretending he had been knocked down, he grabbed him by the arm to lift him up off the grass and he shouted get up, turd, everyone knows you only play because you suck the coach's dick. Ariel burst out laughing. The guy was so extreme that it would have been comical, if it weren't for his criminal expression and the threat of his aluminum cleats.

When the game was over, they shook hands. Sartor was from Córdoba and he greeted him with a warm embrace. Like a tamed mastiff. They arranged to meet after the showers to have dinner in an Argentinian steakhouse owned by a friend. Bassi was in a bad mood because he had only gotten to play the last five minutes. They bring me out just to waste time. Sartor had been living in Spain for five years. Bassi had played in Italy for three before coming over. It's more relaxed here. Sometimes you even have fun playing. Sartor has the face of a B-movie killer. They call enormous, curly-haired Bassi "Gimp" because of his prominent limp.

They drank quite a lot, spoke passionately about Argentinian soccer. Sartor was a Leprosos fan, his first team, while Bassi rooted for Independiente. They walked them back to the hotel. Some drunken fans, who had stopped to piss on the colonnade behind the cathedral, recognized Ariel. They were wearing his team's scarves. In the distance, one was vomiting onto his shoes. Another of the young men, with messy hair and glassy eyes, stepped in front of Ariel. This guy is great. You're the best, the best. *Oé*, *oé*, and they started to sing at the top of their lungs, calling to the others. Ariel and his companions quickened their pace toward the hotel.

But the worst was yet to come. Ariel woke up with a start, hearing shouts in the hallway. It was Charlie's voice. He dressed quickly in sweats and left his room. Curious heads peeked out a nearby door. He saw Charlie, standing naked except for some black briefs, kicking and punching a half-dressed woman crawling along the floor. Ariel ran over and tried to hold his brother back. He was drunk and out of control. It was obvious he had done too much cocaine. During dinner he had gone to the bathroom three times, though no one mentioned it. Two of Ariel's teammates helped him hold Charlie down. The woman, red-headed, was bleeding from her nose and shouting indignantly. I'm going to report you, call the police. Ariel held his brother back as if he were a wild stallion. They think I'm a faggot, those sons of bitches, repeated Charlie.

It took Ariel a while to catch on. Bassi and Sartor had played a joke on Charlie. They had sent that prostitute to his hotel room, as a gift. The drama ensued when Charlie discovered she was a transvestite and, instead of letting her go, he took it personally and started beating her up. Ariel locked his brother in the room and helped the half-naked woman compose herself. Someone gave her a damp towel; she dried her nose and cleaned her face. Ariel apologized, he's drunk, it's probably best if you leave. She calmed down, thanked Ariel for tending to her, and refused the money he offered. No, no, that son of a bitch has already paid me plenty.

Everything would have been forgotten if she hadn't shown up hours later at the hotel manager's office threatening to report the establishment if they didn't give her the name of the guest in that room. Fearing that it was a player, the team delegate was woken up to take care of the matter. It wasn't easy. She wanted to call the press, the police. There in the wee hours of the morning, over the reception desk, they agreed on a sum of money for her to forget the incident.

On the trip back to Madrid, Pujalte exchanged words with Charlie, at the back of the plane, far away from everyone else. Ariel saw them, but wasn't invited to join the conversation. A little while later, Charlie collapsed. The girl was suing the club. She didn't know the name of the player, but the police had issued an injury report. The hotel admitted that the room had been paid for by the team, but claimed not to know which player was using it. Pujalte gave Charlie a week to leave the country. We can buy a few days' time, but then we'll have to give them a name, we have to protect the club. You wouldn't want what happened to that English team in Málaga to happen to us. Around that time, four players from a British team staying in a hotel had been arrested for rape. It was a national scandal until a few days later a shameful agreement was reached with the women in exchange for money. These stupid things can snowball in the press and end up taking us all down, explained Pujalte.

Ariel immediately knew it meant separating himself from Charlie. His serious expression, his irritated silence, his anger at his brother's stupid behavior turned into panic, into sudden, unexpected loneliness. Later it was the car accident and once again the team's protective hand, his dependence on Pujalte. Now his bad performance on the field.

From the front seats, Ariel sees Pujalte walking. He is headed in his direction, although he stops to greet the executives and the players. When he gets to his row, he kneels in the aisle, waits for Ariel to take off his headphones. They told me you went to the hospital to see the girl from the accident. That was stupid. If what you want is to get yourself into more trouble, keep on doing whatever you feel like.

I don't know, just in case, it seemed like the right thing to do, check up on her, replied Ariel. A shiver ran up his spine. The right thing? You'd be better off focusing on playing and leave the rest to us. I don't know how things work in your country, but here it's different. This isn't a banana republic, there are judges here. And with a change in his tone of voice he stands up and jokes around with Osorio, you don't play at all on the field, but you really sock it to that little machine. Then he returns to his seat in the back of the plane.

Ariel feels like a kid caught with his hand in the cookie jar again. He finds Pujalte's authority repugnant but he is more offended by his own submission. His rage contained, he puts his headphones back on. Dragon often repeated a Chinese proverb: "When things go bad, your walking stick will turn into a snake and bite you." Ariel had trusted that that wasn't going to be the case. That at least his walking stick would still be a walking stick. Returning from a defeat, alone with his music, he was afraid he was experiencing a slow, but uninterrupted, fall from grace.

17

The two invalids, says Sylvia, and hops over to her grandmother Aurora's bedside. They hug; Sylvia leans over in spite of her cast. Her grandmother gets excited. What happened, girl? Well, you see, Grandma, I ran over a car. Lorenzo picked her up at the station, but they hadn't let him go onto the platform to help her. The porters would take care of it. After the terrorist attacks in March, the security measures had increased. Atocha Station still kept a corner free for messages, lit candles, and photos of those killed on the tracks. Sylvia appeared, walking along the platform, leaning on her crutches, with a porter carrying her bag. Should we go visit Grandma? She's home now, right? she asked. Lorenzo nodded, give me a kiss, come on. Was Pilar very irritating?

You're missing a lot of school, says Grandma Aurora. Sylvia explains that she doesn't have any exams until December. It's cold. Grandma spreads a blanket over the bed. I'll come pick you up in a little while, okay? says Lorenzo. Then he asks Aurora, where's Papá? He went out for a walk. They hear Lorenzo's footsteps fading away. Your grandfather is so mad . . . It turns out the boiler broke down and no one came to repair it. We have no heat, no hot water. Grandma lifts the blanket. Get in here beside me. Sylvia carefully lies down very close to her and they cover themselves.

They talk about Pilar. Is she happy? Are things going well? Sylvia thought about her during much of her trip back. Her mother is fine. Her mother is happy. Santiago arrived from Paris and brought her a very thin cashmere wrap. Then they all three ate dinner together. The next morning, Pilar took her daughter to Delicías Station. Don't go down until the last minute. There's a terrible draft on the platforms. The fall was colder and more unpleasant than usual. The winter is in a rush, Sylvia heard an older gentleman say as he boarded the train, loaded down with bags of vegetables. Old people often talk about the weather; she's never been the least bit interested in what temperature it'll be the next day. Through the train window, Sylvia watched the continuous metal fence that blocked access to the tracks. It was as if someone had put boundaries on the countryside. The fence, mile after mile, conveyed something demoralizing, as if every inch of the planet were condemned to be fenced in.

Your father is really thin, does he still eat? Aurora asks her. Boy, does he ever, you should see his potbelly. Sylvia asks after her grandmother's pains, if she gets bored all day in bed. I've got visitors all the time, I have more of a social life now than when I'm healthy. It exasperates your grandfather; you know he doesn't like people. That reminds her of something. She asks Sylvia to get her some tickets for the Auditorio. Do you know how to do it over the phone? Of course. Because I get mixed up with those things and your grandfather's not going to do it, I know him.

Grandma Aurora asks her how she's managing with the cast. Fine, the worst part is showering. She tells her how she sits in the tub and wets a sponge and runs it over her body so as not to get the cast wet. She doesn't tell her that she got aroused doing it the other morning, so much so that she was embarrassed. She imagined the sponge was someone else's rough hand, which gave her goose bumps of restless pleasure. What made Sylvia most nervous was identifying that hand as Ariel's. My child,

I bathed that way for years. In a washbasin. And your grandfather used to go to the bathhouse on Bravo Murillo before we built the bathroom in the house. You want me to read the newspaper to you? asks Sylvia. No, no, your grandfather reads it to me in the mornings. I know it annoys him to read aloud, but I like to see the faces he makes over the crime pages. Have you seen the things that happen? It's all husbands killing their wives. And today, what a shame, some pilgrims coming back from the sanctuary of Fátima were killed in a bus accident.

Sylvia offers to read her a book. I started it on the train. That morning, before leaving for the station, Santiago had given it to her. Now you'll have more time to read. I wonder if you'll like it, he had said. What's it called? asks Aurora. Sylvia shows her the cover of the book she's just pulled from her backpack. It's not new. It's been read before. Sylvia likes used books. New books have a pleasant smell, but they're scary. It's like driving on virgin highway.

Sylvia tells her grandmother what she knows of the plot up to that point. There are five daughters of marrying age. A rich heir arrives in their town, and their mother wants to offer them in marriage. There is one, the smartest one, who feels scorned by the rich nobleman's best friend, after hearing him make a disparaging remark about her. And you know that they're going to fall in love, those two. So you are liking it, says her grandmother. For the moment, yeah. Sylvia doesn't admit that several times on the train she had to go back over the pages she'd read, starting again. She's not used to reading, it's a challenge for her.

When she was a little girl, she didn't like her grandmother to read her stories, but preferred she make them up. Her grandmother knew what she wanted to hear. Princesses, monsters, villains, heroes. There was always a little girl with black curls who had a million and one misfortunes before finding love and happiness. Sylvia reads aloud to her grandmother: "That is exactly the question which I expected you to ask. A lady's imagination is very rapid; it jumps from admiration to love, from love to matrimony, in a moment."

When her grandmother falls asleep, Sylvia remains lying beside her for a while, relaxed by the rhythm of Aurora's breathing. Then she gets up and leaves the room. The house was like a refrigerator. Her grandmother's room was at least somewhat warm because of a small electric radiator. The door to her grandfather's room was ajar. She approaches the upright piano. She touches a key without sitting down. She remembers the rigorous classes her grandfather used to give her. He was strict about the posture of her hands, her back, her head. Once he covered her eyes so she would play without looking at the keys. It's a piano, not a typewriter, he used to say. It's not taking dictation, it's listening to someone else's imagination. But her grandfather didn't have the patience, and it seemed she didn't have much talent. One day she asked her mother, please, Mamá, I don't want to study with Grandpa anymore. Let's see when we can catch up on your lessons, he had suggested one Sunday after lunch, but they both knew the classes were over forever.

Her grandfather arrives around eight in the evening. He comes in immaculate as usual, his expression serious, irritable. Did the heating guys call? Nobody called, Sylvia tells him. Through the intercom, Lorenzo says, I'm parked on the sidewalk, ask Sylvia to come down. She goes in to say good-bye to her grandmother, who's awake. I heard a beep from your backpack. Sylvia checks. Oh, it's a message. Her pulse starts racing, but she doesn't say anything. I'm leaving. Her grandfather helps her down the two flights of stairs. I don't know what we're going to do without an elevator here.

"How's that leg?" The message isn't very telling, but at least it's something. And it's from Ariel. Many days have passed. She was sure he'd erased her from his life after visiting the hospital. And what more could she expect? She has the cell phone on her lap as her father drives, but she doesn't know what to write. Have I fallen in love with him? she thinks. Could I be that stupid? She hadn't mentioned his visit, their meeting, to anyone. She hadn't been able to talk through what she was feeling and thinking, she couldn't make light of it. Like everything you keep bottled up, it was growing, growing like an untreated infection. He's handsome, with a baby face, seems like a good person. I'm sixteen years old. He's famous, a soccer star. I didn't ask him. Maybe he's married and has three kids. Soccer players are like that. They seem old at thirty. She'd have to ask her father.

I could talk to Mai about it, she'd think of something clever. But she's obsessed with Mateo and wouldn't be able to put herself in Sylvia's place. She'd have to explain so many things to her. Besides, last weekend her trip to León had just gone okay. We went out with his friends and they didn't pay any attention to me, like my being around bugged them, Mai complained to Sylvia. I'm not going back there, let him come to Madrid if he wants to see me.

Finally she wrote a message: "The worst part is having to drag it around all day." She sends it, biting her lip. She regrets it almost immediately. She should've written something more brilliant. More daring. Something that forces him to respond, that draws him in, something that creates a chain of messages that eventually brings them together. When the phone's beep announces a message received, Lorenzo turns his head. You kids spend all day doing that, what a hassle, you're going to forget how to talk. It's cheaper, Sylvia explains. A second later, she's disappointed as she reads Ariel's response. "Don't let it get you down." Sylvia wants to laugh. Laugh at herself. She looks into the side mirror, searching deep into her eyes. It's broken, cracked. The mirror. It's broken, she says to her father. Yeah, I know, it's been like that for a few days, some son of a bitch.

Ariel's reply brought Sylvia back to reality with a slap in the face. She reminds herself of who he is, who she is. Feet on the ground. She'll have to avoid Ariel slipping in through the cracks of her fantasies. She'll have to watch that he doesn't intrude on her dreams, her musings. That he doesn't find his way into her reading, into the music she listens to. That her free time isn't filled with longing for him to call, for contact that will never happen. She knows that the only pleasure available to her comes with a stab of pain, a sort of dismal resignation. She's sad, but at least the sadness is hers. She created it with her expectations, no one brought it on her, she's no one's victim. She's fine with that suffering, it doesn't bother her. She lies back. To wait. She doesn't know for what.

18

Leandro sat down in the kitchen. He's helping the boiler technician with his work. He doesn't feel like talking. He's mad. The man ignores his discomfort and jabbers on incessantly. He took the metal top off the boiler, revealing the sickly, malnourished belly of the motor, along with the burners that refuse to light. Leandro admires his rough, damp, greasy hands, which move skillfully. He has never known how to use his hands for anything besides extracting music from pianos, correcting his students' positions, sometimes marking a score with a pencil.

He moved his things to sleep in the studio. He cleaned the bedspread of record jackets, papers, scores, and books. He pushed the old newspapers he hadn't finished reading under the bed. He'd rather Aurora slept alone. He's afraid of rolling over in the night and hitting her. He wants her to be comfortable. Also he's ashamed, though he doesn't say it, of grazing her clean body with his, just back from spending an hour or two with Osembe's sweaty and acrid-smelling skin. He has always had respect for Aurora's body. He's watched it age, lose its firmness and vitality, but it has never lost the almost sacred mystery of a dearly loved body. Which is why now, when he brushes against it, he feels dirty and evil.

In recent days, his bad mood has gotten the better of him. Friday night the house was cold and he wanted to turn on the boiler. He couldn't. He called the repair service. They didn't work until Monday. That meant spending the weekend without heat or hot water. They suggested he call an emergency repairman. So he did. A hefty guy came, with a black leather jacket. It was almost eleven at night. He took out a Phillips screwdriver and knocked on various pipes. It's a question of spare parts, you should contact the manufacturer. Leandro explained to him that he had called, but they weren't working until Monday. The man shrugged his shoulders and handed him a bill as he checked his watch. He wore his cell phone on his belt like a gunman.

When Leandro saw that the man was billing him 160 euros, he was shocked. The guy itemized the amount. Emergency house-call, at night, on a weekend, plus the half-hour minimum for labor. Leandro was seized with indignation. He gave him the money, but as he led him to the door he murmured, I'd rather be mugged, you know, I'd rather have a knife put to my neck, at least those people need the money. You guys are the worst. Come on, man, don't say that, the repairman said in an attempt to defend himself, but Leandro refused to listen, slamming the door on him. Aurora's voice was calling out, and he had to explain the situation to her. Okay, don't get upset, there's an electric heater in the attic, see if you can reach it, she said.

The next morning he tried to shower with cold water. He stood inside the bathtub awhile, his hand in the freezing stream, waiting for his body to get used to the temperature. Then he gave up. Somewhat devastated, he sat on the edge of the tub and studied his naked body. Old age was a defeat that was hard to bear. It was disgusting. His whitish skin trembled with cold. His flaccid chest, diminishing body hair. The dark patches on his skin, his arthritic fingers. His bony hands like a sickly person's, the calves, the flabby forearms, as if someone had let go of the cables that kept the skin taut. He recalled those paintings he had always thought little of, where Dalí paints the passage of time as melting viscous matter. Now he was seeing his skin slip away like that, toward the floor like old clothes, leaving only a corpse's skeleton visible.

He thought of Osembe's tender flesh, young and exuberant, of the repugnance she must feel at licking his pale decrepitude. He held up his testicles for a second, his pink, fallen penis, use-less, languid, poultry skin. He couldn't explain the power it still held over him. Who had said that it was the faucet of the soul? It wasn't the erection, now intermittent, unexpected, random, that dragged him toward Osembe all those afternoons; it was something else. The contrast of their bodies, perhaps the escape through physical contact, the feeling of abandoning his own body to possess the body he touches and caresses.

He left the chalet with dismal regret; seized with guilt; later he was flooded with pleasurable memories; then anxiety came over him again, as much as he resisted. Leandro accepted the moment his finger rang the doorbell on number forty as a defeat. But it was such a short gesture, so quick, that it didn't give him time to think, to run away. He felt compelled. He, a man trained in loneliness, used to monotony. He was able to beat the urgency for a day, two, to say no, an emphatic no, to put his mind on other things. But he always ended up succumbing, kneeling before Osembe's black nakedness, before the reflection of her white teeth, before her absent gaze that now, as he studies his own body, he understood as a necessary barrier against disgust.

Leaving the chalet, he despised himself. He considered the female body coarse. He thought of Osembe and told himself she's just a mammal with breasts, muscular and young, a mass of flesh that shouldn't attract me. He denied her all mystery, any secrets. He found her folds dirty, her orifices despicable, he visualized desire as a butcher does a piece he's flaying or a doctor the tissue through which he traces his incision. But that rejection mechanism collapsed under another, a higher order. And so he returned to visit the chalet on Saturday, Sunday, and Monday.

Contemplating his own body turned Leandro's morning into a sad one. He immediately threw himself into pleasing Aurora, tending to her. He read her the newspaper supplement with its absurd leaps in stories, from the painful subsistence in Gaza to a feature on the benefits of chocotherapy, illustrated with photos of models slathered from head to toe. He prepared her a tea and sat with her to listen to the classical radio program. He avoided the news so it wouldn't leave its violent, sinister fingerprints in its wake. As his friend Almendros, who came to visit Aurora often, would say, we old folks tend to see the world as hurtling toward the abyss, without realizing that really we're the ones headed toward the abyss. The world goes on, badly, but it goes on. Leandro often delights in the fact that he'll die before seeing total hate unleashed, before violence swallows up everything. All signs point toward inevitable destruction, but when he expresses his pessimism aloud his friend smiles. It's us, we're the ones on the way out, not the world, Leandro, don't be like those old guys who stupidly console themselves by thinking everything will disappear along with them.

Almendros always reminded him of a cartoon that made them laugh. Two cavemen dressed in animal skins beside their cave, and one says to the other: here we are without pollution, without stress, no traffic jams or noise, and look, our life expectancy is only thirty years. Almendros laughed in spasms. Wasn't it Maurice Chevalier who said old age is horrible, but the only known alternative is worse?

The last afternoon with Osembe, as he fought to maintain his erection, Leandro told her about the news of the sit-in in Nigeria, two hundred women protesting ChevronTexaco. Osembe didn't seem impressed. Where did you read that? In the newspaper, he answered. They only mention bad things about my country in the paper. And she seemed mad, as if no one believed in the beauty of her homeland. My country very rich, she insisted. But she also told him she'd lost a brother in an explosion when he was stealing gasoline from a refinery with some other boys. They pull half a million barrels of petroleum a day from the heart of that country. The politicians steal everything, she said.

Leandro spent the morning repeating to himself, I'm not going, I'm not going, I'm not going. But he went. At a quarter to six, he was already on the sidewalk in front. He usually rang the bell at six sharp and he now considered that time reserved for him. Waiting nearby, he saw Osembe arriving in a taxi. A black man was in the cab with her. He didn't get out. She rang the bell and they opened the door for her.

Do you have a boyfriend? Leandro asked her that evening. My boyfriend is in Benin, she said. Does he know what you do for a living? Osembe nodded. I did this there sometimes, too, the tourists have money. Leandro was surprised he allowed it. He knows that with him it's different. If you aren't from Benin, why does your boyfriend live there? Leandro asked her. Osembe told him about the violence, about a massacre in Kokotown and how she had moved to Benin before coming over to Europe. Leandro imagined she had arrived in a makeshift boat, but Osembe burst out laughing, showing her teeth, as if he'd said something ridiculous. I came on a plane. To Amsterdam. I worked in Italy, first. A friend of mine used to work in Milan. She made a lot of money.

Osembe had come to Spain four months ago in the car of a friend, someone who took care of her. Leandro thought of the man in the taxi. I saw you arrive this evening, he told her, there was a man with you. I don't like to take taxis alone, a friend of mine was raped by a driver. But Leandro insisted on asking her about the man with her, and she ended it with, I don't want a black boyfriend, they're lazy, I want a boyfriend who works. Black guys are good for fucking, they have big dicks, but they don't make good husbands.

Leandro laughed when he heard her categorical, steely opinions. Are you laughing at me? I'm not smart, right? She usually responded to his personal questions vaguely. They spoke lying on the mattress, letting the hour slip away, and when she felt that his questions were pushing the envelope, she put up a barrier, brought her hand to Leandro's penis, and started up the sexual activity again, as a way of capping the conversation.

Leandro knew that the first place where she had worked in Spain was on a highway on the Catalan coast. And from there she came to Madrid by car. Arriving at this chalet, she said, was an accident. They needed an African girl for a good client, a Spanish businessman who was getting into the diamond business in Africa and had to close the deal with an exporting company. After dinner he brought his new partner to the chalet. In Spain it seemed to be a tradition to close business deals with an invitation to a whorehouse. The steakhouse, the after-dinner drink, a cigar, and some hookers. One day Almendros had told him that his daughter worked at a large agricultural mediation company and that after meals she took their out-of-town customers to a trusted brothel. It disgusted her, but it was something imposed, something inherited from her predecessor, and the men didn't seem to mind that it was a woman who accompanied them and took care of the bill.

They had me come in for the man who wanted an African woman. He was drunk, but he paid well and came back two more times, but he had trouble keeping it hard, his cock, because he had had a bad hernia operation, explained Osembe. He was affectionate, but very drunk. They asked me if I wanted to stay. Here you work with good people, it's not like the street, where you do it in cars, sucking guys off in the front seat or in the park, you know? Here there's even a doctor who comes to see us. I don't have AIDS or any disease, she told him in an almost threatening tone.

Do you like this job? Leandro realized he had asked a stupid question. I know it's not right, she said. I know it, but it is just for a short time. Leandro had seen on some lame television program how these women were extorted by networks that paid for their trip to Europe and then demanded one or two years of prostitution. Exploited by threatening their family members back home in their country, they were forced to work until their travel debt was paid off, with their passport held hostage by some compatriot until they earned ten thousand euros to buy their freedom. There were also stories of kidnapping, savage rapes, and blackmail with superstitions or voodoo, where they made a ball with menstrual blood, pubic hair, and nail clippings and then threatened to enslave them with supernatural control. Osembe laughed at the stories he told her. Did you read that in a novel?

They know the girls and they know where their families live, that's enough. Forget about witchcraft. Besides, I don't believe in that, I'm Christian. Aren't you Christian? Leandro shakes his head. She is very surprised. You don't believe in God? Leandro was amused by the question, her almost shocked tone. No. Not really, he replied. I do, I believe God is watching me and I ask him for forgiveness and he knows one day I'll quit all this.

In long sentences Osembe's tongue crashed against her upper lip. She had trouble making certain sounds, but her intonation was very pleasing. And it doesn't bother you to have to be with an old guy like me? asked Leandro. You aren't old. Of course I'm old. There was a silence. She kissed him on the chest, as if she wanted to show him some sort of false loyalty. I guess my money is the same as anyone else's, sighed Leandro. You like money, huh, what do you spend it on? I don't know, clothes, things for me, I send some home. I have brothers and sisters, five. And me and my boyfriend are going to open a store in the New Benin Market or on Victoria Island if things go good for us.

I want to see you outside of here, said Leandro when he finished getting dressed. Give me a phone number. She refused. It's not allowed. All the money would be for you. Osembe shook her head, but with less conviction. Think about it. She said, no, it can't be. Leandro was convinced their conversations were being listened to, that Osembe knew she was being watched. Someone knocked on the door—that was how they announced the time was up. Osembe jumped from the noise, then reacted with an enormous, relaxed, honest smile.

On the street, Leandro felt stupid about the conversation, his attempts to get to know her, to see her away from there. What did he want? Intimacy? For her to tell him her life story, her particular dramas? Share something, get closer? He could pay to have his desire sated, but that was it. Then he had to go back home, call the boiler repair service again, cry helplessly when another day passes and they don't show up, no matter how much he explains that his wife is in bed, sick with a bone disease. He organizes the bills, reads the newspaper, receives a visit from some relative, eats, drinks, washes himself, peeks out onto the street, at other people's lives, trying to reach bedtime peaceful enough to be able to sleep, perhaps dream of something, be it pleasant or unpleasant. And one day disappear. Leandro knew full well that he was seventy-three years old and was paying obscene amounts of money to put his arms around the body of a Nigerian in her twenties. It was a chaotic part of his routine, a time bomb in his daily life.

The repairman is talking to him, this boiler's got some years on it, but once I change this valve, it'll be like new again, you'll see. Leandro shrugs his shoulders. It breaks down every winter. He's been curt with the repairman ever since he arrived. It is his tiny revenge for the humiliating wait of the last few days, with the house turned into an inhospitable freezer, like a cheap motel. The man, his fingers like blood sausages, smiles. Things have to break down, otherwise what would we live on? And besides, now they make things more sophisticated so that not just anybody can fix them. Take cars, for example. Have you noticed? Before, anybody could stick a hand in the motor and patch up the damage, but now you open the hood and you have to have two college degrees just to find the distributor cap. And in the garage there's no repair less than fifty thousand pesetas. Since the euro came in, doesn't sixty euros seem like nothing? Well, that's ten thousand pesetas, which used to be a fortune. Now it's seems like pocket change. Doesn't it seem that way to you? Doesn't it? Huh? Doesn't it seem that way to you?

No, it doesn't seem that way to me.

19

Lorenzo decides to wait on the street. He walks down the police station stairs, scanning the sidewalk. They'll be ten minutes, they had told him. Lorenzo was following an impulse. It had seemed logical for him to stop by the station and check in on the detective, ask if he had made any progress. He'd gone to an interview near there, for a job as a bread deliveryman, but the schedule was dreadful. Starting the day at five in the morning. I have to think it over, he had said. And, with a certain superiority, the man had smiled at him. Don't think it over too long, I've got a line of people waiting. The previous afternoon, at the kitchen table, he had gone over his accounts. He drew up an amount for set monthly expenses, and added a cushion for unexpected ones. He had stopped receiving unemployment compensation two months earlier and managing his money was going to be essential in the coming months. He couldn't remember ever having so little in his bank account.

The first time he opened an account he was still a minor. During the summer, he had worked at a sample trade fair. His father had gone with him to open up a joint account. When Lorenzo deposited his thirty thousand pesetas, Leandro had surprised him. Here, he said, so you'll have something more to get you started. And he gave him a check for 250,000 pesetas. It was some sort of secret gift. Don't say anything to your mother, the last thing she wants is for you to quit school to work, she doesn't want me to encourage you. But, gradually, Lorenzo's life imposed the need for him to make his own money, to be independent. He soon acknowledged his failure at school, his lack of concentration. Óscar told him that his father was hiring at the photosetting company, and he took the job as a salesman. He worked with publishing houses, stores, printers. From the looks on their faces when he told them the news, it was obvious his parents didn't understand his choice. What's the rush? Lorenzo assured them that he would keep studying. And he did, for almost two years. More to keep them happy than out of interest in his studies. He met Pilar when he was seventeen. She was still in college. One day, Lorenzo found himself three years into a serious, tranquil, devoted relationship, and with a job that guaranteed him a stable, fixed income. Then he took the last step, said good-bye to his parents' house, to his youth. He became self-sufficient.

When he discovered there was so little in his bank account, he felt a shiver. He circled four job listings and started calling. In one of them, they were looking for younger people, under thirty. Another one was in Arganda, too far from home. Another was for a real estate agent, a job Lorenzo looked down upon, nothing sadder than showing homes on commission. The fourth was the bread delivery job.

His crime had had a paralyzing effect on him. It was as if he were waiting to be arrested, as if he were waiting every morning for his door to be kicked down and the police to say, come with us. Then he would say good-bye to Sylvia with a devastatingly remorseful, sad look. That's why it didn't seem like such a bad idea to show up at the detective's office. I could always collapse, confess everything, cry over my guilt. At least that'd get me out of this gray area, where I don't know if I'm a real suspect or just a sidetrack in the investigation.

But now he regrets coming. He's out on the street, he didn't leave his name with anyone, the detective hadn't seen him, and he decides it's best not to go back up. What's he going to do? Ask awkward questions? Isn't excessive interest a sign of guilt? Better to stay on the margins. He hasn't returned to the scene of the crime as the clichés dictate. But the scene of the crime has returned to him, hundreds of times.

Lorenzo knew that every Thursday, for many years, Paco and Teresa would dine at Teresa's parents' house. Teresa's uncles and aunts and a couple of old friends were also invited. Paco would join the weekly card game. They would go down to the basement, where there was a bar and a game table, where the heating pipes were exposed and on the walls hung some ad posters from the business. They smoked cigars and drank expensive whisky. They joked around, and sometimes one of them would get wound up, but nobody really talked about anything of importance. Teresa's father, whom Lorenzo had seen only on one fleeting occasion, was a distrustful person, with a cutting sense of humor. Paco sometimes admired him and sometimes despised him, but if he could merge those two emotions the result would have formed an obvious complex. Teresa's father was a confident man who would repeat to anyone listening, I wish I had married my daughter so I could have myself as a father-in-law.

The money was the first reason to attack Paco's house. Lorenzo knew he would find the toolbox in the garage. Maybe Paco didn't even remember that he had seen him take a wad of cash out of there one day. Paco bragged that he got money back each year on his taxes. He wasn't afraid of under-the-table money, just 'cause it's dirty doesn't mean it stains your hands. And if Lorenzo raised any objection, he defended his position. Everybody's the same, lawyers, notary publics, plumbers, don't come to me with your scruples, here the only people who pay all their taxes are people with fixed monthly salaries. Lorenzo knew that the house alarm didn't cover the garage, that the job could be quick. Their Thursday evening outings left him more than three hours to find the toolbox.

He saw Paco's car leave the house. A new, shiny car, a Swedish make. Inside he saw both silhouettes. Teresa was looking at herself in the visor mirror, finishing her hair. When he got close to the gate, the dog started barking, so it was better not to waste time. He jumped over the fence easily, in two attempts. The dog ran to have his back petted. He broke the lock on the side door to get into the garage. He was carrying a saber saw in a sports bag. He put it together and in six turns had gotten the frame off the lock. The dog barked at the noise, but then calmed down again.

Inside the garage he turned on the light. He was wearing latex gloves and put the sports bag down on the ground. He moved tools and cans of paint around on the shelf. But the box he was looking for wasn't behind them. Paco must have changed his hiding place. It had to be around here somewhere. Lorenzo started to search desperately, turning everything over. He was sweating beneath his coveralls.

As he wiped the sweat out of his eyes, he heard Paco's car approaching and the garage door start to rise.

He stopped everything and hid behind the barbecue grill. It was wrapped in a green cover and he wouldn't be seen crouching behind it. The mechanical garage door went up. He dragged the sports bag toward him, but he noticed the saw left on the floor. In that moment, the headlights blinded the garage and the car stopped inside. He didn't understand why Paco was returning. He must have forgotten something. His in-laws' house wasn't far away, he must have left Teresa there and come back. He couldn't ask him why. Now Lorenzo knew that he had come back to die.

Paco left the car door open, which caused the car alarm to sound insistently. He took four steps and stood in front of the messy wall, touched the reshuffled shelves with his fingertips. He turned his head. Lorenzo couldn't see him, but he took the machete out of the bottom of the sports bag. Paco's feet approached and his hand touched the canvas cover on the barbecue grill. Lorenzo jumped up aggressively, leaped onto him, and dealt him two machete blows to the belly. Deep, angry, fierce. The next part was more complicated. Using the blade again wasn't so easy. The two first blows had something of panic, of self-defense. Then they struggled. Paco's eyes discovered Lorenzo's. He didn't scream. But his hands clamped onto Lorenzo's forearms. Lorenzo only stabbed him once more and he did it like a coward, without conviction. Blood was pouring onto the floor, soaking his clothes and covering Lorenzo's hand up to the elbow. Seeing himself like that disoriented Lorenzo, paralyzed him for a second. Enough for Paco to force him to let go of the machete, which fell to the floor. Paco lunged to grab it. Before he could get up, Lorenzo got the saw and, without looking, cut into Paco's back, opening up his suit, which then started oozing blood.

Paco took his time dying. To make sure he wasn't breathing, Lorenzo turned the body over with his foot. He reached for the hose and cleaned off his hands and then his boots and let the water flow freely beside his friend.

It took Lorenzo almost five minutes to move. The car still gave off the monotonous alarm that the door was open. Its persistence was insulting. Lorenzo kicked it closed. He wasn't sure if Paco was dead, but he couldn't kneel beside him, take his pulse, look into his eyes. He had to trust that he was. He put his things away in the bag and decided to forget about the money. He couldn't think. Nothing made any sense. He was sleepwalking, a man without resolve or clear ideas, without a getaway plan. The hose moved like a crazed serpent on the puddle-filled floor.

Lorenzo dragged Paco's body into the car. He laid it down on the backseat. He thought about leaving in the car, but it seemed stupid to drive around with his friend's corpse. Finally he took the hose and stuck it through a slight opening in the window. The car slowly began to fill with water. Lorenzo watched it from the outside, standing in the middle of the garage. The inside turned into a flooded fish tank, drowning Paco's body. The water reached the steering wheel, covered the upholstery, the dashboard, began to rise up the windows. When it began to overflow through the window, Lorenzo decided he needed to leave. How much time had passed? Would someone be on their way to look for Paco, wondering what was taking him so long?

Lorenzo lowered the garage door and trusted that the place would become a swimming pool, that the water would erase any trace of their struggle. He took off his bloodstained coveralls and gloves, while the dog rubbed against him, inviting him to play. He threw everything into the sports bag. He crossed the yard and left as naturally as he could muster.

Inside his car, Lorenzo took off his boots and changed his clothes. He was parked three streets past Paco's house, in front of another single-family home. Driving away, he stopped to throw the saw blade into a dumpster. He threw the body into a different one, a few miles away. The saw had cost him more than seven hundred euros, but it was dangerous to hold on to it. Then he drove to a clearing and poured gasoline over the sports bag and lit it up inside a garbage can, convinced that someone was watching him, that none of what he was doing made much sense.

In front of the police station, he struggles to go back in time, to jump back to the day before Paco's murder. He is unable to get himself moving, to look forward, while suspicion still hangs over him. What was the point of looking for work if he was guilty of a crime? Wasn't it better to just start paying his debt to society now? Or could he forget all about it? Leave it behind without punishment? The guilt was uncomfortable, but the uncertainty was so much more. He thinks about it from every angle and decides not to go back into the police station.

He walks along the street. A man violently argues with a woman; they appear to be on drugs. People stare from a distance, but no one intervenes. At the bus stop is a poster of a model in lingerie. Someone has written on it, above her stomach, in blue marker: "Blowjobs 10 euros." Three students walk noisily down the sidewalk. A man hails a cab. At the stoplight, a girl cleans car windshields while the drivers try to evade her. In his little shelter, a blind lottery-ticket salesman listens to the radio. Two women stroll along, walking together but each having a conversation on her cell phone. Lorenzo feels protected, comforted.

He takes a walk over to his parents' house. He wonders if he should ask to borrow some money from his father, but decides it would be a mistake. It would worry the old man even more. He moves the living room television into his mother's room and while he is doing something, organizing others' lives, he feels better. He realizes that his mood is a question of energy. If you stop, you're sunk. The balance is a question of movement, like those plates spinning on the tip of a cane.

He uses his parents' phone to make a call. It takes him two tries to get the person he's looking for. Hello, I'm Lorenzo, Sylvia's father, the girl who got run over. The man on the other end of the line changes his tone immediately. He becomes cordial, like when they met at the clinic. When Lorenzo tells him why he's calling, the man doesn't seem to have any trouble understanding him. Getting the insurance settlement means waiting and Lorenzo isn't so sure how generous the system is going to be with a girl jaywalking in the middle of the night. He is willing to negotiate an amount and forget about the bureaucracy. He doesn't want to sound anxious or scheming. Have you thought about the amount? Lorenzo would have preferred not to say anything, he didn't want to seem too self-interested or shortchange the amount. Six thousand euros? he asks. Okay, we can discuss it.

He heads home. The walk tires him out and makes him feel anonymous, free. The sidewalk is sown with dry yellow leaves: the mimosas and plane trees are almost bare. He gets out of the elevator on his landing, but before entering his apartment he takes the stairs up to the fifth floor and knocks on Daniela's door. She opens it, surprised. The boy is playing in the living room. I can take you to El Escorial this Sunday. Daniela looks at him, somewhere between amused and distrusting. No, I can't, she says. Lorenzo is silent. This Sunday I can't. My friend's cousin is coming from Ecuador and we have to go pick him up at the airport, we have to be there to receive him. Lorenzo nods. Do you have a car? I can take you both in my car. Daniela searches for something threatening in Lorenzo. Really? Of course, I'd love to help you out. I don't know, it's very kind of you. She hesitates. On the landing they set up a time for Sunday. Lorenzo offers to pick them up at the entrance to the metro that's two blocks away, at ten in the morning. Okay, that's fine . . . Daniela closes the door when the little boy calls her from inside. She barely says good-bye to Lorenzo. She avoids flirting.

20

The meeting turns out to be humiliating. The sport director's administrative office is in the stadium's wing. Ariel goes up in the private elevator with an old club employee who barely speaks, his mouth sunken and his head bowed. The elevator passes the floor that leads to the box seats. They say that sometimes, when games ended in fights or handkerchief waving and the stands demanded someone be held responsible, the executives would take the elevator and lock themselves in the conference room. There, as the fans' disappointment resounded, they would try to hold on to their jobs by firing a coach. That's soccer, thinks Ariel. Power means having other heads that can roll before yours does. Pujalte, Coach Requero, and two other executives he barely knows are waiting for him in the conference room. A secretary has brought them a pitcher of water and three glasses.

The coach speaks first, making a speech devoid of enthusiasm and dominated by the customary clichés: what's best for the team, putting the interests of the group above those of the individual, we understand what it means, but you have to understand the fans. Everything had started a couple of days earlier, when Ariel got a call from Hugo Tocalli, the Argentinian national under-twenty coach asking him to play in the classified round for the World Cup for young players. Ariel had been in the previous game and twice went national with the under-seventeen team. He knew that playing in the World Cup in Holland in June would be a unique opportunity. The Argentinian national team had just won the Olympic Gold in Athens and in the last under-twenty World Cup, in the United Arab Emirates, they had lost in the semifinals to Brazil in a game that left him crying in front of the television. You're talking to me about a juvenile tournament, for boys, a hobby, begins Pujalte. We can't have you miss four essential games. Or send you to Colombia for a qualifying round so you can shine among the up-and-coming. For Ariel it's a commitment he doesn't want to miss, an international championship, a confirmation of his long-term career plan, an indispensable step up. Most of the days I'll be missing are during my Christmas vacation. But Pujalte shakes his head. You are going to have to choose between professionalism and pleasure here. You have to forget about your country already, you're not Feather Burano anymore, okay? It's time to grow up, you came to Spain to grow up, goddamn it, to come into your own as an adult, not to play with kids. Think about the injuries, is the only thing that Coach Requero adds, his head down as he plays with a pen between his fingers. An injury now would be disastrous.

Ariel misses Charlie. Someone who speaks with authority, who slams his fist on the table. Who fearlessly defends Ariel's personal interests, at least what was agreed to in the contract, the permission to play in national championships if you were selected, even in the lower categories. Ariel insists on its importance, in his motivation. But the club isn't giving in. The national team is going to demand I play, and they have every right, the Federation forces clubs to lend their players, Ariel tries to explain. Pujalte interrupts him, of course they force us, that's what we're talking about, you have to voluntarily renounce it. The fan base will appreciate the gesture, your sacrifice. It could be the way you win over fans, wipe away their misgivings. The chosen word, *misgivings*, mortifies Ariel. He doesn't respond, he knows he's lost the battle, but he is surprised that Pujalte finds, in that moment, an opportunity to remind him of the public's criticisms, the whistles when he's pulled out of games, the general lack of enthusiasm around his signing. He continues to listen to a string of superficial justifications. He knows it's just a question of power, that if he were at the height of acclaimed success, he would be able to make demands. But he's not there now. He has to accept that.

The last game had gone better. They scored a penalty kick that gave them the win, but above all he had been active, incisive. His best soccer up to that point. He spoke with Buenos Aires every day and Christmas approaching seemed to encourage him. We'll see each other soon, Charlie told him. He had become close with a couple of players on the team, Osorio and the fullback named Jorge Blai who was married to a model. Jorge put him in touch with an agent who represented celebrities, an amusing, foul-mouthed guy called Arturo Caspe, who invited him to parties and got him a couple of fun offers. They paid him six thousand euros to play a new PlayStation video game against a defender from a rival team in front of the media and another three thousand for going to a party sponsored by an Italian watch company. Husky went with him to some of these events and pointed out what he defined as the cut-rate aristocracy of Madrid's nightlife. People who appear on television, sharing their love lives, their breakups, their mood swings, their changes of hairstyle, even their altered breasts and lips, with the viewing audience, and receiving a fluctuating salary in exchange, depending on their degree of scandalousness. It was Husky who most seemed to enjoy these glamorous outings, though. He stuffed himself with beers and hors d'oeuvres and once in a while saved Ariel from the clutches of some vampiric woman who preyed on celebrities. Yeah, they suck your dick instead of your blood, he explained, but the price is usually higher than just going to a whore.

The day they went to the opening of a nightclub, which had debuted four times that year under different names, Ariel was approached by a striking woman, who seemed to have been reconstructed by someone not only insane, but also afflicted with erotomania. Impossible breasts, swollen lips, accentuated cheekbones, tiny waist. Husky pulled him out of her friendly embrace. This woman comes with her photographer, first she says you're just friends, then that you're involved, later that you dumped her, later that you screwed her six times in one night, later that she cheated on you, and then she tells an afternoon TV program what your cock looks like. Each chapter of her story for a reasonable price. If you want to get laid, ask me for permission first. So Husky, from a distance, nodded or shook his head every time Ariel started a conversation with a woman.

Ariel spent three fun nights with the daughter of a veteran

model, a lovely, multiorgasmic blonde who looked like a twenty-something clone of her mother and shouted so much when she came that instead of having a stiff lower back the next day, his eardrums ached. Then he bedded the waitress at a stylish spot, right in the manager's office, and spent another two or three nights with random women that Husky classified as sluts or desperate. The night can be treacherous, he said, I have a friend who used to say I never went to bed with a horrible woman, but I've woken up next to hundreds.

Ariel didn't much like the smoke, the night, the alcohol, and the girls who were only interested in fame. There was some sort of intersection of interests in those places, a tense lack of genuineness and the threat of wagging tongues. His name would fill thousands of hours of radio and television programs devoted simply to talking about who's dating whom, who's sleeping with whom. It wasn't that different from Argentina, where he'd also been prey for the covers of *Paparazzi*, *Premium*, and *Latinlov*, with a naked spread of some girl who mentioned his name among her many conquests. Around him, he felt the presence of hangers-on, people who went to great lengths to introduce him to someone, who wanted to invite him to an opening night, to a private party, to a fashion show. He got offers to use a gym downtown, a cologne, sunglasses. We've got to take advantage of our moment, said Jorge Blai, soon we'll be yesterday's news.

The big empty house didn't help his mood. At night he watched movies on the DVD player, listened to music, or went online, where he read the Argentinian press or e-mailed with friends from home. In a fit of nostalgia, he wrote to Agustina. In a moment of weakness, he was tempted to invite her to come spend a week in Madrid. He was starting to know places where he could get Argentinian food, Argentinian CDs, Argentinian magazines, where he could have a maté and chat for a while with a university professor or publicist from there who recognized him.

He had become close with Amílcar, the Brazilian midfielder whose career was waning, but who seemed to understand the whole soccer circus. He lived in a big house in an upscale neighborhood. He had met his wife, a beauty from Río de Janeiro who had been Miss Pan de Azúcar in 1993, the year he played for Fluminense. They had three kids. Fernanda would raise her voice and get angry in a comic way, more like an Italian than a Brazilian.

On a clear, bright day, they ate in the sunroom of their house. Fernanda was golden brown, with blond hair. I love Madrid's weather, she said to Ariel. When we got here six years ago, this was a dirty, aggressive, ugly city, but it had its charm. Here everybody talks to you, they're friendly, fun. But now it's getting worse, it's the same chaos, but people don't have the time to be charming. Everything has sped up. Amílcar shook his head. Ignore her, you know how women are, if they're nice to her at the hair salon then Madrid is wonderful; if they don't yield to her at an intersection then Madrid is horrible. He pronounced it *horríbel*.

Fernanda treated Ariel in an easy manner, as if he were a little brother. She had just turned thirty and she confessed to him that she was depressed over something that had happened a couple of weeks before. The Peruvian woman who took care of the kids was at the house and some guys pulled up in a supermarket truck. In five minutes, they had robbed the entire place. The appliances, my family jewels, even the kids' TV, it was awful.

And the worst thing is that they beat up the poor nanny. Can you imagine? She's fifty years old and they kicked her down to the floor. They wanted to know where the money was, the safe, I don't know . . . The poor woman had a terrible time of it. It looks like they were Colombians, that's what the police told me, because in Gladys's room there was a picture of Jesus and they turned it around, it seems they do that so God won't see them, I don't know. What animals.

She and Amílcar argued beguilingly, almost as if they were doing it for Ariel. When we first came to Madrid, she got compliments all the time, and now she feels old because no one says anything anymore. She denied it, that's not it, Latin Americans are very crude. They whistle at you from the scaffoldings, they say very coarse things, Spaniards used to be more subtle. I remember one short, big-headed bald guy with a moustache who passed me on the street and whispered: miss, I would make tea with your menstrual flow, but he said it very respectfully, like someone wishing you a Merry Christmas. Amílcar was counting on retiring in two years and trying to stay on with the team as a coach, but Fernanda wanted to move back to Brazil. I'm sick of soccer, isn't there anything else in the world? I miss Río, I miss being surrounded by the sea and the beach.

Ariel drove with Amílcar in his SUV to pick up his kids at the British school where they studied. The entrance was jammed, cars double-parked. The children came through the door in green uniforms with a crest, in gold relief, on their jackets. For a while Ariel felt comfortable, like he was part of a family.

Ariel played soccer in the yard with the older boy and he left before night fell. In one of the streets of the housing development there was a plaza filled with stores. He stopped in front of a flower shop and sent a message to Sylvia to ask for her address. He ordered a bouquet of flowers from the Dominican employee. Weeks had passed since the accident and he had only gotten in touch with her once, on her cell, to ask how she was doing. He sent her a cheery text message, but she hadn't continued the exchange, she had just replied briefly and rather sharply. Ariel took it to mean that she didn't have a very good impression of him, someone who ran her over and let other people take the blame. She had every right to think little of him. Sylvia responded instantly to his text with her address and at the end a witty remark: "You coming over to sign my cast?"

He dictated the address to the florist's employee and asked him for an envelope to send a note. What kind of envelope? asked the man. Love or friendship? Ariel raised his eyebrows in surprise. The Dominican showed him the different types, decorated with little bows, illustrated with flowers and stenciled borders. It's for a friend, Ariel explained. He held out a sheet of paper and a pen. Ariel couldn't come up with anything to write while being watched. What? You can't think of anything? We have cards that come with messages already in them. Would you like to see some? Ariel shrugged his shoulders and that was when an idea came to him.

Leaving the florist's, he ran to the car. A policewoman was placing a ticket on the windshield. Excuse me, I'm sorry, I just went in to buy flowers for a friend who's been in an accident. The policewoman, without looking up at him, answered, best wishes for a speedy recovery. And she went on to ticket a car a few yards away. You're not very nice, Ariel said to her defiantly. They don't pay me to be nice. I think they do, I think that's part of your job. The woman lifted her head toward him.

What are you, Argentinian? Well, I don't know if in Argentina they pay the police to be nice, but I can assure you that they don't here, said the woman, ending the conversation. Ariel got into his car after tearing up the ticket, but before he pulled out of the park-ing spot another policeman knocked on his window. Are you a soccer player? Ariel nodded, without enthusiasm. The policeman turned over his ticket book and asked for an autograph for his son. For Joserra. My name is Joserra, too, José Ramon. Ariel signed quickly, a scribble and a "good luck." Your partner isn't very nice. The policeman didn't seem surprised by his comment. Did she give you a ticket? Forgive her, it's just that they found a tumor in her husband's colon three days ago and she's taking it really hard. In just two days, she's gone through three books of tickets. Ariel saw the policewoman filling out another ticket in the same row of cars. Anyway, with the dough you guys make I don't think a ticket is too big a deal, right? Ariel replied with a half smile and left.

When the meeting with Pujalte and Requero was over, Ariel walked through the offices. At that time of day, there was a lot of activity. Offices with stuffy atmospheres, the distant noise of a fax, secretaries typing on computers, cell phones going off. You only notice that the place has a relationship to soccer from the photos of legendary players that adorn the hallway and some trophies scattered in the display cases, details that remind you that it isn't just any old company. We'll prepare a press release announcing that you are voluntarily renouncing the tournament for the club's best interests, Pujalte had suggested to him, that right now your only focus is on the team. The fans will eat it up, you'll see. You want to add anything special? Ariel shook his head. No, it's fine like that.

He dials Charlie's cell phone in Buenos Aires, but that early in the day it's still turned off. He calculates that it must be seven in the morning. He only knows one person who's up at that hour. When he sits in his car, he dials Sinbad Colosio's home number. Dragon's voice answers. It's Ariel, the Feather. How are you, Spaniard? What time is it there? Ariel checks his new, enormous watch, a gift from the Italian brand. It's one. Something happen in training? Are you okay, kiddo? Ariel is silent, listens to the old man's breathing on the other end of the line. Everything's fine, I wanted to talk to someone from home, but the only one I know who gets up this early is you. He explains that the club won't let him travel with the under-twenty. He tells him slowly, not wanting to seem fragile. I could force them, but things aren't going so well here and I can't just do whatever I feel like.

Well, he hears him say. They haven't seen your left leg shine yet, right? Once in a while, answers Ariel. You have to win people over, get them on your side. Otherwise . . . Are you coming for Christmas? I hope so. Let's see if we can get together then. There's a long pause, Ariel senses he won't say anything more, but it calms him to hear the cadence of Dragon's breathing.

Do you remember that exercise I used to force the forwards to do over and over? The one with the tire? Ariel remembered. You had to shoot the ball so that it went through the hole in a car tire hung from a rope on the goal's crossbar, from farther and farther away and faster and faster. You remember that at first you all thought it was impossible? But then you'd always manage to find the hole.

The old man seems to have finished talking, but suddenly he adds, it's always the same, at first it seems impossible, but then . . . Yeah. Ariel wants to say something, but he's afraid Dragon will notice he's upset. Did somebody tell you this was easy? He doesn't wait for a reply. It's not easy, you already know that.

It's not easy.

part two

IS THIS LOVE?

1

To save herself the awkward climb up the school stairs with her crutches, Sylvia uses the teachers' elevator. That morning, when she arrived, Don Octavio, the math teacher, got in with her. He was always rod straight; the lack of mobility in his neck forced him to turn his entire body to look either way. When he saw the cast, he asked her, how long do you have to wear it? It's a drag, I think they're taking it off in a week. Oh, well, mine is worse, it's forever. And he pointed to his stiff neck. Was it an accident? asked Sylvia. No, it's something called Bechterew's syndrome, I guess when Mr. Bechterew went to the doctor and they told him he had Bechterew's syndrome, he must have really freaked out, don't you think? He laughed alone, Sylvia chiming in with a delayed smile. He got out on the floor before her. Have a good day. You, too.

During recess Sylvia stays in the classroom. Mai sits on her desk and rests her boots on the edge of Sylvia's chair. The heel of her cast is propped up on a nearby desk. Sylvia has achieved an impressive agility with her crutches. She leans on them when she's standing still, with her bent knee on the handle; she brings them together when she sits down as if they weren't the least bit heavy; she fishes her backpack off the floor using the bottom end of one, and on the street she pushes aside littered paper or cans off the sidewalk as if she were playing hockey. The idle hours have given her time to be alone. Her days, before the accident, hinged completely on her school schedule and Mai's plans. They went home together from school, they hung out in the afternoons, they went over to Mai's house and locked themselves in the "pigsty" to listen to music, or sat in the hall and chatted.

But the last few weeks had been something of a retreat. She lay in bed with headphones on, staring at the glow-in-the-dark stars she had stuck up years earlier, when her room's ceiling aspired to limitlessness. She read for the pleasure of following a story, of losing herself in something beyond her, for the first time. She had overcome the anxiety that usually pulled her attention to her own worries when she had tried to read in the past. She finished the novel that Santiago gave her in six days of marathon reading, sometimes until one eye got red and felt gritty when she blinked. Then she searched the shelves of the study at home, read the first lines of other novels, and made the fatal mistake of asking her father, what should I read? Lorenzo stumbled through the books for twenty minutes, from suggestion to suggestion, with confused enthusiasm, until he held out a thick novel written by a woman. I didn't read it, but your mother loved it. Pilar always carried a book in her purse to read on the way to work.

When Sylvia talked to her mother on the phone, she told Pilar that she'd finished the novel Santiago had given her. That weekend, when she came to visit, Pilar brought her another book. It's from Santiago. He inscribed it for you, he was embarrassed but I insisted. Sylvia opened it to the first page. "Sometimes a book is the best company." His handwriting is strange, but pretty, she told her mother.

On her first day back at school, her classmates circled around her. Some even kissed her on both cheeks. Some, like Nico Verón, signed her cast with obscenities: "What's it like fucking with a cast on?"; others, like Sara Sánchez, with schmaltz:

"From a friend who has missed you"; and some with surprising surrealism, like Rainbow, who wrote: "long life Spain." That first morning, the cast ended up like a graffitied wall, filled with teenage signatures. Dani approached her in class, too, and they chatted for a while in front of Mai, until he had the guts to suggest, if you want I can come by some afternoon and keep you company. Sure, whenever you want, replied Sylvia. Dani left and Mai spat out her diagnosis. That guy is hung up on you.

Two days later, Dani visited her at home. Sylvia took her time letting him in. Her father had just left. Dani sat on the floor, leaning against a piece of furniture. Sylvia lay on the bed, reclining. They talked about school, an upcoming concert, a recent movie, about the beating two skinheads had given Hedgehog Sousa last Friday. Dani brought two beers from the fridge and Sylvia asked him, do you like soccer? Dani was surprised by the question. Just the finals, he said eventually. When someone loses and they cry on the ground and they don't seem so cocky and sure of themselves. Sylvia had seen an ad on TV that afternoon for Ariel's team playing in Turkey. Dani suddenly said, I've been racking my brains over what happened on your birthday. Sorry, I was an idiot. No, I felt ridiculous, he said. Why? I don't know.

After a pause, Sylvia patted the bedspread. Come on, come up. Dani took a while to get comfortable, and when he sat next to her he brushed against her body. Sylvia directed him to lie down beside her. They kissed for a long time, he buried himself beneath her hair, and when he breathed he dampened her neck. Sylvia put her hands on his back. Their bodies moved rhythmically, he was careful not to hit her cast or put all of his weight on it. Their crotches began to rub against each other. Sylvia could feel his excitement through his clothes. Dani lifted her shirt up to her neck and kissed her breasts, taking them out of her bra. Sylvia was uncomfortable with her shirt tangled up around her neck and the elastic of her bra hanging around her shoulder, but she was turned on by the friction and his damp bites. Sylvia put her hand into Dani's pants and ran her fingernails over his ass. They made love with their clothes on, without stopping. The clothes protected them. Sylvia, with an intense pressure in her thighs, gripped Dani when he splattered with a wheeze.

They laughed at the wet stain around his pocket. With my coat on no one will notice it. Do you want to wash up? said Sylvia. No, I should go. He left quickly. Sylvia realized how Dani changed after he came, going from relentless passion to cold discomfort. It was as if he were landing in reality with an abrupt lurch. He went from floating inert to being aware of where he was, of what had happened, of who they were, of the earth spinning on its axis, and of the Canary Islands being an hour behind. Not her. Sylvia would have liked to remain intertwined for a while, for him to twist a finger around her favorite curl, for him to kiss her even if her saliva didn't taste quite as warm after his orgasm. But she had been left alone almost without realizing it.

Her father came home later and found her reading. He noticed that it was a different book than the one he had laboriously recommended. You're not tired? He smelled of smoke and soccer. Who won? We did, said Lorenzo. And how'd that Argentinian guy play, the one you hate so much? Eh, he wasn't too bad. Sylvia finished a chapter before falling asleep.

The day after, Dani wasn't able to meet her eyes. He sat with her and Mai awhile in the classroom and then disappeared before the break was over. She wanted to tell him, relax, I'm not in love with you, but maybe he already knew it. Sylvia again felt stupid about the incident, but calm, with no desire to take their relationship any further.

Now, Sylvia listened to Mai talk about the latest mishaps with her boyfriend. Mateo wanted to go to an antiglobalization march in Vienna, and he had asked her to go with him. It could be romantic, right? A little trip together. Sylvia doesn't say anything. She is thinking about Ariel.

After no contact for weeks, she had gotten a message from him yesterday afternoon. He asked for her address. Sylvia sent it to him and then ran to change her clothes, thinking he would show up at the house. She was tense for more than two hours, she changed her shirt six times, finally deciding on a thick sweater over her bra. She decided that her hair was dirty and she put it up in a ponytail over and over until her wrists hurt. When the doorbell rang, she was about to scream.

At the door was a man holding up a bouquet. Sylvia signed the delivery slip with a disappointed scrawl and was left alone with the flowers. She put them down on the table. There was a little envelope with her name and inside a card that read: "Accept this, please, with a million apologies and a kiss. Ariel." Beside it, folded in half, was a check made out to the bearer for twelve thousand euros. Sylvia dropped onto the sofa. The bouquet was enormous, excessive, impersonal. The brush of the sweater on her skin aroused her. She tore the check into pieces as tiny as confetti and let it fall into the ashtray as if a party had just ended.

Later she sent him a message: "The flowers are lovely. I tore up the check. It's not necessary." Barely a second later, her phone rang. Are you crazy? You have to accept it, it's the least I can do. Sylvia interrupted him. Stop feeling guilty. It was an accident and that's it. Ariel said something about the insurance, but Sylvia didn't let him go on. Your friend took care of it. That's what my father told me. They worked it out. "Your friend" sounded ugly, harsh. There was a pause, which Sylvia cut short. You didn't even invite me to see you play. Ariel asked her if she would like that. She said yes. More than a check. I thought maybe . . . Yeah, I know what you thought. That maybe I was thinking of taking advantage of the fact that you're famous and get some cash out of you. Well, no, you don't have to worry.

On the other end of the line, all she heard was Ariel's breathing. This Sunday we're playing here, he said. Should I leave you two tickets? Is two enough? Yes, agreed Sylvia. And if you score a goal, will you dedicate it to me? Ariel laughed. I doubt I'll score. But if you score, how will I know you're dedicating it to me? I don't know, but I'm telling you I don't think I'll score. You could lift all five fingers in the air, for the five weeks I'm going to spend in this fucking cast. Deal. The flowers are pretty, did you choose them or is there a flower-selecting employee at the club?

When they hung up, Sylvia felt a strange power. She had always been the youngest in the group, used to being told what to do by older friends who imposed their authority. With Ariel she took the initiative. She allowed herself to disparage his check, make jokes, be sarcastic about the bouquet of flowers. It was the first time in her life anyone had ever sent her flowers.

In the afternoon, she took the bouquet to her grandmother Aurora. They are lovely, your grandfather used to bring me flowers every Sunday, from a gypsy woman who set out her wares beside the newspaper stand. But the gypsy left and the flowers stopped coming, oh well.

Sylvia returned home with her father. While he drove, she told him, they gave me two tickets for the soccer game this Sunday, do you want to come? With you? he asked, surprised. Yes, with me. And who gave them to you? Do you want to come or not? Sylvia smiled without moving a muscle on her face.

When recess ends and the classroom fills up again, Mai drags herself lazily away from her friend, toward her class on the upper floor. I'll walk you home later. Sylvia moves her cast to create space for people to pass between the desks. Nadia offers her the last bite of a roll. Rainbow collapses into his seat with a snort of anticipated boredom. The science teacher comes in and closes the door behind him, even though two or three stragglers have yet to make it to class. How's it going? he asks from his desk. But nobody responds.

2

Sometimes he would follow a beautiful woman whom he passed on the street. From fifteen steps behind, he'd delight in her gait, the swinging of her hips, her curves, her rushing about. He speculated on her age, the type of life she led, her family relationships, her job. He fixed his gaze on the wavy hair against her neck or pursued a glimpse of her bust in profile. Sharing the street with these women was enough for him to feel he'd met them; accompanying them for several blocks was like making love. On occasions they would disappear into a doorway, or a car, they'd descend into the metro or enter a store, and Leandro would wait on the sidewalk across the street like a patient lover. Sometimes he followed a woman through the Corte Inglés department store, and studied her through the shelves, floor after floor, and savored her face, with its absent look of someone shopping, unaware she's being watched. He was satisfied with assessing the harmony of a pair of lips, the brush of a sweater over the curve of a breast, or the veiling and unveiling of a knee in play with a skirt. Trailing along in her sensual wake, he sometimes ended up on a bus ride to a strange neighborhood where the woman kissed a man or joined a group of friends, the spell suddenly broken when she was no longer alone.

Watching was admiring. Watching was loving. But never had obsessive sex taken a hold over Leandro like now. He had never felt overtaken by instinct, unable to control his desire. He had never served his sex drive morning, noon, and night. Sex at all hours of the day. The mere gleam off an object was enough to remind him of the sheen of Osembe's skin, a shape could pull his mind to her muscular thighs, a slight sway of flesh reminded him of her breasts, seeing pink painted anywhere suggested the palms of her hands. Any accident was sex. Any gesture was sex. Any movement was sex. The roundness of a cold saucepan, the shape of a bottle placed on the table, the underside of a spoon. Sex. Sex when he woke up aroused, alone in his bed. In the morning shower that reminded him of the quick showers at the chalet before and after making love. Sex at noon when the regular hour of their encounters approached. Sex at night when he returned to his bed repentant, yet the touch of the sheets aroused him again.

Fear was sex, too. The lack of control. The obsession. The shame was sex. The sheer drop he sensed behind his incomprehensible pursuit of the pleasure he enjoyed every evening. Every evening because after the first two weeks, during which every encounter was followed by at least forty-eight hours of anguish, regret, and attempts to forget, his defenses had been defeated. The previous week he had only missed one day. He went on Saturday and Sunday, too. He even went in spite of the persistent rain of the last week of November, which swept the street's pollution and filth, leaving it gleaming under the streetlights. At six in the evening, punctual as an employee, he rang the bell beside the metal door that opened with a groan.

Osembe received him in underwear one day, in street clothes the next. She varied the undressing ceremony, but the process was the same: Leandro's old body assailing her fortress. In Benin she used to work at a stall in the market and on weekends she enjoyed the beach. There she had started to earn a little extra money by going up to the tourists' hotel rooms or by accompanying them to nightclubs. She explained to Leandro that the first Spaniard she ever met was an engineer who worked for an NGO. Andoni, very drunk, but he treated me lovingly. He told her about Spain. He worked in the Delta, on an environmental cleanup project, but every time he was in Benin they met up. His sister had a business selling African handicrafts in Vitoria and Osembe helped him get a good price for the pieces that he brought back in an enormous shipping container once a month. When I arrived in Madrid, I called him. I saw him one day, explained Osembe. He gave me a little money and then he asked me not to call him again. He has a girlfriend here. She also met another Spaniard from the consulate in Lagos, a civil guard who gave her a Real Madrid T-shirt for her little brother and some earrings for her. We used to fuck twice a week in the Sofitel Ikoyi. Spaniards are very affectionate.

On occasion Osembe mentions a name: Festus. Leandro asks her about it, but she never gives more details other than that he is the one who brought her to Madrid. Nothing more. When Leandro asks, do you have a pimp? she laughs, as if it were a ridiculous question. Here I go halfsies with the house. Is he your boyfriend? Are you going to marry him? More laughter. No, not him, how awful. No, I told you already, Africans are not good husbands. Leandro questions her about her gold bracelets, her rings, the necklace around her neck, which she sometimes delicately removes and places on the nightstand. I like jewelry, she says, but she never admits whether they are gifts from anyone. I earn my money. She also changes her hairstyle often, telling him she spent fourteen hours on her day off having her friend do her braids. Her brightly colored underwear is carefully chosen, sometimes even to match her nails, painted with designs that end up chipped and dulled.

He enters Aurora's room with chamomile tea, steam rising from the mug. He puts sugar and jam on the toast she will eat in tiny bites. Leandro caresses the white lock of hair with gray glints that falls toward one side of his wife's face. Yesterday their granddaughter came and washed Aurora's hair in a washbasin of steaming water, massaging her head with delicate hands, and today her hair shines when the light hits it. I have to go to the bank, he tells her. Then I'll come up and read to you. He leaves the room after filling it with the upbeat saraband of one of Mozart's capriccios on the classical radio station.

On the street, he is received by an intense sun that doesn't mollify the cold. A street sweeper smokes a butt beside his pail, dustpan, and bristle brush. He reads a wrinkled, faded sports page and spits green phlegm into the street. They've already hung the Christmas lights along the avenue. Earlier and earlier, someone says every year. He passes by the windows of the various bank branches. He can see the busy employees in their cubicles decorated with friendly advertisements for financial offers and their clients waiting like fish in waterless tanks.

A few days earlier, he had been with Osembe and two other girls, one recently arrived from Guatemala with a huge rear end and lovely sad eyes, and a Valencian he had met on the very first day, and who explained to him that she had been at the chalet longer than anyone else. She had just had her breasts enlarged and she showed them off, firm and plastic, and poured champagne over them during the party. Leandro noticed her gold crucifix, so out of place that it was comical during their frivolous ceremony, which stretched over almost three hours. Naked among all that young flesh, caressed by different hands, hearing whispered voices from three continents, seeing clean smiles, for a moment he felt on top of the world. He emptied his glass onto the girls' skin and then licked their bodies. Drunk and somewhat feverish, Leandro went out into the cold street, convinced that the spiral threatening to pull him down was a reaction against the formal, moderate life he had been leading. That afternoon he paid for his indulgences with his debit card. Three days later, he received a call from his bank. An icily friendly female voice told him the funds had been covered, although they exceeded his balance, so it was urgent that he pass by the office to replace the amount. It was almost an hour before closing time, and in a very low voice Leandro responded, tomorrow, tomorrow I'll be there for sure.

Leandro waits in line in front of the teller's window while an old lady tries to update her bankbook, barely able to see, with blind trust in the woman who tells her her balance. The branch director touches Leandro's shoulder and greets him with fake cordiality. He invites Leandro into his office and as he offers a chair he makes a sign to one of the employees. They talk about Christmas approaching, the weather, the mountains that are already covered in snow, while Leandro thinks that, if the director were an animal, he would be a mosquito, nervous and distrusting. When he asks Leandro about his wife, the conversation turns serious. Bad, to tell the truth, I don't know if you know she broke her hip a month ago . . . Oh my God, I had no idea, how is she? Well, pretty weak, says Leandro, and lets the pause lengthen, her recovery is long and difficult.

Leandro explains that Aurora has to learn to walk again, like a child, but that she doesn't have the strength. The other day, she insisted on sitting but wasn't able to. She couldn't hold herself up. The doctor who visited that morning had tried to be reassuring. It's a normal process, she needs rest. But Aurora went to pieces; that same afternoon she whispered to Leandro, it would be better if I just died now. Leandro took her hand and stroked her face. He talked to her for a long time and it seemed to lift her spirits.

The female employee puts a statement of recent activity in Leandro's account in front of the director. Leandro defuses the alarm growing in the director's eyes. My wife is dying, I have to spend up to the last peseta of my savings on anything that can extend her life or at least make her suffer less. The director points out the almost constant withdrawals from ATMs, the excessive charges on the card. Leandro doesn't say much, just names nurses, expensive medications, second opinions in private clinics. He doesn't say whores, massages, foam baths, paid caresses. He reaches for his wallet and suggests covering the overdraft, but the director stops him. Don't think of it, don't think of it, there's no rush. We put people before numbers, at least in this bank.

Leandro lies naturally, finds it simple to just let himself be dragged along. The bank director pulls out a calculator and scribbles various amounts. He suggests a higher line of credit, which could help Leandro during the coming months. We could take your home as collateral, a part of it, maybe just 50 percent, and that will provide you the liquidity for peace of mind as you face your wife's illness. Otherwise, I don't know if you are familiar with our offer of reverse mortgages.

Leandro hesitates. I'm not sure, I would have to talk to her about it, he says. Here, of course, we are going to give you the best terms on the market, the director assures him. Yeah, but my pension is so ridiculously small, I'm afraid to take on something that size . . . No, Don Leandro, please. Let me explain how our credit system works.

He leaves the branch with the hypothetical bank operation written on a piece of paper. He thinks his entire life story is summed up there, in the intersection of four or five figures. They gave him his most recent statement and Leandro felt a humiliating stab when he recognized the fake name of the whorehouse. Every afternoon with Osembe, every excess, shows up there. A petty amount appears for the tickets to the Joaquín Satrústegui concert that Aurora bought over the phone a few weeks ago; in the end she insisted on getting them. Then the house expenses, the bills. But among them all the withdrawals of money for his vice stand out, accusatory. He is even further debased by the director's expression as he watches him leave the branch, that sort of condescension, respect, pity.

If only they knew.

If only they knew, he thinks, the people who look at him now and see a decent old man bitterly facing his wife's illness, the honest decline of old age, if they only knew his hidden vertigo of moral degradation. If they knew what he knows, that he'll go back to the chalet that afternoon, around five-thirty, and he'll give himself half an hour of doubting, he'll torment himself with anticipated guilt. But he knows in the end he'll ring the bell beside the metal door and he will watch through the frosted glass to the reception room as Osembe arrives with her long stride, her little jump on the final step, her straight-toothed smile as she discovers he's returned, another evening, punctual and vanquished.

Perhaps because of all that, and because when he returns home he finds Aurora more fragile and somber than ever, as he lies down beside her on the bed, instead of consoling her, he breaks out in tears. It is the slow, muffled cry of an old man broken inside. On the radio, Beethoven's adagio from the Emperor Concerto plays, a little bit mosso, and Aurora reminds him that sometimes, long ago, he dared to play it for her. Do you remember? When was the last time you played it? No, I only knew the beginning, he apologizes. Oh yes, I remember now, when Lorenzo decided to quit school and I was so depressed and it seemed like you didn't care and you said that I shouldn't blame people for choosing a different life than the one I would've chosen for them. And I was sad and you played it for me. Aurora dries the tears from Leandro's face with her soft, thin fingers, without even being able to turn toward him. Then they hold hands, lying on top of the bedspread, and she tells him, don't be afraid, everything will be okay, you'll see, I'm going to get better. Why are men always so cowardly?

Why are you so afraid of everything?

3

Her grandstand seat in the stadium is almost at field level, with the grass before her eyes like a damp, springy carpet. Soccer isn't so simple from there. The ball is more intractable. The spaces tiny. The players human. You can smell the sweat, you can hear the groan of a collision and the whistle asking for the ball. Sylvia is seated beside Lorenzo, her leg in a cast. With every breath, steam comes from her mouth. Dress warmly, Lorenzo had told her before leaving the house. He wears a wool cap, but Sylvia is protected by her cascade of curls. They shared the row of comfortably upholstered seats with some players who are sitting the game out and the wives of some others, mass-produced beauties, who instead of following the game keep their eyes fixed on their husbands and shiver slightly every time they are tackled. Look, that's the wife of the Pole who wears number five, points out Lorenzo, they say she spent a hundred thousand euros on a pedigreed dog, but Sylvia doesn't pay attention to the gossip. And the Argentinian? Which one is his girlfriend? she asks. Haven't the slightest.

When Sylvia was fifteen months old and had just started walking, Lorenzo watched her looking at herself in the mirror.

She held a jar of her mother's face cream in her hands and offered it to her own reflection, convinced that it was someone else. Lorenzo dressed while keeping an eye on her. At one point, Sylvia peeked behind the mirror, trying to figure out where the hell the other girl was hiding, the girl who was watching her and also offering her a jar of face cream. She looked for her several times. Lorenzo didn't say anything, didn't explain it to her. He just watched, smiling as he enjoyed his daughter's concentrated calm as she stared at her reflection, unbeknownst to her. Sometimes he remembered that moment and wondered if something as simple as that was happiness.

And another time Lorenzo had taken his daughter to a soccer game. Sylvia was eight years old. After half an hour, she had lost all interest and was playing in her seat, talking to herself, looking around. Being back at the stadium, sitting beside her, sharing the bag of sunflower seeds, his gaze searching for the woman who raucously shouted insults at the referee and his family and trying to find where the cigar smoke was coming from, it felt like he was getting that day back. At the VIP door, Sylvia had picked up an envelope with her name on it that held two tickets. I won them in a radio contest, she told him. Lorenzo helped her get through the turnstiles that led into the stadium. In their special seats, Lorenzo joked, sang the team song out loud, and recited both lineups to her, leaving time to comment on some of the player's particular traits. He was enjoying the luxury of sharing a moment with his daughter again, a rare gift in these days when she's so independent.

Pilar had suffered Sylvia's adolescence before he had. As mother and daughter, they argued and got mad at each other over trivial things. The way she dressed, the long silences, her table manners, her friends. Sylvia turning fifteen had been decisive in Pilar's daring to end their marriage. We still have a lot of life ahead of us and she doesn't need us so much anymore, she had said, suggesting a separation. Lorenzo can't seem to pinpoint when their home stopped being a place of refuge, their family a guarantee of happiness, how their partnership, their love, died. Before he even realized it, the three people living under the same roof were strangers. Each one had their own interests, worries, priorities. In Sylvia's case, that was normal, part of her growing up. But in theirs, as a couple, it was a symptom of something darker, sadder. Passion dies out in small trifling moments, and one day there's none left. Lorenzo sensed that there was a moment when Pilar let go of his hand and decided not to get dragged down with him. She jumped in a parachute from a crashing plane. He was too busy avoiding his own catastrophe to hold on to her. He doesn't blame her for not wanting to share in his breakdown.

In the past, when Lorenzo reflected on his relationship with Pilar, he used to think that she made him a better person. She infected him with her tranquillity, her confidence, her generosity. She allowed him to choose, to establish himself, to grow. She celebrated him each time he made progress. The marriage was a support structure, a driving force. Getting married, living together, having a daughter, those were the natural steps of their harmony. When Sylvia was born, Pilar stopped working, but after a while she needed to escape the house. I feel like my life is on pause, she said. She drifted through unsatisfying jobs until she found her place, but Lorenzo was convinced it was at that moment they started on diverging paths. Paths that crossed at home at night, in shared details about their little girl, in the quick sex on Sunday mornings. The union ended, the coexistence ended, and, as happens, someone new came into her life.

When Pilar announced her escape, Lorenzo couldn't hold on to her. He knew his wife well. Once she had made the decision, there was nothing that could force her to change it. No tears, no promises to change, no emotional blackmail. Pilar's decisions could be slow in coming, but they were rock-solid. She was indulgent, but her sentences were definitive. And that was how it happened. In two days, she no longer lived there, in four there was barely a piece of her clothing, in two weeks they had negotiated the separation and worked out the accounts, done the math, divided expenses, savings. It was easy. She left him almost everything. I'd rather stay in my home, Sylvia told them. Lorenzo took it as a victory, that she had chosen him, but he also knew it was the most comfortable choice for her, as well as the most respectful of her mother's new life. Really, he thought, she is choosing her neighborhood, her friends, her high school, her room, not choosing me over Pilar.

Since the separation, Lorenzo hadn't been with another woman. Sex was something he could do without, something dormant, pushed into a corner. Too many problems. He didn't have enough money for the drinks he'd have to buy to wait out the arrival of a woman lured by his lonely soul or his desperation. He was too proud to admit defeat. He wasn't going to beg in matters of love, either. Everything would work itself out once he recovered his true standing.

Looking for work in a waning field wasn't easy. For three months, he worked as a salesman on commission at a computer company, but the contract expired and Lorenzo found himself out on the street again, without the energy young people have for stringing together six or seven crappy jobs a year. Thanks to a friend's help, he got a position at a telephone equipment distributor, but the workdays were endless and the chemistry with his coworkers was soured by a stupid accident. During one of the little five-a-side soccer games they played on Thursdays after work at a municipal gym, he tackled hard on a disputed ball and one of the young guys at the company, a cocky little guy who often feinted and nutmegged, was badly hurt. He suffered a cranial fracture, a broken collarbone, and a concussion that scared them for a while. Lorenzo apologized a hundred times and they all chalked it up to an unlucky play, but he stopped going to the games, and shortly after he quit the job. He didn't have the energy to make new friends, start new relationships. At that point, he was already considering the heist that would give him back some of what was rightfully his, taking justice into his own hands. Stealing from Paco what Paco had stolen from him, which wasn't only money.

His father had lent him some cash to get over the rough patch: I don't want Sylvia to have to change her lifestyle. He worried that his daughter would suspect his money problems, feel she was a burden, and go live with her mother. It would mean losing everything. For Lorenzo power had always been something physical that travels with you, that's conveyed, like some sort of body odor. That was why he struggled to show everything was the same as always, when really nothing was the same.

So the young woman who took care of the neighbor's kid had showed up at the right moment, when he most needed new people, people who wouldn't judge him for what he had been, but rather for what he could be. Who didn't know about the skids he was coming off, and who could appreciate his ability to bounce back.

When he had offered to drive Daniela to the airport, they agreed to meet at the metro entrance. Lorenzo drove up and she got in with her friend. This is Nancy, said Daniela, introducing them. The young woman's smile was bridled by braces. It was her cousin they were picking up at the airport.

In the arrivals terminal, they waited more than three hours for the flight from Quito and Guayaquil, which had constant delays. A little girl waiting for her father rolled on the floor. Other families waited restlessly, checking the clock, pacing back and forth. All foreign faces, distrusting looks, tension. Sometimes they seemed more like mourners at the door to a morgue than people waiting for an airplane. Daniela and her friend Nancy accepted a bottle of water from Lorenzo to make their waiting more bearable, but that was it. He asked them questions about how they had come to Spain, their working conditions. Neither of them had papers. They both worked without contracts in domestic service. Daniela claimed to be happy with the family on the fifth floor; Nancy was more critical of the family of an old man she took care of. They shared an apartment with three other girlfriends, on the first floor of a building near Atocha Station. Nancy had a daughter in Ecuador, left in the care of her grandmother, whom she sent money to every month. I didn't leave anyone behind, said Daniela, although she explained that she supported her mother and her younger siblings in Loja.

Nancy feared that they were holding her cousin at customs. Daniela reassured her. As time went on, they were more sincerely appreciative that Lorenzo had come with them. It's nothing, it's nothing, he said, but they insisted. They were afraid of the Spanish taxi drivers, who often ripped off foreigners, and if Wilson came with a lot of luggage, going on the metro would be a drag. If you ask someone you know for a favor, said Daniela, they almost feel like they have something over you. Lorenzo didn't say anything. He asked Nancy if she missed her daughter. I'm spoiling her, she answered, she's got the best toys in the neighborhood. Daniela smiled with her cheeks and squinted her lovely indigenous almond-shaped eyes.

Wilson appeared, loaded down with a ton of poorly wrapped packages. He was well built, his face speckled with pockmarks, his hair black and wiry, and he had a wandering eye that observed his surroundings. He wasn't yet thirty, but he hugged his cousin with paternal authority, with one hefty arm, while the other, suspicious, held on to the cart filled with boxes. Lorenzo noticed that Daniela's greeting was somewhat more distant; she stepped forward to exchange a kiss on each cheek. They introduced Lorenzo as an acquaintance who brought us in his car.

Lorenzo went up to their apartment with them. It had a small living room attached to the entryway and a long hallway lined with bedrooms. It was old, with paint on the walls half peeling off, and enormous doors of sagging wood. Two windows in the living room opened onto the back of Atocha Station; the rest faced a dark inner courtyard. When the terrorist attack happened, the windows shook. It was horrible, explained Nancy. We were looking for a friend, for many hours we thought she was dead, but then she turned up in a hospital, with one leg destroyed. She was lucky, they're going to give her papers.

Daniela and Nancy insisted Lorenzo stay for lunch, and they prepared a stew with rice and goat meat they called *seco*, accompanied by a two-liter bottle of Coca-Cola. In spite of the large iron radiators along the walls, there was a small butane heater in the room. While the girls bustled about in the kitchen, Lorenzo talked to Wilson on the sofa, which that night would transform into his bed. He was coming without work, with a tourist visa, but convinced that the next day he'd find something. Noticing Lorenzo's interest in his situation, Wilson asks him, and what do you do? Lorenzo grew visibly worried before answering. Right now nothing, I'm unemployed. But Wilson took it as great news. Why don't we do something together? Hauling, anything. In Ecuador, Wilson worked as a driver. From trucks to limos, for a little while I worked as a bodyguard, too, for a guy who had an enormous hacienda in San Borondón. But your license from there won't be valid here, Lorenzo told him. Well, answered Wilson, and he added an open smile, I could use your license, we look a bit alike, don't you think? Except for the crazy eye. Lorenzo laughed.

Wilson faded a bit after eating, subdued by the time difference. By then Lorenzo was already captivated by his outlook. He had listened to his offers. If you had a van, tomorrow we'd already be working as a little business, keep me in mind for whatever you need. What else do I have to do except stay here at home with these five chicks, and Wilson smiled as if they shared a secret. Lorenzo made excuses, I'm looking for a different type of work, but I'll think about it. Then he went down with Nancy and Daniela and two of the other roommates to a nearby bar, an Ecuadorian bar. He was the only foreigner in the place, which was attached to a Dominican-owned business where immigrants could call home cheaply. The bar was called Bar Pichincha, spelled out in orange adhesive letters stuck on the plate-glass window. Its old sign, Los Amigos, was still hanging in front of the building, above the door, unreachable it seemed, except for the rock that had broken it. It was a wide space with a tall bar, a terrazzo floor, and metal tables where many of the customers were still finishing their meals.

No one looked at Lorenzo as he approached the bar and the girls clustered around him, but he felt uncomfortable, foreign in that place belonging to another latitude. The music transported him to another country, as did the faces. Daniela wore a tight black shirt, with silver embroidered letters that read MIAMI, which were sometimes covered by a lock of her straight hair. People approached to talk to Nancy or Daniela and soon Lorenzo found himself alone with his iced coffee. Daniela realized and went back over to him. We come here a lot. Sure, of course, he said. They started a private conversation, on the side. He asked her about her job; she talked about the rest of the neighbors in the building. About the man in 2B who once, insolently, rubbed up against her in the elevator. It was gross, sometimes Spaniards think we're all whores or something like that. Lorenzo smiles. The guy from 2B? He's a retired military man. Retired? Maybe from the army, not from the other thing. She said "dother," melding the two words. They both laughed, but she covered her mouth, as if she got a charge of shame from saying it.

Daniela told him that almost every Sunday morning she went to church, but she'd made an exception that day to accompany her friend. Are you religious? she asked him suddenly. Lorenzo shrugged his shoulders. Yes, well, I believe in God, but I'm not practicing . . . A lot of people in Spain are like that, she said. It's like they don't need God anymore. But if you don't believe in God, you don't believe in anything. Lorenzo didn't really know what to say. He looked around him. It didn't seem like the right place for a mystical conversation. She continued, and to think it was the Spaniards who brought religion to the Americas. Yes, among other things, said Lorenzo. The dance music resonated.

A burly guy approached the bar to one side of Lorenzo. As he leaned onto the counter he pushed Lorenzo, on purpose. Lorenzo turned to look at him, but said nothing. The guy fixed his defiant, deep black eyes on him. He was thick, not very tall, with the physical decisiveness of a refrigerator. I've got to go, said Lorenzo. Don't pay any attention to him, they drink too much and they get aggressive. No, no, it's not because of that, said Lorenzo after moving toward her and away from the guy at the bar. My daughter is at home and her leg's still in a cast.

He said good-bye to Nancy, who was chatting vivaciously with her friends, and Daniela felt the need to accompany him to the door, as if she were protecting him. Thanks again. It was nothing, said Lorenzo. Tell Wilson he should call me if he needs anything. Daniela seemed surprised, ah, okay, but I don't have your phone number. Lorenzo searched his jacket for a pen. It's okay, she said, I know where you live. They said good-bye with a kiss on each cheek. On the second one, Lorenzo's nose brushed her hair. It smelled of chamomile.

Lorenzo met up with Sylvia, who had eaten at her grandparents' house. He had called earlier, don't wait for me, I'm out with some friends. He felt a bit embarrassed about lying to his father, but he found it hard to explain that he was having lunch with the girl who took care of the kid who lived upstairs. Sylvia was with her grandmother, in the bedroom. They were playing checkers on the bed with the board tilted and the pieces sliding.

Leandro walked through the hallway, restless. Lorenzo spoke to him about Aurora's condition. Her spirits seem better. She likes seeing her granddaughter, said Leandro, with her she pretends she's feeling good. I think I'm going to buy a van, he said to his father, I want to start something on my own, I'm tired of working for other people. Lorenzo didn't get the enthusiasm he was hoping for out of Leandro. His father offered him money, although we aren't doing too well right now. No, no, refused Lorenzo, I have some, I made some, but he chose to hide that it was from Sylvia's settlement.

The first day that Sylvia got into the van it was on their way to the game. I was tired of the car, at least with this I can look for little jobs. It was chaotic approaching the stadium, but he wanted to leave Sylvia in a nearby bar so she wouldn't have to walk too far. Lorenzo's friends, Óscar and Lalo, met up with them. It was their usual meeting place. The bar filled up when there was still an hour until the game started. Seven draft beers, a call came out, another round over here. Checking Sylvia's tickets, one of them let out a whistle. What good seats, if you stretch out your hand you can grab the players.

And it was almost true. Although Ariel rarely came close to that area. In the second half, Sylvia had to strain her eyes to see him from her seat. The game wasn't going brilliantly. Lorenzo had to explain some plays to Sylvia, but she wasn't paying attention. They're making mincemeat out of number ten. Number ten was Ariel Burano. Right before the end of the game, it was that player who took advantage of a muddle in the penalty box to edge the ball into the net. Sylvia lifted two fists to celebrate the goal. Lorenzo held her tightly in his arms and they both let loose with untempered joy. It was number ten, she says.

Lorenzo feels his daughter's body glued to his and savors the moment. When she was a little girl, he squeezed her in his arms or tickled her and gave her affectionate bites, but as she left childhood behind their regular contact was also lost.

He was always envious of Pilar because she shared Sylvia's most intimate moments. He remembers the night Pilar told him that she had found her crying in bed. Why was she crying? Pilar smiled, but her eyes were damp. She says she doesn't want to grow up, that it scares her. She doesn't want to stop being the way she is. And what did you tell her? asked Lorenzo. Pilar had shrugged her shoulders. What do you want me to tell her, she's right. And the next morning Lorenzo had gone to wake her up to take her to school and he tried to talk to her about it. She didn't seem too interested in listening, as if the alleged trauma had vanished overnight. In spite of everything, Lorenzo told her, you'll see, life always has good things, at any age. If I had stayed a child forever, I never would have met your mother and you never would have been born. Sylvia reflected for a moment at the school entrance. Yeah, but when you were little you didn't know everything that was going to happen later, that's the bad part. Sylvia couldn't have been more than eight or nine years old.

After freeing himself from the embrace of his teammates, who had buried him beneath their bodies beside the corner flag, Ariel Burano runs toward the middle of the field and celebrates the public's applause. The goal is the work of number ten Ariel Burano Costa, announces a euphoric voice over the loudspeaker. An ugly goal, but it counts just as much as a pretty one, says Lorenzo. Let's see if those assholes open up a bit now and there are more chances at goals. But it's not going to happen.

The game cools off. The last few minutes go by with hardly any opportunities; both teams seem to accept the results. With five minutes in the game, Ariel is substituted. He walks toward the sideline in no rush. He is applauded, although some whistles are heard. Why are they whistling? asks Sylvia. After he made a goal. Lorenzo shrugs. There's something about him people don't like. Too artistic.

4

Ariel lets the hot water run over his body. But he still can't get the chill out of his bones. When things go well, the condensed steam in the locker room, in the shower area, looks like heaven, the promised paradise. One guy whistles, another jokes, someone imitates a woman's voice, another asks for the shampoo. There's no trace of that thick silence, of the low gazes, the twisted expressions of when they lose. They call the Czech goalie Cannelloni for the size of his cock and that night he can't escape Lastra's joking, who screams, I'll bring you the hand broom so you can scrub the foreskin. Last Sunday Ariel had scored the winning goal in their stadium and this Saturday the second one was earned as part of his play. In Valladolid, with a wind that shifted the ball in midair, they had to mark the lines of the goal area in red because the field froze. Ariel had the feeling he was playing on razor blades. Right on the end line, he eluded tackle by two fullbacks and he faced the goalie with barely any angle. He took a step back and passed it to a forward who barely had to blow on the ball to get it into the net. They call it the "death pass," because scoring is something like killing. When the team embrace broke up, Matuoko came over to Ariel in an aside and patted his cheek, that was your goal, man.

From that moment on, every time the Ghanaian touched the ball, the younger fans made monkey shrieks, ooh, ooh, ooh, to insult the player. They moved their hands like macaques and the voice over the loudspeaker begged them to stop with the racist insults because it could result in a fine for the local team. Last week, in his own stadium, Ariel also had to hear whistles from the fans, in the area reserved for an extreme right-wing group that goes by the name of Young Honor. The board of directors treats them with kid gloves because they are loyal and passionate, they travel with the team at ridiculous discounts, and their organization has their own office in the stadium. Last season they had taken the team's bus by storm on the way back from a game that had ended in defeat. They threatened the players and insulted them with shouts of mercenary and slacker. He had made a date to meet them in their office on the first floor of the stadium. Ariel passed Husky on the way out of the locker room that morning. Are you going to give them an interview and take pictures with them? he asked, shocked. I know everybody does it, but come, look, and he showed him their Web site on his laptop. Nazi symbols, the usual threatening, bullying tone hidden behind the team colors. Most of the players on staff were posing in photographs with the scarves and insignias of the group in an exercise of submission. Ariel found an excuse and got out of his commitment through one of the press employees. So when he heard the whistles and shouts of Indian, spic, he didn't feel too hurt. The atmosphere around soccer is the same everywhere.

Matuoko, for example, was fighting against an accepted fact: a black player had never succeeded on their team.

Ariel dresses quickly and tucks his long wet hair into a wool cap. The visiting locker room, sad, tiled in white like a public restroom, contrasts with their home locker room, which was renovated with no expense spared. Some credentialed journalists and recently showered players mill around. He wants to say hi to one they call "Python" Tancredi, a guy from Santa Fé who inherited the nickname from the legendary Ardiles, even though he had been such a slow center halfback that in *La Nación* someone wrote that "it would take more than ninety minutes and two overtimes for Tancredi to reach a free ball." Journalists sometimes showed off their wit cruelly. They say that Python sent a gift to the newspaper's staff, his stool in a glass jar. Tancredi has been in Spain for six years and he greets Ariel with a hug and a kiss on each cheek. You getting used to it? Dude, you see how chilly the reception is here.

They talk about plans for Christmas. Python has four children and he says, no way am I putting them all on a plane. I bring my parents here and my in-laws, let them do the traveling. In Buenos Aires you need protection, a bodyguard, it's disgusting. You can't even trust the cops. Tancredi lifts his hands in an Italian gesture, bringing together the tips of all five fingers, did you know there are 143 crimes reported every hour? The country's gone to shit. The last time I was there, I stopped in a service station with my old man and up come two ghetto muggers with a blade this big, no, no, I'm staying here. Ariel says that he's going home, his mother's health is too delicate to withstand such a long flight. Have you met "Tiger" Lavalle? Python asks him. Ariel shakes his head. It's traditional for goalkeepers in Argentina to be called Crazy, Monkey, Cat, or Tiger. Tiger Lavalle is a veteran goalie from Carcarañá who arrived in Spain after years in the Mexican league. Anarchic and genius, he shoots the penalty kicks and is equally loved and hated. The press adores him because amid all the usual clichéd answers his are always uninhibited pearls, happy discoveries. Ariel doesn't know him personally. We haven't played against his team yet, he says to Python. He's the one who does the most to unite all the Argentinians here, he explains to Ariel, he always gets us together with some excuse, it's nice.

From the end of the hall, the delegate makes a sign to Ariel with his head when the team is heading toward the bus. Ariel says good-bye to Python. He crosses with the others toward the street. From the fences the kids ask for autographs, throw photos, but it's too cold and they barely stop. On the bus, they choose a martial arts movie, with katana fights and impossible jumps in slow motion. Ariel turns on his cell phone. He brought a book, *No Logo*, that Marcelo Polti sent him with such an excessive inscription that it filled the first three pages and that said, among other things: "So you can be aware that those brand-name sneakers you advertise and get the kids all worked up about are contributing to the world's inequality." But Ariel gets nauseous reading on the highway. He isn't much of a reader. Sometimes his father used to say, I must have done something really wrong for my kids to believe that books bite.

They head back toward Madrid on the bus, with a couple of sandwiches and a piece of fruit, a bottle of water and the beer someone managed to sneak in. They emptied out Jorge Blai's hair gel into his shoe since he usually spends twenty minutes in front of the mirror before going out to meet the press, and they didn't want him to make them wait that night. He reminds Ariel of Turco Majluf, who used an entire tin of Lordchesseny for every San Lorenzo game. It's Poggio, the substitute goalie, who comes up with these cruel jokes. Sometimes Amílcar justifies it, he has to do something, they pay him a million euros to eat sunflower seeds on the bench, he's the luckiest guy in the world. And there is some truth to that, because the first day Ariel was with him on the bench he admired the skill with which Poggio removed the shells and wolfed them down, even with his goalie gloves on.

The seat next to Ariel is empty, across the aisle from Dani Vilar, who sometimes makes common courtesy look like pulling teeth. They look at each other but don't say anything. His father has Alzheimer's and he's going through a difficult time, is how the other teammates justify it. He often misses training as a show of hierarchy that no one dares challenge. It is dark outside. One of the center fullbacks, Carreras, gets up and opens his sports bag, then starts showing pieces of clothing to his teammates. They are from his parents' store and he promises them good prices. There are T-shirts, sweatshirts, sweaters, many of them brand names. Someone shouts, with what you earn you're selling clothes? But he says it's to help out his parents. Everyone on the team knows he's cheap and they tease him about it. To dribble past Carreras, they say, you just have to toss a euro to the right and head for the left. They laugh at his expense for a while, he shouts above the laughter, we're talking about 30 percent off here, eh, 30 percent.

Last Sunday when Ariel turned on his cell after the game he got a message from Sylvia. "Congratulations on the goal. I had a great time. Thanks for the tickets." He replied, "You brought me luck." Then he remembered that he hadn't given her their sign. She wrote: "I don't know if you dedicated the goal to me because everybody stood up and I couldn't see anything." "I forgot, I owe you one," he wrote. The response was slow in coming: "Next time I'd rather you take me out for a drink. I like soccer but not that much." "Done deal, whenever you want," wrote Ariel. "My social life is as busy as a cloistered nun's. You choose a day that works for you." "Tomorrow?" he wrote. They settled on having dinner the next day. "I'll take you to the best Argentinian restaurant in Madrid," he suggested.

When Ariel wrote the last message, he remembered Sylvia's curly hair, her white face with lively eyes, but little more. He felt a slight hint of regret, as if he'd made an awkward date. Yet he felt it was fair compensation for the pain he had caused her. That night he dined with Osorio and Blai and two of the Brazilians on the team. Later they wanted to drag him to a nightclub on the outskirts of town, it's right by your house. But Ariel wanted to call Buenos Aires. We have to celebrate your first goal, they insisted. I don't want to celebrate the first goal as if it's going to be the last, all right? said Ariel as he left. Ah, you never know if there'll be more, Blai said, do you know how many goals I've scored in six years of playing: three. Not much to celebrate. And two in your own side, Osorio managed to say before getting slapped in the stomach.

Ariel agreed to meet Sylvia on the staircase of the main post office. It seemed natural to both of them to meet somewhere close to the place where the accident happened. It could be understood as going back to where they began. He was late, the traffic was exasperating, and while he was trying to zigzag through the cars a taxi driver cursed angrily at him. In order to get close to the building, which from his vantage point looked like a huge umbrella stand, he had to maneuver illegally. He saw Sylvia sitting on the third step, her cast resting on the stone. He honked his horn. There were policeman directing traffic beside the Cibeles fountain and it was impossible to stop for long. As she turned her face, Sylvia's hair floated on the wind. She stood up deftly. She carried just one crutch and it seemed rude to Ariel that he watched her walk toward the car without getting out to help her. He opened the door from inside. I don't think this was a good meeting place, she said. People have started their Christmas shopping, they're insane. Totally, agreed Ariel. Sylvia held the crutch like a cane. Ariel drove toward the Puerta de Alcalá, entering the traffic jam again.

Sylvia tilted her head to the side. It's strange to be sitting inside this car. Although it's better than being plastered onto the windshield. Ariel asked about her leg, about the pain, about the awkwardness of the cast. The worst is when it itches inside and you start to scratch on the plaster as if that would help. Ariel had turned down the music and only muffled sounds could be heard. I made a reservation at an awesome restaurant, but then I thought it would be better to go to my house, he said. Do you like Argentinian empanadas? We can buy some on the way . . . Really Ariel was uncomfortable imagining himself in a restaurant being watched by everyone, that someone would think they were on a romantic date. But her reaction was a long silence. Your house? she finally asked. I don't know. Ariel realized his tactlessness. I only thought since restaurants are a madhouse, the people, all that, but you're right, let's go . . . Of course, you get recognized everywhere you go. The conversation sped up and Ariel gave too many explanations. No, no, let's go to your house, you're right, she said in the end. Are you sure? If you don't feel . . . No, no, let's go, I don't want you to spend the night signing autographs.

But in the store where they stopped to order the empanadas, Ariel saw there were two tables in the back, beside a shelf of Italian pastas. He went to get Sylvia from the car. Let's eat here, there's nobody else, it'll be good. The owners of the place were two nice Argentinian women who explained that they didn't have a restaurant license, just takeaway, but they served people while they waited and got around the law that way. Sylvia ordered a beer and Ariel a glass of wine from Mendoza. They settled in the back, surrounded by displayed products. Every once in a while, someone came in to buy something and Ariel's gaze searched for the door. It took him a while to relax. Sylvia seemed more comfortable. She asked him questions. About the game. About his soccer career. How he got started. How he came to Spain. Ariel talked for a long time, while she stared into his eyes. He pushed his hair back and sometimes she imitated his gesture, putting a section of curls behind her ear. Then Sylvia leaned her elbows on the table and put her hands on her cheeks. She was lovely in that gesture of relaxed observation. And Ariel realized that in all that time he had only been talking about himself. I talk too much, he said. The big Argentinian sin. No, it's interesting, she said. Before I met you I thought soccer players were mass-produced, I don't know, in industrial factories, all cut from the same pattern. And that they always forgot to add the brains, of course, he added.

One of the owners lowered the metal gate. No, no, relax, go on, we're locking up but we still have to clean and close out the register, you're not in the way, she said. That sort of isolation made them feel more comfortable. So *choclo* is corn, said Sylvia after biting into an empanada. Yeah, all the different food names are confusing. Do you miss your family? she asked. Yeah, of course, he said. Maybe I'll bring them over, if I get settled here. One of the owners brought an open bottle of wine and sat with them. She had come to Spain three years ago. The devaluation of the peso ruined me, and here I couldn't find work as an actress, so I was teaching acting. But it didn't go well for her and she partnered with a friend to import products from over there. Ariel wondered if the women were a couple, but he didn't dare ask. During the rest of the evening, she monopolized the conversation. She talked about her country, remembering people. She made fun of a singer, cursed a politician, laughed at the last plastic surgery a television hostess had done. They're gonna have to operate on her kids so they don't look adopted.

The place was called Buenos Aires–Madrid and it was still being renovated. The rent was so high they couldn't afford to continue the work. One of the women, the quieter one, finished tidying up the stock. The other one talked a blue streak. She cursed the American president's reelection and then she insisted that more than ever the world needed a new Che. I don't know, she said, Subcomandante Marcos leaves me a little cold, always wearing a mask and all that. There were moments when Ariel's gaze sought out Sylvia's eyes and he shot her a subtle ironic expression about the woman and her incessant talking or the obvious moustache beneath her nose. Ariel brought a finger to his face to discreetly point out the facial hair and make Sylvia laugh. But they both appreciated the interruption. It allowed them to study each other without explanation, look at each other without speaking, to share something.

As they left, Ariel told her, I'm warning you, Argentinians never shut up. Sylvia was impressed, what a talker. And did you notice? The dictionary is too short for that lady, she needs a new one and quick. They walked to the car. It was quarter to eleven. That's my curfew, I can't stay out much past it. I'll drive you home, he offered. Sylvia guided Ariel along the streets of Madrid. At a stoplight, she raised enough courage to ask him. Do you live alone? Now I do, yeah, he said. There was a silence. Keep going, straight ahead, she indicated. My brother was here, but he had to go back. I live on the outskirts, in Las Rozas. In one of those big houses? Ariel nodded. Do you like movies? I have a gigantic screen and I watch a ton of them up there, if you want to, one day . . . I don't like movies much, she said. Everybody likes movies, he said, surprised. I don't know, after five minutes I already know what's going to happen, I get bored, they're so repetitive. Ariel smiled. I've never heard that reasoning before. Everything repeats itself, right? he managed to say, then he regretted having said it, it didn't make much sense. No, in life you never know what's going to happen the next minute, but in the movies you can see what's coming. Just from the cast you already know if they're going to hook up or not, who's the bad guy. Oh, well, you mean American movies, sighed Ariel. People like them so much because they're predictable, they already know what they're gonna see. Like people who go to the beach for their vacations: what they want is sun and waves. And if you give them something else they get mad. If you come to my house someday, I'll put on a different kind of movie, you'll see. Okay, she said. I have a friend, Marcelo, a musician, he's very famous back home, he always says that if you do what the audience wants, you'd have to compose the same song over and over.

They got to Sylvia's street, but she let the car pass her door before telling him to stop. I really live back there, but I didn't want anyone to see me get out of a car like this. You don't like it? It's really flashy. Flashy? Kinda tacky, typical of a soccer player. I guess it impresses girls, but it makes me embarrassed, she said. My brother picked it out, I know it's tacky, Ariel apologized. I'll help you out, wait. Ariel got out of the car and opened Sylvia's door, then held her crutch as she got out.

They exchanged a kiss on each cheek. I had a really good time, she said. You don't like my car, you don't like movies, you're a tough one. Ariel smiled. Sylvia gathered herself to ask, you really think so? It's a joke, he explained. Well, thanks for inviting me, she said, initiating their good-bye. My pleasure. I guess it must be a drag for you to have to escort a paralytic around. The cast suits you, said Ariel, and then he smiled. Well, they're taking it off next week, so if you like it that much you'll have to run me over again.

Neither of them managed to quite say good-bye for the evening. Call me whenever you want, said Ariel. You call me, I don't want to be a pain in the ass. Sylvia headed off, trying to look agile in spite of the crutch. Ariel went back into the car and, looking into the rearview mirror, erased his smile, which he thought looked stupid, innocent, and captivated. He didn't start the engine until he saw her disappear, a moment after she waved to him.

They hadn't spoken again since that Monday night. Ariel had thought about her throughout the week, but he felt uncomfortable setting up another date. It was obvious they had been flirting as if she weren't sixteen years old, as if they were getting together for some reason beyond his trying to make up for having hit her. She was a smart, attractive girl, but Ariel could see her childish side, that dangerous inertia that could lead her to fall in love with him, to fantasize about a relationship that was never going to happen. On the bus, when he turned on his cell phone, he figured a message from her would appear. But it didn't. She gave no signs of life. And he shouldn't give any, either.

He wasn't going to give any.

He looks at his watch. It's almost twelve. He can't yet see the lights of the city from the bus window. He writes a message: "You want to come see a movie tomorrow at my house? That way you can tell me what happens in the end." He searches through his phonebook for Sylvia's name and sends it. It's Saturday night. Surely she's out with some friends from school. Ariel feels like that would be more appropriate for his age, too, more than sharing the bus with his teammates, surrounded by the sound of the blows of an action hero who, at the end of the movie, as always, will solve all his problems with a fantastic display of physical power.

5

She raises the neck of her sweater so that it covers her mouth. Her breath burns when it comes into contact with the wool. It's a pleasant sensation. The stone step's cold reaches her thighs through her pants. She shouldn't have sat down. But he makes her wait. He always makes her wait. To be punctual in Madrid, you have to take the metro. It must be hard to be on time with all that traffic. Why didn't she want him to pick her up at home? No, she thought, it's better if he doesn't. She worries that her father or some neighbor would see her getting into that car. That's why she's sitting on the steps of the post office again. It is a horrible place to meet, I know, but it's our place, isn't it?

The last time they went out together, she got into the car and Ariel drove to his house. It seemed far, but at this time of night it only takes a second, he said. Sylvia was nervous and her foot tapped the floor mat. It had taken them almost a week to get in touch again after their first dinner together. She was about to give up hope. Or, better put, she had given up hope several times. On Tuesday a message beep sounded; it was Mai. She had just arrived in Vienna with her boyfriend. On Wednesday someone called quite late. It was Dani, sounding drunk. I never know how to talk to you, he said. Sylvia didn't know either. Just like normal, I guess. Friday, on the way home, she saw a silver car identical to Ariel's. She approached it, coming as close as the edge of the sidewalk. It was driven by a somewhat pudgy fortysomething man, gelled hair, sunglasses, beside him a woman who seemed like a standard accessory with the car. On Saturday night, she thought that the incoming message on her phone would be from Alba or Nadia asking her if she was up for going out with some people from school, but it was him. He was inviting her to watch a movie at his house. She said yes. Of course.

What to think. What was he looking for? What was she looking for? The obsessive teenage perspective couldn't be right. It might be deceiving. The typical mirage. Thinking it's something it's not. Desire forces you to see what desire reveals. And reality? He calls me. He talks to me. The normal thing would be that I didn't exist, Sylvia thought, that I ceased to exist after the accident, and yet . . . He's friendly. He's just being friendly.

He's being friendly, I've fallen in love.

Her thoughts wandered. She couldn't concentrate. In class the symptoms were clear. On television footage of the presidents' summit meeting in Vienna was aired, the city overtaken by riot police. Shields and protective helmets straight out of a futuristic movie. Policemen charging. Mai didn't answer her last message. But Sylvia wasn't too worried. She'd be back on Sunday.

The first time he took her to his house, they entered through the garage. On the basement level was a room converted into a gym. He heated up some meatballs for dinner. They were good, but it was ridiculous to eat meatballs in that living room, with Ariel standing while he suggested movies to watch until she picked one, this one. He turned off the lights, took out a liter bottle of beer and two cups, the title credits appeared, but Sylvia's attention wasn't on the screen: it was on Ariel. His arm rested on the back of the sofa, like an attempted embrace, a caress that never arrived, never would arrive. And Sylvia wondered if her socks had any holes before taking off her boots, making herself comfortable, curling up on the sofa to see if he would decide to hug her. They had taken her cast off that same morning. Well, this way I feel a little less guilty, said Ariel when he saw her. She still needed the crutch to rest her foot safely, but she had gotten her mobility back.

They watched the movie. It was fun. A real mix-up about two con men. Halfway through he asked her, do you know how it's going to end yet? Well, one of these two is not what he appears to be, that's obvious. Ariel smiles. Have you seen it before? she asks. Yeah, but that doesn't matter to me. I like it. I don't mind knowing how movies end. It's the same in soccer, if it was only the end result that mattered each team could shoot five penalty kicks at the beginning and then go home. No, what's important is the game. Sylvia shrugs her shoulders, nervous. Why was he talking about soccer? She brought a lock of hair to her mouth, biting it again and again. What was he thinking about her? He must have invited her out as a curiosity. A sharp, funny Spanish girl. Like some sort of witty, flirtatious niece. He was talking about soccer, but with a professorial air, he talks to me like I'm a little girl. Sometimes Sylvia lost the thread of the film, focusing on how miserable she felt.

When the movie ended, Sylvia looked through the mountains of CDs. A ton of Argentinian groups. Names she didn't know, Intoxicados, Los Redondos, La Renga, the Libertines, Bersuit, Callejeros, Spineta, Vicentico. Put on something you like, she asked. He put on the latest record by his friend Marcelo. He sent me this but it's not on sale yet. Listen, it's super-good. Sylvia sat down, took another sip of beer. The lyrics . . . said Ariel, the guy's world is crazy, totally his own. His sentences ended on a high note, as if the last syllables were ringing in the air. I barely listen to any music in Spanish, she said. I like it better when I don't understand the words. I don't know, it's like everything sounds more corny, more simplistic when it's in your own language. Are you crazy? he said. And he repeated the verses: "Tangled in the vines of your jungle, I search for the path that brings me back, sanity before I lose it, lose my sight in the fog, the rope where I hang myself every Monday when my team loses, Madrid is so far away, Ariel." He's talking about me there. Ariel looked at her, without sitting down. Pretty, right? Sylvia was defensive, yeah, I don't know. A little corny. Everything sounds corny if I can understand it. Disagreeing was a way to take a stance. A bit feeble, she said after another band. I hate those groups that look tough with their long hair and tattoos and all those trappings, but then what they sing is pure marmalade, drippy little ballads. Ariel interpreted it as a declaration of her taste, and he searched for a more aggressive band. They come from a shantytown, the poorest in Buenos Aires, he told her. They sounded strong, guitar-heavy. Sylvia liked them better. I see, you're into rock from the slums, he remarked. At least the noise covers up the simple lyrics a little. Ariel laughed. I wouldn't call Marcelo simple, he's been in analysis for twenty years. He's a nutcase. He told me there are people who've done their doctoral theses on just one of his songs. Now he keeps insisting I visit an analyst friend of his who lives in Madrid.

Sylvia found it uncomfortable to listen to music with Ariel's smile fixed on her, his eyes questioning. She nodded, saying, good, or, I like this. The situation was sort of like a test. He asked her what her favorite music was and she named groups he had never heard of. All British or American. You'll have to play them for me, he said, almost to be polite. Sylvia took it as an invitation to continue meeting. He served her beer every once in a while, but always from the other side of the coffee table, its lower shelf filled with magazines and sports newspapers. Sylvia flipped through one, but the cover models were too beautiful, retouched by a computer in search of fabricated perfection, not a trace of pimples, folds, wrinkles, real skin. I made the cover of this one. Ariel holds out a magazine with his photo on it. Don't even think about reading it, the interview is horrible.

They talked for a while more, even though the music played loudly and he changed the songs before they ended, as if he wanted to give her an overview in twenty minutes. It got late, too late. Sylvia said, how am I going to get out of here? It was twenty to eleven. But Ariel insisted on taking her. He took the car out of the garage and Sylvia went through the door to the yard, to avoid the steps. How ridiculous that she had to leave so early. She was sure the night was just starting for him. She got into the car like a childish Cinderella. They got back onto the now deserted highway toward the city. The same music, by his friend Marcelo, was playing. I like it so much that I made a copy for the car, he explained. The return trip seemed to obliterate what had happened that evening. When we get to my house, thought Sylvia, it will be as if we never met. It was a strange feeling. A retraced route that went back to the beginning. Nothing had happened, because there was nothing to happen. Sylvia looked at the highway and started biting on a lock of hair again. In the city, Ariel asked her about her parents. I live with my father, just us. My mother left him six months ago. And without Ariel saying anything, Sylvia felt obliged to add, they're good people. The marriage just fell apart. I don't know, sometimes I think they stayed married just for me, and they couldn't find anything else to keep them together. Sylvia put her hair behind her ears, her sad eyes. He looked at her twice, still driving.

When they got to the doorway, Ariel drove past it. Wouldn't want anyone to see you getting out of this flashy car, he joked. They both laughed. Thanks for the movie. We can do it again whenever you feel like it. Sure, whenever you want. Ariel went over his schedule. Tomorrow we're on the road, we're playing in Italy on Wednesday, but when we get back, I don't know,

I'll call you, we'll talk. Okay, was all Sylvia said. They kissed on each cheek, she enveloped him in her hair, he broke away delicately. Ariel helped her out, I had a good time, I don't have that many people here I can watch a movie and have a beer with. Sylvia walked toward her door with a victorious smile.

In the elevator, alone, on the way up to her apartment, leaning on the crutch, somewhat dizzy from the beer, she kissed herself full on the lips in the mirror. Then she thought, I'm stupid.

Thursday, after coming back from the game in Italy, he wrote her a message. "Another movie?" he suggested. "The works," she answered, and then she regretted having written it. The works? It sounded brassy. She also regretted having painted her lips in muted purple, the lips that were hidden beneath the neck of her wool sweater at that moment, at six p.m., sitting in the cold on the frozen steps, waiting to see the silvery reflection of Ariel's car appear in what was now their usual meeting place. She felt that she was exposing her intentions in too obvious a way. Her love. In the purple, in her easy availability, in her enthusiasm. She was nervous.

6

The hospital makes Leandro sick. In the waiting room, there are only old people. It's like a microcosm in extinction. He's surprised no one has yet shot a science fiction film of a future time where there are just old people left, waiting for transplants, or who've only survived because of some medical discovery. Maybe someone has; it's been a long time since he's paid attention to what's in theaters. Some woman was speaking loudly, animatedly, about her illness. Another responds, my sister-in-law had the same thing. Another, hope is the last thing to go. The nurse tolerates the rebuke of a man who says he's been waiting for an hour, then she gathers up the referral slips of the recent arrivals, asks for patience, and calls for the next three on the list.

Leandro's expression is the opposite of Aurora's. In her wheelchair, she firmly maintains her dignity, her head held high, her shoulders lifted. Only her inert hands, resting white among the rain of age spots, give away that she is the one who's ill. Leandro buries his head, his gaze lowered, his shoulders fallen. Last Saturday his piano student, Luis, had said he was having trouble finding time for classes during his exams at university and he would stop coming for a while. Sure, sure, replied Leandro, but he felt like that was the end of his work life. In the best years, he had had up to five or six private students spread out in classes throughout the week. Since he retired, he had reduced the number, but he'd never had less than three. Last year he limited it to one, Luis, a polite and attentive young man who showed up every Saturday at eleven. In the academy they recommended Leandro as an instructor, and he was lazy about advertising or looking for students. When he lost his last student, he said to himself, that's it, this is the end, another chapter closed. He was quiet during that last class, so much so that young Luis felt obliged to try to cheer him up, maybe after exams I'll start up again.

The last few days, he had barely left the house. He kept watch over Aurora's fragility, waiting for her bursts of high spirits, while he fulfilled her absurd requests: calling acquaintances for their birthdays, paying Benita the extra hour from last Thursday. At times she came out of her sleepiness or interrupted her reading to organize the routine, look and see how we're doing for oil, we might need some, or, you have to help Benita with the upper shelves in the kitchen, she can't reach. Leandro watched as the maid stood on a stool to laboriously clean off the grease that had accumulated out of sight, while she shouted, for two inches, yes sir, for just two inches they denied me the dwarf pension. Now, that's bad luck, at least being so short could have done me some good, but no. Leandro was familiar with her personal misfortunes. A husband dead from emphysema, in his prime; a laughable pension; a daughter lost to drugs who, at twenty-two, had thrown herself out the window; and a truck driver son imprisoned in Portugal for some shady smuggling affair. They hid something in his cargo, but he refused to turn in his bosses. That tiny woman showed too much strength, brightening the house with her vibrant shouting; sometimes she sang a *copla* while she vacuumed, and Leandro, who was frightened by the combination of the two sounds, fled to the street in search of peace. When she finished her work, Benita stopped by Aurora's bed and said good-bye raucously. She pinched her cheeks hard, that'll give you a little color, you're very pale, or she repeatedly told her the worst thing is staying still, from still to dead there's only a hair's breadth.

Leandro went out to take a walk around the neighborhood, taking advantage of the hours of clean winter sun. He wandered haphazardly in the Mercado Maravillas, among the stalls he's known forever but where he avoids familiarity. On the street, he caught the performance of Gypsy women selling clothing, lipsticks, scarves. Sometimes he would lose himself in the small streets and his steps would lead him to the Tuning Fork

Academy, and during class hours he would listen to some music theory or piano student playing with young, tentative fingers. For thirty-three years, he had taught classes there.

His worry over the state of his finances had kept him away from the chalet. He had gone to great lengths in taking care of Aurora, as if that task would keep him from temptation. On some afternoons, he locked himself in his room to listen to a record and fantasized that he was done with his disgraceful behavior. His son, Lorenzo, stops by the house every day and asks him if everything's okay. Can you manage everything, Papá? Ask for help if you need it, please.

One Sunday he found his granddaughter seated at the piano and he sat beside her. He helped her determine the notes to the melody she sang softly with some English words, as if composing a song in the air.

Aurora asks him to wait outside, they'll do tests and weird things, it's best if you don't come in, and she forces him to stay on the other side of a door with a sign on it warning about radioactive levels. Leandro amuses himself in the hallway, rubbing each of his fingers with the other hand, walking up and down to avoid going back into the waiting room filled with chance conversations.

Where did it happen, when, Leandro doesn't understand how the wall rose up between them, that protective area where they don't get involved in the other's suffering, in what the other is feeling. Aurora, so open, alive, sincere, always available, happy, enthusiastic, but reserved when it came to anything that could affect him, inconvenience him. She had respected his space, his silence, his lack of implication, and she had done her best to keep anything from disturbing it. Now Leandro is ashamed of having a relationship like that. His wife isn't going to share her fear and pain with him and it may be that she needs to, but she'll keep it inside, she'll act strong and self-sufficient, because that is what she learned to do at his side.

Perhaps they'd established that way of being right when they met. Leandro was twenty-three years old and visiting an office in the former Ministry of Education headquarters to try to get financial help in postponing his studies so he could travel to Paris. He went from window to window, with a written recommendation he showed to anyone willing to read it. Aurora was hammering away at a typewriter, and she was the one who noticed him and offered to help, even though she was just a temporary secretary. Maybe Leandro already sensed he was ill-equipped to face those challenges, that he needed someone to resolve the domestic catastrophes, the smallest fears. Aurora took an interest in his case when Leandro, sitting on a wooden bench, rubbing his frozen hands together, was only expecting to get a final no to his request. He told her he was looking for a scholarship for a school in Paris and she asked him about his field of study. He said classical piano. And Aurora's eyes, on that day so many years ago, opened enormously wide, and it seemed as if Leandro held the only key capable of opening them that way.

Classical piano.

Leandro always thought it had been those two words that had opened up Aurora's heart. He said them with smug intention. Madrid, 1953, classical piano. It was like talking about life on other planets. Aurora read the recommendation written by some luminary and asked him to wait a moment. She disappeared down a back hallway and was gone quite a while. So long that when she came back, Leandro responded to her smile with, are you sure I'm not wasting a lot of your time? But Aurora shook her head. I hate my job, any interruption is a stroke of luck.

In spite of Aurora's good intentions, Leandro only got a few kind words and promises that never materialized. On the street, that first day, he took his leave of Aurora with a proper squeeze of her hands, and he headed off, raising the lapels of his coat. He didn't look back to see her in the dark doorway. He didn't want to force himself to be nice or thank her for her effort. That was how he presented himself as a romantic candidate, laden with silences, an aura of mystery, and a very hidden warmth. When he walked away from those offices on Calle Trafalgar, he knew he would see her again, that he would go looking for her behind that window to offer her the nothing he had to offer, the little he had to say. I don't think I thanked you enough for all you did for me, he went to tell her two days later. Then she blushed like a schoolgirl.

They strolled that afternoon along the downtown sidewalks. Leandro faded out his on-again, off-again passion for a ballerina he had met at the ballet auditions where he worked as a pianist for hire. Aurora dashed all the hopes of a young colleague of her father's, whom her father had insisted on inviting over to eat at the house so he could moon at her over his soup with his solicitous husband eyes. After six months of reading *Primer Plano* to choose what movie to see, of avoiding puddles on the street or the stench of bums on the sidewalk, of listening to the radio together, Aurora handed over her savings and told him, go to Paris and give it a shot. At that point they knew they were in love, but their financial future was not at all secure. Joaquín's letters to Leandro promised him a shared destiny.

After the war, Joaquín's father reappeared like the living dead, but victorious and heroic. Nothing like those who came back from the front or the internment camps like languid shadows. Rumormongers said he had been leading a double life romantically and was now purging his sins by becoming a devoted father who dragged everyone in his path to daily Mass. He magnanimously helped the less fortunate in the neighborhood and from the first day he insisted that Leandro share piano classes with his son Joaquín.

Three afternoons a week, an old professor, who had lost his post at the conservatory for socialist sympathies, came over. Too old to be sent to the firing squad, too stubborn to change ideas now, was how he had described himself once in a very rare glint of intimacy with his students. Don Alonso tried to discipline the two boys in front of the piano. They learned as much from their lessons as from his taciturn sadness, the bitter gratitude with which he received his payment from Joaquín's father at the end of class, the careful way he put away the worn scores in his leather satchel that was coming unstitched. Leandro always thought of Don Alonso, and his exercises for the left hand, affectionately. He remembered one afternoon when the professor told them about music schools in Russia, about the discipline of their conservatories, the natural selection of talent from the entire country, and he spoke in such a quiet, guilty voice that it was as if he were telling them about an orgy in forbidden brothels. He also remembered the silences, deep as wells. Even though Leandro and Joaquín, at eleven and twelve years old, were devoted almost exclusively to life's joys, they still noticed their professor's downbeaten integrity.

That parallel life with Joaquín, seated in front of the piano, had perhaps given Leandro false expectations. Their families were quite different, their economic realities even more so. As Joaquín started to squander money on entertainment, Leandro was working to help his widowed mother. And the thousands of hours shared on the street and later in the cafés, all the conversations and the confidences, would be left behind when Joaquín went to Paris.

From Paris, Leandro wrote two long letters to Aurora. They were few compared to what she was expecting, but they were very expressive in their bitterness. Leandro didn't earn a spot at the conservatory, nor did he manage to establish himself in the city. Joaquín had a celebrated teacher, an Austrian émigré who spoke leaden French, for whom Leandro auditioned. He had the courage to take on Mozart's *Jeunehomme* piano concerto and she asked him why he was playing that piece. Leandro answered the same thing he still thinks today, that it is perhaps the most beautiful piece ever composed for piano. The woman's declaration at the end of his audition was devastating. We didn't choose this profession to make beautiful things sound conventional. Leandro went back to Madrid after three months. His mother's health had worsened and he missed Aurora. Joaquín told him something that even then sounded like a compassionate lie, you can achieve the same thing in Madrid as I can here.

Aurora and Leandro began an official courtship, happy and intimate, isolated from the world and its limitations. They were waiting for Leandro to finish school before marrying and living together. He could string together two or three jobs and get a salary that would allow them to pay the rent comfortably. She kept her secretarial job until she got pregnant. When Leandro's mother died, they sold her apartment and bought another one in the Plaza Condesa de Gavia. By then Aurora had already grown accustomed to Leandro's reserve. It was enough for Aurora to know that he felt much more for her than he was ever able to express. Then she was fueled by her baby's energy, by the newborn's vitality.

By then Joaquín was flying solo. He had an agent and had moved to Vienna for some master classes and to assist Bruno Seidlhofer and give his first performances. His letters were increasingly shorter and more infrequent. There he spent time with pianists such as Friedrich Gulda, Alfred Brendel, Ingrid Haebler, Walter Klien, Jörg Demus, Paul Badura-Skoda. Yesterday I saw Glenn Gould play, he wrote to Leandro, in a concert where he destroyed Bach, as usual. Or he went to the Staatsoper to see Clemens Krauss or Furtwängler conduct and to see pianists like Fischer and Alfred Cortot, who they had listened to countless times on a recording from the 1930s of the twenty-four Chopin preludes that Don Alonso had taught them to revere. Shortly after, Joaquín would sign a contract with the Westminster record label and Leandro would become an old childhood friend in a Madrid he visited as little as possible, especially after his public declarations against the regime became frequent and well-known in his adopted Paris.

Returning home that morning, Leandro just led the attendants up the stairs as they carried her. On each of the steps that he had traveled over thousands of times, he sees the shadow of what they once were and thinks that Aurora's legs will never again walk up to their apartment, loaded down with a child in her arms or shopping bags. Leandro helps her get undressed and comfortable in bed. A little later, he will place a tray of food on her lap and settle into the nearby armchair. They will listen to the radio news of the day. Aurora will not share the details the doctor gave her with him. Neither will Leandro confess his pressing need to leave, to go back to the chalet where Osembe works. After two weeks of abstinence, he will see her again that evening.

7

Around noon on Saturday, Lorenzo is setting the table for the midday meal. Sylvia is surprised. It's early. Are you going to the stadium? No, but I have plans, he answers cryptically. She cooks some pasta and two steaks and they eat in front of some celebrity gossip show and the start of the news. Sylvia tells him that she is going to spend the afternoon at her grandmother's house.

Have you talked to your mother lately? Sylvia nods. Do you have exams soon? In two weeks. Are you studying? I do what I can.

Two hours later, Lorenzo waits for Daniela in front of her door. When he sees her, he notices she's got makeup on, a bit of violet eye shadow and lip liner. She's wearing tight elastic pants and a fuchsia T-shirt beneath a jean jacket. Her damp hair falls over her back. A large canvas bag hangs from her shoulder. You look very pretty.

One Monday Lorenzo had waited for that uncertain hour of the morning when everyone is occupied with chores and the unemployed stand out with their slow gait along the side-walks and their overly persistent gazes into shop windows. He went up the stairs to the floor above and rang the bell. Daniela opened the door. Behind her you could hear the television and the boy's gurgling in front of cartoons. Once again she wore that challenging expression, somewhat put out, but pleasant. She stepped forward across the doorway, as if that ensured she was not committing any wrongdoing in their home.

Pardon the intrusion, but I think I have something for your friend. Wilson? Lorenzo nodded. Tell him to call me. It's a little job he might be interested in. I'll tell him, thanks.

The conversation ended quickly, but she remained there, with the trace of a half smile. Lorenzo took the plunge. And one other thing, would you like to go to El Escorial this Saturday? I'd love to take you, remember I promised you I would? I don't know, this Saturday . . . Daniela lets her thoughts drift. You don't have to . . . You can bring your friend, if you want. I don't know if she'll be able to. Ask her, I'd love to. Okay, I'll let you know.

Lorenzo apologized again for having come up and then disappeared down the stairs. Half an hour later, his cell phone rang. It was Wilson. He hadn't gotten more than sporadic construction jobs, nothing regular, every morning he waited early in a plaza in Usera for the vans that picked up daily workers. I get in line there, I stick out my chest to show off my muscles, and lower my face to hide my crazy eye. Lorenzo explained that that afternoon he was going to start emptying out a house and the money would depend on how long it took them to do it.

The job opportunity came up during a dinner with friends at Óscar's house. Lalo had mentioned an apartment that the real estate agency he worked for had just bought. It belonged to one of those old men who obsessively hoarded trash, upsetting his neighbors. Why do they do that? someone asked. I remember an old lady in my neighborhood who lived with a million cats, she was like that, too. Diogenes syndrome, said Ana. It's a psychological disorder called Diogenes syndrome. It's becoming more and more common. Óscar said that it must be some kind of social rejection, something you did when you hated your environment. Craziness. Fear of the void, said Ana, they're all old people who live alone. Well, we have to empty it out this week, and you can't imagine how creeped out we are about what we might find there, there must be at least six tons of garbage, said Lalo. I'll take care of it, said Lorenzo, to everyone's surprise.

Lorenzo explained he was planning on setting up a small moving and transport business and if it paid well, cleaning out this apartment could be the perfect job to start with. When he noticed his friends' looks, he felt offended. Isn't that a decent job? Sure, man, of course, it's just a little surprising. Surprising? I have to make a living somehow. I don't know if you guys noticed, but I'm scraping the bottom of the barrel here.

Yeah, of course. And they avoided one another's eyes, as if it were a contest to see who could hold out the longest without saying anything. Lorenzo didn't want the conversation to die out like that. He insisted. I'll take care of cleaning it up and emptying it out, and depending on the hours it takes we'll negotiate a price. But you're going to do it yourself? asked Lalo. The place must be infected.

That was when Lorenzo remembered Wilson and he turned it into, I know some Ecuadorians who can lend me a hand. He felt his friends breathe easier, as if the delegation of work elevated him in the business hierarchy, steering them clear of the degrading image of their friend hunched over, picking up the accumulated crap from a mentally unbalanced old man. Lorenzo was improvising out loud. I'm thinking about setting up a fleet of vans, something small, but the market is definitely there.

It doesn't sound like such a bad idea to me, said Óscar. Oh, man, I was imagining you with lumbago, messed up after a week, admitted Ana. Well, let's talk about it on Monday, said Lalo, feigning enthusiasm.

Wilson waited in the van while Lorenzo went up to Lalo's office at the real estate agency. His friend handed him the keys to the apartment. He wrote down the address on a slip of paper. He was still uncomfortable. I'll need an invoice and all that. Of course, of course. You're sure the owner's not still in there . . . No, man, no, everything's been past the notaries. The apartment is ours. As far as the money, you'll let me know . . . Do you need something for the initial expenses?

Lorenzo and Wilson went up the stairs to the apartment. The peephole had been pulled out and sealed with black masking tape. Before they managed to open the door, trying each of the keys Lalo had given them, a female neighbor emerged from the opposite apartment. We're from the agency, Lorenzo said to reassure her. I can't believe you're going to cart away all that shit. The smell is unbearable.

It was nothing compared to the stench that came out once the door was opened. We need masks, said Wilson. The amount of objects piled up in the apartment made it almost impossible to walk through. On top of the sofa and the television, the regular furnishings of any home, there was a layer of junk, accrued garbage, stuff piled high until the whole apartment was submerged. There was furniture of different sizes, chairs, old newspapers, plastic bags filled with who knows what.

You think there are rats? wondered Wilson. Or worse. And the place isn't bad. Wait and see how much dough they ask for once it's cleaned up, answered Lorenzo. By then he had already transformed into a professional. I've got to buy masks, garbage bags, gloves, shovels, coveralls, add a couple more employees. And after lifting up some boards and seeing a stampeding army of cockroaches, he added an insecticide bomb.

It took them two entire days to empty the apartment. The sewer smell was intense and unpleasant. They parked the van on the sidewalk and filled it with overflowing bags of garbage, drove to a nearby dump and emptied it there, and then went back to start again. The junk seemed to never end. Newspapers and magazines that went back to 1985, as if dating the start of the old man's dementia. During one of their breaks, the neighbor chatted with Lorenzo and Wilson and the two other Ecuadorians who had joined their team, told them the little she knew about the man. First his appearance had started to get sloppy and then little by little his house went downhill. Women? No, she couldn't remember any. She was sure he used to work for the post office, but in the last few years he didn't seem to have any schedule. He was just as likely to head out early in the morning as to not leave the house for days. No noises or fuss. But when neighbors started to criticize his behavior, complaining about the smell and the dangerous accumulation of junk, he tore out his peephole and covered it up. Another day he threatened the president of the building with a knife. And the police got tired of coming over with social workers, until finally they issued the eviction order. Then the real estate agency showed up and, no one really knows how, managed to buy the apartment.

Beneath one of the dressers was a huge wooden box filled with photos of women, cut out as if by a child. It must have taken years because there were so many. The women in the photographs weren't nude or particularly beautiful; they didn't really seem to have been specifically chosen. They were all women, though. They were precisely cut out. He took no shortcuts in his useless high-detail task. They looked like old paper dolls. There was also a collection of metro tickets, held together in bundles by crumbling rubber bands that broke at the touch. In drawers were pins, empty bottles, and advertising flyers.

In the kitchen, there was only enough silverware and dishes for one person. One cup, one plate, and one set of fork, knife, and spoon. A radical declaration of solitude. Hundreds of rags and plastic bags balled up. The senseless obsession for saving seemed only to grow in relation to the uselessness of the objects. Whole collections of nothing. There wasn't much organic garbage and the worst smell came from the broken toilet with its relentlessly dripping cistern. The bathtub was a pool of rust, the toilet was missing a lid, and yet there were mountains of empty bottles of shower gel and soap. In the kitchen, one slip of paper was stuck to the door of the fridge, with a telephone number and the name Gloria.

Lorenzo saved the piece of paper, and on his break the second day he dialed the number. Gloria? he asked the voice that answered. Yes, that's me, said a woman. She must have been about forty years old. Look, sorry, apologized Lorenzo. I'm calling from Altos de Pereda, number forty-three, apartment 1A. From the home of Mr. Jaime Castilla Prieto. Lorenzo had memorized the former owner's name. What do you want? asked the woman.

Lorenzo beat around the bush, trying to get information. He said he was emptying out the house and had found her number jotted on a piece of paper. Why call me? I've never been in that house. I don't know anyone by that name. But your number was on a piece of paper, on the refrigerator door . . . I don't know why . . .

Lorenzo insisted on how strange it was that she didn't know the place or the man who kept her phone number as his only visible contact. It was, it seemed, the sole bit of information that tied him to the real world. But the woman, this Gloria, denied any relationship with him. Her refusal turned out to be sincere, surprised, somewhat concerned. Lorenzo realized he was beginning to upset the woman and he apologized and said goodbye. It was weird.

In his own way, the guy who lived here was organized, pointed out Wilson when they had paused for a moment. The everyday objects were striking, fossils of a conventional life that appeared as they removed the layers of accumulated junk. A stationary bicycle pushed beneath the bed, hangers, shoes in good shape. Why live like that? Why end up that way? Lorenzo felt dizzy and afraid, as he asked himself these questions on his way to the dump. Finally he consoled himself with Wilson's answer. The guy let himself go. And why not?

And why not?

The last vanload was filled with things Wilson or Lorenzo deemed to have some value. Small, cute pieces of furniture, a sideboard, three wristwatches, some glass bottles. In that final load, Lorenzo filled a cardboard suitcase with some small-format records, two or three books, and the enormous collection of cutout photos.

At the last minute, he called his friend Lalo. That's it, the apartment is empty. Tomorrow I'll give you the invoice, okay?

Lorenzo brought Wilson's buddies back to near Tetuán. Then they both went to an antique dealer in the Rastro district who had said he would have a look at the furniture. This isn't worth the effort, thought Lorenzo when he heard the amount the guy offered him for the pieces. Wilson was more skillful, bargaining boldly until he got the final price up by a few euros. Wilson insisted on accompanying Lorenzo to a gas station to wash the van, to try to get rid of the unpleasant smell. The Ecuadorian scrubbed the back as if it were his. Lorenzo felt strangely pleased. He liked the guy. Once in a while, Wilson would say something funny and laugh through his teeth. When Lorenzo took Wilson home, he asked for a favor. Can you ask Daniela to please come down for a minute? I have to ask her something, he justified when Wilson smiled at him knowingly.

Lorenzo waited in the darkness, parked at the entrance to a nearby garage. Daniela came out of the doorway and approached the van, avoiding the headlights' beam. How'd it go? she asked. Exhausting, said Lorenzo. Wilson will tell you.

Outside work Daniela seemed more relaxed. Her loose, damp hair fell around her eyes. Yeah, well, okay, she said suddenly.

It took Lorenzo a little while to realize that was her reply to his invitation for Saturday. So I'll pick you up after lunch? Okay.

Lorenzo started the engine and she left, a half smile still on her face. Lorenzo watched her walk back inside. She didn't swing her hips as she walked; instead she seemed propelled by small defiant impulses. She knows I'm watching her, thought Lorenzo.

Then he passed by his parents' house. Leandro and Aurora were having dinner in her room. A simple potato frittata. Lorenzo noticed their subdued intimacy. He was happy, exhausted by the job. I'm only here for a minute, I gotta go home and shower, he explained. You sure you don't want dinner? No, no. He asked how they were. He got angry because they hadn't asked him to go to the hospital with them and then was giddily evasive about the job. When I get it more established, I tell you about it, was all he'd say, convinced that sounded good. What did the doctor say? he asked his father on his way to the door.

Nothing, just a regular checkup.

At home a note from Sylvia was waiting for him. "I'm study-ing at Mai's house, see you later." Studying. Lorenzo smiled to himself.

After showering he got in bed. He tossed and turned. Ex-hausted, but wired with excitement. It took him a while to fall asleep. He got up to take the Barbie doll from the back of the nearby walk-in closet. He went back to bed with her. Under the sheets, he caressed her plastic curves. But he was too tired to masturbate and he fell asleep with the doll resting on his belly.

He was awoken early in the morning by the sound of the front door opening. Sylvia's light steps. Lorenzo checked the alarm clock on the bedside table. Almost three. Was she going out with some boy? Let's hope she knows what she's doing. I'll have to talk to Pilar. I'll ask her. She'll confess to her mother. He couldn't get back to sleep. He waited long enough for Sylvia to get into bed, then ventured over to her room. Do you know what time it is, Sylvia? I lost track of time. Well, that's obvious. I got caught up over at Mai's. I don't want you coming home so late, I worry. Okay, let me sleep. Lorenzo noticed her body, a woman's body, beneath the sheets. He wondered if some boy was enjoying her curves and then he put the thought out of his mind. It disturbed him. He related it to his own sexuality. Wor-rying about his daughter didn't keep him from masturbating with the doll once he got back to his bedroom and then putting her away, ashamed, at the back of the closet.

When on Saturday, after lunch, Daniela walks out of her door and hops into Lorenzo's van, he restrains the impulse to greet her too effusively. He just smiles in response to her smile. Is El Esco-rial very far? No, an hour, tops. Ah, I thought it was further.

No, no, it's very close.

8

He went down to the garage as quickly as he could. He didn't want to be late for practice. He took the sheets out of the washing machine. He didn't really know what to do with them. They were still damp. He spread them out on a rack. It's cold outside.

At practice his hands are freezing. His legs feel heavy. He didn't get enough sleep. Flashes of the previous night come back to him.

What am I doing? She's underage. She's sixteen years old. Yet Ariel's lips didn't part from Sylvia's. She broke the tension, bringing Ariel's hand to the back of her head, burying it beneath the weight of her hair. Ariel reached to caress her full neck. What was going to happen? It was Sylvia who pulled apart for a moment, searched out Ariel's eyes and smiled.

I'm crazy, right?

Ariel ran his fingers over her cheek. It was soft, spotless. His gesture had something of the way one strokes a child. We're not going to do anything, he said.

Sylvia lowered her head, embarrassed. Ariel wanted to run his fingers over her lips, but he didn't dare. Sylvia trapped a lock of her hair in the corner of her mouth and bit on it. Ariel stroked her hands and pushed away the hair. Why do you do that? I don't know. You don't have to be nervous. Are you comfortable? Do you want anything else? I don't know, another beer . . .

Ariel's trip to the kitchen gave them both a few seconds. Sylvia leaned back on the sofa. Ariel knows that overly passionate kisses reveal the fear that lies behind them. Once he made out for hours with a girl he had met at a concert, they shared incredibly ardent kisses, but she fled in terror when he tried to take her clothes off. That memory, together with Sylvia's spontaneous, fervent kisses, alarmed him. No, he wasn't going to do it. The refrigerator's cold air brought him back to his senses. When he sat down on the sofa he was a few inches further away from Sylvia. Hardly anything, but to her it must have seemed like miles.

It'd probably be best if I take you home, he said, and she nodded. It's twelve-thirty.

My father is going to kill me. Do you have practice early tomorrow?

At ten. When he explained that it was over by one and then he had the afternoon off, Sylvia let out a whistle and said something like, that's the life. Of course I'm a big fan of siesta time, I already was in Buenos Aires. I need to sleep, at least an hour. Then they talked about the game on Saturday. In Seville. They were traveling on Friday. It'll be on TV if you want to watch it. I'm not that big a fan, really. I thought you might like to see me . . . The conversation passed like a screen of rain between them. Ariel touched his nose with one finger and Sylvia bit the fingernail on her thumb.

Did you invite me over because you're into me? Sylvia's question brought back the lost heat, her eyes opened like a green sky. I invited you over because I like you . . . yeah, because I'm into you. But I didn't you bring you here to get you into bed.

Ariel didn't move, kept his distance. She smiled, nervous. Her lips puckered as she drank from the bottle and Ariel wanted to kiss her again. Why was that so crazy? He was only four years older than her, but to Ariel the difference seemed insurmountable. He remembered a teammate telling him that soccer players are like dogs, at thirty we're ancient.

Ariel established some physical distance as a safety barrier. She managed to break it and run her finger over the scar on his eyebrow. War injury, he said, it happened in practice a couple of years ago. It's a pretty brutal exercise, to get you to lose your fear of tackling headfirst. They bounce a ball against the ground between two players who are standing very close together and the winner is the one who manages to head the ball first. You know, those kind of tests designed to see who's got bigger balls.

Can I see your room?

My room?

Sylvia stood up nimbly. She placed herself in front of him and held out a hand. Ariel hesitated for a second, took it, and got up with her. They left the television on, the movie's music resonating through the living room, and headed upstairs. This way, he said, and she got in front of him. Ariel could make out the bones of her back beneath the wool sweater. The corner of a piece of paper sticking out of the back pocket of her jeans. Ariel bit his lower lip. He pointed to the second door. It was ajar. Sylvia pushed it open, revealing the made bed and the mess of compact discs beside the CD player on the floor. She sat on the bed and chose a CD. He put it on. From the streetlight, an orange glow filtered in, illuminating the room. The walls were bare except for a photograph of the New York skyline in a thin black wood frame. Ariel was embarrassed about that picture, a holdover from the last tenant.

He saw Sylvia take off her sweater and let her hair fall messily over her face. She didn't fix her curls after tossing the sweater on the floor, just scratched them in an ironic gesture.

To be honest, it would be nice if you held me.

Ariel smiled. She acted in such a cerebral way that it was impossible for him to feel uncomfortable. They drew closer together and he put his arms around her shoulders. She sought out his lips and found them.

Sylvia had three worn bracelets on her wrist.

I don't know what we're going to do, but after tonight you don't have to ever see me again if you don't want to. Sylvia tried to remain composed as she spoke. She seemed less nervous than he was. They dropped onto the mattress and their kissing extended into a muddled embrace. She took off his shirt first and kissed his shoulders. Ariel lifted up her shirt and after pulling it over her curls he undid her bra. Sylvia's breasts gushed out, dominating with their bright whiteness and the vivid pink of their nipples. She seemed to retreat. The process was slow, with pauses. Clothing is always a pain in the neck, it's not designed to look good coming off, thought Ariel.

He unbuttoned the fly of her jeans and she let him do it. He pulled down the fabric that tangled around her thighs. Sylvia drew him up. She didn't want Ariel's face right there in front of her crotch like a neighbor on a narrow street. She hugged him tight, as if she wanted to immobilize him, while she managed to kick her jeans off her ankles. Then he watched as she pulled back the sheets and hurried into the bed. Ariel sat on the edge to take off his clothes.

Do you have any condoms?

Ariel nodded and left the room for a second. Sylvia saw, without wanting to stare, Ariel's supermuscular legs. When they met again beneath the sheets, Sylvia ran her hands over his athletic body. His toasted skin contrasted with Sylvia's whiteness. Her hand, after evasive caresses, reached Ariel's penis. She didn't go so far as to touch it with her fingers, she backed off and lay down, as if she wanted to be taken without being too aware of what was going to happen.

But Ariel didn't lie on top of Sylvia. He didn't want to ask, are you a virgin? He did bring his hand down to her sex. She was wet and receptive. He touched her delicately, using his middle finger to penetrate her. In a instant, Sylvia closed her eyes and started to melt with pleasure. She grabbed his arm and moaned, until she let out a scream followed quickly by another and then another, more contained, one that made her collapse and open her eyes with a smile. Ariel dropped his head down beside her.

Sylvia recovered the feeling of her own body weight. The moments before she seemed to have somehow been levitating. Ariel tried to make himself comfortable next to her. He placed his arm on the pillow and Sylvia let her neck fall onto it. She covered her breasts with her arm.

Do you want me to do something to you? asked Sylvia timidly. That's okay. Sylvia took on a comic tone. No, no, it's no problem, while I'm here. Blushing, she covers her face with the sheet. You must think I'm stupid.

I hope it was lovely for you.

She was surprised by the adjective. No Spaniard would use it. She told Ariel that her friend Mai sometimes said that Argentinians dripped sugar from their mouths when they spoke. It's something about your tone of voice, here everything sounds more aggressive.

Ariel changed the music. It was a female Brazilian voice, that spread gauzily through the room. Music for fucking. He regretted the choice.

Sylvia caressed his stomach with her hand, then confirmed that he was aroused and she forced herself to jerk him off, even though she found the movements ridiculous, grotesque. Ariel placed his hand around hers and helped her finish.

Then, without them realizing, a very long time passed.

Now I really do have to go, announced Sylvia. She sat on the bed and Ariel was turned on by the subtle way she hid her breasts with her forearm and the sheet. Like in old movies. He watched her start to dress with fiendish speed.

Do you want to take a shower?

I don't want to get home really late.

Sylvia's sweater had ended up on Ariel's side, and as he sat up he held it out to her. Your pullover. Pullover? She smiled. She finished her beer in two sips while Ariel dressed standing.

The car flew along the almost deserted highway. Sylvia lowered the window and stuck out her head. There was a fine mist falling that dampened her face, making her feel refreshed. She didn't tell Ariel that she felt like she had been blushing for three hours and her skin was burning. Her hair flew out behind her, as if it were going to detach from her head. It felt good. The music played between them. They barely spoke.

Sylvia directed him to her neighborhood. What's this area called? asked Ariel. A charming name, Nuevos Ministerios. I bet you've never been with a girl from Nuevos Ministerios before. What about you? Is this your first time with a guy from Floresta?

Ariel was surprised she didn't lean over to kiss him. A brief brush of the cheeks was the whole good-bye. Sylvia said, thanks, I had a really good time. Me, too. Neither of them dares to say, I'll give you a call. Ariel watches her walk toward the brick doorway. She looks fragile in the middle of the well-lit street. He thought perhaps he'd never see her again. He appreciated the effort Sylvia had made to keep herself from getting carried away by her emotions, holding back her desire to open herself up, to let herself go. It made him respect her even more.

He felt closer to Sylvia when he found the vestiges of her visit while changing the sheets. He thought he had been cold, distant, hard with her. Like someone dealing with bureaucracy. The soccer player who fucks the starstruck teenager, hardly making any effort, ignoring anything beyond a new notch on his bedpost. But I didn't fuck her, he argued in his defense. Maybe it was worse that he let her jack him off for such a long time; he even had to make an effort to come so that it wouldn't be humiliating. He tossed the sheets into the washing machine. He waited for it to start running. He didn't want Emilia snooping around and asking for explanations.

In his dream, he saw Sylvia's hair, placed over her breasts, almost completely covering them. He remembered Sylvia's total stillness after her orgasm, not daring to take the next step and reveal having rushed things, and being afraid, regretful. In that moment he wanted to see her again and show her the warmth he hadn't that night.

At practice the ball moves from one teammate to the next and Ariel seems unable to intercept it. At one point the coach approaches the group and in a curt tone says, get with the program, Ariel.

He understands that the coach isn't referring to that play in particular but to his performance in general. And he feels hurt. He is embarrassed to not be focusing, not be devoting himself completely to the team.

As he leaves the field, he signs some autographs for a group of schoolkids waiting behind the fence. One of the girls shouts, you're so handsome, and Ariel looks up at her. Her pubescent face is not quite settled, it's in that somewhat monstrous transitional phase, not yet fully formed. She's surrounded by a gang of her girlfriends, hysterical and shrieking. He doesn't like the group. They've lost that childish charm that can do no wrong. He again remembers his teammate comparing soccer players' lives to dogs'. Our masters outlive us, too.

By that point, he had decided not to see Sylvia again. Distance himself. It is her maturity, unthinkable in a sixteen-year-old, even though it seems like an act, that scares him most about her, that makes her even more dangerous.

9

At six in the evening that Saturday, the sun had yet to shine. It would be one of those rare days where it never appears. Sylvia had arrived at her grandmother's house a little while earlier. Aurora's smile beneath her damp eyes made up for the lazy waste of an afternoon. Mai had gone back to León to spend the weekend, determined to save a relationship she said was heading downhill on the fast track. Their three days in Vienna had been as intense as they were grueling. She had gotten hit by one of the riot policemen's swinging nightsticks and it had fractured her collarbone. Besides a huge bruise, big like a burn, which she proudly displayed, she had spent forty-eight hours in observation in a hospital on the outskirts of the city. She cursed Mateo because he had barely shown any concern for her. This wasn't meant to be our honeymoon, he had said.

The hospital was some kind of jail for people with minor injuries. An Italian with a broken arm, a Greek guy poisoned by a smoke grenade, an American girl with her ankle destroyed by a rubber bullet. It was some sort of veiled incarceration. There, more than twenty-five miles from Vienna, there was no way they were getting back to the protest. And I didn't have my cell phone charger, she whined. That's why I didn't write you, to save battery juice in case Mateo called me. Mai recognized that as selfish, and useless because he didn't even call, and it made her angry at herself. She told Sylvia every last detail of her adventure.

I felt stupid, abandoned. Luckily there was an anarchist from Logroño, really funny and really fat, who had me cracking up the whole time. They had given him fifteen stitches in his head and he wasn't complaining. We really hit it off. He kept telling me, don't complain, just imagine, being an anarchist in Logroño is like selling combs on Mars. Once I jumped into the ring at a bull-fight during the San Roque festival to protest animal torture and demand they put a stop to bullfighting, I was with three or four more environmentalists and that was an honest to god beatdown, yes sir. Plus we were buck naked and one of my testicles ascended from a swift kick, do you have any idea how much that hurts?

In the hospital, after confessing her doubts to the fat anarchist from Logroño, she had resolved to break up with Mateo, but they reconciled on the trip back. Twenty hours on a bus would bring anybody closer, said Mai. In spite of her exhaustion, Mateo's hands beneath the blanket had skillfully saved their relationship. Or at least that was what she insinuated with a crooked smile. Girl, I have the feeling our relationship is purely physical.

Sylvia had wanted to tell her about her night with Ariel, but she never found the right moment. She was afraid of Mai. She talked too much. And if someone at school found out about something like this, they could make her life impossible. In that setting, not doing anything worth talking about was a virtue. Anybody who stood out ran the risk of having rumors made up about them. Like that poor sophmore girl who they swore was charging for blowjobs in the boys' bathroom, and half the school said she had disappeared because she couldn't take the lie and the other half because her parents had found out it was true. No, it was better to keep your mouth shut. Every time she got over her reluctance and decided to talk to Mai about it, she luckily found her friend still caught up in her own problems. What do you think, is going to see him this weekend a sign I'm totally whipped, or do you think it's okay for me to fight to keep the relationship from going to shit?

Sylvia's reply was laconic. Go.

She missed her first class the day after her night with Ariel. She put up with her father's anger, his scolding for how late she got home. On her way to class, she checked her cell phone messages, but there was no news from Ariel. Then she remembered his frostiness. She had forced the outcome. He had resisted and she had taken him to the bedroom. He hadn't done anything to keep her there when she wanted to leave in a hurry. He didn't even kiss her when they said goodnight on the street. They barely spoke when he drove her home. It was all strange. Icy.

She had felt dirty, stupid, getting dressed quickly in front of him, with his still-warm semen staining the sheets. She was embarrassed at the absurd swaying of her enormous breasts as she readjusted her bra. And her woman's scent. Ariel hadn't even wanted to make love to her, take her virginity, which she was sure was obvious. It may as well have been broadcast by a PA system installed in her face, judging from the way she acted. That clumsy handjob she had tried to satisfy him with must have seemed like a hysterical attempt to hide her adolescent spinelessness. Every once in a while, she thought of a few minor positive signs. She remembered his hands and skin, his defenseless gesture as he brimmed over, the electrical charge that went through his thigh, his tensed muscles. The pleasure of stroking the bones of his back, of feeling his prominent ribs. She, in comparison, seemed all flabby. Any temptation to send him a message, to remind him of the night before, went up in smoke when she assessed how she had acted, half brazen and half prude.

The more time passed without word from Ariel, the more fatalistic and bleak her version of the events became. I'm just some stupid little girl stuck on a famous soccer player. As if she had a right, in compensation for the accident, to something more than the insurance indemnity.

On Friday Sylvia couldn't take it anymore and in a fit of bravery and heartache she sent him a message. "Good luck with the game." Artificial but neutral. He didn't answer right away. "We'll talk when I get back. Thanks." The thanks reduced the promise, almost to the level of a business transaction. Thanks. It sounded more like a handshake than a kiss. More like goodbye than welcome back. It would have been the final straw if the night he brought her home he had stuck out his hand and said, my pleasure, see you around. And if you want an autographed

T-shirt I can have it sent to your house. If she was tempted, as she sometimes was, to convert Ariel into the love of her life, she could now start acknowledging her failure. She could tell herself, I've lost the man I love.

That night she went out with friends from school. This is what I should be doing, she thought. I should be out on packed streets and not in luxury homes in the suburbs, elegant restaurants, adult bedrooms. A bench overloaded with kids, mixing alcohols, thunderously loud music oozed from dive bars as if it were overflowing, tangled hair, elusive eyes, low-slung jeans, exaggerated laughter, some girls so made-up they look like clowns in heat, boys with their hands in their pockets, friends who slap each other on the back, girls who cover their legs and hips, one group beside another, in some sort of chain that extends along the street, parting reluctantly to let a car through.

In the plaza where they wanted to sit down, a couple of policemen were asking for ID and trying to scare off six inebriated Romanians who were sitting on a dirty bench crammed with bottles and plastic cups in the kiddie park. Inside the bars there was hardly enough room to reach the attractive waitresses who moved along the length of the bar, attending to customers whose eyes they barely met. Her classmates joked around, talking about school, laughing at some teacher, or some student. Nico Verón imitated the math teacher's stiff neck. The same old nostalgia for what had happened just the day before. They listened to the music and waited for someone to say, should we move on? before changing bars.

Her father was nervous all Saturday morning. He spent it rearranging the living room. He was trying to straighten the bookshelf that sagged under the weight of the encyclopedia.

He set the table very early, more like English lunchtime, and Sylvia cooked for them both. She had gotten up late. She wasn't hungry or in good spirits. She asked her father if he was going to the game even though she knew full well his team was playing in Seville.

Before leaving for her grandparents' house, she studied herself in front of the mirror. Even after a shower, her hair still smelled of last night's cigarette smoke. They say that losing your virginity changes your facial expression. Was Ariel's finger enough? Was that it? Was that how it happens? Finally she touches her not-fully-formed jaw. Her cheekbones weren't in sync either. They were still, if you asked her, stuck in that childish rounded shape that made her look perennially fat. Perhaps in her eyes one could make out a vague, fleeting expression, somewhat more mature and adult. As if she were better acquainted with a certain truth. Mai was right when she insisted that boys want to love you, but they run from you. She said it like this: they might have their hands on your tits, but their feet are already about to start running away. They flee. Sylvia wasn't going to block Ariel from fleeing. Or hold him back. The sooner they resolved this absurd accidental relationship, the better. But it was nice, right? she asked herself every once in a while. It was as if she wanted to at least retain the pleasant memory. When he brought her home, she noticed his hand tense on the automatic gearshift. She wanted to caress his fingers, inviting him to relax, but she didn't do it.

Grandma Aurora's smile helps her forget about him. Grandpa Leandro leaves them alone after a little while, to go take his afternoon stroll. They played a game of checkers on the bedspread and halfway through all the pieces slipped off the board and they didn't care enough to start over. You remember when we used to play dolls in your bed and we totally destroyed it?

I'm thinking about cutting my hair, announces Sylvia. Her grandmother tries to get her to change her mind. But it's so pretty. Yeah, but it's a pain in the ass, she says. No matter how I do it, it always looks bad. Aurora strokes her hair and pulls it back. Recently washed, it seems thicker after drying outside in the breeze.

I used to have hair like yours, but I always wore it pulled back. One time I wanted to cut it and your grandfather, who was the only one who had seen it down, practically the only one, asked me why. It's a lot of work, I explained. Taking care of the paintings at the Prado is a lot of work, too, he told me, and nobody considers throwing them away.

Sylvia smiled and looked up at her grandmother.

Your grandfather always had those blunt ways of saying lovely things. He's still that way. Now he says fewer things, that's true, she concedes with an expression of melancholy. The day will come when you decide to cut off your curls, but don't do it because you're in a bad mood.

Aurora's efforts soon wore her out. Do you want me to read to you? No, talk to me, she answered. Sylvia didn't know what to say. She tells her that these last few days, when she tries to read, she turns the pages without getting anything. After three pages, I have to go back and start again, she says.

What's in your head?

Sylvia doesn't tell her, although she'd like to. They talk about her upcoming exams. Her grandmother asks about Lorenzo. If he goes out, if he's taking care of himself, if he spends much time with his friends. Then she says that she and Grandpa have never been good at keeping up friendships. He doesn't care, he enjoys being alone, but sometimes I miss having people around. Your grandfather loves Manolo Almendros, but he never calls him. It's Manolo who has to call, to come over with his wife to spend an afternoon or for lunch once in a while, and he calls me first to make sure it's not a bother and so I can stock up on the chocolates he likes.

She points out a nearby jewelry case for Sylvia to bring over. They go through the pieces inside. Her grandmother explains the history of a watch and a pendant. This is a bracelet your grandfather gave me in a fit of romanticism, one of those very rare moments when we seemed like a normal couple. If you like something, I'll give it to you, for you to keep.

Sylvia is disturbed by the idea of inheriting something while her grandmother is still alive. She holds some earrings up to her ears but puts them back in the box. Where would she go with them on?

Some day you'll have to dress up . . . Of course, now you kids go around with rings in your nose and belly buttons. Boy, have things changed. And in other places, Grandma, in other places too . . . Tell me . . . Really? Okay, there are girls who pierce their tongues, and their clitorises. Their what? A ring? Yeah, or a little silver ball. Doesn't it hurt when they . . . ? I don't think so. No, of course, it must be some tribal thing, thinks Aurora out loud, as if coming out of her shock.

A little while later, her grandmother falls asleep. Sylvia reads over the notes from history class that she has in her backpack. Her grandfather comes in from the street, his hair mussed by the wind and his face chapped from the cold. Sylvia has supper with them and then walks back home.

Saturday nights depress her, it's like there's some obligation to have a good time. At the door to a car, three young men are putting on sixteenth-century costumes for their university musical group. One of them is bald and has a potbelly; his body is like a mandolin. Further on is a boy crying on a curb, the girl beside him holding his glasses and trying to console him. Her eyes meet Sylvia's, and she takes it to mean that the girl has just broken up with him.

She lies down on the sofa to watch the game on TV. Ariel is grabbed by a defender who sticks to him like glue. When he throws Ariel to the ground, the referee complains, gesturing for him to get up without stopping the game. Sylvia finds the referee ridiculous, as if he belonged to a different reality than the players. He looks like an uptight, aristocratic gentleman, with an impossible string of eccentric last names. They must be chosen for their freaky last names, she thinks. This one's called Poblano Berrueco.

Ariel's jersey was pulled out of his shorts by the grab. It's astonishing how small he looks next to the defender marking him, as if he were a child. When he runs, his hair rises up, straight with sweat.

All the commentators do is point out the jersey number in possession of the ball and highlight obvious idiocies. One of them says that a goal would change the score. The other that the tie only shows neither team is superior. With seven minutes to go, Ariel falls in the goal area and the referee awards a penalty kick. The commentators argue, let's see the replay. Sylvia thinks it was Ariel who sought out the fullback's leg and let himself fall. She's amused by his faking it. Is he like that in everything? she wonders.

The goal is scored by another player. A sturdy Brazilian defender, who's old enough to be the rest of the team's father. Ariel is substituted. When he steps over the side line he exchanges an affectionate smack with his teammate heading onto the pitch. The camera shows Ariel walking toward the bench. He lowers his socks and gets a pat on the back from the coach. He is soaked in sweat when he sits down and he covers himself with a sweatshirt. The commentator says, this kid needs to adapt to being here so he can really open up the bag of tricks he's surely got in him. Sylvia thinks that maybe he'll be a real star soon. One of his teammates whispers something into his ear and Ariel smiles.

There is an American movie on after the game. Sylvia doesn't feel like getting up off the sofa. A guy spends ten years of his life in prison for a crime he didn't commit. When he gets out, his only obsession is finding the real culprit. Her father comes home during the eighth fight. He sits down next to Sylvia for a while. He looks tired, sad.

Your team won, Sylvia tells him.

Lorenzo nods. In the movie, the man is punching three mean-looking guys who have cornered him in an alley. When Sylvia gets up to go to bed, he says, turn it off, turn it off, I'm going to sleep, too.

Sylvia puts on her headphones and sings above the music. She feels like masturbating but she doesn't. She falls asleep with the headphones on. She'll take them off later with a swipe of her hand. On the bedside table lies her cell phone, recharging. Silent.

At dawn she feels alone. And cold. She twists and turns in bed. Finally she breaks out in sobs, hugging the pillow. She stifles herself against it.

On Sunday she calls her mother. She had gone with Santiago to a conference in Córdoba and on the way back she stopped in Madrid so they could have lunch together. They talk about exams and about work with Santiago. Pilar looks happy. She jokes with Sylvia about boys. I scare boys, she says. It must be the hair.

Santiago shows up at the end to pick up Pilar. He brought a couple of books for Sylvia, and he takes them out of his satchel. Do you have these already? Sylvia flips through them and shakes her head. I only wish I had read them when I was sixteen like you are now, but then all I wanted to do was play basketball, he says.

When they say good-bye, Pilar's hug is over the top. Sylvia's grateful for it, but shies away. Her mother rubs her back, as if she wanted to convey something she doesn't know how to say. Take care of yourself, okay, please. Can she tell I'm sad? thinks Sylvia.

That afternoon she starts reading the thickest of the books. There is nothing in it that makes her think of Ariel. The plot is too distant from her life. On page seventeen, she closes it. She opens the other one. "I've always felt drawn to places where I've lived, my old houses and neighborhoods."

From the living room, she hears the murmur of the radio. Her father is listening to *Back-to-Back Sports*. Goals and incidents on every field, interlaced with advertising geared toward men. It's not hard for Sylvia to figure out why Sunday afternoons are so sad.

Mai will interrupt her shortly with a call from the bus. I broke up with Mateo, I can't take it anymore. He decided to move to Barcelona. You think I'm gonna waste my time with a guy who makes plans without including me? What difference does it make to you if he lives in Barcelona or in León? Sylvia will ask her. It's not that, man, it's the thought behind it, fuck. Couples are supposed to want to share everything with each other, isn't that the point?

Mai will talk for a while longer on the other end of the line. Sylvia won't pay much attention to her. Finally, almost out of obligation, her friend will ask her, and how are you?

I've been better, Sylvia will respond. Honestly, I've been better.

10

Leandro doesn't walk, he flees. He turns the corner onto a deserted street and now he's coming out at the intersection that crosses Arturo Soria. He goes down the wide sidewalk until he gets to the bus stop. Leandro quickly regrets his decision. The madam had greeted him with even more of a lipsticked smile than usual. She led him into the little reception room to tell him, we've had a little problem with your check from the other day. It bounced.

Leandro was surprised. He wasn't expecting to hear that. She downplayed the incident. Leandro didn't have cash on him and he offered to write a new check. Anything not to leave a trail on his credit card. I told you before I prefer cash, the woman warned. Just two blocks away there's an ATM. In that case, I'll come back some other day, threatened Leandro.

Okay, okay, we're not going to start losing trust in you over some little accident, are we now?

Mari Luz accepted the signed check that Leandro extended with a trembling hand. She had left the room while he was writing it. She would have hesitated if she had seen how shaky he was. She brought him the returned check from the bank and added a mechanical, almost insulting, I'll go call Valentina right away. He said, today I'd rather have a different one. He said, it just like that, without thinking about it too much. I just feel like a change today. Okay, I'll have the girls come through. Have a seat. Would you like something to drink?

Leandro shook his head and sat on the sofa after taking off his coat. It was hot.

He didn't give much thought to choosing. He asked the first one who came in to go up with him. She was Slavic, with shoulder-length blond hair, willowy, not much chest on her. They went to a room. She promptly undressed and then she undressed him. The shower ritual was different this time, and the girl indicated he should sit on the bidet. There she washed his penis and asshole with shower gel, as if she were finishing up the day's dishes. She spoke good Spanish although her voice was dissonant, running out of steam halfway through her sentences. She tried to act nice. She switched with him and sat astride the bidet, rubbing her shaved pubis with a hand full of white foam.

Lying on the bed, the girl started to grate on Leandro. Her voice was too high-pitched, not very sexy. It broke into an absurd, almost ridiculous, crowing, every sentence like the shriek of a broody hen. The girl was too skinny and he could see the outline of her bones. She ran her blond hair over his chest, nibbled on his nipples, and caressed the flaccid skin around his old belly.

After the days of abstinence during which he had resisted breaking away to the chalet, his visits had become almost daily.

A relapse. On Sunday he stayed home out of an insurmountable sense of shame, and Aurora had a couple of visits that allowed him to lock himself in his room. Seeing Osembe again after two weeks was pleasant. She was affectionate, and asked why he'd been away. He explained that his wife was sick and Osembe didn't make him feel ridiculous, there, naked in bed at a brothel, talking about his wife's illness. Osembe devoted herself fully to his pleasure. That afternoon he returned home with his guilt tempered by the feeling that he'd had a really good time. Besides, he told himself, I won't go back for a good long while. But he returned the next evening. And the one after that. And Osembe went back to her old way of satisfying him. The latter half of each encounter turned into a brief chat where they each shared some private details.

On Monday they used the Jacuzzi again, even though Leandro was uncomfortable about its cleanliness and the fact that the tub wasn't white. He enjoyed being close to Osembe. The foamy water played off her skin and offered him stimulating glimpses. Back on the street, he felt the evening's cold go right through him. He thought he was getting sick.

He imagined himself in bed, feverish. Then he thought how there'd be no one to take care of him. Now it wouldn't be like those old bouts of flu or stomach virus that he spent in bed with Aurora anxious to offer him something to eat, his medicines at the right time, more heat when he needed it. Now he would be a neglected patient. And it seemed like just punishment.

But he didn't get sick. And after lunch the next day he left Aurora dozing with the murmur of a cheery afternoon radio program in the background. Before entering the chalet, from the sidewalk across the street, he saw a man bringing in boxes from the supermarket and then some bags from the dry cleaners.

Maybe they were laundered sheets, he said to himself. He didn't go in until fifteen minutes after seeing the man leave in a dark van. The chalet presented its usual lowered shades like closed eyelashes, the same air of discretion, silence, almost neglect. But that afternoon he got angry with Osembe.

She received him sleepily but solicitously. She was almost naked; maybe she had just finished with another client. She washed him clumsily between giggles and Leandro thought she had taken drugs or was drunk. They lay on the bed and she was excessive. Sometimes she let out silly laughs and said affectionate things that sounded mocking with all her laughter. With two fingers, she shook Leandro's penis for a while as if it were a talking doll. In its flaccidness it looked like a perverse, insulting puppet show.

Leandro felt exposed and ridiculed. He tried to control his desire, to convey his displeasure. But she applied herself in a laborious fellatio. She nibbled on Leandro's penis and several times he felt the border where pain and pleasure brush past each other. She filled her mouth with saliva and rinsed and dampened his half-erect member. The sounds were unpleasant and worked against her diligent efforts. What's wrong today? she said. Don't you like me anymore, darling? she asked. Then she just wagged Leandro's penis with an aggressive hand, as if it were a tiring and absurd task, like shaking a dead bladder.

Leandro grabbed her hard by the wrist. Relax, he said. That's enough. She resisted, but he forced her to lie down beside him. He waited a second for their breathing to calm after the struggle.

I want to see you outside of here, Leandro told her. That's not allowed. Give me a phone number. You'll make more money. It will all be for you. Don't talk, Osembe told him, and moved her head as if warning him to be careful. Don't you see you'd make twice or three times what you are making? How much do they take out here?

Leandro traveled over Osembe's body. In response to his delicate nibbles, she laughed or let out muffled screams. Leandro slid down to her sex and tried to tame her. He felt he was failing in his attempts to give her pleasure, didn't notice her pink folds moistening. She seemed made of stone. I'm so stupid, he thought.

He stood up, dressed without his usual shower, and left the room without leaving a tip. Osembe didn't say anything and Leandro suspected she was dozing on the bed.

Downstairs he paid in cash. He answered with a concise yes to the madam's did everything go well? He had felt a desire to hit Osembe, to slap her, to make her mad or irritated, to finally see, maybe, a real glimpse of her as a person. But he was glad he hadn't. Any conflict in those places always ended unpleasantly.

Along the street, he struggled to contain his fury. The people he passed seemed terribly ugly, unpleasant, awkward. The hedge of flowers seemed tacky and lacking personality, the sidewalk poorly drawn. He preferred the gray streets of old Madrid. The shape of cars seemed ridiculous; the climate, inhospitable; the chipped tree trunks, depressing. The city transmitted life, but a grotesque, obscene life. The stores weren't very tempting, with rickety signs or cheap neon. The advertising on bus stops was invaded by the same frigid beauty, and most of the cold faces he saw were demoralizingly common.

I'm not going back, he told himself. From the first day, he had been attracted to Osembe's haughty disdain, the cruelty in her empty and indifferent gaze. But the smoothness of her skin was addictive. He knew he would never have her, that she would never think of him or worry in the least about her dirty old customer, that the loyalty of his visits would never soften the absent heart of that chalet. The sexual pleasure she conceded him was the product of an automatic professionalism; the hands that ran over his body only caressed the money it gave them. Money she'd spend on manicures, hair salons, cosmetics, clothes, jewelry, because from everything he could make out about Osembe, she was a girl removed from the seriousness of her destiny, the complacent survivor of a shipwreck.

If someday he let that stupid vice ruin his life, he would have the consolation of knowing he had done it consciously, that he hadn't been tricked into going to the chalet or into those arms. It was a chosen downfall, a voluntary and obsessive descent that deserved no mercy, that wasn't sustained by romantic justifications.

When he got home that night, his anger turned into peace and devotion. He read to Aurora beside the bed, he made broth for her, and he kissed her on the cheek when he said good night. He wondered if he would have done all that with the same disposition if he hadn't just come from staring his moral misery in the face, seeing how low he had sunk. He wondered if there had to be a fundamental contrast in life's events. If what was good was only good because of the lurking presence of the bad, the lovely beside the ugly, the right beside the wrong.

I'm going to get better, don't worry, Aurora said when she noticed Leandro was down in the dumps. He turned off the light. In the dark, he felt dirty and disgusted with himself. She was making a huge mistake in her interpretation of the reason behind his sadness. I'm not suffering over you, but over me, he thought, wounded.

Leandro went to sleep with Osembe's dried saliva on his skin. He wished to wake up dead, liberated. But he woke up healthy and hale, in good spirits even. And that same evening he was beneath the body of a flat, bony Ukrainian woman, who said her name was Tania and whom Leandro had chosen to get back at Osembe, even though he suspected she wasn't bothered in the least by this gesture. What was he expecting? Jealousy? He quickly regretted it as he watched himself fake it in order to seem like something close to a satisfied customer. At least with Osembe he didn't feel conditioned into a role.

Leandro had to focus to come at the end. I can dress myself, he says when she offers to help him with her horrible rook's voice. Leandro looks at his soft, pale body, the body of an old man, the age spots around his chest. Why do I do this? Why am I destroying myself this way? I didn't work all my life, read, study, live with a lovely, dynamic woman, struggle to have a decent, emancipated life to end up a despicable wreck in an uptown whorehouse. Am I going to ruin my life? he asks himself. He places his head between his hands on his knees, like a boxer who's been served a knockout punch, minutes before losing everything.

He senses the inner warning that keeps him from crying. The voice that reminds him that guilty lamenting isn't sincere, either. He is too familiar with resorting to guilt. He was old friends with remorse, but he dealt with it by remembering that everything is transient.

Outside a bird sings and the murmur of paid sex in some nearby room arrives from the hallway. Tania had gone to the bathroom and was standing, waiting for him so they could leave the room together. No one should walk alone; everything was choreographed to avoid unwanted encounters. Would Osembe know he was there? And what would that make her feel? Indifference, surely. Maybe a stab of annoyance at losing easy money. But all the customers were the same, she had told him one day. Although he did have an unusual facet. His age, his decrepitude, this elderly lust, the persistence in his ways, his guilt infinitely more pronounced than in any other slave to an out-of-control sexual appetite. She'd have trouble finding someone worse than him.

He runs his fingers through his hair in front of the mirror. Again the sensation of being in a schoolboy's room. No one would suspect the immense desolation he hides. He sees a dead man at the back of his eyes. Leandro gives himself an intelligent stare that helps him control any emotion. Cold.

In the hallway between rooms, Leandro hears a door opening, something unusual. Osembe sticks out her head. She is wearing a cream-colored dress that ends halfway down her thighs, is tight at the hips, and opens into two wide straps on her shoulders, revealing cleavage. The dress is somewhat unpleasant in its artificiality, but it highlights her splendid body. Her eyes are filled with tiny red veins.

You're cheating on me today, huh? Leandro doesn't feel like answering. He starts to go down the stairs. She puts her long raspberry-colored fingernails on his shoulder. Tomorrow is my birthday. If you come we'll have a special party. Want to?

Leandro understands the scene as a pathetic triumph. He shrugs his shoulders. Is it a provocation? Or maybe a small victory?

The madam relieves Tania at the bottom of the stairs. She guides Leandro to the door. I hope there won't be any problems with the check, right? Leandro firmly assures her that there won't be. But she shows her smile with a twisted, worn tooth.

Don't let me down, old man, don't let me down.

The phrase has a dose of both disdain and threat to it. Leandro feels insulted and leaves the chalet with strength, without giving in. It is the end. He will never go back to that place. He even shoots a glance back at the metal door to fix it in his memory. At the large veiled window, too. Soon it will all be a shadow. He feels someone's gaze behind a venetian blind, senses a presence behind the strips. Never again. No one is so stupid as to let themselves be beaten when the enemy has showed its weapons and its obvious superiority. It would be suicide. He heads off with a lively step, reborn. He is fleeing.

And he knows it.

11

On Sunday Lorenzo has lunch at his parents' house. He has made an overcooked rice dish that sticks to the spoon when he serves it. The two men have arranged themselves around Aurora's bed and when she praises the food after barely eating a few grains of rice, Lorenzo feels the need to insult his own cooking. Well, we could use it as paste and wallpaper the room, too. Sylvia is having lunch with her mother, who is passing through the city. And, as always, Lorenzo felt a stab of jealousy. He feels awkward about not being able to take his daughter to restaurants except for the place downstairs where the fixed-price menu costs nine euros. He knows that Santiago will show up and try to win over Sylvia with the same air of power and confidence that captivated Pilar. His important manner, his chitchat, his gifts of books that she now reads in spite of never having shown an interest in reading before.

When Pilar announced she was leaving him and there was another man in her life, Lorenzo wasn't surprised it was Santiago. It's not that unusual, he said then, taking great pains to hurt her as much as possible, for a secretary to get involved with her boss. He didn't manage to offend Pilar with his comment. And maybe that irritated Lorenzo even more. In the days following, he did something that he's still ashamed of. He is not even sure if Pilar knows the story. Maybe Santiago never told her.

Lorenzo had barely met Santiago on the few occasions he passed by Pilar's office near the Plaza de la Independencia. Before Santiago was her boss, Pilar used to joke at dinners with friends, I think I have the most boring job in the world. But Marta, Óscar's wife, who worked at the Ministry of Justice, shot back, I'm the secretary to a subsecretary, where does that leave me? A sub-subsecretary? And they all laughed, as if their laughter would banish Pilar's endless job frustration.

Lorenzo waited one day near the office, and when he saw Santiago emerge from the building he confronted him. Do you want to talk? Let's have a cup of coffee. Santiago's civilized air only riled him up more. Lorenzo gave him a shove, which he received without response, holding on to the wall. He said something else. Something conciliatory. Lorenzo shouted at him. Why are you doing this to me? Huh? Why are you doing this to me? Santiago reflexively covered his face with his hands. What do you think, I'm going to hit you? Lorenzo recriminated. And he angrily slapped Santiago's arms as if he just wanted to make him feel inferior. It sent his brown plastic-framed glasses to the ground, almost by accident. They didn't break. Someone passing by on the street stopped to look. Santiago picked up his glasses, put them on, and started to walk away, with firm steps but not running. Lorenzo didn't follow him. He only repeated, I'm not going to hit you. But Santiago didn't turn around to look at him, he was far away.

Lorenzo never understood what he had wanted to do, what he was looking for in that confrontation. He was only trying to force Santiago to notice the injury he had caused him. You are happy at my expense, because you stole everything from me. In time he was ashamed of his violence, his stupidity. It humiliated him. Santiago had to know the cost of his happiness, the price the other man had to pay. Lorenzo wanted to present himself to Santiago as something more than just Pilar's ex, as a real, wounded person.

But his discomfort that Sunday as he eats with his parents doesn't date back that far. It has more to do with the previous afternoon.

On the esplanade of the monastery at El Escorial, surrounded by groups of tourists on their way back to buses parked nearby, Lorenzo asked Daniela, did you like it? She confessed to mostly being impressed by how enormous and old it was.

Spaniards are crazy, right? Lorenzo thought to say. Something like this erected in the middle of nowhere just because some demented king wanted to purge his guilt.

He told Daniela about the origins of the monastery, Saint Lorenzo's martyrdom, the very building being shaped as a torture grill, Philip II's shame for winning the Battle of San Quintín on the saint's day, all Internet facts he had read hastily on Sylvia's computer.

Daniela told him she had felt the same feeling of smallness on a school trip to visit the Church of the Company of Jesus in Quito, in the middle of the city's historic center. The effect on her of the sun coming through the windows and the very explicit paintings depicting the fate of the infidels, which convinced the natives of the greatness of the Catholic God. Then she went back to visit after the fire, with the blackened walls, and it was even more impressive.

Lorenzo made general comments, mixing up dates and names, in some sort of well-intentioned speech that seemed more like a presentation by a flunking student. When he tried to say something about the Spanish arrival in Ecuador and the missionary spirit that erected enormous churches and convents, Daniela corrected him with a certain sweetness, Hernán Cortés didn't have anything to do with any of that, I think you mean Pizarro. Yes, of course, Pizarro, well, it's the same thing. He also pretended to know the names of Sucre, and the date of independence declared on the slopes of the Pichincha volcano. He even straight-out lied, insisting that of course he had heard of Rumiñahui. A long time ago, in school.

He wasn't able to answer all her questions as they toured the site. Well, I think the king married several times, I don't know if it was three or four, he said in front of the sepulchers. Yes, of course he was very religious, look at the tiny bed he slept in. Once in a while, he managed to read the caption beside a painting before she did and then he would show off, this is his father, Charles V. But it was the Spanish entrepreneurial spirit, their enlightened madness, that Lorenzo highlighted in his aimless lecture, as if he wanted, in Daniela's eyes, to draw a parallel between him and those cruel but magnetic men filled with fruitful projects. And boy were they fruitful, Francisco de Aguirre had up to fifty children, she said, with an irony Lorenzo didn't quite get. The monastery soon closed its doors and they were pushed to the library. Lorenzo was pointing out, not quite accurately, Ecuador on an old globe when the beadle urged them to leave. That's so typical of functionaries, look at this schedule. How can they close such a popular monument at six in the evening, something that's a national point of pride?

They sat on the low wall that served as a fence to watch the sun set between the mountains behind the monastery. The view was lovely. Daniela told him about her days at school in Loja. She explained that she knew the history of Spain well because of an aggressive and authoritarian nun from Pamplona, her greatest teacher. She hit us with a thick missal, here, right on the crown of the head. But she also taught us how the light of God had led the Spaniards through the seas and jungles to spread their faith through the New World, naming the cities they conquered for saints. The soldiers had fatally strayed from their God and had given themselves over to the lust for riches, to vice, madness, and sex, and in the end they had perished sick and punished.

That woman, Leonor Azpiroz, said Daniela with a remarkably precise memory, once hit me in the middle of class. As she passed through the rows, she discovered that my book was in poor shape, it had been through many hands before mine. It was a Spanish catechism entitled *He Is with You*. She made me stand up and then she slapped me. That is not how we treat school materials, she said. I remember being filled with rage, it wasn't my fault, I had gotten the book that way, and when I got home I stomped on the crucifix we had made in arts and crafts out of clothespins. But the next day she saw the bitterness in my eyes

and she sought me out to hug me, she took my face in her hands
and said, little Indian girl, you have the face of a saint, don't let
that change over the first injustice you encounter in your life.
She was a wise woman, a wise Salesian who could see inside
you.

Lorenzo took the opportunity Daniela's confession afforded
him to ask about her family. She told him about a sick mother
who devoted herself to caring for all her brothers and sisters. Daniela had come to Spain and had the responsibility of
sending money home. When they spoke on the telephone, her
mother could hardly contain her emotion. I pray for you, she
told Daniela.

I have a sister, a bit older than me, who makes my mother
suffer in every way possible. She takes after my father, I think.
We don't ever see her anymore. She came to Spain before I did,
but she never calls or anything. She got in with a bad crowd. My
mother was very generous with me about that, she told me go
to Spain but don't do it for me, do it for yourself and earn honest money, even if it's not a lot. Be decent and God will reward
you. What do you think, challenged Lorenzo, that I don't know
how some people make money, even right in the neighborhood?
It's very difficult to compete with people who break the rules.

Then Lorenzo remembered a T-shirt he had barely noticed
the day he saw Daniela wearing it. HE MAKES ME HAPPY, it read.
And he'd had the feeling it was referring to him. But now it was
clear it was about her firm religious beliefs. He felt he should
warn her that he didn't believe in God or go to Mass. Seeing her
somewhat distant expression, Lorenzo launched into a confusing explanation, saying he believed in the existence of God, but
not a God as understood by believers, but a more ethereal and

personal one, like a God who lives inside each person. When he felt that his words might not be getting him anywhere, he decided to drop the conversation, saying, it's not that I think about these things very often.

In response Daniela told him, this structure could only be the result of true faith, the desire to honor God above all things. And Lorenzo looked up to see the immense esplanade and the monastery catching the sun's last rays of the day. In his own way, he thought about the intrinsic Spanishness of its spartan construction, although he lacked the perspective to see it as a glacial leviathan of granite that broke with the pine-filled mountains surrounding it.

Daniela felt cold and Lorenzo put an arm around her shoulders. Should we head back? he asked her. It's probably best, she replied.

They walked along the side of the highway in search of the van he had parked on the far shoulder. On Sundays we go to a church near our house, Daniela told him, the pastor is very intelligent. Lorenzo took it as a veiled invitation, but didn't say anything.

They got into the van. Lorenzo drove along the street that bordered the monastery and at every speed bump he couldn't help but cast a sidelong glance at Daniela's breasts bouncing up and down. Meanwhile, she talked to him about the parish. Every day there are more Spaniards. Sometimes Spaniards think these churches are just for South American wetbacks, but now they come in, they hear us sing, and some of them join. Do you know what they tell me? That religion here was always sad. You celebrate God with happiness, laughter, Lorenzo dared to interject. The last Mass he had been to was probably at Lalo's father's funeral, almost fifteen years ago.

The highway back to Madrid goes through fields fenced with stone, and Lorenzo and Daniela stare straight ahead. Not looking at each other allows them to speak more honestly.

Your people are more cheerful in everything, Lorenzo heard himself say. And a second later he felt he had gone too far. Appearances can be deceiving, Daniela corrected. We suffer a lot. People only see the partying and dancing and all that, but there's another side to it. I bet you know a Colombian woman. Colombian? No, why? asked Lorenzo. You'd like them better than me, that's for sure, said Daniela, still looking straight ahead, as if she wanted to challenge him. They are shameless, nothing stops them. Well, I don't want to generalize . . .

Lorenzo felt a stab of anxiety. He was carrying a good bit of money in his wallet, thinking that she would want to go out dancing, or to a restaurant or somewhere for some fun. Now he realized his mistake.

A few days earlier, he had passed by his friend Lalo's office to get paid for clearing out the apartment. Actually, he confessed to his friend, I left the amount blank, I don't know what to put. Lalo skillfully drew up an invoice on his computer and asked Lorenzo to peek over at it. Does that seem fair to you?

It's a bit more than what I was thinking, Lorenzo admitted.

Lalo printed the invoice on his computer and took the money out of a drawer in his desk. Don't worry, that was what we had anticipated, I swear. They went for a cup of coffee. The morning was bright, but the café was dark, with windows only at the front. Lorenzo asked Lalo about the owner of the apartment. There are some personal objects that should maybe be given to him, but, of course, now that you've sent him to live under a bridge . . .

Lorenzo's statement sounded like a direct accusation. Lalo justified himself. Not at all, we set him up in a residence for the elderly. I don't really know him, it was all handled by a guy in sales. It's one of those things that when they tell you about it, about the whole mess with the neighbors, the police reports, you think it's going to be incredibly complicated, that it's best not to get involved, but then it turns out to be really simple. In barely two weeks it was resolved. You know what I thought afterward? That actually nobody had offered to buy the guy's apartment and really he was wanting to sell. It's simple, right? The best place for him is in a home. I don't know, seems like a guy who lost his marbles. Somebody talked about an accident . . .

Do you know what home he's in? Sure, in the office I have all the information, you want it? No, well . . . Lorenzo didn't want to show too much interest. When you empty out a house like that you feel kind of sorry about it, you think you're destroying someone's life, everything they've accumulated in a life.

In my job, Lalo explained, you see things that break your heart in two. Think about it, a lot of times their apartment is the last thing people have. My boss always says something brilliant: your monthly installments can't be paid in pity. And it's true, life is a cycle, in the end . . . No matter how bad you feel about it. A living person moves into a dead person's house; when things are going bad for one person, they're going better for somebody else. That's life.

He walked Lalo back to his office. His friend explained that after the renovations in the apartment they could sell it, in that neighborhood, for four times what they'd paid. It's just one of those things that worked out well for us, he confessed to Lorenzo. Then he got the information on the home where the former owner was now living. Jaime Castilla Prieto, the name is completely normal, he remarked. And don't feel like you have to bring him anything, the guy is totally cuckoo, and Lalo made a vague gesture with his hand. Lorenzo shrugged his shoulders.

It was the money he'd gotten from Lalo that was burning in Lorenzo's pocket on Saturday. The heat in the van smelled of fuel. When Daniela told him she hardly knew the outskirts of Madrid, Lorenzo told her how, just a few years ago, it had been pastureland for sheep and cows.

Daniela confessed that going anywhere made her panicky. She didn't have papers and she didn't want to meet the police in a train station or on some trip. They keep you locked away for two days and then they write you up an order of expulsion. She had come to Madrid two years earlier on a tourist visa, her only plan being to send money to her mother. Someday I want to have my own house, but not one of those enormous homes that other immigrants build with money from Spain, I don't want to show off like they do, just something simple, pretty. Lorenzo asked her what her first steps were when she arrived in the country.

You already know Nancy. She helped me a lot. At first I took care of an elderly woman. You know that gray-haired man who has an interview show on TV in the afternoons?

Lorenzo nodded vaguely, but it took him a while to figure out who Daniela was talking about. Well, I took care of his mother. They didn't give me any days off. Not even Sunday afternoons. The family hardly ever came to see the woman. And I had nothing to eat. Do you know what I lived off of? You know those chocolate cookies, Príncipe brand? Two or three a day, that was it. I had terrible anemia and one day I fainted in the woman's house. They put me in the hospital. And the TV host came right over and without even asking how I felt, he started threatening to make my life impossible and that he'd have me kicked out of the country if I said anything. He even went so far as to tell me he was a friend of the king. Right there in the hospital, he fired me.

All you ate were chocolate cookies? You could have died, said Lorenzo, shocked. No way, I got fat as a cow. Look at me. You're not fat, not at all . . . My mami sees the photos I send her and she writes back, hey, fatty, you ate my daughter, where's my daughter? They both laugh.

Then I took care of a family's three children, but the oldest one, a nine-year-old, was hyperactive. He abused me, he insulted me, he pulled my hair, he kicked me. One day I just didn't show up, I didn't even have the guts to quit. I didn't want to tell the kid's parents the things he did. One day he told me I was his slave and that I had only come to Spain to clean up his poop. It was wrong, but I just left. He had the devil inside him, I swear that kid had the devil inside him.

Lorenzo said something to console her, it's not the kid's fault, it's the parents' fault. Then she told him about her current job. They're a young couple, good people. And the boy is delightful. He's like my own son to me. I barely know them, I just say hi on the stairs, confessed Lorenzo. I think he's an administrative assistant at a company or something like that.

Daniela shrugged her shoulders. In Spain people live really well, they like to go out, be on the streets. One day the woman I work for explained it to me: we don't want our son to steal our social life from us. That's why I stay some nights until they come home from eating out or going to the movies. They are sweet. They seem happy.

Yeah, well, just like you said, Lorenzo replied, there are all kinds. But here people are happy, I do think so . . . Except on the metro, Daniela smiled. On the metro everybody's so serious, they don't look at one another, they don't say hello. They all read or look at the floor like they're embarrassed. Like when you'd get onto the elevator with me, and you'd lower your head and I'd think, what shoes am I wearing? Ay, I hope they're clean.

After they laughed, there was a silence. Daniela asked Lorenzo about his separation, about how he manages to handle his life and take care of his daughter, if he misses his wife. Lorenzo responded honestly, but not without a slight tinge of self-indulgence.

I made a mistake, he admitted. At one point I thought my life would always be the way it was then. With my wife, my daughter, my work. I couldn't conceive of it changing. And maybe I wasn't careful enough. It was a mistake.

The silence that followed seemed to end the conversation. Soon the highway emptied out into an expressway. The faster cars passed Lorenzo's van on the way to Madrid. When passing the exit for Aravaca and Pozuelo, Daniela told him she had a lot of friends who worked around there. Lorenzo told her that in Aravaca he had met the last shepherd in Madrid. Mr. Jorge. Every Christmas we used to buy a lamb from him for New Year's dinner. They put up a block of terraced housing behind his pen and the city government forced him to get rid of the sheep. When I was fifteen years old. You weren't born yet.

Don't exaggerate. Daniela smiled. I'm thirty-one. I'm not so young anymore. Well, you look it, said Lorenzo. Look, this is where the president lives, he pointed as they passed the Moncloa Palace. Do you like the president? Daniela asked him. Bah, all politicians are the same . . . No, no, corrected Daniela, in Ecuador they're worse. There isn't a decent one there . . . They're four families, they all have to go. They're rats. Rats? Corrupt.

As they entered Madrid, Lorenzo suggested they go out for dinner. Daniela said, you've already spent a lot of money. And then added that she was tired. You don't want to go out dancing? I bet you're gonna go out dancing with your friends now, joked Lorenzo. No, no. Really, no, she added. And he couldn't get her to change her mind.

When they arrived at her door, Lorenzo turned off the engine and the headlights. Thank you so much for the trip, Daniela said to him.

The combination of the two long lines of her eyes with the line of her mouth was lovely. Her hair fell over one side, breaking the almond shape. She put her hand on the door handle and Lorenzo leaned over, governed by a force he couldn't control. He took her by the shoulders and tried to kiss her on the lips, but she only offered her cheek, no-man's-land. But the kiss lasted until she moved her neck away.

I knew you were going to do that, Lorenzo. It was the first time Daniela had spoken his name. I didn't come for this, I don't want you to think . . .

It was Daniela who apologized, as if she judged herself for having aroused Lorenzo. He felt uncomfortable, he tried to be tender. I like you, forgive me if . . . but I like you and I . . . Men only want one thing, Daniela told him, and then they cause a lot of pain . . .

Daniela spoke sweetly and her features became more beautiful to Lorenzo's eyes. When he kissed her, his forearm brushed her breast and it gave him a shiver. Lorenzo wanted to hold her, to reassure her, but she took control of the situation with an authority that left Lorenzo paralyzed.

I'm not upset, I just want you to know that I . . .

And Daniela's silence seemed to explain it all.

Thank you for a very nice evening, she said, and hopped out of the van. She walked toward her doorway. Lorenzo felt a stab in his chest, like a cruel pinch. He was slow to start the car up and drove like a sleepwalker toward his house. When they had gone through one of the rooms at the monastery, among the biblical tapestries woven in gold, Daniela had turned toward Lorenzo and said, in a very soft voice, like a whisper, thanks for what you've done for Wilson. Then, feeling her breath very close to his face, Lorenzo had wanted to sleep with her, take off her clothes, make love to her.

He understood his mistake, his precipitation. He sensed wounds in Daniela that he had been oblivious to, but the rejection still made him feel bad, desolate.

It was Saturday night, but Lorenzo went home early. He felt he was driving in the opposite direction from the rest of humanity.

When he got home, the soccer game was already over. He watched an American movie beside his daughter for a little while. Her Saturday got screwed up, too, he thought, but he didn't ask any questions.

Sunday ended with the same feeling of emptiness it had started with. On Monday he sleeps in. He finds a note from Sylvia underneath two oranges placed next to the juicer. "I won't be home for lunch." He hears chairs moving in the apartment upstairs and thinks it's a coded message from Daniela, communicating her disdain.

Wilson calls while Lorenzo's having breakfast. He's got a moving job and asks if he wants to join him with his van. Yeah, sure, great. Tomorrow at eight, then. Lorenzo writes the address down on Sylvia's note. You'll have to get up early, sorry, because I can see now that you're not an early riser, says Wilson on the other end of the line. I got up a while ago, says Lorenzo in his defense. Your voice is weak, you sound like you're still in bed. You know what my old lady used to call it? Pillow voice.

Lorenzo showers and shaves listening to the radio. In the news they don't mention him. In front of the mirror, he says, I am a murderer. It's strange how easy it is for him to forget it, leave it behind. Buried in the day-to-day. I am a murderer. Looking at his freshly shaved face, he wonders, have I changed? And he repeats it to himself.

Have I changed that much?

He has gas. He'd had a bad night. He squats to try to release the air. He lies down on the floor and massages his belly. He lifts his legs up. Then he thought, I'm not the man I once was, am I? In that absurd position, with his back on the damp bathmat, he hears the doorbell. The noises in the apartment upstairs have stopped and he is confident for a moment that Daniela had come down to see him, maybe to apologize. I was abrupt with you the other night.

But when he looks through the peephole, his heart starts racing. Detective Baldasano is accompanied by four policemen. They're here to arrest me, it's all over. For a second he's glad. The anguish is over. Then comes the insecurity. Losing it all. He doesn't want to take too long to open the door and he ends up opening it brusquely. The detective speaks in a reassuring tone.

Good morning, forgive the intrusion. Lorenzo invites them in while he checks to see if any neighbors are peeking from the stairwell. We have a search warrant. It'll be a few minutes. Are you alone? Lorenzo closes the door behind them.

Yes, I'm alone.

12

It was him. He's the one who started it. He sent the first message at sundown on Sunday. "Hello. You want to get together tomorrow?" Almost all the soccer games of the day on both continents were over by then. The results would allow his team to move up three spots in the standings. "OK, but not too late." At night he'd watch the rebroadcast games in the Argentinian league. But he still had some hours to kill. "At five? In the usual spot?" He knew he would eventually send the message to Sylvia, but he tried to put it off as long as he could. I want to see her. "OK." She conveyed a strange calmness. It was her clean gaze, her almost childish mannerisms, the lack of calculation, a certain innocence. He remembered her trembling caresses, somewhat furtive, her unfamiliar body, her kisses where she lets her head drop, partly terrified and partly aroused, her nervous, tentative smile. It all seemed so close that Ariel couldn't believe he'd let so many days pass before seeing her again.

She responded instantly to the messages. They were short, direct. Of course. I set the cold tone, admitted Ariel. "But not too late," she had written. It was a subtle way of saying, we won't end up in bed this time. And Ariel understood that. The night has its own rules. Theirs will be an evening love, like teenagers, he thought. With orders to be home before eleven.

On Saturday he had experienced the tedium that precedes a game. Expectant tedium. A stroll through the street with hundreds of kids asking for autographs, lunch with the team, the tactical discussion, the fifteen-minute prep video of the rival team, the nap, the brutally harsh conversations of men in a group. Lastra had come up with a new nickname for the coach. Lolailo. It's like in songs, he explained, when they don't know what to say, there's always a chorus that goes lolailo. That's what it seemed like to them, that once he'd used up the three concepts and three details that they had to look out for in their rival, the coach would start talking to himself, repeating the chorus. And in a whisper some of the players murmured lolailo, to make the guys who couldn't hold it in burst out laughing. A bit childish, but effective. The technical staff appreciated a good atmosphere. When the joke spread, Lastro turned to one of the younger guys. Don't you say a word of this, we all know you're a stool pigeon. The boy tried to deny his bad reputation, but the group imposed its own law.

He had tried to nap, but Osorio, his roommate, called his girlfriend and spent two hours whispering sweet nothings into his cell phone. When he hung up he turned toward Ariel, she's already got a car out of me, the bitch. Then he became engrossed in playing a video game on his PlayStation. Amílcar came to find Ariel for a coffee. Someone said that Matuoko was fucking a local celebrity in his room, somebody related to a duke of who-knows-where. The Spaniards all seemed to know her from television. She called him up on the phone in his room, just like that, brazen as can be, said Matuoko's roommate. The chick must be fortysomething, but she's amazing, said another.

They loaded the bags into the bus, since they'd go straight from the stadium to the airport. Don't leave anything in the hotel, warned the delegate. This guy left his blow-up doll, shouted one of the players. And you and your fucking mother, they answered from the back of the bus. When a frantic Matuoko was among the last to board, his teammates received him with a burst of applause that he acknowledged with a show of his enormous teeth and pink gums. The coach lowered his head, somewhat somber. The head of equipment told two or three very celebrated jokes. My wife screams so much when she's screwing, sometimes I hear her from the bar. Some people put on headphones; others chatted.

At the entrance to the stadium, a group of local fans insulted them, showing their fists. They threw oranges that burst open against the bus windows. A drunk fat guy lowered his pants and showed them an ugly, hairy ass. Paco, don't look, you might like it, shouted Lastra between laughs. I prefer your fucking mother, answered Paco from his seat up front.

The hour and a half before the game seemed to last forever. Warm-up on the field. The murmur of the people who started to fill the stands. Changing in the locker room. The smell of lotions. Ariel kicked around a ball made of two knee socks with one foot. One, two, three, four, he kept it in the air, passing it from one foot to the other. Some players watched him, smiling. Another shouted, on the field, man, on the field. Then they waited in the hall from the locker room. That was the moment when Ariel felt the most nervous. Someone shouted, come on, come on, come on. We have to win. Let's go, let's go, let's go, guys, we have to win, we have no choice, the goalie coach reminded them. If things get ugly, strike hard, advised the second coach.

The game was grueling. The play was interrupted by constant fouls. The team playmaker kept the ball close to his foot instead of making long passes. Dragon used to ridicule that kind of player, they're mailmen, he used to say, they come up beside you, shake your hand, ask you about your kids, and nothing can get them to let go of the ball. You should touch the ball a lot but hold on to it as little as possible. Ariel grew frustrated by the lack of passing. His marker followed the first feint and when Ariel recovered the ball unexpectedly he got knocked down. The referee showed the defender a yellow card halfway through the first half and that kept him off Ariel's back a bit. Three or four times he went over the sideline and managed to cross the ball. But it seemed like Matuoko's headers were badly placed, as if he couldn't locate the goal. His shots were high and off-mark. On one rebound, Ariel took a chance with a bicycle kick, but the goalie managed to knock it the other way from above the crossbar. It would have been a gorgeous goal, the kind they replay on TV for days.

Finally, because of an awkward clearance, a ball came over to him near the penalty box. He moved into the box and toward the endline, searching for a teammate coming up behind him. He saw the fullback going down to the ground to take the ball off him and he just had to make his foot meet up with the defender's leg. Ariel fell in the box and the referee whistled the penalty shot. Amílcar scored with a powerful shot at mid-height.

Then the coach decided to maintain the team's advantage by switching Ariel for a defender. He didn't mind. He sat on the bench. The coach said something to him that Ariel didn't understand. The substitute goalie, who was working on his fifth bag of sunflower seeds, whispered into his ear, lolailo lolailo, and they both laughed.

In the airport, two passengers complained angrily about the wait. It's outrageous, they've had us here for an hour. One of the center midfielders shot him a look filled with sarcasm, relax, don't have a heart attack. The man looked at him with fury and disdain, and the delegate started gathering the players so none of them got left behind. During the flight, some of the journalists who shared the plane with them came over to congratulate Ariel. Husky dropped onto the arm of his seat, you must be happy. Ariel nodded vaguely. You want to have a drink when we get there? Ariel looked at his watch. They would land in Madrid around one. It's Saturday night, you won, the referee bought your dive, Husky said, what more do you want?

Ariel smiled. It wasn't a dive. The guy touched me.

He thought it'd be good to go out. His teammates joked with the flight attendants, who smiled, somewhat embarrassed but flirtatious. One of them, her hair dyed a reddish tint, was waiting on Ariel. Can I have a tea? She smiled at him. Thanks a million, he said. As she headed back toward the cabin, a player shouted, don't run, there's enough cock here for everybody. Soon the attendant brought Ariel the tea. I'm sorry, we don't have any maté, she said. Ariel smiled with his green eyes. At some point later, from a distance, they locked gazes and she waved. Ariel's seatmate elbowed him. Are you flirting with the flight attendant?

You know the saying? Flight attendants and nurses, condoms in their purses. Ariel laughed. The player was a substitute who hardly played, though he'd been in the club for three years. I'm from Murcia. Have you ever been to Murcia? Ariel shook his head. Land of milk and honeys. And the guy started cracking up again. Ariel decided to listen to music. He was about to put on his headphones.

Dude, you have to come some day, I've got a mansion there, near La Manga, that you would not believe. What are you doing for Christmas? You going to Buenos Aires? Ariel hesitated, that was his plan, but he hadn't hammered it out yet. And you think such a long trip is worth it? For the four vacation days the sons of bitches give us? My parents are there. They say it's crime-ridden. I read about the soccer player whose father got kidnapped. And I used to play with an Argentinian, Lavalle, you know him? When he went to Buenos Aires he took two bodyguards with him. He made it out to be pretty fucked up.

The vice president, a young lawyer with a pale blue tie, got up and said, the prez called and asked me to convey his congratulations. And our bonuses? shouted a player, he should double 'em. People laughed at the remark. You know that at the Christmas dinner I'll give you each a gift. The team applauded sarcastically, sure they'd get a fountain pen or a watch. Ariel wanted to put on his headphones, but he didn't want to offend his seatmate, who showed no signs of reading his car magazine. My wife is pregnant, he told him then, the fifth. You know what they say, the fifth one can't be bad. It's the middle one that turns out screwy. He doesn't even want to hear the word *soccer*. Ever since he was real little he's been playing with his sister's dolls and my wife, the bitch, goes around saying the kid is gay. You think you can say that? The kid is only nine years old, well, she says you can, that you're born gay and she's fine with it. And

I've tried to talk to the school psychologist several times, but she won't have it. Don't laugh, this is serious, fuck, I really get embarrassed sometimes. One day he says to me, do you always have to wear that jersey, can't you change the colors? Imagine how screwy this kid's head is.

A bit later, the conversation devolved into politics. I don't vote, his teammate told him, but if I did it would be because somebody like Pinochet or Franco was running; for me, if I'm gonna get robbed, I rather it be by someone with authority, someone who'll get tough on all the scum around here.

Before landing, the stewardess collected the trays and had everyone put their tables in the upright position. On Ariel's she placed a coaster with her cell phone number written on it. Ariel put it in his pocket before it caught the eye of his seatmate, who was then talking about why the Spanish national soccer team usually lost. It could be because Spaniards aren't competitive by nature, but, fuck, we've got Ballesteros and Fernando Alonso, they're from here, Spaniards, not Martians. What do they say in Argentina about our team? Ariel shrugged his shoulders, well, everybody there knows it's because of that guy, the one with the bass drum, that guy is *mufa*. *Mufa*? asked his teammate with exaggerated interest. Yeah, *mufa*, brings bad luck. A jinx? Yeah, that's it, the guy with the drum is a jinx. No shit, no shit. But everybody there knows that, insisted Ariel to the astonishment of his teammate. You mean M . . . No, no, don't name names. Ariel knocked on his head as if it were wood. We had a president that was *mufa*, and they had to beg him not to go to the national games.

When the airplane's wheels touched the runway asphalt, there was an immediate commotion. People undoing their seatbelts, reaching for their suitcases, turning on their cell phones. Ariel watched as his seatmate turned on two different cell phones. Two? he asked. Shit, one for my wife and one for all the others, you wouldn't want to get a call mixed up. Our goalie two years ago sent a pornographic message to his wife by mistake. You can't imagine the scene. The guy was slick, especially for a Catalan, and when we asked him how he patched things up, he said he had made her believe it was meant for her, to spice up their relationship a bit, breathe some life into it, the asshole. And you should meet my old lady, she's a piece of work, she goes through my messages, my address book. When I screw some random chick, I stop at the gas station on my way home and rub gasoline on myself, she can sniff out perfume a mile away.

Ariel searched for the flight attendant among the tangle of heads, as if he wanted to have a last look at her. Now I'm screwing one of the salesgirls at the club store, one of the brunettes, the curviest one, I'll introduce you to her. I got her the job, and it's an awesome one. You know what turns the little slut on, when I fuck her with my uniform on. I don't know, it makes her hot . . . but with shin guards and everything, what a scene. Once you scratch the surface, you find out women are very slutty.

They got out of the plane and Ariel felt relieved to be rid of the conversation. The flight attendant said good-bye in the breezeway with a nod of her head, biting her lip that she had glossed in bright pink.

They picked up their suitcases from the baggage carousel while the head of equipment organized his assistants so Ariel wouldn't have to carry a single piece of luggage. Husky was waiting for him beside the Civil Guard's control booth. Let's go to a place near here, I'll lead, said Husky, speaking quickly. Didn't you have a flashier car? Ariel told him about the conversation he'd had on the plane. He used to be a decent player, the kind who dedicate themselves and get their jerseys sweaty, but he's not getting the Nobel Prize in physics this year, he's old now, Husky said. Look, there it is, the Malevo. It's a horrible place, but this is where the action is.

At Husky's insistence, they parked in a pedestrian crossing. Who's going to give you a ticket now? On the street, Ariel pulled out the airplane coaster from his pocket and showed it to Husky. The flight attendant's number? And now you tell me? Tell her to bring a friend, but what are you waiting for? Husky dialed the number on Ariel's phone, but there was no answer. What were you thinking? She must have gone off to fuck the pilot, like always.

They settled in at the back of the bar. The music was deafening. Husky drank beer like it was going out of style. He teased Ariel indignantly for having let the flight attendant get away. A little later the door to the place opened and to their surprise they saw Matuoko come in, accompanied by a woman with reddish hair. It's her, said Ariel. It's the flight attendant.

They waved from a distance and watched them sit at the other side of the bar. Well, looks like she passed out her number to the entire team, said Husky. There's no way I could compete with that guy, said Ariel in his defense, you haven't seen him naked, he has a perfect body. Showering next to him is depressing, admitted Ariel. Husky made a disgusted face, don't go on, thinking about a group of naked men makes me want to puke.

They talked about soccer for a while, without taking their eyes off Matuoko's moves on the flight attendant. Every once in a while, she looked toward Ariel and smiled, almost with a trace of apology. Young men came over every so often, to tell him their stories, shake his hand. They all had their line, now my girlfriend is becoming a fan, I played in the juvenile leagues, you need someone in midfield that can bring some life into the team, I'd sign another goalie. Someone even said, from under his breath, less partying and more sweating that jersey. The whole jersey-sweating thing is one of the most overrated things in soccer, don't you think? Husky asked him. Ariel remembered that Dragon would tell them, you've played very badly, you ran too much, if this sport was about running they'd sign the hundred-yard sprint champion. Then another guy shouted from the end of the bar, fewer nightclubs and more goals, and Husky challenged him. What does that have to do with it? The best players in the world have always been serious party animals. What you need, Ariel, is to be more of a layabout. Sometimes you don't even seem Argentinian. In the goal area, what shows are the nighttime hours spent around a bar, in every dribble, the delinquent comes out. Two years ago, a group of fans showed up at practice with a big sign that said fewer hookers and more allegiance to the team colors. It's people's fantasy, that you guys are out there living it up as if you had three balls and you can't let them down, it's like when some Hollywood actor says his life is very sad, boy, do they ream him a new one, people don't want to hear that, they already have their own fucked-up lives.

The alcohol ended up arousing Ariel. A girl split off from her group of friends to come over and say hi. Husky encouraged him. Come on, give her a kiss on each cheek, don't be shy.

Ariel focused on the girl, who didn't stop talking. She put her tanned hand on Ariel's thigh and whispered in his ear things like that she wasn't really into soccer. Husky continued his jokes, are you sure you don't have a friend who likes ugly guys? I can assure you I look a lot better naked. When Ariel leaned over the girl and said, wouldn't we be better off just me and you somewhere? she smiled proudly. Let me finish my cigarette and we'll go, okay?

The girl lived in a white brick building in the north, near the Chamartín Station. She shared an apartment with three friends. She studied business management. Her family was from Burgos. No blow jobs, eh, I'm telling you that from the get-go, she told Ariel in the elevator, when he grabbed her roughly by the hair. Ariel had a hard time getting her clothes off, the girl had put music on and was dancing in her panties and bra as if she were showing off her body. I'm crazy, I never do this, I'm crazy, she kept repeating. Ariel took slow sips on a can of beer she had brought him from the refrigerator. Their lovemaking was out of sync. She turned up the music as if she didn't want to hear herself, just the trilling of Celine Dion. Ariel didn't understand what he was doing with a woman he didn't really desire, who wasn't particularly beautiful and didn't attract him any more than the alcohol dictated. The girl said, whisper dirty things in my ear, ay, I love your accent, and then she asked him to spank her bottom, not so hard, like that, like that. Ariel felt ridiculous. He hated her kisses and when he had finished and yanked off the condom he could only think about escaping to his car parked on the street. By that point the girl, who had come in the midst of what seemed like an attack of the hiccups, was moaning weepily in bed. I never do this, shit, I have a boyfriend in Burgos, now what do I tell José Carlos? Huh? What do I tell José Carlos now?

Ariel got lost trying to navigate the outlying highways. He went back to the city center as if he could only find his way from there. In the Plaza de Colón he was stopped at a sobriety checkpoint. The policeman approached the driver's side window. Ariel lowered it with his best smile. I got lost on my way to Las Rozas.

I bet you've knocked back a few, haven't you? I'll let you go because we won, eh. He called his partner over, you'll see, he's a big fan. Ariel gave them a couple of signed photos that he had in the glove compartment. Then he received some confusing directions to the nearest highway entrance. The cop sent him on his way with an alrighty then, good luck, we're gonna get back to hunting for drunks.

The sun was already coming up as he got into bed. It took him a while to fall asleep. He was wiped. He woke up at three-thirty. He answered his e-mails. Marcelo wanted to get together with him during Christmas vacation, and told him that he was going to compose a song about an eighteen-year-old girl who killed a twenty-one-year-old kid in a suburban disco. It seems she didn't want to dance with him, they got into an argument, he insulted her, she took a knife out of her sneaker and killed him. Fifteen years in the slammer. But what Marcelo liked was the girl had written that very night in her diary, "Today I really fucked up. I stabbed a guy and I'm really scared." Someone has to write the great Argentinian song and it has to come out of things like that. Ariel wrote back, count me in for the Christmas barbecue.

After a little, while he couldn't find any excuse not to write Sylvia a message.

"Hello. You want to get together tomorrow?"

He picks her up at five. He finds her gorgeous when she approaches the car window. She's a girl, he tells himself. It's starting to rain and two Chinese guys are selling umbrellas by the stoplight. Sylvia's face is freezing. It's cold, she seems to justify, as she blushes. Her pink lips stand out against the paleness of her face. She's wearing a thick wool sweater, and when she takes it off it lifts part of the shirt underneath with it, revealing the skin of her belly. Her jeans are black. They go to a downtown coffee shop, kind of swank, she says. There is a piano that no one plays. Let's sit here, she points, but he prefers to be away from the large window. Oh, sure, says Sylvia.

A pompous waiter comes over. She orders Coca-Cola, he a beer. I saw the game, congratulations, Sylvia says. He says thank you. Are you becoming a fan? It's your fault, and she smiles above the glass.

I felt terrible the other night, after I dropped you off, begins Ariel. Sylvia shrugs her shoulders. He continues. This is a little confusing for me . . . A mess, she says. But I wanted us to talk, Ariel goes on. Was this a good time for you to get together? Anything's better than studying for my exams, she replies. I have three this week. Maybe today's not a good day for you, he insists, awkwardly. Today's perfect for me.

Ariel looks around. He once again feels her strange authority. She always manages to gain control of the conversation, leaving him behind like a slow fullback. Sylvia sticks an ice cube in her mouth and then drops it back in the glass. She drank her Coke quickly. There is a moment of silence that Sylvia breaks with a smile.

I don't think we're going to be able to kiss here, she says to Ariel.

All of a sudden they've relaxed. Their knees are brushing against each other beneath the table. Sylvia extends her hand over the tabletop so he can put his above it. Ariel hesitates. When the waiter approaches, they avoid contact. He brings the check and asks Ariel for an autograph. For my son, I don't like soccer. What's his name? asks Ariel. Pedro Luis, but put Pololo, that's what we call him.

Ariel signs, trying to hold back his laughter, tears in his eyes. Sylvia covers her face when she sees his hand trembling. They leave and double over, bursting with laughter. In the car they are still joking about the terrible life of a boy who grows up with the name Pololo. With that name I wouldn't be surprised if he ends up throwing himself off a bridge or busting into a McDonald's and killing thirty people, for revenge, says Sylvia.

In the underground parking garage at the Plaza Santa Ana, they kiss. Ariel keeps a watch out when he hears any sound. This is where bosses come to fuck their secretaries in their cars, says Sylvia. He secretly feared someone would film them with a cell phone. It had happened to a teammate a few weeks ago. They kiss for so long, sunk into the seat, that the time runs out on Ariel's garage ticket and he has to pay extra to the attendant, who is in a bad mood because someone took a shit in the nearby toilet and the smell is unbearable. What did that guy have in his guts? Damn, whatever it is, it's rotten. When he gives Ariel the receipt, he recognizes him and says, let's see if you've got enough time to get out now, because if you're this slow on the field, we're really in trouble.

They get to his house as dusk falls. They make love leisurely, with extended preambles exploring skin, studying it as if their bodies were the subject of an upcoming test. They remain in an embrace, stroking each other. Ariel can't remember ever being better, but he tells her, I'm scared shitless, you're underage, I don't know what I'm doing.

Sylvia places herself on top of him. She wants to reassure him. Her breasts are half covered by her hair, which he pushes away. They are lovely, and she tenses her shoulders. I'm in love with you, she says to Ariel, I don't think that's a bad thing. You're only four years older than me, you're not my grandfather.

Take me home early, she asks him shortly after. I don't want another lecture from my father. Can I see you tomorrow? asks Ariel. Sure, but if you don't mind I'll bring my notes and look them over a little. I can't help you out, I was a horrible student.

In the car, parked at the beginning of Sylvia's street, their mouths don't seem to want to separate. They want to be together even as she gets out of the car. She has her hands hidden in the sleeves of her sweater, Japanese style. When Ariel goes back home, he has Sylvia's fractured moan stuck in his ear.

The fractured moan of someone losing their virginity.

13

Two weeks pass in a heartbeat. Sylvia says good-bye to Ariel. It is almost one. Christmas break from school has already started and that gives her freedom to stay out somewhat later. They are in the car, in front of a car repair shop. How long until I see you again? she had asked him a second earlier. Eight days. We have training on the second. Sylvia wanted to go with him to the airport the next day. Sure, he joked, so we can make the cover of the gossip magazines for the Christmas special.

These constant references to the impossibility of their relationship make Sylvia uncomfortable. For Ariel it was something insurmountable. You're sixteen years old, he would repeat as if it were a sentence, a definitive obstacle. Age is corrected by time, she would say to him.

They went to the movies twice. In the darkness, they held hands and shared popcorn, but on the way out he distanced himself. Sometimes, annoyed, she would joke and approach him, asking in a loud voice, aren't you that Argentinian soccer player? Alone on his way to the parking lot, he signed several autographs and listened to someone's tactical advice for the next game. You have such patience, said Sylvia.

His house was a refuge. They went in through the garage and found the house had been tidied by Emilia on her daily rounds. She's on guard, Ariel confessed to Sylvia, this morning she told me that nights are for resting, that I'm still very young. Well, imagine if she met *me*, joked Sylvia.

She no longer felt so inhibited at his place. The night they made love for the first time, she wanted to leave the second it was over. She found everything threatening. She was afraid she had stained the sheets with blood and when Ariel discreetly removed the condom, she heard it land on the wood tabletop with a comic, ridiculous sound. Love wasn't an emotion, then; it was sticky fluids, smells, saliva.

Sylvia warned Mai that her father could call someday to ask if they were together. Only then did Mai realize she had gone too long without asking Sylvia about her personal life. I met a guy, she had said, I'll tell you about it later. Mai, who wore dreadlocks as dried and frayed as seaweed, shrieked in the yard during recess, oh my God. But Sylvia had already revealed her secret to someone else before her.

It was almost accidental. Dani found her in the hallway. This weekend I have tickets for a pretty good concert. Sylvia's expression twisted. I don't think I'm going to go out, I have to cram. Come on, you can study later . . . Dani insisted. I'm going out with somebody, Dani. Saying it made Sylvia feel relieved, secure. Her mirage could be real. She said it in a very soft voice so no one else would hear. Daniel nodded and smiled. I'm happy for you, he managed to murmur. Well, I'm happier for him, actually. They went down to the yard together, but there they separated.

Telling Mai didn't have the magic eloquence of the first time. She had decided against confessing to her father that one day when he came into her room, euphoric, and they had talked for a while about music. She didn't tell her mother, either, in any of their phone calls where they spoke about exams and plans for Christmas. Or her grandmother on her Sunday visit, right before going to see the game. Going to the game because Ariel had invited her to the stadium.

The game dragged. Her feet were cold and she kept them from freezing by stamping against the cement floor. It was strange to see Ariel on the field. He looked like someone else. A figure in the distance, different, older. She didn't feel that he was hers when the entire stadium whistled at him or clapped at the capricious final result of a play. Near her seat were teammates not playing in that game and a few wives and girlfriends of players who preferred the cold of the stadium to watching the game from home or on the television in the players' bar. They were all beautiful in the same way, somewhere between good genes and daily workouts in the gym. Like their husbands, they seemed older than they were; in the case of the women it was because of their pretentious, expensive way of dressing and their excessive makeup.

Ariel's team won handily. For Sylvia the stadium atmosphere was the most appealing. She missed the television replays and the close-ups that helped her follow the game. She couldn't even figure out how the third goal, which Ariel scored, had come about. She did see Ariel, after the embrace of his teammates, run toward the central circle with a lock of hair between his teeth in an aside to Sylvia that only she could understand. She blushed there in her private box seat and looked around her. She was relieved that none of the eighty thousand spectators could possibly suspect the gesture was meant for her.

The fans protested the referee's decisions and applauded the offensive plays. They ate and drank nonstop; some had brought sandwiches wrapped in aluminum foil from home. There were those who smoked cigars and an area where the youngest fans gathered to tirelessly sing and cheer their team on. Their noisy presence gave them their authority in the stadium.

After the game, they were barely together an hour. In the car parked on a dark street. He had a dinner with his teammates that he couldn't miss. It's Christmas dinner. Are they fun? Sylvia asked him. Well, the president gives us a little speech and an expensive watch, then most people get drunk and end up throwing croquettes at the ceiling fans. Have you ever seen what happens when you throw a croquette at a fan? Is it funny? Oh yeah, everything gets all sticky.

Sylvia's nose ran from the cold and he lent her money for a taxi. When she left the car, he said, you didn't congratulate me on my goal, but she walked a few steps without answering and then turned with a lock of hair in her mouth. That night the temperature dipped to freezing.

They saw each other on Monday and early on Thursday they said good-bye in front of Sylvia's door. The next morning, Ariel flew to Buenos Aires. I hate Christmas, this year more than ever, Sylvia says to him. The car that several weeks ago had run her down was now the car she didn't want to get out of, whose appearance in the traffic around the Cibeles fountain she celebrated with a marked increase in her pulse.

Ariel says good-bye with a flash of his headlights and waits for her to go inside the building.

Sylvia lies down on her bed in silence. She has a bad feeling. The trip will separate them. She is terrified that Ariel's doubts will grow without her beside him. Everything will conspire to make him forget her. They are a couple that no one else knows exists. It is a private relationship, one that can be made to disappear very easily. Such different lives will end up pulling them apart. Sylvia knows this. She wants to think that it won't be that way, but she can't manage to convince herself.

There is no future for us, she says. We barely share anything, a bed and long conversations about a song, a movie, trivial things. This is the end.

Christmas is death.

14

Leandro's hand doesn't shake. And that frightens him. It should be shaking. Otherwise what have I become? He looks at the veins of his hands to make sure blood still runs through them.

He signs.

His signature is a quick stroke, like the flight of a dragonfly. It's the two initials of his first and last names, Leandro Roque. He liked it when he was young, when he imagined it was a name destined for fame. When he practiced his signature in Joaquín's house, dipping the pen in the inkwell of his father's office.

At that point, the old military man was already retired and he fantasized all day about the possibility of writing his memoirs. When the sun warmed the street, he would go out for a stroll, showing off his manners, his war wound, his cordial greeting, his prodigious generosity with everyone. He paid for Leandro's piano lessons; he helped Pedro on the third floor set up a sawmill with a few thousand pesetas; he got the son of the blind woman who sold lottery tickets at the market out of summer military service; he paid for sewing lessons and a Singer machine for the daughter of the guy who fried strips of dough; and he had taken care of the studies of Agustín, a young man who came to visit him some afternoons, who had been his charge since wartime and eventually became a high school Greek teacher.

Once in a while, Leandro wondered if that neighborhood patronage was born of an innate decision or if it was the result of some guilty drive, a way to make up for all the damage caused. Because he never spoke about the war, about his mysterious adventure. In those years, few people talked about the war, except to mention it abstractly as an evil that had darkened everything and to tell, for the umpteenth time, some funny, or grotesque, anecdote almost always having to do with being cold or hungry. Cold and hunger being two enemies devoid of ideology in that recent, uncomfortable war.

Now he was writing that same signature sixty years later. A signature designed for the end of musical scores or for fan autographs but that had only seen bills, irrelevant documents, and forgettable administrative operations.

At the signing, he was surrounded by the bank's branch director, the employee in charge of the matter, and a notary who didn't meet his eye and arrived twenty minutes late. On the way there, Leandro had crossed through various states of being. Ups and downs, depression and euphoria. The morning of Osembe's birthday, he had gone to the bank to start the loan process. We need several documents, the deeds to the house, your wife's signature, medical certificates. The bank employee had written down a complete list of everything he would need, with the handwriting of a diligent university student.

Tomorrow I can bring all the papers, Leandro had said to the director, who responded with an expression Leandro hadn't liked. Icing on the cake. What did he mean by that? The director added that later everything would be in the hands of the risk department so they could okay the transaction.

To Leandro the risk department was a sarcastic title. He was about to burst out laughing. It wasn't that much of a risk, giving him money with their apartment as collateral. They called it a reverse mortgage, with that ability words have to obscure the truth. The reverse meant death. The day they died they would lose the apartment, no big deal, that same day they'd have lost everything anyway.

He knew that branch on Calle Bravo Murillo from the days he first came to live in the neighborhood, as a newlywed. He had seen it go through renovations, grow and change names according to the evolution of bank mergers. He had seen the staff retire and move on, young people arrive who would get old prematurely in their dark jobs filled with vacuous smiles and forced cordiality. The branch director, with his insectlike appearance, gave him explanations. Everything about him was fake. One could just as easily take him for a pervert, a stand-up family man, or a skeet shooter. The world seemed to end in his striped tie. As soon as you bring me the papers I'll put the wheels in motion. The previous director, Velarde, had at least flanked his desk with family photos that gave him a real air. He was straightforward and coarse, a real chatterbox. The first time he noticed that Leandro's profession was listed as musician, he commented, that must be very unstable, right? And later, over the years when the account stayed afloat with the always-punctual salary from the academy, he never missed the chance to say, you're always surrounded by music, what luck, and, all I've got are numbers, nothing but numbers. Leandro must have heard him repeat that remark close to seven hundred times.

That same evening Osembe invited the girls to her room, they opened champagne and toasted in plastic cups during what seemed to be a break from work. When Mari Luz, the madam, left the room, two of them pushed Leandro onto the bed and tickled him like a game between teenagers. Four or five had to leave for clients, but of the twelve four stayed, extending the party through the whole hour. Let's see, you have to choose the most beautiful, they said to Leandro, or, you're very serious, this is a party. When they finished the bottle, Osembe asked Leandro if he would treat them to another and one of the Spanish girls went down for more champagne.

They forced him to drink a long slug from the bottle. They took off his clothes. You've never done anything like this before, huh, grandpa? They ran their breasts over his face and laughed their asses off. At one point, the madam came up to let them know their laughter was above the acceptable levels. Leandro tried to vomit in the toilet when the drink made him dizzy, but he couldn't. The girls put him into bed for a little nap. They covered him with towels.

Leandro awoke with his mouth dry. Outside night was falling. His clothes were piled up sloppily on a chair. Old faded pants, a blue sweater, the shirt with the worn-out collar, a winter undershirt, socks both inside one shoe. He dressed and went out into the hallway. The little reception room was closed and through the frosted glass he saw two young men sitting on the sofa.

The madam came out to meet him. Come over here, you had a fabulous time, huh? she said with a crow's smile, and she stuck him in another tiny little receiving room. That's fifteen hundred euros, she said to him, and Leandro waited for the punch line, but there wasn't one. Shocked, he only managed to say, I didn't organize the party. The party was the first toast, everything else was on your tab, the girls spent their work time with you. And I'm giving you a discount, if I charged you what I should . . . come on, okay, write out a check for a thousand euros and we'll leave it at that, the patience one has to have . . .

Leandro, leaning on the little table, filled out the check. The doorbell rang and the madam left again for a few minutes. Come on out now, Mari Luz said to him when she came back to pick up the check. This is a really bad time, it's when all the offices let out.

That night, after dinner with Aurora, after turning off the television when her slow, monotone breathing revealed she'd fallen asleep, Leandro gathered the bank papers. He dug in the files at the far end of the shelf, bound by slack rubber bands. He reread the deed to the house from 1955, when the apartment cost barely more than the amount he had squandered that afternoon. The signing had taken place in a notary's office on Calle Santa Engracia. He remembers the nervous walk there with Aurora, and the building's owner, a man who had made his fortune in an automobile-importing business backed by several important military men. It was a warm autumn day and he was concerned whether he would be able to make the installment payments. The city couldn't have then suspected the chaotic evolution that would make its limits grow and expand. The disappearance of the night watchmen, the coal merchants, the knife sharpeners on bicycles, the large arched plazas with open workshops, the dairies, the bath houses.

He didn't go back to the chalet for two days. When he did, it was at his usual time. He was surprised when the bus driver greeted him, as if he were already a regular on the route, and when he recognized some familiar faces among the passengers. No one thought he was anything less than a respectable, upright elderly man, well-preserved in his slenderness. No one could possibly imagine the shameful routine I'm carrying out, thought Leandro. But that day the routine was interrupted when the madam stopped him at the door to the house and didn't let him enter. The last check was returned, this is very serious, said Mari Luz without a hint of sympathy. Here we are again.

Leandro tried to say something, to excuse himself on the porch. From the door to the garage, a rectangular structure separated from the house, a man let himself be seen. He looked imposing, with gray hair and light eyes. It seemed to be a scene designed to frighten Leandro. The man was stock-still, he didn't move toward him, but he didn't hide himself, either.

Let's handle it like this, explained the madam, don't come back until you have the cash in hand. And it'll all be taken care of, that way there are no misunderstandings, you know how the banks can be. Leandro turned, but the woman held him by the forearm, authoritatively. But do come back, don't leave this debt outstanding, eh. We wouldn't want to have to come to your house for it . . .

The notary reads him the terms of the loan and as he closes the document he says, with his lethargic enunciation, Don Leandro Roque, do you know that you are signing a borrower's loan in the form of a reverse mortgage using your ownership of the apartment on Calle Condesa de Gavia as a guarantee? I know. I will ask you for the power of attorney signed by your wife, who is not present due to illness, which is confirmed by a document signed by a medical professional. The notary then recites what he sees, as if he were advancing through a jungle, hacking out a path with machete blows to reach the clearing of the signature.

Leandro had gone through the pitiful step of putting some documents in front of Aurora's face, documents he only vaguely explained. Aurora signed without asking questions, with her weak hand that could barely hold the pen. Then she asked for the bedpan and Leandro solicitously slid it beneath her body, purging himself, he thought, of some of the malice he was causing. Her urine hitting the plastic gave Leandro reasons to justify his behavior.

The next morning, Leandro went to the hospital to get the certificates he needed. He was surprised the doctor had him come into his office, he had insisted to the nurse that all he needed was a signature and he didn't want to be a bother, but the doctor wanted to greet him.

How is your wife feeling? Weak, but in good spirits, Leandro heard himself say, seated on the edge of the chair without taking off his coat. The nurse will bring the paper as soon as she stamps it with the hospital seal. The doctor looked into his eyes. I have a problem with your wife, you know? Leandro shook his head, sincerely intrigued. Your wife is very brave. Women in general are braver than us, right? Maybe . . . yes, said Leandro. Your wife doesn't want anyone in her family to know what is really going on with her. I don't want to alarm you or your son. Hers is an attitude I understand and respect, but I don't think it's fair. What do you think?

Leandro nodded. For a second he had a feeling the doctor knew everything about him. That he could X-ray him with a single glance, bare his soul, and point out the black recesses with the tip of his pen. He felt uncomfortable, helpless. What strange power doctors have, even over the healthy.

I don't know what you know about your wife's state, or what she's told you. Well, Leandro rationalizes, some bone thing, I guess with her age and what you told me about osteoporosis . . . The doctor interrupts him. Your wife has truly resilient cancer that would have finished her off months ago if not for her reserve of strength, I don't know where she gets it from. Anybody else would be depressed, grieving, and finished, but either she fakes it really well or, honestly, you are married to an exceptional woman. There is no chance she'll ever walk again, I already told your son, she let me go that far. What she won't let me tell you is that she has very little time left, and it's not going to be fun. She's going to burn out like a candle. Her lucidity, even, will start to break down.

And do you know why I'm telling you all this? Because I believe that if those around her know how serious her case is, they'll put all their efforts and means into at least making the little conscious time she has left enjoyable, happy, full. These are the hard things about this profession, frankly, sometimes I'm forced to break a promise I've made to a patient, but I guess you'd agree with me when I tell you that in the end each person has to be responsible for the decisions they make. What can you do? I only have one answer: try to make her happy.

He leaves the notary's office and the air is crisp. The bank director offers to share a taxi with him and they set out from the outer curve of Bernabéu Stadium toward the bank. On the radio is the monotonous litany of the schoolchildren who sing out the Christmas lottery numbers. Someone makes a predictable joke about the jackpot. Leandro wants to get out. It's as if he feels oppressed by all the fake kindness that gilds reality.

It'd be good for me to have some cash in the house for an emergency, explains Leandro as he gets out of the taxi at the entrance to the branch. Sure, of course, Marga can help you. Leandro fills out a paper that quickly transfers into several bills. The manager accompanies him to the door. I suggest you keep an eye out, she explains, there are muggers around here, and they prey on retirees and the elderly. I think it's so unfair that they go after the most helpless. They hit them or push them and then they steal their money. And the woman waits there, defending him with her watchful gaze from any possible attack while he crosses the street.

Leandro walks toward his house with the bulging envelope in the inner pocket of his coat. The money seems to beat to the rhythm of his heart, as if it were alive. He goes up the stairs too quickly, and when he gets to his apartment he is worn out. Benita is putting away the cleaning supplies, although she always forgets the glass cleaner on the arm of the sofa and the duster on top of a radiator. I left some potatoes and meat in the pan, you just have to heat them up. Someone called asking for you but didn't want to leave a message, said that you would know who was calling, asked if I was your wife. Do you know what I answered? I wish . . . sorry, it just came out that way.

Leandro wasn't paying much attention to Benita but he smiles along. She raised her voice too much because she was deaf in one ear from her husband's beatings. But her laughter doesn't distract Leandro. He is upset about the call.

Aurora begrudgingly eats the stew Benita cooked. Leandro doesn't tell her anything about his conversation with the doctor. He goes through the daily routine of bringing the radio over so she can listen to the classical music program. The only change from his usual behavior is that when the hostess announces a Brahms piece, he explains to Aurora that the composer had written it while he was having an affair with Clara, Schumann's wife. Schumann was a marvelous pianist, he says, and he tells her two anecdotes about the composer.

He knows how much she enjoys his commentary. Leandro doesn't want to feel bad about having rationed out the few, simple pleasures his wife had asked him for in all those years as a couple. And he had been so miserly.

Leandro remembers in detail the night, years earlier, when he came home from the academy and she asked him how his day had been, and he replied with a laconic good. Then his wife broke the silence with a slight moan and Leandro realized she was crying. Even though he asked her why, she didn't answer right away. She only said that she was expecting something more than a good when she asked about his day. Aurora had gone to her room. She never repeated the complaint so overtly. Leandro knows that the countdown set by her illness couldn't make up for an entire life. He trusted that the sum of all the good moments made a profitable balance of their years together, but she'd never be able to forgive him for what he had denied her, his stupid stinginess of emotion. She hadn't deserved it, she had worked to create a livelier, full atmosphere.

Leandro separated out the money he would bring to settle the debt at the chalet. And with that, I will fill in this hole in my life. Like someone covering up a crack, like someone blocking a well, like the displaced earth that in time will get mixed back up with the dirt around it. It will be his Christmas present, his renunciation, his last visit to the chalet.

15

Lorenzo hadn't been back to that upper part of the Tetuán neighborhood since the days he played soccer with other kids on the open stretches of ground. He had seen the outskirts of the Plaza de Castilla grow, but the side street he was now on had barely changed. Humble, clustered houses, some low-lying housing, almost redbrick shanties, that revealed the poor neighborhood it had been. From some streets, he could see the plaza's leaning towers and beneath the clock of the old water tower on the canal a defiant glass building owned by a bank or a big company. When he and Pilar were looking for a house, they even considered the rich strip on the other side of the plaza. But by then the prices were already prohibitive and he had an immediate feeling of nostalgia looking at them. Nostalgia for a kind of life and city that they would never enjoy.

Finally they found the apartment on Calle Alenza. Pilar was pregnant and they had ruled out leaving Madrid. Lorenzo didn't know if moving to Saragossa had been hard for her or easy, if it was something she accepted as part of Santiago's delusions of grandeur, his social climbing, or as another advantage of distancing herself from her past with Lorenzo.

He looks at his watch. It is three minutes past eleven and the cold off the street isn't conducive to much waiting. Lorenzo is in front of the place, which is lined with people. It must have been an old workshop. A wide elevated platform barely ten inches above the sidewalk is crammed with chairs arranged on either side of a central walkway. Old, not particularly elegant folding chairs. The entrance is a glass and aluminum door, almost completely covered by taped-up posters, advertisements, photocopies. On the door an ugly sign composed of orange adhesive letters reads: THE CHURCH OF THE SECOND RESURRECTION. There is a muted television screen showing images of religious acts. The largest poster on the door says: GOD IS CALLING, ARE YOU GOING TO ANSWER? And the somewhat naïve drawing depicts a cell phone.

Lorenzo watches the people who go in. Mostly Latin Americans, women in their Sunday best, men who have tamed their thick manes of hair with shiny gel. Some have tattoos peeking out from beneath their clean, brightly colored shirts. The doorway is crowded with kids playing on the sidewalk, their complexions dark and their accents local, dotted with the strong Madrid *j*.

By then Lorenzo begins to worry that Daniela isn't going to show up. A man approaches the door to call the kids in, and when he sees Lorenzo he comes up to him cordially. The service is about to start, join us if you'd like. Lorenzo goes into the last row, still standing.

Days earlier he had watched, beside Detective Baldasano, his house being searched. His state of mind had been much less calm. He was surprised at how unscientific it all was, seeing four men spread out through the rooms, particularly insistent on going through Lorenzo's clothes, deep in his closet. The work lasted barely twenty minutes, during which Baldasano looked out the living room window onto the street. He put out his cigarillos under the kitchen tap. The policemen took some of Lorenzo's clothing in sealed plastic bags and left the apartment in a disorderly fashion. Baldasano insisted on inviting him for a coffee in a nearby bar. Do you know the Rubio? It's right around here.

There was a fish tank with shellfish in the window and a lobster that looked more like a pet than something available to customers. He ordered a coffee with milk. The kitchen spat out the smoke of reheated oil. The bar concealed tapas: potato frittata, anchovies, potato salad, meatballs, and soft *empanadillas* sweating grease beneath the glass display cases. Baldasano waved from a distance to another man who was sitting at the end of the bar and flipping through a sports newspaper. Maybe another cop. Lorenzo tried to locate their pistols, near their armpits. They both wore thick jackets, but not coats.

Baldasano smoked his short cigarillos. His skin was lined along the chin and he had a scar hidden on his neck. The first thing he did was reassure Lorenzo. I just wanted to have a chat with you, I don't want you to think that a search incriminates you in any definitive way. Lorenzo felt nervous, but he adopted a passive attitude.

The detective explained to him that every investigation proceeds by fencing in the territory. More than following leads we rule out possibilities. In Lorenzo's particular case, he had called him in mostly just to close, once and for all, the trail that led to him from Paco's corpse. Of course, you have to understand that our evidence rules out bands of marauders or the robbery motive. We are convinced it was someone in his circle, someone who knew him, who knew for example that on Thursday nights he wasn't home, and that makes the investigation more complicated. The idea of organized crime doesn't hold water.

Lorenzo realized that the strategy was quite simple. It consisted of pressuring him to see if he'd collapse.

Closing the circle, continued the detective, one arrives at the conclusion that we are dealing with a hired killer. Someone who had something against Mr. Garrido. Economic problems, romantic problems, who knows. Maybe everything was precipitated by the victim's unexpected return home. Or it was a paid job, these days you can hire a Romanian or Bulgarian thug for chump change. And the guy who killed him was a big lug, he wore a size twelve shoe, I can tell you that.

Yeah, Lorenzo felt obliged to say.

From the time when you were close friends, I'm sure you can remember people, powerful people that Mr. Garrido didn't get along with, who he owed money, something that could give us a lead.

A long time ago . . . Lorenzo produced two or three names of large companies at random, debts from the final months of the business that suddenly came into his head. The detective didn't take notes. All he did was brush the ash of his cigarillo on the base of the ashtray. Bit by bit his interest in what Lorenzo was saying languished.

Mr. Garrido had a relationship with a married woman. The wife of an acquaintance. Something sporadic, but ugly. You know, these things . . . You and your wife just separated, too. Was there also . . . ? Lorenzo shook his head at the vulgar gesture Baldasano made with his hands. We weren't good, things weren't going well for me, and my wife and I grew apart and then she met someone else. Yeah, the detective hastened to say, out of the frying pan, into the fire.

They talked about the neighborhood, of the widespread fixation on Colombian gangs, the payback deaths that were never resolved. Until the detective, as if declaring the end of a ceasefire, went back to Lorenzo's personal life. I was surprised you were free this morning. Are you working? I do some little jobs, but I don't have steady work. Mr. Garrido's wife told me you have a little girl. Not so little anymore, she's fifteen, sixteen already . . . At that age they're only girls in their heads, the rest is a woman.

The comment made Lorenzo uncomfortable. He comes to hunt me, to provoke me. Otherwise, it wouldn't make sense for him to waste his time like this.

I'm going to be honest with you, because I can see you're worried. There is only one thing that surprises me about you. You are going through a bad patch, financially, I mean, I don't know if in other ways, too. My experience tells me these situations occur when someone suddenly, cornered by problems, reacts unexpectedly. Somehow you could blame Mr. Garrido, Paco, for your current state. You don't have a family that can help you, you're not in an easy situation . . . How old are you? Forty-five, answered Lorenzo. That's still quite young.

Look, detective, I know that you think I might have been able to do something like that, Lorenzo spoke confidently, but you don't know me. Violence terrifies me, paralyzes me. I see a street fight and I'm sick for two days. I'm going to tell you something. A while ago, years now, from my car I saw some young men, one of those bands of young kids, run and chase another kid. And they threw him to the ground and they kicked him furiously, you can't imagine it, it was a terrible thing. Kicking him in the head, the ribs. I couldn't do anything to stop it, they left him there on the ground, like an old rag. It made me sick. It's something I still can't forget. That violence.

Lorenzo was telling him about a real episode. It had happened years ago. Sylvia was a baby then and maybe her being so young had made him feel the aggression as something personal and terrifying. The detective observed him carefully and sat up in his metal chair. Yet Mr. Garrido's wife told us that, once, you almost hit her husband. That's not true. It was an argument. I didn't even touch him. But you were about to. She saw you. I know you know what I'm referring to.

Lorenzo shrugged his shoulders. He was surprised at the insistence of Paco's wife in pointing to him as a suspect. Her intuition was so dead-on that it hurt.

Look, the detective told him, if I thought you were guilty or a suspect I would have stuck you in the can for a few days, I would have hounded you with some incriminating leads, and I wouldn't be here having a coffee with you. The only thing I'm saying is that it intrigues me how the crime coincides with your bad patch.

Once again the cop's veiled insinuations. He thinks I'm guilty, but he doesn't have anything on me. He's digging around like a dog, but he can't find what he's looking for. He's hoping I give myself away, that something will sink me, that I'll lower my guard.

The detective spoke again. I've seen it all, husbands reporting their wife's disappearance and fifteen minutes later collapsing, swearing they killed her by accident, lifelong friendships ending in a fraction of a second, a junkie son who kills his parents with an ax. I'm not distrusting by nature, but life has shown me that I can't close any door. I don't want to make you waste more time, but I'm going to tell you the truth. I'd like to take you off my list of suspects, but I can't manage to eliminate your name. There is always something that tells me it could be you. Do you know what's probably the biggest strike against you? Deep down you think Mr. Garrido deserved to die. I can see it a mile away. Friendship is like love in that way, a double-edged sword, wonderful on one side and deadly on the other. Those are emotions with a horrible flip side.

He lit another cigarillo after offering one to Lorenzo, who turned it down. You bought a van. You're planning on starting over, huh? Lorenzo shrugged. I wish you luck. We still haven't managed to find the guy who bought your old car, because you switched cars right around the time of the murder, right? Yeah, I think so. I might have to take some more of your time later on, there are some DNA tests pending, you know, these modern things. You can't imagine how much we hate those fucking television dramas, now people show up at the police stations and they basically think you're useless if you don't come out of the laboratory with the guilty party's name. Boy, would I like to give them a tour around the lab so they can see the crappy shit we've got to work with. Everything in this country has gotten so modern, except us . . . Well, I won't take up any more of your time. Don't worry, I'll pay.

Lorenzo realized that was his way of saying good-bye. He got up slowly, they shook hands, and Lorenzo left the bar.

He felt constant fear during the following days. He barely slept. He was hounded by memories of the murder and the detective's presence at every turn. He heard a distant echo when he spoke on the telephone; he was convinced someone was always following him, keeping their steps in time with his so they wouldn't be discovered.

He heard Sylvia come home at dawn and he could make out the sound of a car engine heading off when the gate closed with a metal clang. Maybe someone was watching the door.

He had trouble answering his friends' messages. He didn't go near Daniela because he thought the detective was shamelessly watching his advances, that he enjoyed stalking him. He heard her move around the apartment upstairs, take the boy out for a walk, but he didn't try to bump into her in the stairwell. He even went so far as to think that ten or twelve years in prison wouldn't be worse than what he was living through those days.

Wilson got him two or three moving jobs and they worked together with the van. In a corner in the back, there was still that cardboard suitcase from the apartment they had emptied out. One day around noon, he drove along the airport highway toward the senior citizens' home. At the reception desk, which was covered with papers, he explained that he had come to deliver some belongings to a resident. When he mentioned the man's name, Don Jaime, the woman seemed to show more interest. It was obvious he didn't get many visitors. I took care of emptying out his apartment, and I wanted to return some things to him. The woman jotted down Lorenzo's name and the number of his ID on a file card and gave him the room number on the third floor.

The place was more ugly than sordid. He knocked on the door. Even though nobody answered, he opened it. He found the man sitting on the mattress, watching television. He hadn't imagined him like that. Stout, immaculately clean, with a dreamy gaze on his kind face, not dangerous in the least. His face was shaved in irregular patches. At first glance, there was no trace of insanity or eccentricity. Lorenzo explained why he had come and placed the suitcase beside him. The man looked at him and seemed to understand, but he made no gestures of acquiescence nor did he open his mouth to say anything.

Inside the suitcase were the watches, the clippings, some records, but Lorenzo didn't open it to show him the contents.

You can keep it all, said the man suddenly. I don't need anything, thanks. I'd rather you have it, Lorenzo tried to explain. I also found this. Lorenzo still had the piece of paper with the telephone number in his wallet. It was on the door of your refrigerator, maybe it was important to you, he said to the man.

That's Gloria's phone number, was all he said. As if it explained everything. Lorenzo nodded. I called her, but she told me she didn't know you. That's true, nodded the man. Lorenzo left the piece of paper on the bedside table, giving it an importance that perhaps it didn't have. The man spoke again. Someone called my house one day. It was a young woman, in a hurry. I could barely talk to her. She told me, I'm Gloria, take down my number in case you need anything. I wrote it on that paper. But you never met her? Never. It must have been a mistake. She dialed the wrong number and thought she was talking to someone she knew. So why'd you keep the paper with her number?

The man sighed deeply, as if he had no easy answer to the question. It kept me company, he said finally. Sometimes I would call her, but I never dared to speak. I listened to the woman, to Gloria, answer and wait and then hang up on me.

Lorenzo, without really knowing why, used the long silence to sit delicately on the bed beside the man. Without brushing against him. He stayed there a good long while. The man watched television and when a gossip program ended he said, now comes the news, and he turned off the television with a remote control that he had in the pocket of his pajama top.

They spent a few minutes more in silence. Lorenzo asked him if he needed anything, if he was feeling okay. The man nodded. I'm fine.

Lorenzo stood up. He heard the nearby highway as if it were running through the middle of the home's tiny yard. And every two minutes an airplane made the walls tremble. They were very close to the airport, near the old Ciudad Pegaso.

Maybe I'll come back some other day.

There was no one at the entrance desk. It was lunchtime. An old woman was sitting in a wheelchair on the path in the garden. From behind, her badly combed white hair looked like a resting dog.

At home Sylvia was locked in her room. Music flooded the house. Lorenzo knocked on her door and she invited him in.

Did you eat? he asked Sylvia. No, but I'll fix myself something. Lorenzo waited a second before turning around. He paid attention to the music. Saturated guitars. A woman's voice, powerful, strident, imitating the singer from the Pretenders. What's this band?

Sylvia showed him the CD cover. A brunette, wearing a white shirt without shoulder pads. Lorenzo left her room for a moment and came back with a CD. Put on number six, he told Sylvia. She, somewhat lazily, stood up and did as she was asked. See how they're similar? Do you know this band?

Sylvia shook her head. They both remained there, listening to the song together.

All the music today only makes sense when you know what came before, explained Lorenzo. Now it's a little softer, a little more conventional, and all cut from the same pattern. They don't make bands like they used to.

Sylvia knew the kind of music her father liked. Bands with legendary names, the Rolling Stones, the Beatles, Pink Floyd, Led Zeppelin. When Pilar left him, like a teenager, he listened to the same Queen song over and over, with that singer's extreme voice. Sylvia would sometimes stop in the stairwell, before opening the door to the apartment, so as not to interrupt his exorcism. She heard him sing loudly over the recording. Too much love will kill you. Then he stopped, got over it. Just like you can have a love song, you can have a breakup song.

I remember one day when your grandfather asked me to put on some of my music for him to listen to, Lorenzo told her. I chose something by the Stones. I think it was "Honky Tonk Women" or something like that. He sat down and listened to it on the record player, paying full attention. And then he said, it's good. In my opinion, the harmony is very predictable, but you know that taste is a form of memory, so you only appreciate what you know. I'd have to hear it more. And then he looked sad, like your grandfather does sometimes. Parents and kids have never understood each other's music.

I like some of your stuff, Sylvia reassured him. She named Bob Dylan. Recently she had heard him at Ariel's house. It seems his friend Marcelo Polti was obsessed with Dylan and he had turned Ariel on to him.

Lorenzo picked up his CD. This chick was so hot, he said, pointing to the singer on the cover. She was virile, strong and stringy, but we loved her. I'll lend it to you if you want. Okay, Sylvia said, but it sounded more like a consolation than real interest. She was pleased to find her father talkative, expansive, more animated than she'd seen him the last few days. So much so that Lorenzo dared to ask, Well, you never tell me anything about your life these days. Have you got a boyfriend? Because with these hours you're keeping . . . I'm on vacation, Papá. So if you did have one you'd tell me? I don't know, it depends, if it was something serious . . . And what do you call something serious? Everything is serious, he said. No, everything is not serious, maintained Sylvia, convinced.

A few months ago, a friend of Lalo's told us over dinner that one day she found her daughter, who must be about your age, necking with a girl, this wildly passionate thing on a street bench, near where they live, smoking a joint, I don't even know what else, and the lady was super-pissed at her daughter because she hadn't told her anything, even though they have a really good relationship. I told her that kids don't ever tell their parents anything. Right? I never told mine.

The conversation bored Sylvia. But she appreciated her father's effort, possibly contrived, to access a part of her private life.

One day, when I still lived with your grandparents, I came home for dinner and my father tells me, that girl called a little while ago, your girlfriend. And I hadn't told them anything, they hadn't even met Pilar, but my father said your girlfriend so naturally that it killed me. They asked me what her name was, I said Pilar, and your grandmother said, I wonder if she'll come up to the house one day so we can meet her. And one day she came up to the house and I introduced her. I don't know, it just seems normal to me, no big confessions, "Papá, I have something important to tell you," he said in falsetto.

Sylvia shrugged her shoulders. I don't know, are you trying to get something out of me or what? she asked her father. No, no, not at all, I just felt like telling you, we're talking, right?

Lorenzo left the room. His burst of energy drove him to cook something beyond his skills, even with the help of one of the cookbooks that adorned a nearby shelf. Sylvia headed out a bit later. Lorenzo didn't hear her come back until late at night. After one.

The liturgy began with group singing. The pastor took center stage. He greets those present and talks to them with a syrupy accent Lorenzo can't quite place. He tells them it's Sunday and on this day we give the Lord our reflection, our thoughts, and our joy in this shared space of church. He speaks straightforwardly and makes eye contact with the parishioners. He's wearing a white shirt buttoned all the way up. In the first row sits a stocky guy, his rear end spilling over both sides of the folding chair, holding a guitar in his big mitts. He plays a song Lorenzo thinks he's heard before. Someone told me that life is quite short, and that fate mocks us, and someone told me life is filled with duties, and sometimes it will fill us with pain, but someone also told me that God still loves us, he still loves us. God still loves us.

The door opens and Lorenzo turns to see Daniela come in. She is surprised to see him there, but she doesn't walk toward him. She moves along the side wall and joins the people in the first rows. Lorenzo can just make out when she discreetly greets them and joins the ceremony. He doesn't take his eyes off her. Daniela barely turns a couple of times to check that he's still there. On one occasion, she does it while singing, along with everyone else, a song about God's mercy for the poor.

The pastor talks about everyday life, of God's presence in the most trivial things, of his definitive presence in daily events. At the bottom of the wastepaper basket where you throw the remains of the day, he is there; in the stairs of the metro and in the elevator he watches to see how you react with strangers; forget those endless discussions about the soul and faith, imagine him in every corner of your lives. But he isn't judging, he already knows you, he is accompanying you so that you don't ever forget him. Do you see those security cameras they put in certain buildings? Well, God has those cameras installed inside us. Every once in a while, the parishioners answer him out loud, as if they were striking up a conversation. And then they break out again in songs and clapping.

Any believer is a pastor of souls. You are pastors, in the street, at work, in your family. You can see the light that illuminates the invisible. That is our mission. To save ourselves and save as many of the people around us as possible. We are neighborhood missionaries.

When the service ends, the group moves the chairs and chats for a while in a circle before escaping into the street. Some of them bring packages of rice, beans, or eggs and leave them in plastic bags on the pastor's table. We will hand it out, of course, he tells them. Daniela approaches Lorenzo with the pastor and introduces them. Welcome, the man says, I hope to see you back here often. Thank you, replies Lorenzo.

He goes out to the street with Daniela. He suggests they take a walk. But she says that she has to stay to prepare the bags of food for the needy, to help the pastor hand them out among the poor. If I had known, I would have brought something. No, it's not required, explains Daniela. They remain standing for a moment on the sidewalk.

I didn't want the other night to end badly. Maybe I went too fast, Lorenzo starts to apologize. But it's important to me that we don't let that come between us. I want to get to know you better. For you to get to know me, too. Lorenzo hears himself, he sounds ridiculous, influenced by the pastor's way of speaking. It might seem weird to you, but I don't want to let you get away, like something passing through my life I didn't really get to know. That's why I'm here, I wanted to tell you that. Wilson told me this was your church. Wilson knows the way? Daniela smiles. I thought he only knew how to get to the bars.

Lorenzo ignores the comment and stares into Daniela's eyes, as if he were waiting for something that hadn't arrived.

You're very lonely, aren't you? she asks him. You're very lonely.

16

Ariel extends the seat back and tries to sleep. In first class, there is a lot of space, and beside him a man in a suit reads a business newspaper as he sips on a sherry. Like on the flight out, the plane is filled with Argentinian families that live in Spain, on their way back from Christmas holidays. In line to get onto the airplane were advertising executives, university professors, the solidly middle-class, mixing with more humble travelers holding big bags and showing tense expressions when they had to show their passports. January 2, the beginning of the year, always creates some sort of wide-ranging hope, like a blank page.

In the last row of first class, stretched out to full length, with a mask over his eyes, amid thunderous snores, sleeps Humberto Hernán Panzeroni, the goalie of an Andalusian team. He had come over earlier to greet Ariel effusively when he saw they were on the same flight.

Humberto is big, a veteran of the Spanish league, where he's spent almost six years. He was chosen as the third goalie of the Argentinian national team in the last few World Cups. He sat on the arm of Ariel's seat to talk to him and every time a flight attendant passed by he turned; it wasn't clear if it was to let her pass or to flirt. I hate traveling in first class, they send the experienced flight attendants up here, the tender young things are in coach, the world's upside down. He had one incisor a different shade of white than the rest of his teeth and Ariel remembered that he'd lost a tooth in a collision with one of his fullbacks. Ariel had seen it on television.

I have my wife back there with the three kids, in first class they charge an arm and a leg. For the baby who doesn't even have his own seat they charge a thousand euros. They talked for a while about the latest in their profession, the state of the country, and then Humberto announced that he was starting to feel the effects of the pills and he stretched out to sleep.

The days in Buenos Aires had been intense and they reminded Ariel of everything he missed. He thought about Sylvia; they even spoke on the phone. It was four in the morning in Buenos Aires and Sylvia answered the call with a mix of euphoria and nervousness.

In Ezeiza, when he arrived, his brother Charlie was waiting for him at the entrance to the breezeway, chatting with the ground flight attendant. He leaped onto Ariel and squeezed him tightly in his arms, blocking the exit for the rest of the passengers. He took Ariel's carry-on and put it over his shoulder. You've changed, he said, now you look like the older brother. When they passed a girl dressed as Santa Claus with tight short shorts handing out flyers, Charlie elbowed him. He took him in a new car to his parents' house. I'm testing it out, if I like it I'll keep it. You know now I go around as the brother of Arielito Burano, the Feather who scores goals in Spain, Charlie felt obligated to explain. Here Madrid goals get noticed, not everybody scores those.

On the way home, Charlie brought him up to date on family affairs. Their mother was in a delicate state again, with some depression, taking iron pills or copper or I don't know what, and the old man is fine, spending his free time locked up in the little workshop as if it were his life's business. He mentioned the new names in local politics, he told him about the hardships of close friends, so-and-so's mother died, they kidnapped so-and-so's son, so-and-so's store closed, the so-and-sos went to Spain . . . If there's nothing bad to talk about here, people get mad.

Ariel was listening to his brother, but he didn't take his eyes off the city emerging beside the highway. He had missed it, the way the houses are arranged, the serrated profile of the buildings, the different colors, the familiar advertisements, the streetlights high up above the streets, the elevated railroad, the stores along the avenue. In the neighborhood, a few days' worth of trash was accumulated beside the trees, because of the strike, Charlie explained, and they had changed the door to a metal one with a video alarm system. Things aren't as bad as people are going to tell you they are, predicted Charlie. And take off your sweater, it's eighty-six degrees, boiling.

At home they received him with tears. His nephews had grown and Ariel told them, I don't know if the T-shirts I brought you will fit. He gave his father a bag filled with nougat candy, sloe gin, and vacuum-sealed Jabugo ham and his sister-in-law the magazine *Hola*. Did you win the Apertura? his father asked, and everyone laughed. Ariel told them the league championship in Spain didn't end until June. And who cares anyway, said his father. You know the painter Dalí said soccer wouldn't improve until the ball was hexagonal. Maybe that would suit me even better, said Ariel. His mother had gained too much weight. Ariel found her old and tired.

Do they stop you on the street, do people recognize you? asked his sister-in-law. Oh man, explained Charlie, in Spain they ask you for autographs everywhere, on a napkin, a bus ticket, on their T-shirts. You remember the little kid who asked you to sign his report card?

On the street, Ariel enjoyed people watching, the good weather. Soon the heat would really set in. A lot of his friends had gone out of town to the beaches for the summer. They invited him to Villa Gesell, the beach house of some close friends, but he wanted to stay in Buenos Aires. As he was sitting at an outside café table on a corner near Recoleta, they would yell at him every once in a while from the opposite sidewalk, you're brilliant! Or someone would give him the thumbs-up from a car window or ask him, are the Spaniards treatin' you right?

He wanted to use his week's vacation to get together with friends. What are we doing for New Year's? Something at home, mellow, suggested Charlie. He talked to his brother about his adjustment to Spain, the team's playing, about his needs. They told me you have a girlfriend, he said suddenly. Who told you? I have my informants. Ariel didn't really know how much his brother knew and all he said was, yeah, well, there's a girl, but nothing . . . Later he guessed that maybe Charlie was talking to Emilia.

He went back to his apartment in Belgrano. Walter had it better decorated than when he lived there. He even used the roof, which Ariel had barely taken advantage of. He had put in a hammock up there. They scaled seven metal steps on a shaky ladder and settled in with a thermos of maté. The building, near Monumental Stadium, rubbed elbows with the the highest ones in the area. All with acrylic super-balconies, expensive lounge chairs, and privileged views of the river that looked like the sea. It's so great up here, said Ariel, in Madrid I live in a really different kind of place.

Marcelo invited him to a barbecue with friends, all of them *cuervos*, he warned. *Cuervo* meaning a San Lorenzo fan. He played Ariel his latest tracks from the studio, told him that he might be traveling to Madrid on his new tour: Express

Kidnapping. I got together a fabulous band, I'm pleased. He looked happy, sure of himself. The record just came out, and it's already pirated in every corner of the Web, and what's more you have to make nice and thank all those fucking people who rob you, but, well, as they used to say, it's better to get robbed than killed. Ariel wanted to leave early, but Marcelo insisted, today the unemployed are going to be protesting, stay, there's nothing to do out on the street. It's organized by the Bloque Piquetero Nacional, the Corrientes Clasista y Combativa, the Frente Darío Santillán, the PTS, the MAS. Ariel was refamiliarizing himself with local politics.

They had a family dinner on Christmas Eve. Santa brought gifts after midnight and at four in the morning Ariel was turning in bed, unable to sleep, listening to the birds and some nearby generator, the elevated train passing by the house, the murmur of the highway. His room now seemed like a schoolkid's room, a place trapped in time, as if it no longer belonged to him. His childhood trophies, the photographs of juvenile teams on the walls, the boxes filled with games, the few books. All his life he dreamed of playing professional soccer and now that he was, he felt like he wasn't enjoying it the way he used to. He liked practice more than playing; in the morning when he got to the field he found the grass fresh, welcoming, without the pressure of games. Then he enjoyed the ball, his teammates, the exercises. He found the actual games laborious, difficult. Only in bursts did he get the fulfillment he used to have, when playing was a pleasure and just a pleasure. The stadium often transformed into a pressurized bubble, where he found it hard to breathe, to fly. When he remembered feeling happy, it was always with his hand on the nape of Sylvia's neck, lost among her curls, her peculiarly shaped eyes of intriguing, intelligent green, pulling him in, the expression at the corner of her mouth right after she said something defiant and funny. From thousands of miles away, he was aroused by the memory of Sylvia's busty body, running over it in his mind to savor it again.

He took a long walk with his father to Chacabuco Park. They talked about his mother's health. Otherwise, we'd come visit you, I mean it, but she can't get on a plane now, with her blood pressure the way it is. She looks fatter, Ariel confided. It's the medicine and she doesn't exercise, she never leaves the house.

He pored over the local press. Suddenly he felt strange, a newcomer to a city he felt he didn't really know. It was similar to how he felt in Madrid. He had managed to not belong anywhere, to be a stranger everywhere. He drove along Avenida Nazca toward Bajo Flores, he was held up by a passing train, and he edged along the Nuevo Gasómetro to catch the entrance to Avenida Varela. The neighborhood of Soldati, bleaker than ever, the same message painted on the wall: ENOUGH OF LOW WAGES ALREADY. The family that owned El Golazo carwash was getting their barbecue ready on the sidewalk. The security guard opened the gate for him, you back on the job? Just here for Christmas. He parked Charlie's pickup beside the pregame dormitories, he remembered the Saturday barbecues beneath the deck, with the team enthusiasm; he really missed that. He crossed beneath the portrait of "Balls Out" Zubeldía, who exactly thirty years earlier won the national championship for San Lorenzo. The walls bore reminders of the winning team: Anhielo, Piris, Villar, Glaria, Telch "the Sheep," Olguín, Scotta, Chazarreta, Beltrán, Cocco, Ortiz. Ariel was surprised to find a framed photo of himself beside the glorious matadors, as that dream team was called. Did you see your photo yet? asked Cholo, the grounds manager. They hugged. Cholo went into the locker room with him, everyone's on vacation. It was humble, with the religious imagery, the thermoses of maté, the little lacquered wood lockers, the piled-up sneakers. It must be more luxurious over there, huh? It's another world, Cholo, it's another world.

He called Agustina. It was an obligation. He had called her a few times from Spain, in moments of desperation, after his brother left. On one occasion, he was about to offer her a ticket and invite her to visit, but he stopped himself when he realized how selfish he was being, having people at his disposal on a whim. The worst call was the last, one night when he came home drunk, after going out with Husky. He suddenly felt the need to talk to her, to go back down that path, and he was crude and unpleasant and ended up jerking off while he begged her to say dirty things into the phone. Since then he hadn't had the guts to call her again, except for a cold, brief apology, but he felt that it was rude not to see her while he was in the city.

They went out in the early evening. Ariel had plans to dine with some friends and he didn't want the night to turn into a temptation. It would only hurt her to prolong something that was over. They met near Lavalle Plaza and she said, you look like a tourist. I am a tourist now, he said in defense. I even wanted to take a walk before we met up. They talked about superficial things. Agustina had chosen her ivory earrings, her ponytail, and her lipstick with extreme care, but she quickly understood that the date wasn't going to end with them getting back together. Ariel established a clinical distance during the two hours. Agustina managed to get him to talk about Sylvia.

I don't know, I don't think it's a relationship that's going anywhere, but it helps me be more relaxed, comfortable, to be able to speak intimately with someone. She nodded while she listened to him. His words hurt her, but she pretended they didn't. Ariel said, you know when you love someone so much that you try to protect them from the pain you could cause them, out of fear because you know yourself, but the other person only sees the wonderful side. And Agustina felt like saying, I know what you mean, I know that feeling, but she only said that the best thing was to just enjoy yourself, to not get worked up thinking too far ahead.

I should vaccinate her against me, he said, with a smile.

Maybe she doesn't want the vaccine.

And Ariel realized he was talking about Sylvia, but Agustina was talking about herself. They said good-bye a bit later, she put her hand on his cheek and said, take care of her, and she managed to make Ariel feel guilty for not having done the same with her.

Ariel's friends took him out to eat and he was in rare form. He told them anecdotes about the Mexican halfback who burned out his car driving it in first gear for twenty-five miles, convinced it was an automatic; the one about the inside right forward from Mendoza who played in the Second Division on the Canary Islands and had gotten so fat that fans sang "go on a diet" to the music of "Guantanamera"; the one about the substitute goalie on his team who ate sunflower seeds at a dizzying rate, and with his gloves on; the teammate whose feet stank so bad that they hid his sneakers in the garbage; about the Pole Wlasavsky, nicknamed Bert, and his collection of gold Rolexes; the one about the wife of the goalie coach who would get drunk in the stadium VIP bar; the gay referee who called certain players before a game to tell them he was a big fan and invite them out for dinner; the one about the right halfback from Paraguay, on a team in Extremadura, who was suspended for three games after telling the press he thought Bin Laden was an admirable public figure; about a Brazilian coach who insisted the team captain play with a radio transmitter in his ear and halfway through it had picked up the announcer's broadcast and the poor guy went crazy.

The fun ended when the restaurant television broadcast news of a fire in a nightclub in the capital where a lot of kids had died; the exact number wouldn't be known for days. It was a packed concert hall without security measures, where the bathrooms were used as a daycare so the post-teenage parents could enjoy the music. It burned down because of some fireworks lit inside while the emergency doors were closed and padlocked to keep people without tickets out.

That night he called Sylvia. She shouted from inside some dive. He tried to whisper in his room, right next to his parents'. I miss you, Ariel told her, but they could barely hear each other.

The next day, he went to spend the morning with Dragon. The country was shaken by the fire the night before. His wife fixed them a maté and they sat on the sofa, in front of the television. You don't know how good it is that you're getting far away from here. Everything is corrupt. If they start to investigate this nightclub thing, they won't find one person from the first to the last who did one thing right and clean. It makes me mad.

After a while, they turned off the television. How long are those bastards going to keep squeezing people's pain to fill their segments? He asked about Spain, but Ariel confessed that he didn't much follow the current events there. After the train bombings, do they hate the North Africans? asked the coach. No, I don't think so, answered Ariel, doesn't look like it.

Dragon told him that he was considering the idea of retiring, I haven't got much steam left. He had a son barely two years older than Ariel who had had a bad year. Later he alluded to a drug problem. He wondered if he should leave the city, get a change of scenery, he liked the time he spent at his country house. In the unkempt yard, an old soccer goal made of squared wooden posts rose among the goosefoot. Dragon had rescued it from an abandoned school in the area. All my life trying to teach boys and it turns out I did the worst job with my own, he said bitterly.

Dragon told him that he had seen a few games on cable. You look tense, as if you have one eye on the stands. Just play, don't get weighed down with responsibility. You have to always remember the pleasure of the game, always. Yours is an absurd job, if you don't enjoy it, there's no point. You can't start thinking, you freeze up. The smart thing to do is to know how to manage your own anxiety. Look at what's going on in the world, if you stop to think, you'll shoot yourself, it's enough to make you start dodging and weaving when you remember those kids from the Cromañón nightclub.

He wanted Ariel to stay for lunch, but he had made plans with Charlie. They said good-bye in high spirits. Score goals, all the Spaniards want is goals. At the car window, Dragon leaned over to speak. The most important businesses are devoted to things you can't touch, intangible things. Look, the most profitable company in the world is the Catholic Church and then there's soccer. They both live off people with faith, and that's all. Isn't it crazy?

Charlie took him out to eat at an elegant restaurant in Puerto Madero and introduced him to a lovely woman who had become his regular lover. She worked at Channel Once, in production, and they wanted to interview Ariel before he went back to Madrid. That same afternoon, they recorded an insipid, stupid conversation strolling through the port. In the car, on the way home, Charlie said to his brother, don't judge me, I can tell you're judging me and you have no right. When you get to where I am you might be worse, much worse than me, so save your morality lectures. Ariel lifted his middle finger and they both laughed.

It was a sad Christmas. When you turned on the television all you saw were the relatives of those who died in the nightclub clustered together for three days at the morgue without any information. The brother of a player Ariel knew was among the missing. And several days before, a giant tsunami in Southeast Asia had left more than 400,000 people dead in its wake. The news aired coverage of the dramatic stories with fragments of video recorded by tourists, images interrupted when the tsunami reached them with a fatal slap.

His last evening in Buenos Aires, Ariel cut his walk short because the Casa Rosada was surrounded by riot police. They were expecting a protest. Walter invited him to the tenth barbecue in six days. There he ran into an old teammate from San Lorenzo, a midfielder who played for the Corinthians. Around his neck, he wore a gold necklace with a little soccer ball pendant. It's nice. I had it made by a jeweler in Rosario, a guy who makes one-of-a-kind stuff.

In the airport, Charlie and his older son saw him off. His mother had bought him two big bags of yerba maté at the last minute and he packed it in his hand luggage. On the plane, he doesn't sleep. He tosses around the idea of breaking up with Sylvia, of putting out that strange fire. He's decided to focus on his work, not get distracted by other things.

When he gets off the plane, he says good-bye to Humberto. He woke up with his mouth dry and his eyes foggy. When do we play against each other? But neither of them remembers the game schedule. Well, we'll definitely see each other at Tiger Lavalle's birthday, that you can't miss.

At customs a kid with a small backpack on his shoulder asks him for help. The police are detaining him, he doesn't have enough cash and no particular address to go to. He is very nervous, worked up. I didn't bring enough dough, just for that they want to screw me. Ariel talks to the policeman at the window. There's nothing we can do. Ariel wants to help, he turns to another policeman, who recognizes him instantly. I don't know, is there something that can be done? The policeman smiles at him, don't get into trouble, that's my advice. Ariel thinks it over, gives the little money he has in his wallet to the kid, and passes through customs.

When he goes out with his suitcases, he still feels uncomfortable, disturbed by the situation. He has to stop and sign a couple of autographs for two boys. He looks up and, behind the line of people waiting for the recent arrivals, he sees Sylvia. She smiles at him but doesn't approach. He walks toward her, but Sylvia evades him. She walks behind him as he heads toward the parking lot and they maintain the distance through the entire path of moving sidewalks. He turns every once in a while and they smile at each other. They don't say anything, but it's as if they are embracing from afar. As if they are making love, each from their own space, she ten feet behind.

The parking lot is ice-cold. It had dipped below freezing that night. Ariel finds his car. They kiss inside it. They only separate when she tries to put on the heat, turning the buttons on the dashboard to the maximum. I'm gonna freeze. She pulls on the sleeves of her sweater.

He slips his fingers underneath Sylvia's curls and caresses her neck. Happy New Year, she says.

part three

IS THIS ME?

1

Sylvia leads a double life. In one she sits at the back of a classroom, at a green desk with chipped edges that touches her classmate Alba's desk. During the morning, different teachers try to leave a small mark on her and the other kids. Sometimes in the form of notes in a notebook, other times as a fact they'll remember until the day after the test, and rarely as a piece of knowledge that will be with them all their lives. The math teacher is setting up a vectors problem on the blackboard. He had a strong start to the semester, his passion still intact after years of teaching. Everything is mathematics, he told them. Math applies to when you buy, when you sell, when you grow, when you get old, when you leave home, when you find a job, when you fall in love, when you listen to a new song. Everything is mathematics. Life is mathematics, adding and subtracting, division, multiplication, if you understand math you'll understand life a little better. And when he saw them laugh, he added, tell me something that isn't math, come on. My ass, muttered "the Tank" Palazón, and they all laughed harder. God, said Nico Verón, is God math? Don Octavio stopped for a second, but he didn't seem surprised. God is the solution to an equation that has no solution. But today the class wasn't paying attention to Don Octavio.

When the morning ends, Sylvia will walk home. Maybe with Mai, maybe with other schoolmates, who will scatter at each intersection. She'll make lunch for her father and herself or eat something he's prepared. She'll lock herself in her room to listen to music, study for a test, answer some text messages, or search the Web to find the lyrics to some song, chat, or just surf. She will count the seconds until the time comes to switch to her other life.

Her second life takes place at Ariel's big house, where they watch some movie on the plasma screen, chat with a beer and music in the background, challenge each other in a video game. Then they'll eat the stew Emilia left for him, or pick up thin-crust pizzas from an Italian restaurant where they make a fuss over Ariel, or order in Japanese or Argentinian from a deli that delivers to their area. They undo the bed to make love. It's nothing like the thin cold sheets Sylvia returns to later, where love is just a memory and a worn teddy bear with soft fur, a survivor from her childhood. The two lives develop on different planets or on different stages, with Sylvia playing two almost opposite roles. Sometimes the planets brush past each other, sending off a spark. Like one day when they were buying music and movies in the Fnac store on Callao. From a distance, they showed each other the covers, she some popular British group, he a band that sings in Spanish. In the checkout line, they stand one behind the other and then Mai appears, surprised to see Sylvia, didn't you say you were going to your grandmother's house? And Sylvia lies, I slipped out for a while. She's already gotten used to lying and she does it quite naturally. And when Mai insists on having a drink together, Sylvia is evasive, and when Mai points to Ariel, who is paying in front of them at the register, she says, isn't that the soccer player, the Argentinan one? I have no idea. Well, he is super-cute. Yeah. And Sylvia gets rid of Mai in spite of the uncomfortable suspicion. I know you're not telling me the whole truth, you're going to see your boyfriend. I wonder when you're going to introduce me to him, or is it that you're keeping him hidden for a reason, he's a hunchback, he's a count, I don't know? And they laugh. Later Sylvia manages to meet up with Ariel in the parking garage.

It happens again when Ariel bumps into a teammate at a red light. They talk from their cars, through the windows, joking until the guy points at Sylvia with his eyes. She's a friend's daughter, Ariel couldn't think of anything better to say, and Sylvia spends the afternoon making jokes about the incident. And does your friend know what you do with his daughter? It's in those accidental moments when the two lives seem, more than ever, irreconcilable.

On other occasions, Sylvia finds the contrast of fleeing one life for another entertaining. Today she left English class in a hurry. Her explanation to the teacher seemed to drag on forever, while he pulled on the hairs of his sideburns in a nervous tic. She took the metro to a meeting with a real estate agent to see an apartment near the Bilbao traffic circle. Are we waiting for anyone else? asks the agent, when she finds herself with a client carrying a school backpack. No, in the end my father's not going to be able to make it, explains Sylvia as the elevator ascends to the penthouse. She amuses herself by playing the role of a millionaire's daughter. My father doesn't have time for these things, he lets me choose. The agent abandons her reluctance and opens the door to the apartment after searching in her purse for the keys.

Sylvia walks through the apartment while, from a distance, the agent tells her about the benefits of its recent renovation. High ceilings, wood-framed windows, a striking terrace with views of the rooftops. I love it, but my father said not to pay more than a million euros, that's his limit. That's going to be difficult, reasons the agent, but, of course, if a large part of it is under the table we can negotiate. Of course, says Sylvia, most of it will be under the table.

It's been a few weeks since Ariel decided to move to the city. He's tired of being isolated in a housing complex where the most exciting encounter is with a neighbor who's decided to jog in the mornings after a mild attack of angina. This way we could see each other easily, without so much driving, it's ridiculous, Sylvia told him one day when Ariel was yawning with exhaustion along the highway to drop her off at her house. Ariel assigned his financial adviser to draw up a list of possible apartments. They ruled out several from the photos online and the place that Sylvia is now visiting, allowing her a fun stint as a millionaire, is the one they liked best.

A little while later, Ariel picks her up in front of the Roxy movie theater. Sylvia gets into the car. I loved it. I would knock down a wall to make the living room bigger, what do you want three bedrooms for? She told me if you pay for part of it in cash under the table, they'll let you have it for a million euros. Ariel has no problem with that; a substantial part of his contract is paid into an account in Gibraltar. Sylvia is surprised he never pays with cards or takes out money from the ATM. He always has large amounts of cash on him. He calls his financial adviser from the car. He closes the deal. That neighborhood is a good investment, the guy tells him. Sylvia smiles and rests her foot on the dashboard.

That night they joke around in the gym installed in the basement of Ariel's house. He lifts weights with his legs while she walks on the treadmill. She gets tired easily. He tells her, you're gonna get a fat ass if you don't do a little exercise and she reproaches him, I don't want to be the typical stuck-up rich girl-friend of a soccer player who spends the morning in the gym and the afternoon shopping and at the salon. They aren't all like that, Amílcar's wife is really great. The exception, Sylvia tells him, but all the rest . . . What's the deal, do they kick you off the team if you hook up with someone different? Can't a soccer player have an ugly but smart girlfriend? Ariel smiles without stopping his exercise, well, I'm going to be the first. Sylvia threatens to drop a five-pound weight on his crotch.

Gyms depress me. They're like torture chambers, she says. In my neighborhood, there's one that fills up in the afternoon with crazy wannabe boxers who end up in skinhead gangs, kicking the crap out of immigrants. One day I went with a friend of mine and there was a guy in one corner, with his hand stuck in the pocket of his sweatpants jerking off, I swear, while he watched the chicks on stationary bikes.

Ariel's cell phone rings and Sylvia hands it to him. She can't help looking at the name on the screen. Husky. Ariel chides her for her curiosity and answers. What's up, how are you? Oh yeah? No, I haven't read it. It says that? Of course, because he's perfect, he never makes mistakes. What a son of a bitch. And where is this interview? No, no, whatever, I don't want to read it.

Sylvia listens to him talk. She smiles at the thought of how soccer has become a priority in her life. She plans her nights out with friends and her studying around the league calendar. Something that no one close to her would have suspected. And she's up-to-date on all the soccer scene commentary and back-stabbing. My father would be proud, she thinks.

By the way, I bought an apartment downtown, Ariel tells Husky. What do you mean a soccer player can't live downtown?

And where do we have to live? In the locker room? Go screw yourself. Yeah, sure, I'm crazy, and that's coming from you, the sanest guy on the planet.

Who's Husky? asks Sylvia when Ariel hangs up. He says an interview with my coach came out where he explains how some of the newly signed players aren't producing the way they hoped, he's talking about me, of course. What a dick. He never takes responsibility. If I play well, he was right to bring me over, if I play badly, I'm of no use to him. Dragon always told me, never trust stupid-looking people.

Who's Dragon? A coach from back home that I had as a kid. And what did Husky say about the apartment? Nothing, that I won't be able to live downtown because of all the people, the whole autograph thing . . . His name is Raúl, but everybody calls him Husky. He's a journalist. And you can be friends with a journalist? Sylvia asks him. Why not? And if one day he has to talk about you? Well, then he'll talk about me. Yes, insists Sylvia, but if he has to say bad things about you . . . Well, then he will, I understand . . . Ah, so you take criticism well, like the comment your coach made, and Sylvia smiles. It's different, that's the typical son of a bitch trying to shift the responsibility for his mistakes onto everyone else. There are a lot of those, most of them are like that. They don't say anything to your face, but then they insinuate in the press like it was nothing. Was I the one who signed an injured French midfielder who hasn't been able to train with us all year? Or two fucking Brazilians who just sit around scratching their balls?

Ariel stops exercising. I'm gonna take a shower. Sylvia watches him leave the basement. Maybe he's mad, she thinks. She knows how tense his work makes him. The good thing about winning on a Sunday is that you know that week the press will leave you alone, he told her one day, they'll mess with the team that lost. If I were jealous, thinks Sylvia, I would be jealous of his job, of fucking soccer. Sometimes she uses that expression. It's her way of establishing the rivalry. It's her and fucking soccer fighting over Ariel's life. But she is aware that it's essential to him. I would be nothing without soccer, he had confessed to her. Hey, what would I be without soccer? An uneducated employee, an everyman? I can't allow myself the luxury of not appreciating what makes me special. And sometimes she sees him lose himself in the game on television, isolate himself from the world, as if he were playing with his eyes. Should we order some dinner? she asks, and he answers, if they'd pull their lines together they'd be harder to attack.

Other times he gets calls on his cell phone and talks for a long time. Always about the same thing. Fucking soccer. About the play, a rival's game, what they told him about the Argentinian championship, about someone's statements, an article criticizing them, a comment made by the president's wife. Don't be a baby, he says sometimes when he hangs up and she says, if I knew you were going to spend the evening talking on your cell I would have stayed home.

Sylvia knows when Ariel needs to withdraw from reality in order to dedicate himself entirely to his work. At those times she feels vertigo. As if she were falling from way up high with nothing to grab on to. Alone, like she is in her relationship with Ariel, hanging in the air, beside the trail he has left in his wake. She feels like the special guest on a distant, gravity-free planet, which she'll disappear from as soon as Ariel loosens his hold on her, when he no longer takes her fingers between his as he drives.

Often she finds herself overcome by sadness, her eyes damp. She knows that dependence is love's worst enemy. But there is little she can do; she can't settle into Ariel's life, into her other life, and stop being who she really is. She enjoys when they get out of the car and walk down the street with other people. When they sit in a movie theater and a couple arriving late makes themselves comfortable nearby and when they take refuge in a café and someone comes over to greet Ariel. Then she feels like everybody else.

The month of February came with fifteen spring days. People sit outside in the Plaza Santa Ana. A few afternoons they lay out in Ariel's garden, carefully trimmed each week by Luciano, with a view of the branches silhouetted against the sky. They felt like all the other young people.

Sylvia goes straight from the basement to the garden through the garage door. She sits on the edge of the pool where leaves float on the greenish water. She leans her hands on the grass and lets herself fall backward. She feels how her hair hangs down her back and is rustled by the breeze. She stays there until he finds her. Ariel walks on the grass, his hair wet. He is wearing the sandals she hates and as he approaches they slap with each step. He sits behind her and holds her by the shoulders.

What are you thinking?

It takes Sylvia a little while to tell him that she'd like to go out, to meet people, to do something together. Ariel moves his face from one side to the other so that it brushes against her hair. Should I make some pasta and we can watch a movie? he suggests. Sylvia nods. She is cold and he wraps her up in his arms.

During the movie, Sylvia falls asleep, overcome by tiredness. She rests her head on the arm of the sofa. Ariel carries her up to his room. He undresses her delicately and she, although smiling, pretends to be asleep. When he takes off her pants and drops them onto the floor, Ariel brings his face to her sex. She picks up one knee and leaves her leg bent like a mountain towering over him.

They both seem to be more relaxed knowing their time is limited. In less than an hour, they will have to comply with her strict curfew.

But that night, Ariel's caresses put Sylvia to sleep. She will wake up disoriented and surprised, with the light of a sunny dawn in that early spring. Ariel will be sleeping beside her, facedown, with one arm tangled in the pillow. Slight noises can be heard from the floor downstairs, some footsteps, a chair scratching along the kitchen floor, a faucet running. Sylvia, panicked, will elbow Ariel hard in the ribs, twice. She is trying to wake him up.

Ari, Ari, it's daylight. It's the morning. Fuck. It's the morning.

2

How strange to encounter your reflection all of a sudden and have it be alien to you. Recognize yourself in it, know that it's you, but at the same time feel like someone else. Leandro had dampened his gray hair to comb it back into place, tight against his skull. Who is it that looks back at him from the mirror? He washes up before leaving for the chalet, where he will once again meet Osembe. Spotless, like a decent old man on his way to Mass or some conference, with a sweater beneath his jacket, because today he'll skip the coat, it's so nice out. Often, when he combs his hair in front of the mirror in the chalet, which is so similar to the one at home, Osembe comes over and musses it with a childish naughtiness that somehow feels absurdly normal. As if a moment later they were going to stroll arm in arm down the street, stopping in front of a store window or maybe going into the supermarket to buy some fish for dinner. He looks at his watch. It's time to go.

In the last few weeks, Aurora hasn't been able to get up. She doesn't trust her strength and, even though several times she's sat at the edge of the mattress, she hasn't dared to get out of bed. For her, terra firma no longer exists. Leandro even has a hard time getting her comfortable in the wheelchair. In the mornings, he fills up a large bowl of water and places it on her thighs. Aurora spends a long time washing her face and dampening her hair and neck. Her skin gets easily chapped and she asks for the lotion to moisturize her arms and face. Leandro sometimes does her legs while Aurora lifts her nightgown to reveal her fragile, pale extremities. Leandro, leaning over her, looks at the fabric pulled halfway up her thighs. On other occasions he washes her feet with hot water. While they are still damp, Leandro trims her nails, resting the sole against his thighs. You don't have to do that, it's okay, she would say. Benita can do it. No, no, it's no problem. And Leandro continued, wanting to see his actions as some sort of penance, kneeling before his wife.

On New Year's Day, Aurora felt almost constant pains and the emergency doctor sent an ambulance. She spent two days in the hospital and they discharged her with a daily dose of sedatives that made her doze most of the day. Any time she felt better, Aurora avoided taking them. Leandro would insist, you don't have to withstand the pain, there's no point. I'm better today, I don't need them, she would say. Lorenzo was shocked one afternoon when he visited and saw his mother's sedated state. Leandro took him to the kitchen. I spoke to the doctor, she only has months to live. Lorenzo dropped his head into his hands. It's better not to tell Sylvia anything, continued Leandro.

Benita changed the sheets every day, and spoke with Aurora in a big, cheerful voice. I'm handicapped, not deaf, Aurora reminded her when Benita would repeat the same thing three times increasingly louder. She talks to her the way people talk to the sick or the foreign, thought Leandro. Twice a week, a Colombian masseuse came to help Aurora loosen up her muscles. She gives her a slap on the thigh at the end and always says the same thing, well, now you've done your two- or two-and-a-half-mile walk, since that's the passive exercise equivalent.

Leandro spends his mornings taking walks, buying things off Benita's lists, and reading the newspaper to Aurora. Sometimes he skips over the delicate paragraphs. Every week a precarious boat filled with immigrants crashes into the rocks on the coast and the sea spits out twenty-odd corpses onto the southern beaches. Almost every day a driver or a group of friends or an entire family loses their lives in cars. A prisoner glues his hand to his girlfriend's with industrial-strength glue during their conjugal visit to demand a switch to open prison. There are deaths in the Middle East, meetings of international leaders, constant political arguments, cultural prizes, detailed information about the soccer championship, news on the economy and television programs. Reading the newspaper is a routine Leandro doesn't dare break. It would feel like the world is ending. Once in a while he'll read her an interview and she'll say that's very good, a simple comment that inspires Leandro to continue.

Together they watched the Christmas reports on the tsunami that devoured the virgin beaches of Thailand and Indonesia. They looked at the cold images, almost something out of fiction, without saying anything to each other, and they, too, felt overwhelmed by nature.

Once a week, two women from the neighborhood visit. On those afternoons, Leandro disappears. Sometimes to the chalet. Since New Year's he never went more than once a week, he had established that limit, and when he feels the urge and is about to break his promise to himself he locks himself in his room and puts music on the record player at a deafening volume until six o'clock passes. Sometimes he masturbates looking at old photos in a book of nudes.

On New Year's Eve, they ate the traditional twelve grapes in Aurora's bedroom. Lorenzo and Sylvia were there, even though they both left shortly after. Leandro stayed with Aurora to watch the New Year's concert on television. Two days later, he asked Osembe if she was going on vacation. These days there's a lot of work, she answered. They had added some more Russian and Bulgarian girls at the chalet, who laughed with strident peals in the adjacent rooms. Fucking Russians, Leandro heard her mutter one day. What did you say? Nothing, nothing. But Leandro wanted to understand what bothered her about the recent arrivals.

One afternoon in mid-January, Aurora received her friends at home. She was so weak that she had barely been able to greet them when they came in. Leandro left them alone. A little while later, he was lying in bed at the brothel with Osembe. My wife is dying, he said suddenly. Osembe dropped down by his side and stroked his face with her fingertips. She's dying and it makes me feel so bad spending the afternoon here. Why? she asked. You have to forget.

But I don't forget, was the only thing Leandro managed to say. I don't make you forget? For a little while? she asked him as if feigning hurt pride.

Leandro didn't respond. Osembe wanted to know more. It's her bones, he answered. You have to rub cloves of garlic all over her body, on her legs and arms. Raw, quartered cloves of garlic, rub her with them good and hard. Leandro smiled as he listened. Don't laugh, it is very good to do.

These conversations ended up arousing Leandro. Especially when he noticed Osembe relaxing, no longer a whore for those brief moments of trivial chatting. That turned him on more than all the lovey-dovey erotic foreplay. He lay on top of her then, as if all of a sudden he was overcome with sex. And it took her a few minutes to understand his fit of lust.

That evening he went back home in time to say good-bye to Aurora's friends and thank them for their visit. She was dozing in the room and Leandro approached to kiss her. Aurora opened her eyes. Are you here already? He didn't respond, just sat on the bed.

Are you using a different shower gel? she asked suddenly. You smell different. I used a sample that came with the newspaper. He remembered how she used to pull off the sample packets of cosmetics in the Sunday newspaper supplement. It's a bit strong, she said, but Leandro felt he hadn't managed to assuage his wife's suspicions and he lied more. I rinsed off when I came home, I was sweaty from my walk.

He had showered after making love with Osembe, he had felt invaded by the scent of her body. He wouldn't do it again. Most days he just soaped up his crotch, he was put off by the idea of sharing the bathroom with all kinds of clients. To combat the smell of woman and strange perfumes that impregnated his skin, he walked quickly along the street, making himself sweat in a unwarranted race.

The unexpected good weather in February tempted Leandro into extending his walks. In the morning hours, when Benita's cleaning was most annoying, he went down and trolled the neighborhood. There was always frenetic activity. Delivery trucks, people shopping, nannies taking kids for walks in strollers loaded down with plastic bags. One morning Leandro had followed a petite young woman who looked like she was Latin American, her hair loose down her back and wearing a short denim skirt, all the way to Calle Teruel. She was pushing a baby carriage that couldn't be hers; she wasn't more than twenty years old, and phenomenally proportioned. She stopped leisurely in front of the windows of shoe shops and clothing stores, with the baby asleep. Leandro kept a prudent distance but accompanied her on her walk. When she turned to one side, he observed her lovely features. It was rare to find that delicateness in a neighborhood where vulgarity reigned, filled with coarse faces, leathery skins. Leandro appreciated the girl as a strange pearl, dropped there thanks to the generous capriciousness of beauty's allocation. Following her took him almost an hour. When she arrived at what seemed to be her door, she stopped and waited. Leandro, afraid of disturbing her, walked past. She didn't pay him much attention. She had vivacious black eyes that found Leandro invisible. She opened the glass door and disappeared inside the entryway.

Retirees sat on benches along the street, talking about soccer and politics with clichéd ideas that were almost always wrong, in Leandro's opinion. Their ideas were limited to what they'd heard on the radio. Some of them returned home with bags of groceries lifted high, as if they were doing exercise, and others strolled with a young grandchild by the hand or used a cane rather than give up their daily walk, their gaze lost in the distance, sometimes talking to themselves beneath their visors. Leandro made an effort to distance himself from that group of dying urban birds.

Leandro preferred to walk at a good clip. The main obstacles were vendors or the disabled elderly who leaned on the arms of Latin American caretakers. Sometimes he got as far as the wide sidewalks of Santa Engracia, where the neighborhood grew posher and more boring. There doormen controlled their dominions, their eyes following girls from the Catholic school nearby or shooting a hostile look at a passing Moroccan. Young Central Americans handed out advertising flyers at the entrance to the metro, the area sprinkled with pedestrians' lack of interest in their course offerings or neighborhood restaurants. The sound of traffic was constant, but Leandro was upset when he heard the grating sound of jackhammers, a welding workshop, and a tile saw. The closest park on Calle Tenerife was far and dirty with dog shit and trash and Leandro felt more comfortable in the hustle of people racing about than those who just sat and watched the morning go by.

Leandro walked toward the chalet, relaxing his pace so as not to arrive early. The door opens for him after he rings the bell. Mari Luz comes out to receive him, ah, it's you, come in, come on in. She leads him to the little receiving room. Excuse me for a second. She disappears and Leandro is left alone for a few minutes, sitting on the sofa like someone waiting for the dentist. When Mari Luz returns she says, well, I'll have the girls come through, okay?

No, no, is Valentina free? Leandro reserves Osembe's real name for himself. If not, I'll wait, he says with obvious command of the situation. But he isn't prepared for the response from the madam, who turns her made-up mask to one side before answering. Ah, didn't I tell you? Sorry, but Valentina doesn't work here anymore. What?

You heard me, the black girl doesn't work here anymore.

3

If someone is watching me from a distance, at this point they must be completely confused. When nothing I do makes sense to me, the most logical thing to think is that it must be even more inscrutable to someone observing from the outside.

This is what Lorenzo thinks as he attends the procession of the Ecuadorian saint Marianita de Jesús through the nearby streets of the Plaza de la Remonta. He barely knows anything about her, her tears of blood shed a hundred years earlier, her life of affliction and martyrdom to become, through suffering, sainted by God. For weeks now, after that strange face-off he'd had with Detective Baldasano, and after he had gotten over his fear of being arrested at any moment, Lorenzo has been convinced that someone is following him, spying on his calls, watching his every movement. This feeling, which at first made him feel panicky, only intrigues him now. It sometimes forces him into an exercise of identifying with his pursuer, trying to share his perspective. One Lorenzo separates from the other Lorenzo, as if he had to draw up a full report on his own activities and the result is only a confused jumble of actions without any particular connection. What is he doing? Where is he trying to go? What is he looking for? The game becomes fun when he himself doesn't even know why he is where he is. Daniela had said, let's go see the procession, my mother would like it if I sent her photos.

The members of Daniela's church aren't there. Neither is the pastor with the sweet voice and the nose so hooked that it looks like a padlock on his face. Daniela had bought a disposable camera, wrapped in yellow cardboard. Lorenzo takes a picture and turns the little wheel, advancing the film with a ratchet noise. Daniela is in the foreground and behind her is the saint's image raised aloft. Smile a little, he says, and she does, her mouth taking on the shape of a double-edged blade. Lorenzo looks around him for a moment. Yes, it is definitely hard to explain what he is doing there. There are few Spaniards. A couple of discreet men, one with gray hair and the other stocky, who accompany their Ecuadorian girlfriends. Before, when he saw one of those couples, he looked at the Spanish men with suspicion, a certain disdain even. Is that me now? he wonders.

Lorenzo spends long hours at his parents' house, at his mother's side. He knows she has only months to live and what at first was infrequent anguish and pain is now almost routine. Week after week, Aurora's hours of consciousness decrease. Her dying shows at the height of her cheekbones and in her emaciated mouth. As if her skeleton were gaining final authority inch by inch. He understands that she wants to hide the gravity of her condition from everyone; she never liked being the center of attention. She always accepted a supporting role beside her husband. What was important was his career, his peace of mind, his space. Kids, don't make too much noise, Papá is listening to music or preparing his class, she would say to Lorenzo and his friends. Let's go take a walk so your father can be alone for a little while, she would say at other times. Let your Papá read in peace, your father isn't feeling well lately—phrases Lorenzo remembered well. Later she also assumed a supporting role with regard to him, as her son. His education, his life, his fun were important to her, but she was never possessive or scheming. Now she made a great effort to keep her illness a personal struggle that didn't affect others. She seemed to be saying, relax, don't worry that I'm quietly dying little by little, go on with your things, don't change your plans for me.

Lorenzo liked to stand beside his mother's bed, organize her night table, where her glasses and some books were jumbled among the medicine boxes and the glass of water. What would his pursuer say? Here we see a son watching his mother die without a big display of pain, a son sorrowfully witnessing the ritual of letting go of the person who gave him life, unable to do anything to repay her.

It would be interesting to know what those eyes were thinking when they watched him make some ridiculous purchase at the supermarket. Some cans of sardines, eggs, beers, canned goods, the yogurts Sylvia liked. What would they think of a man sleeping alone for months now, left by his wife, who doesn't pull down the covers on her side, who just folds the corner of his bedspread and gets into the bed without touching the pillow that was hers, as if there were a glass barrier that kept him from taking complete possession of what was still a marriage bed in spite of the definitive absence of the other half? That inhospitable house that's like a cave when Sylvia's not there, and she's there increasingly less and less. On some days when she left the house, she was resplendent, as if she had become a mature, beautiful, independent woman. Other days she was the same old lazy girl, curled up like a cat on her pillow in the childish warmth of her room with some reddish, ardent pimple on her forehead or chin.

He related to her in the same vacillating way. Days of monosyllables and evasive responses, and then afternoons filled with jokes, sharing the kitchen table or watching a soccer game on TV and arguing because she defended, for example, the quick Argentinian winger he criticized for his lack of connection to the team and his futile feints. He was a father with a teenage daughter he knew almost nothing about, who would be the last in knowing what all her close friends, and maybe even her mother, surely knew. But he hadn't told her about his relationship with Daniela, either.

It was undoubtedly the most confusing chapter in his life up to that point. If they were dating, it was a very strange relationship. They walked separately down the street, they said good night at the door with a kiss on each cheek. The evenings they went out, they took long walks, Daniela strolling, almost dragging her feet. They would go in some café or a store where she'd try on shoes or a skirt, and then they'd leave without buying anything, either because of the price or her stubborn insistence that everything looked bad on her, I have fat legs, my feet are too small. Although sometimes a conversation would provoke her splendid smile, it was difficult to breach the distance, to bring down the invisible wall that separated them. One would have thought they were just friends if not for the languid expression Lorenzo adopted as he watched her leave and his sadness on the way home.

On weekends they spent hours together, sometimes with her friends. Then more time was spent looking at store windows or trying on a pair of pants or a shirt. She only let him treat her once in a while. They would troll through the bazaars, eat at cheap restaurants. On Sunday mornings, they went to her church and chatted with the other attendees while the kids ran between chairs. Afterward they organized the bags of food, like little ration sacks they handed out to those who came to pick them up, some with honorable expressions attached to accepting charity.

On other days, they walked alone through the paths of Retiro Park and she stopped to greet some Ecuadorian acquaintance who looked at Lorenzo as if he were judging a usurper. If he mentioned something about the cutting stares her fellow countrymen gave him, she only said, pay no mind, they're men.

It took me a long time to be able to tolerate those dominating looks from men, Daniela explained to him one day. You think I don't feel those eyes that grope you in front and in back? Making you feel like a dirty whore they have the right to enjoy. Men are always very aggressive.

Lorenzo felt forced to defend them. He said that violence wasn't always behind those looks; sometimes they can be admiring.

If a man wants to flatter you, she explained, he only has to gaze into your eyes, he doesn't have to linger on your breasts and hips and hound you. The same men that give you challenging looks when you're with me would rape me with their eyes if they found me alone.

Daniela's attitude, sensitive to any kind of sexual approach, in spite of the sensuality she exuded almost effortlessly, forced Lorenzo to apologize if his arm brushed hers or if their knees bumped under the table or if he touched her thigh when going to switch gears in the van. In the bazaar, when she tried on a necklace or some earrings, he would tell her, they look good on you, but when they parted he only dared to say, sleep well. In her way, Daniela's most affectionate gesture toward Lorenzo had been one afternoon, when coming through the door and walking toward him, she had shown him her cell phone and said, did you know I included you in the four numbers I can call for free?

Work wasn't much easier to define. Wilson had a small entourage of three or four Ecuadorians that he directed authoritatively during moves and pickups. Lorenzo had made a business card with his name and cell phone number beneath a succinct definition of the word *transport*. Often, though, his work was just taking Wilson to the airport and picking up a group of newly arrived Ecuadorians in the van. It was some kind of profitable collective taxi. Lorenzo drove around the terminal to avoid police surveillance and Wilson rang his cell phone as a signal when the passengers were ready. They dropped them off around the city and made sixty or seventy euros off the books. Wilson smiled at Lorenzo with his mismatched eyes and explained, when you come to a strange land, you always trust a fellow countryman.

Lorenzo would have liked to know if Detective Baldasano was aware of his activities and if they increased his suspicions or perhaps convinced him that Lorenzo should be taken off the list of suspects in Paco's murder. Seeing him exhausting himself over a few euros, working a full day for negligible pay, should surprise him. In case he had positioned someone to follow him around, Lorenzo made sure his days were very complicated, with no set hours or predictable routines, filled with patchy little jobs. It was surprising for someone who not long before had always held down stable jobs. If you are watching me, thought Lorenzo, welcome to the lowest rung of the labor ladder. He was amazed to see himself surrounded by Ecuadorians, with his shirt sweaty, working on sidewalks around the city.

Daniela sometimes took him to the Casa de Campo Park on Saturday afternoons. There they'd meet up with Wilson and her friends, buy something to drink in the makeshift stands, and snack on *humitas*, *arepas*, or *empanaditas* cooked in smoking oil. As the sun set, they'd sit and listen to the dance music that came out of some nearby car with the doors open. Wilson hadn't been in the country long, but he was already recognized by the entire community. Lorenzo was a sort of local partner for his entrepreneurial abilities, his aggressive need to make money. That's why I'm here, my friend, to rake it in, was all he would say.

There it wasn't uncommon to find someone had drank too much or had left the soccer game on the sandy field near the lake with a grudge. Sometimes rivalries were unleashed amid races that lifted clouds of dust. If someone got violent, the others held him back. But the alcohol took its toll. One of those afternoons, it was Wilson who was involved. Daniela and her friends, among them Wilson's cousin Nancy, pulled him out of a fight and took him home, stinking drunk, in the van. At the door, Lorenzo wanted to help them, but Wilson said he could get upstairs on his own. The next day, Daniela told Lorenzo that he had drank even more at home and he'd attacked them when they asked him to stop drinking. The girls all took shelter in Daniela's room, but they heard him destroying the furniture with punches and kicks until he collapsed. The next day, they were unyielding, even though he apologized a million times, and that very day he moved out.

Wilson then convinced Lorenzo to rent an apartment. Lorenzo would be the face that dealt with the owner; people don't want to rent to us, and they won't have any problem with you. They found an old apartment without an elevator on Calle Artistas. Lorenzo signed a contract with a trusting elderly woman whose legs were so swollen that she didn't go with him to look at the apartment. She just gave him the keys and waited in the entryway. In just a few days, Wilson had set himself up in the best room and rented out the rest of the apartment to five other Ecuadorians. Two of them were married, but with no kids. It was a perfect deal for him. He had free housing and he even made some money to split with Lorenzo. A deal is a deal and a partner is a partner, he said as he handed him the first payment.

By the second week, Wilson had put a mattress in a walk-in closet and was renting it out by the night. Sometimes he closed a deal with one of the new arrivals they picked up at the airport. It's only fifteen euros, brother, he announced, until you find something better. Lorenzo had to sort out a call from the owner, who had been informed by a neighbor that the apartment was a nest of spics, as she herself put it. No, no, Lorenzo reassured her, they're doing some work for me, but as soon as they're done they'll leave and me and my family will move in.

And three days before the month ended, Lorenzo reassured her again with a punctual rent payment accompanied by a small tray of cakes, a detail Wilson had suggested. I have two sons, the woman explained to him, one is a soldier in San Fernando and the other works in construction, in Valencia, but they go months without coming to see me, they were the ones who convinced me to rent. And you are doing the right thing, ma'am, you enjoy the rent money, Lorenzo told her, and don't let the neighbors breed bad blood.

Wilson was enterprising. He had convinced Lorenzo to become a moneylender to three families. We are their guardian angels, not opportunists, he explained. They fronted them the money needed to rent an apartment and pay the deposit, which was always excessive because of the landlords' distrust, and Wilson took care of collecting the installments with their mandatory interest. You think the banks are better than us? They wouldn't even let these poor people wipe their feet on the welcome mat. The amount he had lent out was up to three thousand euros. Are they gonna pay? asked Lorenzo.

Do you know any poor person who doesn't pay their debts? They know we're doing them a good deed, helping others, Wilson convinced him.

Lorenzo could never have imagined when he picked Wilson up at the airport, silent, nostalgic, out of place, that he would become a daily presence in Lorenzo's life. But he admired Wilson's ability to remake himself, to find yet another formula for multiplying a euro. You are my lucky charm, Wilson would say to him. To thrive here, you need a local partner.

Daniela was the only one who didn't seem seduced by Wilson. He drinks too much. Even though after his violent outburst he'd promised to quit alcohol, she still avoided him. Lorenzo didn't talk to her about his stable partnership with Wilson; he knew that she didn't trust him. Drink emboldens, Daniela would say. I suffered through that with my papá. A man who drinks is a weak man.

Wilson justified himself to Lorenzo. That Indian girl is very uptight. What's the harm in a few drinks after work? Lorenzo tried to get more information out of him about Daniela, but Wilson was evasive. Over there I didn't know her very well, either. Or he got more mysterious, saying, I think that Indian girl is a saint. You may be right, conceded Lorenzo. Looking into Daniela's eyes is quite an experience. It's as if they wash you clean. Wilson burst out laughing.

Lorenzo feels like someone hovering over a well-protected treasure, without daring to touch it for fear it might vanish. He remains cautiously close to Daniela's fortress, searching for the way to make his decisive siege. He doesn't know if someone is observing his shy advances or if Daniela herself mocks his attentions. They could be seen as just the innocent maneuverings of a man in love, or at least that's how he sees it when he views himself from a distance.

4

The game you dream of is always better than the actual game. The stands of old Highbury Stadium embrace the fans' constant chanting. It is some sort of pagan praying maintained in a murmur and only broken during the difficult plays. Then it rises to a roar. When they get to the grounds, he's surprised at how close the surrounding houses are, as if the stadium were an intrinsic part of the neighborhood. Dragon always told them, if you want to quiet the rival supporters, hold on to the ball. The first ten minutes, don't even worry about scoring, but keep passing the ball, one- or two-touch, right and left, in fifteen minutes the crowd will be deflated and already whistling at their own players. Trust me, hold on to the ball, the crowd is like a petty, demanding wife who's only loyal when you're playing well.

They lose because of two goals on free kicks at the very start of the game. Even though Ariel's team put on the pressure, no space opened up. The other team sent quick passes to a striker who received them in the goal area, brought the ball down to the ground, and guarded it while he waited for a foul or the arrival of a player from the midfield.

Dragon said that soccer was a game of memory where all the situations had been seen before, but there were infinite ways to resolve them. As kids he would tell them, if you're bored on the bus, imagine what you would do in the face of a particular play, maybe one day it will save the game.

Ariel had become more integrated with the team. He dared to whistle to ask for the ball, and he noticed that during difficult plays his teammates started looking for him. His left leg was the only guarantee of escaping the defenders, a can opener against the fullbacks. That was soccer, ten against ten until someone breaks the dead heat. You lack concentration, the coach told them at halftime. We lack a system, he thought. There was no practiced model to use against the rival team. Their attack was structured like a chaotic lottery.

Coach Requero immersed himself in his notebooks. He had the Amisco system, which studied a particular player with eight cameras, then broke down the movements, analyzed the highs and lows of his success, and with that information the coach seemed satisfied, as if the discoverer of the theory of relativity were, in comparison with him, uninformed.

The routine: travel, concentration, game, press conference, obsessive opinions based on the most recent results, the invocation of abstract concepts like streaks, luck, crisis. In Spain they talked so much about soccer that it was impossible to emerge unscathed from the rain of words. Seventy thousand pairs of eyes fell on him when he received the ball. And there was frustration in every pair when the imagined play failed to match up to the real one.

He came back from Buenos Aires convinced he was going to break up with Sylvia. But her appearance at the airport changed everything. That long walk to the parking lot, keeping their distance, made all his desires to hold her come rushing back. Sylvia's proximity transformed everything. There was no loneliness or pressure, no anguish or anxiety, only the shadow of a full life. He was living a fake existence, in a city where he had no roots, and Sylvia had shown up and given it meaning. The waiting, the distance, the return trip, the training schedule, the hasty shower in the mornings, even his nap now had importance. Because he had someone to talk to, someone to laugh with, someone to feel close to.

Sylvia took possession of the house, of that empty, soulless house that Ariel wanted to leave as soon as possible. I have a five-year contract, they might be the best years of my life, and I don't want to spend them in this unfriendly house, pushing open these ugly doors in ugly doorframes with ugly handles, with these narrow stairs that lead to an ugly bedroom where I've never felt at home.

Now the corners of the anonymous house hide Sylvia's smile, a gesture of her hands. Even the throw pillows piled up on one end of the sofa held her presence long after she'd gone.

Ariel decided to buy an apartment in the real world, the world he had no right to be in. At least he could look at it from his terrace, like he had envied that rooftop in Belgrano Walter now enjoyed. Just like he loved the time spent with Sylvia, people-watching from a bar or from his car. It was a break from that obsessive gaze others fixed on him.

If you could see the people in the stadium, Sylvia told him one day, when you get the ball they lift their butts up a little off their seats, like they're levitating. It's like they're moving with you on the field, whether it's an old man with a hacking cough or a guy who smokes cigars or a teenager eating sunflower seeds. And they all fall back into their seats when you lose the ball, as if it were rehearsed, you ruined their fantasy. It makes sense when they curse you up and down, of course . . .

Sylvia was watching it all for the first time. She asked questions, she wanted to know stuff, she noticed the over-the-top details that everyone else saw as normal. She repeated his answer in a television interview, noticed his constant gesture of running his hand over his sock as if it were falling down, the way he pressed his upper lip when he didn't like a play, or gazed toward the sky to avoid the stands. There were times when Ariel didn't really indulge her curiosity, responding only in monosyllables; then she felt instantly belittled. The demands on Ariel never let up. This will consume me and when there's nothing left of me that surprises her, she'll leave me behind forever, thought Ariel one day.

She recognized his moods instantly. Sometimes Ariel felt overwhelmed. He appreciated Sylvia's youthful intensity, but he needed breaks. She defined his absence as fucking soccer. Sometimes she said to him, if they took soccer away from you, you'd be empty.

Sylvia maintained the modesty of their first days together, which was attractive to Ariel. Nothing was easy and what happened the day before wasn't something that could be taken for granted the next time they got together. One afternoon, because theirs was an afternoon love, she might let Ariel caress the entire length of her body with his tongue, but the next day she might ask him to turn off the light before taking off her bra and *bombachas*, as she liked to say, having picked up the Argentinian word for panties. One day her hands were barriers and on another they were curious and demanding. Then, she would say things to Ariel that made him laugh unexpectedly: a dick is a pretty absurd thing; it looks like a turkey's wattle, don't you think? Did you notice that our feet make love at their own pace, not coordinating with the rest of our bodies?

Sylvia was capable of stopping him mid-caress and saying suddenly, I know you want me to suck you off now, but I don't feel like it, okay? Or if he threw himself onto her, she'd stop him, you already ran me over once, all right. Other times she'd interrupt their long kiss before going up to his room, I think we don't know how to love each other any other way, I'm not in the mood to fuck today.

Perhaps they were adolescent games, but Ariel preferred to take part in them. He didn't want to be in charge. He was afraid, sometimes, of turning Sylvia into too sexual a woman, of raising the bar of his desire too high. He remembered a teammate from his Buenos Aires team who had broken up with his lifelong girlfriend and had confessed to Ariel, somewhere between irritated and ironic, I don't know what I'm complaining about, I was the one who turned her into a whore, when I met her she was just a little girl, and I molded her into someone who needed to have a ready cock nearby all the time, and she went looking for it elsewhere when I wasn't around. "Dragonfly" Arias's girlfriend cheated on him, the others said, but Ariel never forgot his complaint.

Every afternoon they went through the security check into the housing complex and Sylvia asked him for those tacky sunglasses he always wore, to protect herself from the guard's gaze. They're horrible, but they pay me thirty thousand euros a year to wear them once in a while, Ariel said as he put them back in the glove compartment. Sylvia laughed. And when are they going to tattoo some brand name on your forehead, while they're at it . . .

Emilia, of course, had let a few hints drop to make him aware that she knew he wasn't alone at night. Today I left meat for two in the fridge. A few days ago, Sylvia had spent the night at his house. They were awoken by the sunrise. She was terrified at how her father would react. They dressed quickly. Ariel tried to calm her down. He avoided running into Emilia, who had already started to bustle about the kitchen. Ariel kept her occupied while Sylvia went to the garage unseen. On the way home, Sylvia cursed. I don't know what I'm going to say to my father. The traffic jam on the highway made everything worse. It turned them into something they didn't want to be. Her into a fraught teenager talking to her father on the phone, telling him that she had fallen asleep at a girlfriend's house. And him into an inconvenienced, shifty lover.

A little while later, he dropped her on a corner near her high school and Ariel felt ridiculous again. He read the newspaper in a café, surrounded by construction workers. He confirmed the greasiness of *porras*, the fried dough he had seen people eating for breakfast so many times in Madrid. One of the articles mentioned him: "Ariel Burano has seized up and he's nothing like the unstoppable young man who played in San Lorenzo. There is no trace of that player with frenetic jinks who knew how to mark the pace of the game. The Argentinian is now a sloppy player flustered when he has the ball at his feet." The worst thing was he was convinced everyone had read the article and agreed with it.

This Wednesday you guys are gonna win, right? said the man with sunken eyes and yellow teeth working behind the bar. Throw us a bone, come on. Ariel smiled and nodded, to reassure him. In Madrid older men had that punishing air to them, they never gave a compliment without a threat hidden behind it. This year we'll do a double or you'll all be sent to dig ditches. There was no bar that didn't have a photo of the team and a pile of sports newspapers getting stale along with the day's tapas. Soccer spread like hope or a curse. People gave it such an exaggerated importance that Ariel suspected they didn't truly care.

They lose the game. The referee marks the end with a cruel triple whistle. Ariel thinks of the guy in the café. They haven't been eliminated, but the next matchup makes it complicated, an Italian team or a Spanish rival that knows how to play you where it hurts. They hadn't had time to do more than look at London through the bus window, the roundabouts, the huge airport.

All cities look the same to him. In Heathrow Ariel watches a family sleeping on an airport bench, their flight delayed. They look like Pakistanis. An obese woman eats chocolate bonbons. As they board, the pilot greets them with, you lost, huh? From the looks on your faces. I don't really follow football, honestly. The flight attendants seem tired. They return to Madrid after midnight, doomed to train the next day like unruly schoolboys. Amid whispers, the vice president invites a few players to have one last drink at a topless bar near Colón. Ariel isn't in the mood for anything, but the laughter of some teammate or other and the naked dancers arouse him enough to buy time in a private room with a Brazilian with a tattoo of an eagle on her back. After a short dance she gives him quick fellatio. Ariel lets himself do it; anything that can separate him from Sylvia is welcome. He needs to focus on his work, get everything else out of his head. I don't want to see her anymore, I shouldn't see her anymore.

5

Sylvia opens the door to her apartment. Her key ring is an *A* encircled in metal. A gift from Mai, she explains to Dani. I don't know if my father's here. It's three in the afternoon and from the kitchen echoes the TV news theme song. Sylvia peeks into the kitchen and finds her father sitting down. Hello, Papá, this is Dani. Come in, come in. Lorenzo stands up and extends his hand. Dani shakes it, somewhat uncomfortable. Then he sits down. There's plenty of food, says Lorenzo. Sylvia takes the plates and glasses out of the dishwasher. It is a tacit agreement she and her father have, to use the dishwasher as a cabinet, and when it's completely empty, they put the dirty dishes from the sink in there and turn it on again.

Water? asks Sylvia as she fills the pitcher from the tap. Okay, he says. The television shows the charred corpses of the passengers on a Russian plane brought down by Chechen terrorists. Fuck, how horrible. Lorenzo watches Dani, who has started eating. You guys in the same class? No, I'm in the grade above. He's in Mai's class, explains Sylvia.

Dani accepts Lorenzo's curious looks. But he's not completely sure how to interpret them. Two days earlier, Lorenzo was coming out of the shower when Sylvia called him on the phone. She hadn't slept at home. I fell asleep at Mai's, she lied, and then I didn't want to call you so late. When she came back from school at lunchtime, Lorenzo meet her. He found her with messy hair, a forced smile, and sleepy body language. Lorenzo didn't exert his authority, avoided getting irritated. Come on, let's eat.

You were with a boy and you spent the night with him, obviously, said Lorenzo before she decided to speak. At his house? He lives alone? His parents weren't there, lied Sylvia. Can I meet him? I have a right . . . Papá . . . I'm not going to interrogate him or anything like that, just see his face, I just want to meet him face-to-face.

She thought he would forget all about it in the following days. Ariel was playing a game in London and Sylvia took that time to spend the afternoons at home, go to bed early, study. But her father insisted. When are you going to bring him over? Sylvia wanted to get out of it, but Lorenzo was serious. Look, Sylvia, I am not going to let you be out all night with someone I don't know. I imagine you are taking precautions and not doing anything stupid, but I'll feel better about it if I've met him. Sylvia imagined, with amusement, her father's surprise if she introduced him to Ariel. Would he ask him for an autograph? Would he tell him he needs to help the defense more? Or would he be furious at him?

I'm not going to start laying some embarrassing father shit on him, Sylvia, I just want to meet him. Is that so weird? Would you rather I just tell you to be home at a certain time and that's it? Come on, I just want to have a look at him, I'm sure he's a great kid, knowing your good taste.

Sylvia smiled. Worried about my daughter? No, no, what I'm worried about is that you're not going to make it to Champions' League final. She was still imagining the scene with her father. My father wants to meet you, she would tell Ariel, you're lucky, he roots for your team.

Which is why, when at lunchtime recess that morning she was walking with Mai toward their usual corner at the back of the schoolyard, against the cement wall, and Dani joined them to chat, Sylvia forced the situation. Do you guys wanna come over for lunch today?

Mai shook her head, I can't. In exchange for Vienna I promised my mother I'd go to the dentist, and the appointment is this afternoon. After six years, it's about time, right? If he threatens to put braces on me, I swear I'll strangle him. In her class there were three boys who wore braces and Mai jokingly called them the metalworkers. Dani tells them that his dentist is a woman and when she leans over to fill his cavities he looks down her shirt. One day she got me right in the eye with the silver crucifix she wears around her neck, almost took my eye out. Divine punishment, said Mai.

And you? You coming? Sylvia looked into Dani's eyes. He let a few seconds pass. Okay, he said. Mai opened her eyes super-wide, to comic effect. The look was just for Sylvia, who stifled her laughter.

On the way to her house, Sylvia felt she was being cruel to Dani. He was walking with a spring in his step while talking a blue streak about music and Web sites. He had a half-empty backpack hanging over one shoulder and both hands in his pockets. If my father starts to ask you ridiculous questions, said Sylvia with a smile, just play along, you know how they can be. Deep down she was enjoying this game.

Sylvia interrupts her father's attempts to strike up a conversation. When he mentions something about international terrorism, she says, what an entertaining topic for the lunch table. When he asks about school, she responds, after spending the morning in that hellhole you don't expect us to want to chat about it, do you? When he questions Dani about his future schooling, Papá, let him eat in peace. Lorenzo is in a rush and finally has to leave. A pleasure to meet you, he says, and extends his hand to Dani with surprising virility. He kisses Sylvia on each cheek.

I think he thought I was your boyfriend, says Dani when they are left alone. Did you see the way he shook my hand? Like he was thinking, I trust you with my daughter, the girl I love most in this world.

The weatherman talks about a drop in temperature. The weather depresses me, says Sylvia, laughing. Don't you find it depressing? The way the world is, we don't really need to worry about whether it'll be sunny or windy tomorrow, but if we'll be alive, right? Sylvia flips through channels. The African baby recently adopted by a famous Hollywood couple is going to have a wax figure in the London museum. Can you think of anything more depressing than a wax museum? asks Dani. It's like a morgue of people who are alive. She turns off the TV.

In Sylvia's room, Dani has a hard time getting comfortable. He looks over CD covers while Sylvia puts one on. I have to burn some discs for you, a friend of mine went to Valencia this summer, to the Campus Party technology fair, and he spent the week downloading movies and music. This year I might go with him, even though I'm not really into all those computer nerds. You and Mai could come, now that your father's met me. They both laugh.

Actually it's my fault, confesses Sylvia, I promised my father that one day I'd introduce him to the guy I'm seeing and he thought that you were him. Sylvia brings her desk chair over so he can sit down.

I hope he liked me. I think so. Imagine if now he makes a big scene, like I forbid you to see that punk again . . . I don't think so, says Sylvia. He probably wouldn't have liked the other guy as much . . . Is he that bad? It's not that. He's older. Older than your father? No, come on. So? But he's twenty . . . Mother-fucker, fucking cradle robber . . . I'm just kidding. Dani smiled.

Soon they change the topic. And how's school going? she asks Dani. I don't know, I'm so out of it. I hope I don't fuck up too bad. I have to pass somehow. Dani swivels the chair. The stupidest fuckup ever is getting left back . . . spending another year there.

Sylvia's cell rings. It's Ariel. I'll call you in a little while, okay? she says. I'm in the middle of something. She hangs up and for a little while they don't say anything.

I guess that's every girl's dream, says Dani, going out with someone your father wouldn't like.

Sylvia laughs. For a second, she's about to tell Dani everything, tell him the truth about Ariel. But then it seems like un-
necessary torture. Sylvia looks at Dani and feels the strangeness
in his expression; she knows he has fallen in love with her. And
that makes Sylvia feel good and bad at the same time. Powerful
and fragile.

I must have bad luck, confesses Dani, fathers like me. Except
my own, of course. Last year for my birthday he gave me tickets for the Formula 1, all excited, a fantastic plan according to
him, a weekend in Barcelona. Bah, I got pissed off, and I told
him he could shove them up his ass, that I wasn't going to waste
a weekend on that stupid shit. Boy, did he lose it then . . . One
day you have to come to my house, I have good music. I don't
know if your father will like me, replies Sylvia. Sure, he'll start
hitting on you. Soon as he sees some tits . . .

And he doesn't finish his sentence. Sylvia shrank into her
T-shirt. She's still smiling. Suddenly, Dani takes a step toward
her and puts a hand on her shoulder. His hand is shaking. Her
skin glows at the height of her collarbone.

Sylvia offers Dani a beer. She goes to the kitchen to get it.
She calls Ariel. She explains that she's with her father and can't
talk. From her room, Dani listens to the distant murmur of Sylvia talking on the phone. She makes a date with Ariel for an
hour later, on the corner of her street.

When she comes back from the kitchen, Sylvia is light-years
away from the conversation with Dani. She steals a sip of his
beer and he drinks quickly. As if he wants to vanish after his
failed advance. I could fall in love with him, Sylvia thinks,
maybe in another life.

Ariel brought Sylvia a gift. A T-shirt that says LONDON inside a bull's eye. I think you have an idealized image of me, she

jokes. No way is this going to fit, I'm fat. You're not fat, don't be silly. Try it on.

He drives. She takes off her sweatshirt, is wearing only her bra for a moment, and then puts on the T-shirt Ariel bought in the airport store. It fits Sylvia's body like a glove. It's perfect, he says. If someone can manage to talk to me for five minutes with this T-shirt on and not look at my boobs, they deserve to win a free trip for two to the Caribbean.

You're such an idiot . . .

Behind the Gran Vía there is a little café where they fix him a maté. She tries it again and burns her tongue for the millionth time. *Está recaliente*, she says, it's super-hot, in her fake Argentinian slang. Honestly, the shirt is a bit much. I told you, she says. It's too tight around your *lolas*. Sylvia likes that word for tits.

While they're there, Sylvia doesn't know where to put her arms. She crosses them, puts them around her neck, hugs herself with her hands on her shoulders, unable to find a position she feels comfortable in. He smiles. Sylvia tells him that her father was insisting she introduce him to her boyfriend. Today I brought a friend home for lunch and he thought he was my boyfriend, you can't imagine how ridiculous it was. And what friend is that? Are you jealous? she asks, amused. I don't know, should I be?

Sylvia smiles. He does seem jealous. What am I going to do? she says, my father wants to meet the boy that is keeping me out so late at night. I thought about sitting him in front of the TV for the next game and saying that's him, number ten.

And what do you think your father would say? asks Ariel.

He'd start jumping up and down, he'd put on the team scarf and do the wave. I don't know, I guess he'd take you to the nearest police station. Ariel goes silent. Then he brings his face up to Sylvia's and kisses her by the ear, delicately brushing aside her hair. Don't be afraid, he whispers. I can't help it, she says, backing away a little. Every time we're apart for a couple of days I think I'm never going to see you again, that you're never going to call. Yeah, says Ariel, but he doesn't say anything more.

You don't have to feel tied to me, you know, when you get tired, just tell me and no hard feelings, says Sylvia, stringing her sentences together. I'll go back to the real world and that's it. And I'll stop charbroiling my tongue every fucking time you make me try that shit, she says, moving away from the metal maté straw with a comic expression.

So this isn't the real world to you? he asks.

Being with you, well, honestly, I don't know. It's definitely not the normal world. But I like it, you know. It's more like a dream.

Did I tell you that tomorrow I'm signing for the apartment? They'll give me the keys.

Really? That fast? You already got all the money together?

You're gonna laugh. Last week the president paid me the bonuses he owed me. He opened a drawer and told me, here, and he handed me an envelope filled with five-hundred-euro bills. My bonuses are outside of my contract, all under the table. And then he starts chatting with me. He asked me, how are things in Argentina? I have a partner who wants us to start buying up land in Patagonia, down there in penguin land where everything is really cheap.

Sylvia shakes her head. They'll fill it up with housing developments, like here.

That night she wants to go home early. At ten they are parked in front of her door. They kiss. Sylvia's cell phone rings. It's her mother. Sylvia answers. Ariel is silent. Then he looks out the window. When she hangs up, Sylvia says that was my mother, my father called to tell her that he met my boyfriend and he's a very nice boy.

This kid is starting to get under my skin, jokes Ariel. I might have to go wait for him at the school door and beat his head in.

Sylvia thinks about her father, who for once thinks he has more privileged information than Pilar. My God, she says to Ariel, my parents are crazy, now they're happy I have a boyfriend.

A great kid, by the way, he says sarcastically. Good-looking, polite, nice eyes. He wears glasses, corrects Sylvia. Ah, he's an intellectual to boot. Probably wears flannel shirts buttoned all the way up to the top . . .

They kiss quickly. Suddenly it seems that Ariel is in a rush, it makes him uncomfortable to be in the car idling for so long. A minute before a gang of kids looked at the model and made loud comments. She realizes he's uncomfortable and says, I'm leaving, I'm leaving. See you tomorrow? To celebrate your new place? Ariel nods vaguely.

Sylvia takes the elevator up to her apartment. She opens the door. She's expecting to find her father there, but he's not back yet. The place is dark and Sylvia doesn't turn on the light on the way to her room. She takes off her sweatshirt and looks at herself in the mirror with the London T-shirt on. A bit much, she remembers. She sighs and lets all her hair fall in front of her face. It seems absurd to get into bed and set the alarm for school. Her teenage bed seems ridiculous, and the schoolgirl's desk with her computer. Dani's beer can is still there. Suddenly she is filled with a fear of the empty house, as if it might collapse around her.

She opens a book and reads in bed. She answers a message from Mai that she got hours ago. It said: "wot happened w/ Dani? He is way into U, he'd eat ur boogers, no complaints." Sylvia had received it when Ariel was with her. She didn't say anything to him, just a friend of mine, she's crazy.

To Sylvia, Dani and Ariel are two people she can't even imagine comparing. There is no competition between them, although she noticed a slight pinch of jealousy in both of them at the vague presence of the other. Maybe when Ariel dumps me I'll hook up with Dani, thinks Sylvia suddenly, not understanding how she comes up with these calculating reflections. Her idea surprises her. It would be out of spite, obviously.

You are cold, girl, you need to loosen up, Mai tells her sometimes. But in her relationship with Ariel, she'd rather not let herself get completely caught up. She'd rather swim near the edge of the pool, like a child who's just learned the stroke.

Something Dani told her that afternoon comes into her mind, when he was parodying his father. He is a totally predictable guy, the only intelligent thing I ever heard him say in my life is every year the winters are shorter. How stupid. And yet that phrase now comes into Sylvia's head. Every year the winters are shorter.

Her father comes home, noisily. When he sees the light beneath Sylvia's door, he knocks. He finds her lying in bed, with the book in her hands. Sylvia leans back. She had gotten into bed with the London T-shirt on. He's a very nice kid, he says. Come on, Papá, I'm tired. They talk a bit more. Lorenzo notices the T-shirt when the sheets slide toward Sylvia's lap. Isn't that a little tight? I'm just wearing it around the house, she answers.

Her father leaves. Sylvia places her hand on her stomach, stroking around her belly button. When Ariel takes off her clothes, she likes to feel the strength of his embrace. It's one of the few moments when she feels beautiful.

6

The taxi arrives on time. The intercom buzzer rings and Leandro rushes to answer. He is finishing the knot on his burgundy tie. It's here, he shouts. From Aurora's bedroom comes the wheelchair. She is wearing a dress and some flats. On top she wears a shawl gathered in her lap. Lorenzo pushes his mother, who had combed her ash-gray hair in front of the mirror. Aurora's smile as she advances along the hallway moves Leandro. Only the forced climb down the two flights of stairs carrying the wheelchair taints the delicacy of the moment. I'll take the front wheels, you grab hold tight to the back, manages Lorenzo. Shit, goddamn it, hold on.

The taxi, outfitted for wheelchairs, has its platform ready at sidewalk height. Leandro places his wife's wheelchair on it and the mechanism lifts her up and places her safely in the back of the minivan. I feel like a crate of fruit, comments Aurora while she's being lifted up. Lorenzo says good-bye to his parents through the window, as the driver closes the sliding door and runs back to the steering wheel. Have a good time. Are you sure you don't mind waiting for us? his father asks him. No, no,

I'm going to watch TV. Lorenzo points upward. I'll wait for you to come back so I can help you with the chair. That morning his father had called, what a hassle, I don't know how to do it, your mother wants to go out. Lorenzo had calmed him down, no problem, it'll be good for her to do something.

You look lovely, Mamá, Lorenzo had told her when he got to the house. His mother had just smiled. Leandro is tense. The chair makes everything harder and, as always, he feels gripped by his uselessness, his inability to deal with difficulties. Aurora's expression turns pleasant when she sees the activity on the street. To the Auditorio? Are you going to a concert? asks the friendly taxi driver. A fine rain leaves streaks on the windows. To top it all off, it's raining, thinks Leandro.

When is Joaquín's concert? Aurora had asked him that morning in the middle of his reading her an article about the private security guard strike. Eh? We had tickets, right? Yes, yes, but it doesn't matter. Did it already happen? For a moment, the expression on her face clouds over. Aurora makes a real effort not to lose track of dates in spite of the fact that for her every day is the same.

It's today, this evening, he said.

She was decided. Of course, let's go. And that was the beginning of Leandro's anxiety about organizing it. Calling his son, finding a handicapped-accessible taxi, planning the movements and the schedule. He knew Aurora wasn't going to let him miss it, but he was surprised by her decision to go. I feel like getting out.

She chose her dress, his clothes, even the tie. After her nap, it seemed that the usually quiet house was filled with furious activity. Lorenzo would arrive at six-thirty to help them with everything. Did you call the taxi? Yes, yes, it'll be here at seven.

In front of the Auditorio, people were already gathering half an hour before the concert. Leandro holds the tickets. When they open the doors, he pushes the chair until he finds an usher. I'm sorry, but when I bought the tickets my wife wasn't yet handicapped. Don't worry, we'll try to work it out. The employee checks with a coworker and returns to seat them on one side. Will you be okay here? Leandro looks up at the stage. Would it be possible to be on the other side? Of course. Because of the pianist's hands, you know? The usher nods and crosses in front of the first row to the opposite end. When Leandro sits down, he turns his head toward Aurora and asks, okay? She reassures him with a nod.

In recent years, since Leandro retired, they'd gone to more concerts and they had seen the seats filled with a wider range of people than in years past. There are so many young people studying music these days, she said happily. Leandro reserved his opinion. Music had become an almost ubiquitous student hobby. But there was a huge leap from hobby to studying music in a disciplined way toward a future. Sometimes he joked in conversations with friends, music is like the gym or judo, that's all, but when a kid shows real aptitude they discourage him, they don't want to ruin his future as an engineer or a businessman.

He greets a few familiar faces, then he prepares his concentration for the recital. Aurora turns around to look behind her every once in a while, happy to find herself out in public after so many weeks of immobility. Leandro was worried. Would she feel okay? In the last week, she had occasionally asked him for some painkillers, but she wasn't able to explain where the pains were.

He had been afraid to leave her alone for the first time. At night he slept more lightly, in case she called him from the room. The doctor had visited, put on a patient expression, and recommended they keep up the massages, they're always enjoyable, right?

Leandro had still not gotten over his surprise at hearing the madam at the chalet tell him, with an almost offensive sarcasm, Valentina doesn't work here anymore. It had taken him a few minutes to react. The woman offered him a drink, but he didn't want anything. Well, you already know the other girls, none of them will disappoint you. Or do you only like chocolate? Leandro wasn't ready for her jokes. He scratched his head for a second and dared to ask, is something wrong with Valentina? What happened?

She wasn't right here, black girls don't know how to be in places like this. I'm not saying it to be racist, it's just the plain truth.

After several questions that only got half answered, Leandro managed to find out what happened. It seems that the day before, it must have been five in the morning, one of her last clients of the night had gotten into bed with Osembe. When the guy left, he couldn't find his car. A Mercedes, to top it all off, said Mari Luz. It wasn't parked where he left it and when he stuck his hand in his pocket he couldn't find the keys, either, so it wasn't too hard to connect the dots. He came back to the chalet, and made quite a scene, that the black girl must have taken his keys, and I don't know what else. We had to get serious with him. Leandro thought it was her way of saying they called in the guy who watched over the place, the same one he had seen that afternoon at the garage gate.

Of course Valentina had already disappeared. I'm sure she took advantage of the guy being distracted and threw someone the keys through the window, down to the street, piece of cake. The madam continued explaining undramatically. The man got aggressive and I had to tell him, come on, if you want to go to the police, go ahead and quit bluffing. The only good thing about this business is that nobody wants to get the police involved. We all have too much to hide, right? What was that about the stone? Let he who is without sin throw the first one, right? So the man left, I felt bad for him, really, because I know the black girl robbed him, with some accomplice, who knows. The thing is she won't be back here, and it's for the best because that's one less problem for you. A thief around here is the worst thing you could have.

Leandro tried to get Mari Luz to give him a contact number, an address, something to find Osembe. Even if I had some phone number, I wouldn't give it to you, she told him. Take my advice, don't go looking for trouble, you've got plenty as it is. If you want to have some fun, you got plenty to choose from here, there are new girls you haven't even met. Sit down, have a drink. Why get obsessed with one when the world is full of pretty girls?

When Leandro began to insist, you must have something, a phone number, a last name, I don't think it's so hard, the madam ended his visit. Look, forget about it, that girl's no good, getting rid of her was the best thing that could have happened to us. And as she spoke she pushed him toward the door, as if Leandro were an annoying Sunday visitor. On the street, a woman passed by, staring at him. Leandro thought he could see her wagging her head, as if she were judging him.

Why did he want to see Osembe again? What was it about her? Was there something about her he hadn't yet got his fill of ? He knew very little about her. He remembered that she had once mentioned she lived in Móstoles, near Coimbra Park, but to Leandro that sounded like a foreign land, a new city.

On a long walk with his friend Almendros, he dared to ask, don't you have a son in Móstoles? No, in Leganés, he said, but it's pretty much the same thing, why? It's my son, lied Leandro, he's thinking about selling his apartment and moving someplace cheaper. He should think about it, he should really think about it. Yeah, I'll tell him.

The loudspeaker announces that the concert is about to begin and Leandro looks at the program in his hand. Two parts divided into a first half of pieces by Granados, his waltzes, and a second with Schumann's "Kreisleriana" and Schubert's "Musical Moments." Joaquín hadn't played for more than a year because of chronic tendinitis in his left wrist. It had been almost ten years since they'd seen him in person. The last time was after a performance of the symphonic orchestra where Joaquín played as the soloist in Mozart's Concerto no. 25. Leandro had envied his naturalness, the polish of his execution, although he had thought, I prefer Brendel. Then he felt somewhat ashamed of his judgment. They invited him to the cocktail party afterward and Joaquín was friendly with him, as always. He asked for Leandro's phone number again, as he had done the last four times they saw each other, but he never called. He played in Madrid on two more occasions, but Leandro didn't go to the concerts.

Joaquín comes out on stage and applause accompanies his smiling wave and vigorous walk toward the instrument. He pushes back the tails of his coat and sits in front of the keyboard. There is the deepest silence, which he allows to build, broken only by the crunch of the wood or a woman's cough. Aurora looks at Leandro and smiles to see him concentrating. He plays the armrest of the chair and brushes Aurora's hand through her shawl. Joaquín places his fingers on the keys and the music rises up from his delicate left hand. He has his back to them, but Leandro can make out his profile. His hair is white and thick as ever. His straight back is a powerful presence that extends in perfect continuation of the piano. His feet are together, leaning forward on the tips of shiny shoes with gray heels.

When the music envelops the blond wood auditorium, Aurora closes her eyes. Leandro remembers the teenage friend he shared his life with on the streets, in their open houses. He doesn't really know why he remembers the afternoon when they shut themselves in, sitting beside his father's radio to listen to Horowitz play the "Funérailles" by Liszt and then trying to imitate the octaves with great swings of their arms. And on that same program "Patética" by Tchaikovsky was played. They turned up the volume the way they always did when they were alone in the house. The music echoed loudly and could be heard from the street. By then they had both decided to become professional musicians and at barely fifteen they devoted themselves to it with enthusiasm and snobbery. Joaquín's eyes that afternoon were flooded with tears. It is God playing, he said grandiloquently.

That could be where the great distance between them lay. Leandro was incapable of such emotional exhibitionism. His friend spoke without fear in the midst of some sort of torrent, he let himself get carried away by what he was listening to, what he was playing. He had no problem with shouting, no, no, when a performer played a piece differently than how he felt it should be approached. Years before, their teacher, Don Alonso, would repeat to them, afternoon after afternoon, the same correction, no, no, emotion is not enough, intensity isn't enough, it has to go hand in hand with precision, precision. Forget about poetry, this is sweat and science. And yet when he noticed an excessively cold and technical way of playing he would repeat to them in German the now classic quote by Beethoven that introduces "Missa Solemnis." *Von Herzen, möge es wieder zu Herzen gehen,* let that which flows from the heart reach your soul.

Joaquín's mistakes were huge mistakes, but hopeful ones. That was how the teacher defined them when someone asked. Leandro began to feel that a breach was opening up between them, the same abyss between someone who plays like the angels and someone who correctly interprets a score. The professors they studied with in the conservatory barely corrected Leandro. But they gave Joaquín torrential explanations to win him over with their critiques. They knew it was a challenge to guide such spectacular, extraordinary talent. Many times Leandro surprised himself by thinking, how unfair, I'm the one who struggled to play, the underdog, the one who fought not to give it up, and the success will go to him, as if it broke with some poetic sense of justice. For Joaquín life was easy, satisfying, comfortable. Soon Leandro got a job as a copyist and handed over his meager wages to his mother. Joaquín wasn't forced to do that.

He invited Leandro over to listen to Bach records, paid his way into concerts, bought him drinks in bars, included him in plans and outings that Leandro couldn't afford himself. Joaquín was the only one who allowed himself the brashness of getting up in the middle of a concert and walking out along the row of seated audience members as he muttered, I can stand it, but Beethoven can't. Then came Paris and the distance. Aurora's appearance that filled his orphaned free time. The slow shift of his friend becoming someone foreign. I'm more French now than the French, Joaquín would say to him when he returned to Madrid and mocked the pious provincialism of his hometown. I chose Paris, those born there don't have to work at it, but I do, I want to stop being what I was before I went there.

When his parents died, Joaquín's visits became more infrequent. He would ask Aurora, behind Leandro's back, if they needed anything, once his international success was already confirmed. In Austria they gave him the Hans von Bülow medal in the mid-sixties. Leandro never felt jealous, he was pleased to have shared in the rise of someone gifted, he was pleased by Joaquín's success, and he never thought it took anything away from him. Leandro defended Joaquín if in a conversation among musicians someone committed the typical injustice of discounting him, usually for being local. But he stopped writing him, stopped keeping him up-to-date on his life, and even though the countless ties that bound them wouldn't fade until many years later, in the sixties the gulf between them was so great that Leandro began to hide the fact that he knew him when his name came up. Often, like now, if he went to one of Joaquín's concerts it was at Aurora's insistence. He didn't have time to call you, you have to be the one to make the first step, don't mistake his lack of contact for a lack of affection. But the day came when Leandro realized he was just another audience member watching that man up on stage.

At one time, their hands had been placed together on the old Pleyel piano. The same piano Leandro bought from Joaquín's father to bring home when no one played it anymore. It pleases me for you to inherit it, the old man had told him. Joaquín's hands were still capable of moving through a score and extracting its pleasure for an auditorium full of people, they still had the constitution and the strength, the fingertips reinforced with glue and Band-Aids. Leandro's hands had grown tame, in order to be the correct working instrument for an academy teacher. For years Leandro thought his friend believed he'd been wounded by the sting of failure, by the unfairness of art, and he struggled to show him that wasn't the case. Until one day he discovered his friend wasn't thinking about him, wasn't noticing him, wasn't suffering over him. What's more, he might have even forgotten that Leandro was a pianist, too. He didn't grasp, of course, that they shared the same profession.

At the intermission, Aurora wants a drink of water and Leandro goes toward the bar with her. The usher asks if everything is okay and in the vestibule a boy comes out to greet them. It is Luis, his former student. His last student. Hello. The boy greets them both, not letting his gaze linger on Aurora's chair. Leandro had always been irritated by Luis's perfect image. He dressed tastefully, his manners were always correct, and he had a deliberate way of speaking. A couple of times, Leandro had warned him that music had to be accepted as something superior, not like an escort, but more like a goddess to be worshipped. But the boy always took refuge in his confessed lack of ambition. I already know I won't go far, but I want to play as well as I can. He was an applied student who progressed at his own pace. Leandro knew he wanted to finish college and not to make music his profession, so he wasn't surprised when he dropped the classes. Are you enjoying the concert? the young man asks. Yes, yes, of course, replies Leandro. Very much, says Aurora. Okay, I'll see you later, says Luis before heading off.

Leandro hands Aurora the water and he quickly drinks a glass of wine. The sharp taste does him good, perks him up. The tone of surrounding conversations had risen, bit by bit, and now echoes in the hallway. Leandro wonders if Joaquín still has the peculiar habit of washing his hands with warm water during the intermission and lying down with his shoes off on the hard floor with his legs up on the seat of a chair at a perfect right angle. His wife would fix him a tea, which he would drink barely two sips of before returning to the stage. Aurora holds out the almost empty glass. Do you want more? No, no. Leandro quickly finishes the wine.

When both of their heads are at the same height, back in their places again, Aurora asks him, do you like Schumann, too? Who doesn't? What he is about to play now is masterful, but Schumann suffered a lot, from a very young age, a tortured soul as they'd say now. She nods as if she wished the class would never end. Do you remember when we were dating, we saw that German movie about his life, *Träumerei*?

The second half of the concert is fast, goes by quickly. Joaquín plays the "Kreisleriana" barely using the pedal, combining the most unbridled, violent movements with odd ones, which he plays excruciatingly slowly. If someone coughs during one of them, they get a recriminating look. Soon drops of sweat start to slide down his forehead. For the first time, he uses a nearby towel. When he finishes, the audience, on their feet, demand another piece and he sits and plays solemnly, letting himself get tangled in the more disturbing harmonies of Fantasy and Fugue for Organ in G minor. The audience really gets into the somber atmosphere, letting themselves be transported. Serious things are always more valued, thinks Leandro, who finds the approach predictable. Yet everyone smiles as if it were a nod to levity when Joaquín chooses to close the performance with a Jerome Kern song whose swing borders on jazzy improvisation. The shift in mood leads to a boisterous send-off in which Joaquín offers several versions of the grateful nod of the head. Their applause has a metallic resonance. Leandro looks at Aurora, who also smiles as she claps with barely any strength.

When the audience begins to file out, Leandro lifts the brake on Aurora's chair. Are you going to say anything to him? she asks. No, no, Lorenzo is waiting for us at home. He doesn't care either way, let's go, you can't leave without going backstage and just saying hi. Leandro changes his expression and, somewhat nervous, looks around. When he finds the usher he asks, is this the way backstage? I don't know if you can, go over to that door. She points to an entrance flanked by two or three employees. Leandro doesn't feel like going through the filter, giving explanations. Luis comes over to them when the seats are almost empty. I wanted to ask you something, it seems like this semester isn't going to be too difficult and I'm thinking about taking lessons again and I don't know if you . . .

Leandro looks at the boy, who stops in the middle of his explanation. I don't know if I . . . Luis lifts his hands in a gesture similar to pleading, it could be whenever it's convenient for you, I don't want to do that many hours, I'd rather finish my degree . . . Leandro looks at the boy. There is a blond girl waiting for him. She is pretty, she belongs to a new generation of girls, like his granddaughter, who have nothing in common with the serene women of his adolescent years, the silent land of bowed heads. The girl, as she waits, runs a finger over the fabric on the back of a seat. Okay, call me and we'll see. The boy beams and before leaving he bends over Aurora's chair to say warmly, a pleasure to see you again. Leandro watches him go back over to the girl and put his arm around her hips. Aurora always knew how to win over Leandro's few students who came to the house. She'd open the door for them, lead them to the room, offer them something to drink, and, often, before saying good-bye again at the door, once class was over, she would say confidentially, he's not as much of an ogre as he seems. The money would come in handy, was the only thing Leandro said to Aurora as he watched them head off.

The woman guarding the entrance to the dressing rooms asks for his name when Leandro requests permission to say hi to Joaquín. She is a little while in returning and when she does she gestures for him to enter. Leandro goes to push the wheelchair, but the woman says, the chair, too? There are stairs . . . You go ahead, says Aurora quickly. Leandro wants to protest, but Aurora insists. I can wait here, right? she asks the woman. If he isn't too long . . .

Leandro goes down the stairs to a lit hallway. He can hear voices and laughter. Leandro isn't in any hurry to reach the dressing room. When he sees him, Joaquín leaves the group circled around him and walks over to Leandro. Well, what a surprise, I didn't have time to call you, I just got in yesterday and I can never find your number. He gives Leandro a big hug, engulfing him in his arms. He has splashed water on his thick, snow-white hair and taken off his jacket. He turns toward his wife, twenty years younger, thin, with very pale skin, blue eyes, you remember Leandro, Jacqueline? She greets him with her fragile hand extended, of course, of course.

Joaquín is cordial. He asks about Aurora and Leandro explains that she's not in very good health. He doesn't want to tell him that she is waiting upstairs, stuck in a wheelchair. He finds Jacqueline's aged, with a certain strain she didn't have before, as if she is holding on tight to her beauty as it slips away. She wasn't prepared to stop being a radiant statue, and the surgical machinations on her face were disastrous. Leandro doesn't want to prolong his visit. Joaquín holds him by the elbow and takes part in another conversation while he turns toward Leandro and unleashes a barrage of rhetorical questions, your son doing well? And your granddaughter? How are you handling getting old, I can't stand it, Madrid is unrecognizable, when they finish all the construction it's going to look like some other city, they'll have to rebuild it again, Jacqueline wants us to buy a house in Majorca now, she fell in love with the island, how long has it been since we've seen each other? You're so lucky to be retired, I can't . . .

When Leandro insists on saying good-bye, Joaquín brings his face to his friend's ear. I'm going to be in Madrid for three days giving a master class for the foundation of I don't know which bank, why don't you call me and we can have a coffee. Jacqueline, give our cell phone number to Leandro, I want to talk to you about something, call me. Jacqueline hands him a business card with a number written on the back. I have the mornings free, is the last thing Joaquín tells him. Before Leandro leaves the dressing room, he has already turned around to merge effusively with the elbow of some other acquaintance. He liked to touch elbows, avoid having hands touch his. He protected those hands from any contact, using them only to gesture, raising them to the height of his eyes, as if he were conceding them the same relevance as his lively and intelligent clear gaze.

In the taxi on the way home, Leandro is curious about why exactly Joaquín wanted to see him. Maybe it was just another formality. Aurora seems tired but happy. He's the same as ever, was all she had said about Joaquín. And it was true. Joaquín even still wore those shirts with his initials sewn above the pocket. Leandro had always considered that a detail somewhat inappropriate to an elegant person, no matter how necessary it might be when traveling so much and not trusting dry cleaners. He knew Joaquín, ever since he was young, liked to brag that the initials of his full name, Joaquín Satrústegui Bausán, JSB, were the same as Johann Sebastian Bach's. He's the only person I wouldn't mind switching shirts with, he had said to Leandro years earlier, the first time he had made a comment about the monogrammed shirts. That was when he still traveled to Spain with his first wife, a German journalist he divorced when he met Jacqueline. Without really understanding why, Leandro suddenly thought of the different initials with which Bach ended all his compositions. SDG. It wasn't a personal stamp, but rather a fit of Christian modesty. Joaquín, on the other hand, didn't share that virtue. It was a Latin phrase, *Soli Deo Gloria*, something like Glory Only to God. Unlike so many who dream of having all the glory for themselves. Leandro erases the cruel thought before getting out of the taxi and ringing the intercom for Lorenzo. We're here.

7

Lorenzo looks at his friends, who feel scrutinized. He does so brazenly, searching out their eyes. Challenging them. None of the four meet his gaze. Lorenzo thought of it right when he arrived. If I stare at them, they won't dare stare at Daniela. They are six in the dining room of Óscar's house. The extendible table is covered by a white tablecloth striped with colors. On the wall are three engravings with wooden frames. They used to live in a tiny apartment near the Retiro. Taking advantage of the market increases, they managed to sell it at a good price and move into a recently built building in Ventas. They have a communal garden area and pool. Fifteen years ago, we bought the apartment for twelve million and we sold it for sixty. How is that possible? asks Daniela. Ana stops to clarify that they are talking about pesetas and then tells her about the factors that cause sales to increase. Nobody rents here, the banks love people with debts, explains Lalo, more cynically. That's how they control us.

In the middle of the week, Óscar had called Lorenzo to invite him over for dinner. So you can see the new apartment now that it's finished. Lorenzo didn't think too long before saying, can I bring someone? They joked for a while about women, but Lorenzo didn't give him any details about Daniela. He only said, I'm like a teenager in love. Daniela, on the other hand, was reluctant to go. They're your friends, they're going to think it's strange that you're with someone like me. Hey, come on, don't invent stupid stories, they're great people, you'll see. On the way to Óscar's house, Lorenzo told her they had met years ago, at college, and that Óscar and his wife, Ana, didn't have any children even though they'd been together for years. Lalo is my oldest friend, we went to elementary school together, he knows my parents. You'll see, we are nothing alike. Marta, his wife, is a child psychologist and they have a nine-year-old son.

When Ana opened the door and saw Lorenzo with Daniela, she smiled radiantly. He introduced them. Welcome, said Ana, and then she seemed embarrassed when Lorenzo explained that Daniela had already been living in Spain for almost three years. Lorenzo wanted to make clear he wasn't going to tolerate any special treatment of Daniela. When Marta vaguely asked Daniela during dinner, how are things going, he felt forced to interrupt, don't expect one of those tragic stories you hear on the news, Daniela shares an apartment with some friends and has a great job. I can't complain, she added. What do you do? asked Lalo. I take care of an eight-month-old boy, and before Marta or Lalo could add anything, Lorenzo was already explaining that Daniela worked in the apartment above his.

Lorenzo's friends went to great lengths to be tactful. They didn't hound Daniela with questions and even less so when they saw that Lorenzo was on the defensive. They joked about the food and about a couple of news items that were perfect for an inane conversation. In sporadic questions, someone asked Daniela about her family, her hometown, and if she missed her country. To Lorenzo's satisfaction, his friends seemed tenser than Daniela. When Lalo asked her if she was planning on visiting her country soon, Lorenzo felt the need to explain, she can't, she still doesn't have papers.

It's a strange feeling, described Daniela, like being in a cage with the doors open, and I don't dare leave. I'd love to see my mamá, but I don't know if I'd be able to come back in.

Well, it seems like there's going to be a legalization, said Óscar. You think so? corrected Ana, I think people want them to keep working without papers, they're cheaper that way.

Lorenzo keeps his gaze fixed on his friends. Daniela isn't inhibited. After a somewhat shy start, she dares to ask Marta about her job as a child psychologist. She had worn some stretch jeans that were tight around her powerful thighs. Lorenzo places his hand delicately on the right one. She lowers her hand and caresses his, but doesn't linger. She puts hers back on the table and he pulls away. She is wearing an orange T-shirt glued to her body that stands out vibrantly amid the more discreet decoration. Daniela doesn't taste the wine even though Lalo keeps insisting, it's a wonderful Priorato. No, no, I don't drink alcohol. Lorenzo, on the other hand, refills his glass.

Óscar and Ana seem thrilled with their new house. They have more space. Lorenzo tells them that Sylvia has a boyfriend, the other day she brought him by for lunch. He seems like a really nice kid. But, of course, imagine the scene. It's incredible, explains Marta in a professional tone, now all sexual behaviors have accelerated, kids have to put up with tremendous pressure, we have cases of twelve-year-old girls and boys with an addiction to pornography, and then there's the media, which forces them to feel sexually active. Their lives have been sped up. It's a social thing. What a shame, comments Daniela in a very soft voice. No one contradicts her.

I called Pilar to tell her the news. It bugged her to find out from me something so personal to Sylvia. Well, then she shouldn't have abandoned you guys, interrupts Daniela. She spit out the sentence with a contained aggressiveness that surprises everyone. It is followed by a thick silence. Lorenzo tells them about Pilar. She's fine, well, you know, she loves Sara-gossa. Do you have more family here? asks Óscar in an attempt to redirect the conversation toward Daniela. Yes, a sister, she came over before me, but we hardly see each other, she lives near Castellón. I don't think highly of the life she leads.

No one digs any deeper; they all retract when they sense how harsh Daniela's judgments are. The conversation turns away from her and Lorenzo announces that they'll be leaving early. He goes to the bathroom. He is a bit tipsy and his hemorrhoids have been bothering him for days. He can't take sitting so long. He sensed the awkwardness of the situation, as if Daniela had to pass an exam. Angry, he pees outside of the bowl, staining everything around it. Then he's embarrassed and tries to clean it up with wads of toilet paper that he scrubs along the floor before leaving it sticky and dirty.

They stand up and start their good-byes, the pleased-to-meet-yous, the when-will-we-see-you-agains, the I'll-call-yous. In the elevator, which still smells new, Lorenzo and Daniela are silent until she says, they didn't like me.

You don't like being liked, replies Lorenzo with a smile. She thinks it over.

Lorenzo resists taking her home when they get in the van. It's still early, you must know someplace where we can have a drink. Daniela gives in, she tells him there's salsa every Saturday night at a place her friends go to. Lorenzo starts the car and heads to-ward the neighborhood. It's a place on Calle Fundadores. The traffic is dense at that hour, the Saturday night traffic jam. He has to drive around the area several times before finding a park-ing spot on the sidewalk.

The place is called Seseribó. In Quito there is a salsa place with the same name, Daniela explains. Seseribó is a beautiful god that no one can touch—whoever touches him dies. It seems an Indian fell in love with him and dared to touch him. He died that very instant. They made a drum with the Indian's skin and from it they say music was born. Lorenzo nods while he walks, what a lovely legend.

At the door are two muscular mulattos watching over the street as if it were enemy territory. There are some men nearby hanging around the entrance; it's not clear whether they just came out of the place or if they weren't let in. Lorenzo and Daniela get to the door and the men step aside. He has to pay; she gets in free. In the doorway, one of the guys pats Lorenzo down quickly, from the armpits to the ankles. I don't know if you're going to like it, but this is where we come sometimes, says Daniela while they go down toward the magma of music, smoke, and bodies in motion.

There is barely any space, but Lorenzo and Daniela manage to make their way toward the bar on one side. The music is deafening. Vocals rise over a drum machine, a cry of love betrayed. The chorus is repetitive. The couples dance, sometimes without their hands touching, but with their thighs, knees, the folds of their bodies in contact. The men put one hand at the base of the women's spines to pull their bodies closer together. Is it like this in Ecuador? And she nods above the noise.

Daniela drinks a bottled juice in a tall glass with ice. Lorenzo orders a beer. Domestic? The waiter asks him. Lorenzo shrugs. Club Verde, Club Café, or Brahma. Club Verde, he says finally. He isn't the only Spaniard there, as he had thought when he first came in. He is comforted to see a few dancing and a couple near the main bar. Lorenzo tries to talk to Daniela, and to make himself understood he has to bring his mouth so close to her ear that it brushes her hoop earrings. He doesn't say anything important, just something like, this place is a sauna. Then he begins to follow the rhythm of the nonstop music. For him it's all just salsa, although he listens to Daniela explain with each song, this is a *bachata*, a *cumbia*, a *vallenato*, or just a merengue. It doesn't make sense to be there and not dance, and Lorenzo leads Daniela to the dance floor.

He is surprised that she doesn't object. In fact, she quickly lets the movement of her shoulders get in time with the movement of her hips and knees and allows the music to take hold of her. She lifts her arms in the air and spins around. Lorenzo feels stiff compared to her and tries to wave his arms and wag his hips. He can't get past feeling ridiculous until he grabs hold of Daniela's waist. She runs her hand through her hair and keeps the rhythm.

There is a presenter with a microphone on the other side of the dance floor. He cheers on the dancers, let yourselves go, multiplying the *s*'s in the word until it is coiled like a snake around a tree branch. Most of the women wear tight clothes and most of the men unbuttoned shirts.

Lorenzo can now feel Daniela's breasts against his body. Her thighs mark the sway of both of their bodies. Lorenzo wants to kiss Daniela, but their faces aren't close. Then he has to put his energy into hiding his uncomfortable erection, shrinking his groin back when she brushes it with her hips. Stopping in the middle of the swaying would be like shouting in a place of silent worship. He is pleased Daniela isn't rejecting his proximity or advances, although Lorenzo's hands have been fixed on her hips for quite a while.

He remembers the last time he danced was at the wedding of some friends, with Pilar. And it was more a mockery of dancing itself. She didn't like to dance and neither did he, though they listened to music often. His friend Paco used to say that dancing was the orgy of the poor, but he said it with the same classist disdain as when he stated that making love was for the working class and he preferred getting sucked off. Fucking is work; getting blown, a luxury. Living with a woman is a sentence; seducing her, a hobby. Having a cell phone is great if you're the boss and a kick in the balls if you're an employee. Our point of gravity isn't in our brains, it's in our cocks. Those were typical Paco phrases, his way of speaking. Categorical and sarcastic. He used to say, kick a stray dog and he'll come back for more. And Lorenzo always secretly felt that particular phrase referred to him, to their friendship.

But why is he thinking about him now? Or about Pilar? Yes, he feels they would both scorn this ridiculous image of him, they would mock his sweat and his dance partner. Stray dogs think a kick is a caress, that's what Paco would say about his relationship with Daniela. Like the voice of a cynical, provocative subconscious whispering, why don't you dare tell her the truth, that you just want to fuck her. Maybe neither of them, Paco with his warm disdain and Pilar with her cold demands, would be able to understand that I feel happy right now.

Let's leave, says Daniela. Lorenzo pulls away from her and lets her lead him to the exit. The stairs are filled with people, too. They're in the mood to party, she says. They leave the trancelike atmosphere behind as the cold of the street hits their sweaty bodies. They don't say anything and head toward the van.

I had a really good time, it's been a while since I went dancing, Daniela says when they get to her door. Lorenzo stops her before she gets out, holding her gently by the wrist. Let me come up and sleep with you. Daniela lifts her face toward him, without smiling. The expression in her eyes isn't serious, but rather indulgent. Not tonight. She hops out of the van and before closing the door asks, will I see you tomorrow? If you want to, he replies. Daniela nods, I do, and runs to the door. From inside she waves good-bye to Lorenzo. Not tonight, he thinks, the words resounding like just a postponement of inevitable victory.

He drives home slowly. It's not hard to find a parking spot. The streets of his neighborhood are asleep. There are barely any open after-hours bars or shady spots with cheap neon. The next morning, he would go to Mass and settle down next to Daniela, listening to them sing, but he would be thinking about her movements as they danced, the lust unleashed from her hips.

At home he peeks into Sylvia's room and sees her sleeping facedown, hugging the pillow, her clothes a mess. Lately he finds her so adult, too grown-up for her age. That makes him sad. He wishes he could protect her forever, but she is headed far away, where he won't be able to follow. In bed he makes a valiant attempt to masturbate, but he can't, and after fifteen minutes he gives up on his half-erect cock, red from the furious friction, and sleeps with his mouth dry and a dense smell of cigarette smoke in his hair and on his face and hands.

8

Ariel hears Sylvia paying the pizza delivery guy. The kid glances around behind her back and, seeing the apartment empty, asks innocently, are you a squatter or just allergic to furniture? Sylvia laughs. He is Colombian. A little bit of both, she answers. Sylvia reappears in the living room and Ariel asks her, what did he say? She tells him. She brings over the cans of beer in a plastic bag. Your dinner, Mr. Apartment Owner. And she gives him the change. They even gave us napkins, how thoughtful. They sat on the floor, the wood creaking at their every movement. The house speaks, she said when she first came in.

Ariel had had the keys for a week, but he hadn't come to see the apartment with Sylvia until today. From the terrace, they watched a violet sunset behind the buildings. Spectacular sky, he said. This morning it rained, she explained, and when it rains the twilights in Madrid are clean. Ariel held her by the waist and kissed her on the lips. I thought you were never going to bring me here, Sylvia said, gesturing around the apartment. This week we barely saw each other. Sylvia dropped down into one corner of the terrace. She looked out onto the street. That was when he suggested ordering a pizza and having dinner right there.

Ariel was slow to bring her to the apartment on purpose. Wait until they decorate it, they recommended someone who did the places of several guys on the team, he told her a few days ago. Typical, you buy an apartment and you have it decorated by some snobby bitch who specializes in soccer players' houses. But Ariel didn't want Sylvia to think of his buying the apartment as a commitment between them. He knew it was unfair, but it was one way to avoid misunderstandings.

Last weekend he was glad to be playing out of town, to travel to Valencia. He scored the tying goal against the local team and that gave them the push they needed to win the game in the last few minutes. Ariel didn't celebrate the goal by chewing on a lock of hair, and he didn't find a message from Sylvia on his cell phone when the match was over. They gave them the night off in the city and he went out with his teammates. They ate paella in the private room of a restaurant on the beach and then they were taken to a well-known nightclub. There they sat in a private booth that looked out over the full dance floor, but where no one could bother them. The owner of the place offered them girls, but Amílcar warned his closest buddies, be careful, they record everything here. If you want whores, take them to the hotel with you.

In spite of the warnings, ten minutes later the private room was filled with dissonant laughter. The girls divided up into groups. They are really nice, said the owner, making it clear that they weren't professionals. Ariel talked to one who said her name was Mamen and after a very brief conversation about nothing she let drop, you know what? I'm having an awesome time. Her only worry seemed to be maintaining her blond curl behind her ear and showing off her excessive, uniform tan. I thought Argentinians were more talkative, she said at some point. He smiled. Only with our analysts. When you come from a small country, you must flip over how superpassionate we are about soccer here, right? Ariel felt himself shiver. Amílcar rescued him with a trip to the bathroom. There the right fullback was finishing taking a piss. How's yours? he asked. Too stupid, answered Ariel. Stupid girls turn me on, you're not into them?

Look, for me to fuck one of these sluts I'd have to be incredibly drunk, said Amílcar. Well, your wife is lovely, answered Ariel. That's what you need to do. Find a decent girl who keeps you on a short leash. Now with the money we make you're always gonna have one flitting around, but it's a waste of time. I've been playing fifteen years, if I didn't have the life I've had I'd be in jail somewhere, or retired.

When he went back to the private room, Ariel was glad the girl was talking to some other teammate. Some of them had gone downstairs to dance reggaetón. He sat next to Amílcar and they made sarcastic cracks about their teammates. One of them had been caught by his wife in bed with the nanny. She threw him out of the house.

The next day, they went back by train, most of them dozing, hung over. At the station's exit was a group of people waiting to ask for autographs. It took them almost half an hour to get onto the bus. On the way to the stadium, Ariel looked at the line on a Sunday morning in front of the Prado. I've been in Madrid six months and I still haven't visited the museum, he said to himself. He decided to do it that same week.

He spent the evening at home. Husky stopped by. They watched the last game of the day on television. Husky put on the radio while they watched it on mute. I used to work on the radio, rebroadcasting games. But with this voice, shit, people called in to complain all the time, get rid of that guy who lost his voice. I still think I could have been successful, the Tom Waits of sports newscasting, but the plebs like a commentator to sing out the goals with a trill. I say the plebs because my boss at the station always called the listeners that, the guy used to say to us, now pass me another call from the plebs, or, the plebs are gonna love this bit, we owe it to the plebs, we can't let the plebs down, the plebs want entertainment.

After the Argentinian league game, Ariel took Husky into the city. It made you all nostalgic, Husky said, seeing him so quiet, you shouldn't watch games from your country. The truth is sometimes I wonder what the hell I'm doing here. Money, man, making a lot of money, isn't that enough? More money than you could even imagine when you were a *pibito* in Río de la Plata. Ariel is amused by the ludicrous Argentinian accent Husky puts on.

Turn, turn down this street, wait till you see. Ariel obeyed and drove alongside a sidewalk filled with North African women in lingerie offering themselves up. Go slower, I can't get a good look at them, said Husky. Incredible, right? Some of the women approached the car or gestured at them; the more daring ones went out to meet them and stood in front of the headlights. Stop, stop, shouted Husky, that one is gorgeous. No way, you're shitting me. Dude, they'll give us a quick blowjob for twenty euros. Ariel started to think that he wasn't kidding around.

Most of the girls wore impossibly high heels that clacked against the asphalt. Your disdain for hookers can only mean one thing, said Husky when they had already left the area, that you're in love. What are you talking about, said Ariel evasively. You're in a strange moment of a man's life when his heart has more say than his cock, I don't think it's ever happened to me. How is it? Is it nice? Ariel smiled at Husky's jokes. You fucking idiot, shut up for once.

On the way home, Ariel remembered that it had also been a Sunday, driving alone through the city, when he ran over Sylvia.

He convinced himself he'd be able to resist calling Sylvia for a few days, letting their relationship cool off until she realized herself that it was impossible. She's strong, he told himself, she'll understand.

On Monday Arturo Caspe called to drag him to a dinner, they're giving out awards from some magazine, they need famous people. They sat him at a table with a successful writer and a television host who was trying to seduce a young model. The girl smiled, amused, and shot "save me" looks at Ariel. He played the role of shy and silent. He presented a prize to a tall swimmer whom he enjoyed chatting with for a while afterward. When the dinner was over, he went out with Caspe and his group, mostly actors and television people. They went into a bar behind Callao and met up with the young model there again. They were leaning against the bar. She was nice and smoked incessantly. Her name was Reyes. Ariel took it up a notch. The girl knew Buenos Aires and had friends there. Ariel asked her if she wanted to go somewhere quieter, just you and me. She smiled, exhaling cigarette smoke and told him, you're not going to believe this, but I have a boyfriend I really like and I don't want to go around cheating on him, not even with guys like you, with really cute beauty marks like that. Ariel accepted defeat, they joked around for a minute, and then she left him alone to ponder his failure with a drink before saying good-bye to Caspe's group. He was in a bad mood, embarrassed to have been turned down. It was an appropriate response to his clumsiness and inelegance. Ariel thought about his inability to reach any other kind of girl besides nocturnal predators. Sylvia might have been the only normal girl he'd come in contact with since he arrived in Madrid.

On Wednesday they played a Champions' League game. And even though it was in Madrid, the coach chose to have them spend the night before in a hotel. It was the first game of the qualifying rounds and the German team had a lot of experience in the competition. On Monday he didn't call Sylvia, or on Tuesday. On Wednesday she sent him a message, "good luck tonight." What she didn't say was more telling than what she did, as was usually the case. "Thanks, I've been really busy, I'll call you," he replied.

Ariel played badly. It was nearly impossible for him to break through the German defenders. They played behind the ball, leaving very little space to work between the lines, convinced that a scoreless tie was an excellent result for an away game. A dry cold had settled over the field, I wouldn't be surprised if it snowed, said a veteran when their bus arrived at the stadium. They took Ariel out when there were still twenty minutes left and the stadium whistled as he trotted to the touchline. Good luck, he whispered to the player replacing him. But he didn't have any. The Germans packed their goal area, allowing them to counter with a fast attacker, who overwhelmed the only center back left in a defensive position and scored a goal before Ariel's team had time to react.

Ariel got a hard blow to the knee near the end of the game. The next day he barely practiced. He lay down on a gurney and the top masseur on the team smeared the affected area with magic ointments. He rubbed him with hard hands. Ariel had always been treated by the masseur's assistants up until then, even though Amílcar always told him, don't let any of the young guys touch you, the old man is a wizard.

He talked a lot, but it was relaxing to listen to him. He had stories from every period. He had been with the club for almost thirty years, he was an institution. In his youth he studied with a

Galician masseur who made his own concoctions of herbs, oils, and roots. He still used some of them. Life treating you well? he asked Ariel suddenly. That's the most important thing, the game doesn't work if life's not working. Are you happy here? Have you adapted well? Does it hurt when I press here? He didn't seem to be expecting answers to his questions. You have good ankles, that's important, forwards' ankles take a lot of abuse. Have you ever calculated, for example, the number of kicks in the ankles you can get in a ten-year career? About twenty thousand. Now imagine you got them all at once, twenty thousand kicks in the ankles. A lot of trampoline work, that's what you have to do, but the man is scared you'll get injured jumping and the press would have a field day. Do you have a girl? Are you with a Spanish girl?

Bah, I don't know, evaded Ariel. There is somebody but we're giving it a rest, we're taking it slow.

Women are trouble. But you need someone who loves you, who can talk to you, help you bear the loneliness. It's strange, but when you have sixty thousand people watching you every evening, it's really easy to feel alone, ignored. Shit, it's like poison. You have to be strong. Fuck, I've heard some stories here on this gurney, let me tell you. I've seen kids grow up and become men here and lose their way, too, there are plenty who lose their way and some of them from good stock. Those boos and whistles you got yesterday, they hurt, they cause damage, too, I can tell you that. Don't be afraid to admit it, that'd fuck anybody up, but that's the law. You gotta keep your head held high, defiantly, don't let it get you down now.

Yeah, it fucking hurts, yeah.

Look, this soccer stuff is like riding a train. You got a great seat by the window, all comfy, watching the landscape go by and you never get bored. Until you get to the station, they take you off, and put somebody else in your seat. It all goes real quick. Have you been to the bullfights yet? You have to go see the bulls. You can learn a lot about soccer there. It's just the same. We've had a number of Argentinians here. I don't remember their names, I'm not good with names. They ask me, what was so-and-so like? And I don't remember. Because I do my work here, but I don't deal with soccer players, I deal with people.

Ariel left with his knee loosened up by the massage. He felt consoled, wrapped in the torrent of words. It had been a while since anyone had talked to him for such a long time, in that curt Spanish tone. He called Sylvia from the car, but she didn't answer. It was during school. I'm sure she's mad. If I left Spain right now, he thought, all I would have is the memory of her. Sylvia sitting on her side of the car, driving back into the city some night. That tired, clean smile.

He ate at Amílcar's house. He found the conversation in that filleted Portuguese-accented Spanish sweet, with the strong *r*'s and *j*'s taken out. He told himself that Amílcar had been lucky to find Fernanda and he forced them to tell him how they met. He had called her insistently after getting her number from a friend, but she was resistant. I invited her out to dinner, to lunch, to the movies, to concerts, but she never wanted to come. I was about to throw in the towel, explained Amílcar. Until one day I called her and I said, listen, take my number down and let's just do it this way, I'm never going to call you again, but when you feel like it you can call me. I don't care if it's tomorrow, next month, next year, or thirty years from now, I swear I'll be waiting. It sounded nice, said Fernanda, interrupting him. I should have waited thirty years to see if it was true. Unfortunately, I called him a week later. A week. Can you believe it? I was going nuts, he admitted. She smiled flirtatiously. He tricked me, Fernanda said in her defense, like you all do, putting on your best face. He showed me his good side and then, boy, what it takes to find it again. Sometimes you even think you're with a different person, that they pulled the old switcheroo.

That night, alone at home, amid music and movies, he couldn't concentrate. Ariel knew he would call Sylvia. He did it even though it was late and she answered with a sleepy voice. Tomorrow I'm going to the Prado. I have school, she answered. Damn. What's up, you turned into an intellectual since I saw you last? No, I haven't seen you in a while and I need to look at some art. The things you say always come out so pretty, she said without smiling.

Leaving practice the next day, he confessed to Osorio that he was going to the Prado. Where? You Argentinians are some big flaming faggots. Ariel laughed as he got into the car.

Ariel strolled aimlessly through the rooms of the museum. He spent a long time studying *The Garden of Earthly Delights*, by Bosch, at the end of the main corridor. Then he approached a school group to listen to the docent. The "faithful likeness" was the epitome of the portrait in that period. Most of the great painters worked on salary for their lords and had to make portraits of the nobility and the ladies of the court with their best technique. But Velázquez went beyond that to give free rein to his incredible talent. For example, look at this portrait of the jester Pablo de Valladolid. He led the children to a nearby painting, Ariel following a few steps behind. Spanish art, in all its aspects, heard Ariel, stands out for its ability to depict the disabled, the crazy, the eccentric. The representation of a country based on its darkest, most disastrous side is a deeply Spanish invention.

In the Goya room, Ariel finally saw the originals of paintings he had seen so many times in reproduction. *Saturn Devours His Son*, *Fight with Cudgels*, and *Dog Buried in Sand*. Then he discovered a painting called *Witches' Coven* and he spent a long time looking at it, as if it were a *Guernica* painted more than a hundred years earlier. He doesn't know why, but it's similar to the way he sometimes sees the stands, it reminds him of the crowd. The group of students surround him again, accompanied by the guide's explanations, and now we arrive at the most accurate perspective on our country, nourished on Velázquez and El Greco, at the hands of the Aragonese painter Francisco de Goya.

The students began to lose interest. A group of them noticed Ariel and encircled him with their notebooks open. There were students with pimples, others obese, some with their smiles and faces deformed by growth spurts. What are you doing here? Don't you have practice today? The teacher approached them and got them to disperse efficiently, but without clout. That's enough, can't you see this is a private place? When are you going to learn to respect people? I'm sorry. Ariel thanked him with a nod of the head. It's understandable, it's a bit absurd to run into a soccer player in a museum.

Ariel was about to ask if he could accompany them on the rest of their tour, but the henlike laughter of the kids grew and he decided to head off the other way. In front of the curls of Our Lady of Santa Cruz, before her naked white flesh, caressed by the light and transported to the canvas by desire, before her thighs outlined in marvelous harmony beneath the gauzy fabric, Ariel thought of Sylvia.

Suddenly there was a commotion. The kids seemed to be running wild. Ariel peeked into the adjacent room. One of the girls had fainted; several of the others were putting her on one of the benches. The teacher was repeating, give her room, give her room. A woman who identified herself as a doctor approached. Seeing that Ariel had taken an interest, a couple of boys came over to him. No, it's nothing, she's just anorexic.

When he left, he called Sylvia again. He made a date to pick her up three hours later near her house. Along the wide avenue, the slight wind pushed his hair back as he walked and seemed to be pleasantly caressing him. He had to avoid the gaze of people who recognized him because once you give one autograph you have to give more. The first one was essential to avoiding the rest.

He bought the Argentinian newspaper *Clarín* at a stand near Cibeles. He went up to a restaurant near the Retiro and ate alone at his table. A young Argentinian player on an English team had been robbed at his house in a posh London neighborhood at gunpoint, and they had threatened his family. A cartoonist referred to it in a strip: "Can you believe I come all this way for this . . . when in my own country the robbers are first-rate." Ariel smiled. Then he read the depressing op-eds about the state of the country. When he went to pay, they refused to charge him, it's on the house, it's an honor, come back whenever you like. He walked back to the parking garage. He reclined the seat and in the darkness tried to take a short nap with the music playing softly.

He picked up Sylvia at the spot they had agreed on. At first it was a bit chilly between them, and they didn't greet each other with a kiss. My father could come out at any minute. She smiled and he started the car. They talked for a while about his trip to the museum. He told her about the girl fainting. Sylvia shrugged, at school Mai and I always go to the boys' bathroom because the girls' is full of vomit, there are a ton of anorexics and bulimics, it's a plague. Ariel drives aimlessly. I think we've been past this street already, she said. Where do you want to go? asked Ariel. That was when he suggested going to the apartment. She hid any trace of enthusiasm. The traffic was slow and dense at that hour.

Even though it was cold and the wood floor doubled the freezing atmosphere of the empty house, Sylvia's bare skin was scalding hot. She undressed messily. Her curls brushed Ariel's chest. They made love among the coats and other clothes piled up. It was like baptizing the new house. Their naked legs intertwined. Sylvia puts on his sweater. Now they embrace and the lack of a home around them doesn't seem to matter much. They've created their own nest. In a little while, they'll feel the cold again.

9

The snow falls without sticking along the promenade beside the river. The clock on the enormous building on the opposite shore marks almost five. Sylvia can make out the slanted roof of a small building, almost like a Tyrolean house. Ariel has just laced his fingers through hers. Yesterday you were wearing gloves, Sylvia says. You looked funny, with your wool gloves, like a little old lady. It was incredibly cold. Halfway through the game, Ariel took them off and threw them to the bench, remembering something Dragon used to say when they were kids, a cat with gloves catches no mice.

Sylvia had come to Munich the evening before. She took a taxi to the InterContinental Hotel and at the desk they handed her the key to the double room. An employee insisted on taking up her tiny travel bag and she found herself forced to share the elevator with him. He rewarded her with a friendly smile for having broken the record for lightest luggage in the history of the hotel. She tried to hide her nervousness beneath an indifferent face. She didn't tip the porter, who was slow in leaving, showing her the obvious working mechanisms of the room. Next he's going to show me how to flick the light switch, thought Sylvia. The room was well lit, lined with wood, with a double bed with two feather comforters, one for each half. The Germans had solved the problem of couples stealing the covers from each other at night. She took a long hot bath, with her headphones on, wrapped in steam, her eyes closed. Ariel called to see if everything had gone well. She gave him the room number. Five-twelve. I'll wait for you here, I'm not going out. Where are you? In the bus, on the way to the stadium.

Sylvia watched the game on television. Ariel seemed contaminated by the cold until well into the play. Sylvia, lying on the bed, watched him. She ordered a sandwich during halftime. The waiter who brought it to her room delivered it with some brochures that suggested a raft trip down the Isar River. He explained something to her in English. She said, isn't it too cold? and he explained, there'll be beer and bratwurst.

She called her father. She had already told him she wouldn't be sleeping at home that night. Are you watching the game? Yes, he said. And how are they doing? Scoreless, but if we push it we'll beat them. Sylvia, from what she had seen, found that a pretty optimistic report. Good luck, said Sylvia before saying good-bye.

Ariel had taken care of everything. The electronic ticket in her name at the airport, the hotel reservation. If you want I can send a driver to pick you up with a sign that has your name on it. I'd rather take a taxi. The official version she gave her father was that she was staying at Mai's house to study for an important test. No boyfriends? No, no, I just don't feel like coming home so late, that's all. Mai, on the other hand, had demanded more explanations than her father.

It was the Germans who pushed it in the second half. They crashed a ball so hard into the goal's crossbeam that it looked like it was going to break. In five minutes they shot seven corner kicks into the penalty area. In one of their rebounds, the ball was sent over to Ariel, the target as the only forward. He set off racing; his long run didn't end when the first fullback hit the ground trying to knock the ball off Ariel's foot, since Ariel was able to get around him. Sylvia hugged the pillow tightly. Come on, she shouted, keeping her voice down so she wouldn't alarm the neighboring rooms. Come on, come on. The ball got a bit ahead of Ariel in the dribble, which encouraged the goalie to come out of his box. But Ariel was faster and managed to get the ball just out of the keeper's reach. The goalie didn't hesitate, he knocked Ariel down brutally hard, sending his entire body into his standing leg. Ariel plunged almost into a somersault before hitting the field. Sylvia chewed a lock of hair between her lips.

The goalkeeper was expelled from the game before Ariel recovered from the blow. He looked like he was in pain. Now they're gonna take him to the hospital with a broken leg and I'm gonna be alone in this hotel room in Munich. It's ridiculous, thought Sylvia. But Ariel got up and was still readjusting his socks when a teammate sent the foul shot right into the genitals of a German player who was part of the wall. The game was interrupted again. The Spanish commentator was insisting that the player had gotten a very hard blow to the knee, as the guy twisted on the ground, his hands clamped over his groin. Sylvia would later say to Ariel, if that had been you, you'd have a bag of ice over your balls right now, for sure.

No one managed to score, but Ariel's run was replayed several times and ended up being the play of the game. Although nobody managed to shift the balance of the score in their favor, he had stopped the German assault cold. A psychological blow, said the commentators.

Sylvia found a channel with music videos where women danced pseudo-erotically, showing PG-friendly parts of their perfect anatomy and performing superficial versions of sex acts. She dozed off. The room was hot. How should I receive him? How much longer is he going to be? She had put on the white hotel bathrobe. She was naked underneath, her hair still damp from the bath. She thought about getting dressed, but she didn't do it.

Ariel showed up almost two hours later. He had left the team on the bus, on their way to the airport. He had permission from the sports director and the coach. I have family in Munich, I'd like to spend the day off with them. Would you like to hang out a day in Munich? he had asked Sylvia a few days earlier. Then he explained his plan. I was there once, it's almost like something out of a fairy tale. I played there with the under-seventeens.

They embraced, undressed, made love. Ariel ordered some dinner and the best champagne they had. By the third glass of Veuve Clicquot they were smiling and relaxed. We've got to finish it, he said. They were sitting on the bed. Sylvia's head resting on his belly. He stroked her hair. She had her arm around his bended knee. Were you faking it? What? Were you faking it when you were twisting in pain on the field after the foul the goalie made on you? Well, I had to get the referee to kick him out of the game. You're good at faking, I was worried for a little while.

Before falling asleep, they made love slowly. They stretched out each moment as if they didn't want them to end. Afterward they slept in each other's arms on one edge of the bed, relaxed for the first time, with the whole night ahead of them. They were awakened by the bustling of the cleaning woman in the hallway and the murmur of the elevator. They looked at each other to find something they had never seen. Morning faces, waking up with the eyes of a child. They had breakfast from two abundant trays that made them feel fortunate. Sylvia read him the sentence from the Süddeutsche Zeitung that mentioned Ariel. "*Die Spurts des argentinischen Linksfusses waren elektrisierend, er war zweifellos der inspirierteste Stürmer der Gastmannschaft.*"* Her German was pathetic and they both joked about the words. What did it mean? *Elektrisierend*, it sounds good. Then Sylvia said, I have an idea, do you feel like going on a raft?

They started the journey at the pier where the hotel minivan dropped them off. They had paid for the activity at the reception

---

* The Argentine lefty's galloping was electric, he was without a doubt the best offensive player of the visiting team.

desk. Sylvia was able to make herself understood with the brochure in her hands. In the raft was a gas heater that radiated a bearable temperature thanks to a heat umbrella. The Isar River ran placidly and soon they found themselves with two steins of lager in their hands. They shared the seats with a group of Americans and a young Finnish couple who didn't stop drinking. There was a guy dressed as an American Indian who sang songs in German. Every once in a while, along the shores of the Isar some passerby lifted a hand to greet them. I forgot to bring a camera, said Sylvia. We don't have any photos of us together. The group of Americans took pictures of each other next to the oarsman and the singer. He says he's a Cherokee from the Isar River, translates Sylvia when she hears him speak English. The trip down was almost an hour long. It was pleasant, a cold day but sunny. The last stretch dragged out a bit. Sylvia joked with Ariel. She didn't want to kiss him. You smell like mustard.

The hotel car brought them back to the city. Ariel and Sylvia went for a walk. The streets were comfortable, allowing them to relax their usual furtiveness. When they passed a group that spoke Spanish they lowered their heads and fled onto a side street.

Ariel wore a wool hat that went down to his eyebrows and covered his hair and ears. No one seemed to recognize him among the few people they passed, retirees defying the weather and early darkness. They passed people on bicycles and a dog sniffed in the grass while its owner listened to music. Sylvia didn't say anything, but for the first time in her relationship with Ariel she discovered peace and tranquillity. Normality. His slight accent had hardened somewhat since living in Madrid. She liked to listen to him talk. They went beyond the former

Turkish bath building with the enormous dome and looked at the cable car that divided the street. Sylvia hid her childishness in an intelligent silence. Ariel jumped up on a street bench and said, it's a lovely day.

The airplane leaves at five minutes to eight. On time. Although they board separately, their seats are next to each other. In first class. Ariel jokes with her after takeoff.

Are you Spanish? Yes, what about you? Don't tell me, Uruguayan . . . Buenos Aires. It's not the same thing. You're a soccer player, aren't you? Are you in school? When I can get there. Well, I'm a soccer player when I can make it, too. My name is Sylvia, she introduces herself, and extends a hand, which he shakes. Ariel. Like the detergent brand. Yeah, I get that all the time. He was slow to let go of her soft hand.

Nearby a businessman looks at them over his newspaper. The flight attendant smiles and offers them something to drink.

And you live in Madrid? Don't you miss your country? Sometimes. I've never been to Buenos Aires. Well, you should go. Maybe one day I'll find an Argentinian boyfriend and he'll invite me to go . . . An Argentinian boyfriend? What's wrong with that? You don't recommend them? Sylvia feigns alarm. There's all kinds, I suppose.

They continue to talk, pretending they're strangers. Without realizing it, they experience a certain pleasure in the charade. It's as if they were starting over. The flight attendant asks him for three autographs for some passengers. I'd rather they didn't come over to bother you. Sylvia is surprised by her cordiality. She is reassured by the fact that she is neither young nor pretty. You were the best yesterday, says the businessman as they exit the plane. Thanks, it wasn't much help. Ariel and Sylvia say good-bye in the line for taxis. Are you sure you have money? he asks her in a whisper. They each get into a different taxi. Sylvia and Ariel smile at each other through the windows. Then the cars separate and move apart. At the highway exit, they take opposite directions. It's almost eleven. On the radio someone talks in a bitter tone about the political situation. The buildings surrounding the city are ugly and chaotic. There is a big traffic jam before Avenida de América. It seems a truck charged into a car stopped on the hard shoulder. What was on his mind? asks the taxi driver out loud.

Huh? And Sylvia lifts her head. She doesn't know what he's talking about. In that moment she was remembering Ariel's hand holding hers when they greeted as strangers on the plane. *Elektrisierend*, yes, that was definitely a good description.

10

Leandro returns from an upscale neighborhood where he would never hear a distant radio playing from a window, where a woman would never shake a rug full of lint balls and dirt from a balcony, where no staircase smells of stew and no pressure cookers whistle. The sky today was a gray mass against which the heads of buildings and the tops of trees were silhouetted. The light of day was a filtered shadow, sunless. Leandro walks back home after meeting up with Joaquín.

In Joaquín's apartment, the day's newspapers were on the table. One was open to a page where he was interviewed. The photo showed him pensive, resting his chin on one hand. His hair messy, his eyes lively. The photo makes him look better than he actually does, thought Leandro. He was the living image of dignified, attractive old age. He had arrived punctually to their date. Come up and that way you can see the apartment, Joaquín had told him when they spoke the day before. It was ten in the morning and Joaquín was talking on his cell phone while Jacqueline tidied up the remains of their breakfast and got ready to go out shopping. Beside the newspapers he had placed a mug of steaming tea. Leandro refused the offer. He skimmed the interview. Joaquín spoke of the public's lack of interest in education and culture, of the pleasure of teaching young people. Then he presented a pessimistic view of humanity. Nothing new. The fatalistic vision of those who enjoy an above-average living. The world is getting worse, say those who know that for them it couldn't get better, thinks Leandro.

He smiled when he noticed Joaquín's last answer. In it he spoke of pianists who had influenced his career. I could name classical pianists without whom my profession would have no meaning, and not Horowitz or Rubinstein, by the way, who seem more myth than anything else, but I would be lying if I denied that the pianist I've most admired, tirelessly throughout my life, is Art Tatum. How appropriate, thought Leandro, someone he can't be compared to or measured against. Joaquín closed the cell phone and sat beside him. Don't read that nonsense. Art Tatum, you remember? What was the name of that amazing song we used to play as a duet? Leandro had no trouble coming up with it, "Have You Met Miss Jones?" Exactly. Joaquín has a flirtatious way of toying with his memories, they just piled together in a life filled with emotions and experiences, too many to retain. Then he hummed the melody.

Leandro congratulated him again on the concert. Yes, people left happy, it seems. He asked him about the tendinitis that had kept him from performing. Completely psychosomatic, a horrible thing, now I see a specialized psychotherapist in London. And soon you discover there's a repertoire that you have to start giving up, too debilitating on the hands. You no longer play "Petrushka," said Leandro with a smile. No, no, not the "Hammerklavier" or the "Fantasia Wanderer," we're not up to that sort of thing anymore. It's for young people, now they're real athletes. It's like tennis, every year somebody comes up that hits harder. Leandro reminded him of Don Alonso's obsession with eating and developing muscle mass. He had them lie on the floor to do sit-ups. Joaquín nodded. What did he used to say? Forget inspiration and trust in constitution. He was a funny old guy. *Mens sana in corpore sano* and all those Latin expressions.

That's why I wanted to talk to you. The little details, you always had a better memory than me. Actually what I want is for you to talk to a young man who insists on writing my biography. He's from Granada, but he lives here in Madrid, a very persistent boy, he knows music, he writes well. Your biographer? Leandro asked him. Don't call him that, it sounds ridiculous. My life has no interest beyond the fact that there are few Spanish concert pianists, it's sort of like being an Ethiopian weight lifter, I don't know . . . I have a meeting with him this morning, in a little while, in the bar at the Wellington. I hope we won't have to put up with that pianist, he always plays something by Falla for me, which is, I don't know, fine, I just loathe Falla and he does it in my honor and he ruins my morning with that *Amor Brujo* stuff. But I wanted to see you first, not dump it all on you without asking. We hardly ever see each other anymore.

I hardly ever see anyone, honestly. You know the feeling that you'll never again meet anyone interesting in your life and you don't have time for the ones you already know anyway? It's distressing. Jacqueline says it's all a problem of anxiety. You know me, anxiety is my life, I'm not going to get rid of it now, am I?

Joaquín's wife said good-bye at the door. With her coat already on. A patterned scarf around her neck. I don't know if I'll see you when I come back. Leandro stood up and they meet halfway to exchange a kiss on each cheek. When she left, Joaquín seemed to relax. The expensive perfume left with her. I like this apartment. Joaquín gestured to the lovely place, the windows overlooking the branches of two white mulberry trees, upscale, historic buildings across the street. In a hotel it's different, here I have my space, I can rehearse, relax.

It's lovely, the apartment, said Leandro.

This area costs a fortune. You can't even believe it. Sometimes I come here to get away from Paris and prepare my concerts. Joaquín smiled impishly and Leandro thought he understood what his friend was suggesting with his escapes to Madrid. You know me like no one else does, when that nagging self-criticism springs up, the awareness that I haven't gotten anywhere with what I've tried to accomplish, that I pound on the piano without any art, any class, then you are a fragile man, capable of falling into the arms of any woman who makes you believe that you are what you wanted to be. Sex is nothing more than reconstructing a battered ego. There is nothing worse than an old seducer, but it's better than just being old, what can we do.

Leandro was surprised by his expression of sorrow. Many times Joaquín had tried to explain what attracted him to women, to the wild love affairs, that it had more to do with his insecurity

than with his carnal appetite. Soon he changed his tone and
asked about Aurora, almost in contrast. Leandro was concise,
he spoke of her illness without beating around the bush. She's
really bad, there's no hope. We're so old, for fuck's sake. Now
every year I go to more funerals than concerts. The comment
didn't bother Leandro. He knew the superficiality with which
Joaquín usually faced any serious situation; he had been like that
even as a young man. He avoided the blow. We are strangers
to each other, thought Leandro, we're no longer what we were.

The apartment was somewhat overdone, with molding on
the ceiling. Perfect furniture that hadn't been lived in, a majestic
black Steinway grand piano beside a large picture window. The
enormous living room was the receiving room. A nearby kitchen
and a small hallway led to the only bedroom. They had knocked
down walls to create that sweeping space in the living room.

They talked about the concert, about the previous days,
about the state of the country, about general things and impersonal matters, about his life in Paris. So much mediocrity, we're
so far from those exciting years where everything was ahead
of us, right? Joaquín lit a Cohiba that inundated the room with
bluish smoke. He leaned back and his pant legs revealed the tops
of his socks. He stroked the cigar, giving it small turns with his
fingertips, made space between his lips to house the smoke for
an instant before exhaling it gently.

I guess you're retired from such competitions.

Seeing Leandro's puzzled face, he felt obliged to finish the
sentence, women . . . Leandro lifted his shoulders and smiled.
I've got Jacqueline on top of me all the time, it's not healthy.
Listen, if some day you need to use the apartment all you have to
do is ask, the doorman has keys and is completely trustworthy,

if you want to come by and play the piano, although I suppose you have more interesting things to do, and he let out a guffaw like a complicit whiplash. I mean if you want to impress some woman don't hesitate, eh. We'll talk to Casiano, the doorman, his father used to be the doorman of this building, imagine, it's an inherited post, isn't that sad? He's a very discreet guy.

Joaquín had no children. His way of relating to his wives had always turned him into the object of their caretaking. He was the son and husband to women who accepted the role of mother, lover, and secretary in equal parts. During the long hour they were alone together, Jacqueline called twice to remind Joaquín about his next appointment and some other triviality.

They went down to the street in a painstakingly maintained elevator. It was a portal into the old Madrid, built in that short period when the city aspired to be Paris. The doorman sat in a booth, the radio spitting out advertising jingles. Casiano, I want to introduce you to my friend Leandro, my childhood friend. He is also a pianist. The man greeted him with humble eyes. Once they were out on the street, Joaquín gossiped about the doorman with amusement. He explained to Leandro that he had a son in jail for belonging to a Nazi party and having been involved in the murder of a Basque soccer fan. And all of a sudden, with a cloud of cigar smoke, he changed the subject. Do you still teach piano? I've got the odd student.

In the bar of the Wellington, the pianist spotted Joaquín and a second later dedicated, with a smile, the chords of a Falla piece with clumsy execution and bad taste. You remember when Don Alonso used to say to us, keep it up like that and you'll end up a pianist in a hotel? Well, there you have it. A nervous young man waited, sitting at a table, with a bag that looked almost like a schoolboy's resting on the carpeted floor. This is the boy I told you about, my biographer, as you say. They sat around the table and Joaquín announced he was going to commit the eccentricity of ordering a whisky before noon. Since you guys are the ones that have to talk . . .

There was a tentative attempt at conversation, during which the young man took out of his bag a notebook that he opened, searching for a blank page. Leandro realized he expected something concrete. The boy asked a question to lay the groundwork. I'd like you to tell me about your childhood together, you were both children of wartime. Oy, who can understand that today, right, Leandro? Joaquín smiled. Leandro started to talk about his origins and the building where they lived as boys. The young man put on his glasses and resolutely jotted a heading: childhood friend. Then he underlined it. Leandro felt bad.

He tried to not be too precise. He talked about the enormous social difference after the war and he remembered the generosity of Joaquín's family toward his. It was a moral obligation, interjected Joaquín. Spain was divided into victors and vanquished and the victors were divided into those who had a heart and those who were just scoundrels interested in lining their pockets.

Any special, memorable moment from your adolescence?

Leandro and Joaquín exchanged a look. Leandro's expression was eloquent. It seemed incredible that someone could ask you to sum up a life in two or three anecdotes. The best thing would be if you two could get together one day, without me around, today the idea was that you got a chance to meet. Leandro can tell you things about me even I don't remember. Let's see, there are things that shouldn't be left out, those first piano lessons we shared, then our first jobs and my leaving for France, you came to Paris and lived with me for a year. It was barely three months, clarified Leandro. We had a piano teacher who was a harsh old guy, fun, serious, very serious. You can tell him about all that. Things about the neighborhood, I don't even want to try to remember them. My father, for example, was someone from another era, a model military man, conservative, authoritarian, but more nineteenth-century than of the new fascist Spain.

I think you came to hate your father, almost as an essential stance for your ambitions. Leandro's words shut Joaquín up for a second. You always were very clear on what you wanted to be. It's strange. But I think it's a very important detail. You were a young man who knew what you wanted. That's rare. You molded everything around you. And perhaps your father was a victim of that. And others, maybe myself included, benefited from it, because you were building something that only you were clear on how it had to be constructed. For example, I was your friend, but with a type of friendship that you had created in your mind.

There was a silence. Joaquín ruminated over Leandro's words. He wasn't offended by them, but he didn't understand where they were leading. Then he added, *unaquaeque res, quantum in se est, in suo esse perseverare conatur*. The young man looked at him with eyes big as plates. Spinoza, each thing, insofar as it is in itself, strives to persevere in its being. It's from *Ethics*, my favorite book, one I always keep beside my bed. Don't overthink it, I was something and I could only persevere in being that something. The young man took notes at a furious pace.

Deep down, in the world of children and women that we lived in during the war, without adult men, just the old and unfit, the return of your father was something unexpected and annoying for you, added Leandro.

Joaquín smiled. He agreed. When a boy overcomes the loss of his father and gets used to his absence, you are right that what he least expects is a resurrection, a return to the beginning, I rebelled against returning to the early authority. You will agree with me that the war was for us a very strange moment of total freedom, strange and cruel but freeing, something that was lost with the victory. Leandro nodded and Joaquín continued. It's true, in the image that I wanted of myself, being an orphan was essential. Perhaps that's why, and maybe it was unfair, I never accepted him back again.

The young man took the occasional note. Leandro suddenly remembered a cruel game they would sometimes play during wartime. They ran from the street to a doorway, they called up to an apartment, and a mother would answer and they would announce dramatically, your son, your son was found dead, a bomb went off. And then they'd run off, unaware of the pain they were causing and that their joke would unleash a tragedy until the truth was discovered. Why would we do something like that? Joaquín wondered aloud. I don't know, it was the cruelty of the war, transformed into a fun game by kids. The young man put on his glasses in a shy tic.

Kids are always like that, said Leandro. Then he talked about something else. A hazy memory of the return of Joaquín's father and the evening he took them to see a newsreel at the movies because he could be seen among the people at the back of a shot featuring Franco's elite in Burgos. The movie playing afterward wasn't approved for minors, but they forced his father to let them stay and watch it. Leandro didn't remember the title. But he did remember Carole Lombard was in it, wearing tight elegant gowns that showed off her breasts, and that years later you confessed to me that her presence had awakened desire in you, as it had in me.

So what you're saying is that my father took us to show himself off and politically indoctrinate us and we tended more toward carnal desire, kids are wise. Yes, yes, I remember now. Joaquín took obvious pleasure in hearing about his past. He was attracted to the re-creation of his life by a third party, as if he could situate himself as a spectator.

I think that during our childhood, said Leandro, we create the unmentionable challenges of our lives and the answer to happiness consists in the achievement, or inability to approximate, those childhood goals, maybe not fully articulated or clear, but evident to yourself. Although now you are listening to me as if what I'm saying was nothing more than an obscure memory, I know that you remember very clearly how you were and how you thought as a boy. Leandro continued dispassionately in the face of Joaquín's smile that seemed to say, this all seems too complicated of a psychoanalytical game for the time and the place. Would you believe, I'm the same way, sometimes I surprise myself by feeling that I'm being observed by my younger self.

And? Do you find yourself loyal to what you wanted? Do you think there's anyone who achieves that? asked Joaquín as he stared into Leandro's sunken eyes.

Well, this gentleman didn't come here to hear me talk about myself, just about you. I'm not important at all.

Joaquín laughed, satisfied with Leandro's evasive reply, it was enough for him. They could now focus again on what he was interested in: himself.

Leandro returned home leisurely. He had taken the metro and gotten out at Cuatro Caminos. In his pocket, he has a piece of paper with the young man's phone number. They had made a date to see each other some other day and work in a more methodical manner, and without Joaquín present. But recalling those years had awoken in Leandro the feeling that he was at the end of a journey, that there was nothing left ahead of him. Meeting Aurora had been his salvation from an uncontrollable bitterness, a renewed strength to go forward with a life that wasn't the one he had dreamed of. He feels a sudden flush of tenderness and appreciation for her. And in that same moment he imagines her dead in bed, not breathing, he sees himself enter the house to find her paler than ever, with her eyes veiled and her chest lifeless. He doesn't know if he should quicken his step or just stop. He's afraid, but he continues. Leisurely.

11

He finds his mother sleeping, drugged by tranquilizers. She is never left alone now. If his father has to go out, he calls the cleaning lady or waits for Sylvia to arrive to spend some time with her grandmother. That afternoon Lorenzo called him, I'll come by. His father had gone out a little while ago after a very brief conversation between them in the hallway. How are you? Here, stuck. Lorenzo had been surprised by the answer. Even when his mother was in perfect health, he never felt that his father had much need for the world outside. It more seemed that he found pleasure in the solitude of his room. As he remembered it, his father had always been a homebody annoyed by a weekend excursion to the mountains, relatives visiting, or a commitment that required leaving the house. But it was clear that Aurora's illness was enslaving him and Lorenzo understood that as the reason behind his wanting to get out, to get some air.

He was upset for a few days now, since he had come back from his walk and found Aurora on the floor. You don't know what it was like, he told his son, I thought she was dead. Aurora hadn't been able to control her sphincter, she had dirtied the bed and had been crazy enough to try to stand up. She didn't break any bones in the fall, but the feeling Leandro described of picking her up off the floor, her embarrassment, had been a horrific moment, you have no idea, how terrible. God, it's intense what's happening to your mother, he ended with his eyes flooding with tears.

When the doorbell rings, he knows it is Daniela. She comes up to the apartment and Lorenzo opens the door for her. My mother is alone, but sleeping. Daniela takes off her coat, her workday ended. Lorenzo hangs it on a hook in the entryway. I spent my whole childhood in this house. Daniela looks around with curious eyes, but she's unable to imagine Lorenzo as a child playing on his knees in the hallway near the kitchen door.

The previous Sunday, they had gone to church together and chatted with other couples on the way out. That day there were a lot of children and the pastor talked to them about the possibility of renting a space in another neighborhood with a little yard, so the little ones could enjoy it. We'd have to gather the money between all of us, of course. Later they went to the Retiro to eat. They sat on the grass. Lorenzo's hemorrhoids were really acting up and it took him a while to find a comfortable position.

When he finally did, he was almost leaning on her thigh. I'd like to introduce you to my parents, he then said.

Saturday night they had had dinner in an Ecuadorian restaurant, El Manso, that's what they call Guayaquil, she explained. The owners took away the tables to transform the place into a bar with a little place to dance. They were a friendly couple and they accepted Lorenzo without any prejudice. They knew Daniela well. I come by here and pick up their packages of leftovers that we leave at the church for the needy, without the shame of those soup kitchens, where they have to stand in line right on the street, Daniela explained. It was there, in that restaurant, while some danced and Lorenzo and Daniela made themselves comfortable in a corner, that the police burst in, forty agents for no more than a hundred customers. Those that were standing were forced to line up along the bar. Without the music and with all the lights on, it seemed to have suddenly become dawn. It must have been two in the morning. The few that were seated were forced to stay in their chairs. The policemen demanded documentation, residency permits. As he handed over his ID, Lorenzo said to the agent, this is an outrage. The man lifted his eyes toward him. Are you going to tell me how to do my job? he said in a challenging tone. With a nervous gesture, Daniela begged him not to answer, but Lorenzo did. I don't understand this harassment, these people are having fun, they're not doing anything wrong.

Daniela searched in her bag, as if she were trying to find her wallet. Lorenzo and the agent locked eyes again. Forget it, the policeman said to Daniela. And he continued his inspection at the next table. The result of the raid, of almost forty-five minutes of paralysis, would be a few deportation notices that, in practice, would probably not be enforced. As the police left, the place was plunged into a loaded, sad atmosphere. The scene reminded those present that their stay in the country was provisional and fragile; it spread a stench of uncertainty. We only have a permit as a restaurant, explained the owners, so it's probably best if we shut down for tonight.

They don't want us here, but we're not going to leave, Daniela told him on the street. But now a period of legalization is open, you have to get your papers, insisted Lorenzo. Yes, but it's difficult, the couple I work for still has to be convinced.

Lorenzo came into her entryway with her, to the foot of the stairs. There he embraced her. He searched out her mouth and Daniela gave him a kiss. Lorenzo placed his hand on her back and held her very close. Daniela hid her head on his shoulder. Lorenzo felt her bra strap beneath her clothes.

The walls were of filthy stucco and the mailboxes were bent, several of them broken. The staircase was dirty with peeling paint and the light gave off an annoying buzz. In the dimness, Lorenzo kissed Daniela again, but this time they were long kisses. He sank his fingers into her hair. He mussed it up and caressed the nape of her neck.

They're all up there, it's better if you don't come up, she said. Lorenzo nodded, he wanted to kiss her, but she preferred to leave. Lorenzo accompanied her to the landing. They kissed one last time in silence. He stayed on the other side of the door when she went into the apartment. Daniela smiled at him.

Lorenzo wanted to introduce Daniela to his parents. He could feel their tenseness when they asked him about his work, about how he was feeling, he didn't want them to imagine him alone and depressed, like those recurring images of the unemployed, heads lowered, hands in pockets, the out-of-work as gray victims. I'm dating a girl, he told them suddenly, I'll introduce you to her. His father's surprise, and his mother's, immobile in bed, made him think that they harbored a fear of seeing him alone forever.

He didn't tell them that Daniela was Ecuadorian or that she worked in the apartment above his. Nor that he went with her to a church on Sundays where the pastor spoke intimately with them about life as sacrifice, about renunciation, about happiness, about abstract concepts brought closer with everyday metaphors. At first Lorenzo thought the service was something that she and others like her needed out of some sort of lack. Later, he watched them sing, respond, and laugh when the pastor broke the seriousness of the sermon with something funny, and he realized it was more than that. Daniela talked about God, what God thought, what God would do. God was a companion, but also a watchman.

Lorenzo's parents had never been religious, even when that was the norm in a submissive society. After doing his Communion, Lorenzo doesn't remember having gone back to church with them, and the few times he had asked his father about God or faith, he had always given the same answer, that is something only you can discover, when the time is right.

In religion, as in so many other things, his parents had given him absolute freedom, waiting for Lorenzo to work it out on his own. That was why he felt that what Daniela devoted to God was a measuring stick, the doctrine of behavior. And he wondered, puzzled, if it hadn't come to him, finally, the moment in his life that his father always referred to, the moment of truth, not like something imposed by society, but more like an inner voice.

In church, that last Sunday, Lorenzo had also wondered if the lack of sex in his relationship had something to do with it.

Was Daniela one of those women who compartmentalize sex as dark, dirty? Maybe we have to be married, thought Lorenzo with a smile. It didn't seem that the rest of the couples showed any renunciation or imposed chastity. Quite the opposite: the girls wore tight clothes and showed open smiles. Lorenzo thought that his sexual possibilities might be resolved amid those messy banquets, the euphoric chanting, the mischievous kids, and the parents in their Sunday best with serious, profound expressions.

Aurora opens her eyes and watches Lorenzo's movement around her. Hello, Mamá, look, this is Daniela. His mother looks up and Daniela leans down to kiss her on the cheek. The first thing Aurora notices about Daniela are her almond-shaped eyes. Daniela holds back her straight hair with her hand so it doesn't fall onto Aurora as she bends over.

Have you been here long? No, just a little while. I sleep almost the entire day, she explains to Daniela, I have very strange dreams, very vivid, very real. Aurora tires from speaking. Lorenzo sits on the mattress and takes his mother's hand between his. Don't wear yourself out. Where are you from, Daniela? She answers. Aurora's eyes travel from Daniela to her son. She seems to shiver briefly, like a stab of pain. With a shaking of her head, Aurora tries to convey to them that it was nothing.

The masseuse had come by that morning to exercise her muscles and Aurora was more tired than usual. It's a luxury we can't afford, she says, but Leandro tells me of course we can afford it, that's what I spent my life working for. The doctor had ruled out any aggressive treatment, so it was just a matter of waiting.

Lorenzo tried to keep in touch daily with his father. He suspected that he lacked the strength to face the illness's onslaught without support. If there is anyone unable to live alone, it's my father, thought Lorenzo. He belonged to the group of men who seemed independent, but had no ability to solve the most trivial of tasks. Lorenzo was pleased to see Sylvia find some time to visit her grandmother, read to her, chat with her.

The week before, Lorenzo had gone back to the old folks' home and sat next to the man whose house he had emptied out. What, Don Jaime, don't remember me? I brought you your things in the suitcase, remember? They didn't exchange many sentences. Nothing tied him to the man, beyond the destiny that had brought them together. But that same random chance wouldn't let Lorenzo ignore him. Wilson laughed when Lorenzo told him that he had visited him twice. The crazy guy? What for? I wish I had time to waste like you, he had said.

Lorenzo knew it was important to maintain a link with the outside world. Like that note hung on the fridge with a stranger's phone number.

It's cold. Quite. It's good in here. It's not bad. Those few words could be a normal exchange between them. Pretty much all they said in forty-five minutes. Don't you have any friends, family? But the man didn't usually answer concrete questions. They remained seated. Sometimes one of them lowered the blinds if the sun was glaring in. A nun then entered and took the man by the hand to walk him down to the cafeteria.

Wilson organized the workdays. He took his small notebook out of his pocket, which contained the precise schedule of the day's tasks. Trips to the airport, a move. Wilson settled the money with him after showing Lorenzo the state of their accounts, loans, rents accounted for in the notebook.

When it got cold, Wilson took over an empty warehouse. It was a former commercial space and he piled up some mattresses to turn it into a rental shelter. He waited for his customers until ten-thirty at night and at eight on the dot he was at the door to send them out. He hired some acquaintances to work on the renovation of that temporary hotel of sorts and then he shared the profits with them. If one of the tenants drank too much or made too much noise, he had to show up and calm things down. A boy who helped him with moving jobs also worked as a threatening bodyguard. It was in those moments that he earned his money, when everything didn't look as simple as suggesting to Lorenzo the thousand different ways to make a euro.

Really it's all due to this crossed eye, Wilson explained to him, people take me for crazy. And everybody's more afraid of a crazy guy than of a strong guy. Nobody wants to take on a crazy guy. Like a Swiss army knife, Wilson seemed to have the resource needed for every given occasion. The exact amount of charm and chitchat, the prescribed dose of contained violence and latent threats, the precise skill in every situation. He handled a bundle of rolled-up bills wrapped in a rubber band that became his bracelet when it was time to pay. He turned toward Lorenzo to explain, money is a magnet for money.

They called Lorenzo into the police station to return his belongings to him, some clothes, some shoes. Even though he asked after the detective, they didn't see each other that day. And he hardly ever turned around to check if they were following him or stopped the van suddenly at an entrance to watch the cars behind him pass. Paying his bills was more of an obsession for him. It was also something that his partnership with Wilson guaranteed without many problems.

Lorenzo and Daniela are in Aurora's room when Leandro returns. They greet each other. Leandro likes Daniela. Aurora strokes the girl's hand, you have lovely skin. In the hallway, before leaving, Lorenzo asks his father if he needs anything. Leandro shakes his head.

On the street, Daniela says to Lorenzo, your mother must have been someone very special. Lorenzo nods his head. He remembers what his mother whispered into his ear the second Daniela went out of the room to talk on her cell phone. The important thing is that you're happy.

12

There is no crunch. No electric current running up his leg. Just the feeling that his foot is separating from his body. The rival player falls onto him, with a brush of his breath and sweat and a brusque push to soften the blow against the grass. They are barely fourteen minutes into the game, the time it takes to size up your opponent. The crash was during a simple play. He received the ball with his back to the goal and turned, trying to get clear. The fullback stepped on Ariel's foot as he lay on the grass waiting for someone to kick the ball out. The crowd whistles, as always. They make fun of the injured. My ankle, my ankle, indicates Ariel to the doctor when he kneels beside him.

At the level of the field, Barcelona's stadium is lovely. The stands don't emerge drastically like in other stadiums. Sylvia is at the opposite corner of the field, with a distant perspective on the game. In fact, a minute earlier she had thought that she

428 | DAVID TRUEBA

wouldn't have Ariel close by until the second half. Then she started eating sunflower seeds. Now she sees him leave on a stretcher in a ridiculous little motorized cart driven by a blond girl with a reflective vest. Ariel's coach has sent a player from the bench to warm up. Ariel disappears into the tunnel to the locker rooms.

Sylvia is left alone amid people. She looks around as if she expected Ariel to show up a moment later next to her or to send someone to find her. But nothing happens. The game draws everyone's attention, but not hers.

After the trip to Munich, they were together all the time. The following day, Ariel went to pick her up in an alley by the high school. If a classmate sees me getting into your Porsche, I can start looking for a new high school. Why don't you get a different car? They went to eat at a barbecue place on the highway to La Coruña. She ordered a Coca-Cola, he a white wine. The team doctor won't let us drink Coca-Cola, he says it's the worst, explained Ariel. Any of the few diners could think they were siblings from their attitude. Ariel had said that to her one day, don't freak out, but most people who see us think I'm taking my little sister around Madrid. They ordered pork chops, but Sylvia first ate shrimp, to his horror, I could never eat those. When she takes the head off one of them, the murky liquid squirts into Ariel's face and they both laugh.

Later they went to Ariel's house. They took a hot, messy nap, their bodies burning like heaters. They maintained an uncomfortable embrace that neither of them wanted to break. When night fell, Ariel took Sylvia home.

The next day, Ariel went to Barcelona with the team. Sylvia took a morning flight. Ariel had reserved a room in the same hotel the team was staying in. After an early lunch, Ariel left his teammates shouting as they played cards, drinking coffee, and he escaped to the eighth floor, where Sylvia was waiting for him in bed, surrounded by school notes. She threw them to the floor when she heard him arrive.

It's ridiculous. I can't study, I think about you all the time. Don't blame me when you fail your classes, please. Can I help you? he asked. How much time do we have? We have to be downstairs to go to the stadium in two hours. Sylvia's expression twisted. I have bad news, I have my period. It doesn't matter, this way we can use the time to study. Ariel tried to read a page of her notes. I had my period timed to coincide with your league games, it was a perfect schedule, but today it got screwed up, of course. Don't worry about it, I didn't bring you here to fuck. What are you studying?

Two hours later, his teammates traveled down the hall toward the bus parked at the hotel entrance. The place was filled with fans. The police were discreetly keeping an eye on the surroundings. Kids were asking for autographs. Even violence became part of the routine and they always expected insults from some group, some rocks getting thrown at them near the stadium. *Madrid se quema, se quema Madrid*, Madrid is burning, sang others. If some people didn't want to kill us, there wouldn't be others willing to die for us, a player in Buenos Aires used to say when things sometimes got ugly on the way out of a stadium. There they would keep the local fans in the stadium for thirty minutes postgame to give the visiting team time to get back to their neighborhoods. But the ride with police escort was pleasant; the bus ignored red lights, like they were VIPs in a world that stopped to make them a priority.

Sylvia's gaze found Ariel's when he went out among his teammates. He winked at her; she smiled. He was still on the bus when Sylvia called him on the phone. I'm on the Ramblas, it's full of tourists, she told him. Is it pretty? asked Ariel. There are human statues with costumes on, they remind me of mimes, I don't know why they make me sad. Mimes make you sad? I always want to kill them, said Ariel. Every two steps is a stand selling soccer jerseys, but I don't see yours. Well, I'm on the rival team. Yeah. Sylvia kept describing what she saw. A guy offering cans of drinks that he carried in a backpack, bars open to the street, pets in cages, pigeons that ate parakeets' birdseed, a herd of Japanese tourists with wheeled suitcases, portrait artists who used up charcoal reproducing the impossible faces of their occasional clients and exhibited pathetic caricatures of celebrities. Once, when I was little, my father insisted on having my portrait done on the street, I had to ask my mother to hide it, it was horrible. Sylvia, I have to go, we're getting to the stadium. Good luck.

Ariel went out on the field on the terrazzo stairs. Cleats echoed like horseshoes. Some players crossed themselves, others ripped up a blade of grass when they leaped onto the field, others carried out highly elaborate superstitious rituals. In Argentina he played with a center halfback from Bahía Blanca who went out onto the field with his right foot, then had to place his left hand on the field and kiss the crucifix he wore against his chest five times and say, mother, mother, mother three times. No strategy for feeling protected was too small in this profession, to survive in the void.

Less than an hour later, a car takes him with the doctor to a clinic in the upper part of the city. There he is subjected to an

X-ray that reassures them. It's just a sprain. Two weeks of re-covery, the doctor says, and for the first time Ariel feels able to relax the tense line of his lips. A more serious injury would have left him out of the end of the championship. He knows, like everyone does, that the last ten games are as important as the last ten minutes of each game. No one remembers the dull first half after an electrifying end, no one remembers the whistles in the middle of the season when they hear the ovations at the end of the championship. An old Argentinian midfielder who had come back to San Lorenzo after almost a decade of European soccer always told them, a shitty season is saved by a decisive goal in the last minute of the last game. This amnesiac business was just that absurd.

The doctor speaks calmly to him about the recovery pro-cess. They get into a taxi directly from the clinic to the airport. They gave him a crutch so he doesn't put any weight on the ankle and wrapped it up tightly in a bandage. The doctor asks the driver for the results of the game, and Ariel feels guilty about not having worried all that time about the score. They lost. At the boarding gate, he is joined by his teammates, heads bowed, tired, not in the mood to talk. Everyone asks about his injury, the coach comes over to talk. Ariel finds him cold, he blames him for the result of the game, which complicates their chance for winning the title. Amílcar sits next to him in the waiting area. We missed you on the field, there was nowhere to pass the ball.

Sylvia didn't make the flight. She sends him a late message. I couldn't find a fucking cab in the area. Later she writes again to tell him that she's getting on a flight at almost midnight. In Madrid, Ariel doesn't go with the team to the bus. I'll get a cab, he says to the delegate. He shouldn't drive, so he leaves his car in the parking lot. When enough time has passed, he tells the taxi driver that he forgot something at the airport and he has to go back. The man kindly insists he'll wait for him, but Ariel says it's going to take him a while and gives him a generous tip.

He goes to sit far from the door where Sylvia's flight is set to arrive. Husky calls him on his cell phone. I guess you're already at home, how's your ankle? Ariel chats with him for a while. He's out drinking. He tells him about the game. I didn't travel to cover it because the newspaper's cutting costs. Soon I'll be back to writing about games while I listen to them on the radio like when I started out. Then he says I wish you came back out to play, you playing lame could have done more than some of them with two good legs. I think your team only got in three shots at goal in the whole ninety minutes. In one of them, the goalie almost insisted on scoring a goal on himself, he must have been bored.

Ariel waits another half hour until he gets Sylvia's call. Where are you? He explains. She finds him sad, his forearm resting on the crutch. Is it serious? We'll have to take a cab. Sylvia picks up his bag off the floor and carries it over her shoulder, they walk slowly to the taxi stand. I was about to go out and scalp my ticket. How boring. My substitute didn't do a good job. No, even though he's pretty cute. That guy? They call him "the Mirror" because he spends almost two hours combing his bangs, he's a real pretty boy.

The cabdriver looks into the rearview mirror when they are already out of the airport. Are you out of it for a long time? No, no, nothing broken, luckily, just two weeks. From that point on, Ariel finds himself forced to maintain a long conversation with him, focused particularly on the endemic problems, as the driver calls them, of the team. Sylvia makes mocking gestures, showing two fingers like a pair of scissors for him to cut it short, but Ariel shrugs his shoulders. In my day, says the man, players were on a team for life, it was a marriage, but, now, it's a little like well-paid whores, excuse the expression, they put out for one night and if they lose, well, it's the fans who suffer, because the players couldn't give two shits.

Don't say those things in front of my sister here, please, says Ariel.

A while later, the taxi searches for Sylvia's address. She has her hand on Ariel's thigh, which seems like it's about to bust through the worn denim. Come to my house, he says, stay with me tonight. I can't. The cabbie keeps talking. Soccer today is pure business, money, money, and money, it's the only thing that matters. Ariel decides to get out with her.

They walk to the high step of the doorway. The street is dark. They sit down. Ariel extends his leg. I'd rather be out in the cold than listen to more of that guy's chitchat. I'd invite you up to my house, but my father will be there. This isn't the time of night to introduce me to him. Can you imagine? We can go into his room and wake him up. Sylvia laughs. Look, Papá, look who I brought you. Does it hurt? Ariel shrugs. I don't remember a single day in the last three years that my legs didn't hurt.

Now seriously, there's nothing I'd like more than seeing your room.

13

Sylvia is surprised to hear whispering voices in her father's room. At first she thinks he's talking on the phone, which would be unusual at that time of night. But from her room, while she undresses, she hears a restrained and sporadic female voice. Although the conversation reaches her as an unintelligible murmur, the movement, the brushing of sheets, the squeaking of the bed frame, and a bridled panting convinces her that they are making love. In her bed, she has two feelings. On one hand she is happy her father is with someone. On the other she is terrified by who that someone will be. Although she tries to repress the idea, she wonders if it will be someone whom she will have to develop a new, as of yet undefined, relationship with. Her independent coexistence is threatened. Today the house is a pit stop, a refuge, a rest, she doesn't think she can accept it becoming a couple's home again, and finding herself obliged to participate in their lives.

The tiredness, the hours of missed sleep, helps Sylvia fall asleep in spite of the hushed voices that come from the room next door. She left Ariel at home with his ankle resting on the living room coffee table. That afternoon, Sylvia had found him more worried than other times. Somewhat caught up in himself. Team problems, he explained. The two weeks off had been, at first, good news for Sylvia. They broke the routine of separations and trips. But soon she realized that not playing was tragic for Ariel. Decisive games are coming up, he complained.

That evening they didn't make love. Sylvia had stopped to buy pasta at the Buenos Aires–Madrid deli. On the brick wall, they had hung a long picture with a printed phrase: "There's only one thing Buenos Aires has that Madrid doesn't: Buenos Aires!" How's the chief? asked one of the owners. Fine, recovering from his sprain. Oh, he has a sprain? Yeah, Sylvia explained, he can't play. The girl insisted on giving him a box of *dulces de leche*. He loves them, tell him they're from me.

Ariel saw all the games on television, while Sylvia skimmed through some notes on his lap. Can you call me a taxi? she said when she looked at the clock and was surprised to see it was almost eleven. He gave her money; he always had an envelope around somewhere filled with bills. The trip to her house cost a fortune, but he gave her extra money. You don't have to give me so much, she protested. You paid for the pasta and the cab here. Keep it, and that way you have some for the next few days. But this is three thousand euros, that's quite a chunk of change. So? Aren't you with me for my money? said Ariel. It's obviously not for my brains.

Sylvia leaves the house before there is any movement from her father's room and his door remains closed. The morning of classes holds some charm of normality for Sylvia. She sees her schoolmates and laughs at their jokes more indulgently because she knows that in the evening she will be far away. She enjoys her lunch break with Mai, the conversation with Dani when he joins them. A normal life hemmed in by the gray walls of the high school.

Mai had been a bit low since she broke up with her boyfriend, Mateo. He moved to Barcelona, to a squat. She went to see him with hope of reconciliation. She had gotten Ma+Ma tattooed onto the inside of her arm, in gothic letters. Mai plus Mateo, she explained, but it ended horribly. There I was washing everybody's dishes. The house stunk, there was a group of French kids who had never heard of the invention of the shower, I can't even tell you . . . And on top of it all, they had dogs covered in fleas. Is it completely necessary to be so skanky? Fuck, it's one thing to be against the system and another thing altogether to be against soap. She carried over her annoyance to the small inconveniences of the cafeteria, the schoolyard. She now used her sharp wit for aggravation rather than irony. The failed relationship had made her lose a lot of her self-confidence, even though she talked nonstop. When I came back I showed my mother the tattoo. I did it for you, I told her, and she got all choked up. Sylvia appreciated the interruptions from other students and Dani's arrival, despite the fact that she sometimes detects his sad eyes.

The night Ariel got injured in Barcelona, when they returned to Madrid on different planes, they ended up sneaking into her room. He asked to with a childish smile and she agreed with a challenging expression. Sylvia opened the door without making any noise, but could barely stifle her laughter when Ariel went through the living room, in the half light, hopping with his crutch. From her father's bedroom came some monotonous snores that stopped abruptly when Ariel crashed his crutch against the edge of the coffee table. Is that you? Yeah, Papá. What time is it? Sylvia approached the door. One-thirty, see you tomorrow.

Sylvia put a T-shirt over her desk lamp, creating an orange glow in the room. Ariel looked the place over. The computer on the desk, the messy pile of CDs, the clothes overflowing from the open closet, hanging from the door and the knob, on the chair, and at the foot of the bed. There is a teddy bear on the bed and a yellowed poster of the vegetarian singer of a British band. Who is that? asked Ariel. You still haven't given me a photo of you. They laughed, sitting on the bed, and talked in a whisper. Every once in a while, she lifted up her hand and shushed him, listening to make sure her father wasn't moving around the house. They kissed for a long time. Sylvia noticed his erection beneath his pants. You want me to jerk you off? Ariel threw his head back. How can you ask me that? My God, you're so crazy . . . Then Sylvia led him back to the door of the apartment. They parted in silence on the landing. He waited to call the elevator until she had gone back to her room.

In the afternoon, she stops by to visit her grandmother before taking a cab over to Ariel's apartment. She finds her weak, unable to have a long conversation. Your father came to introduce us to the girl he's dating. Her grandmother's remark surprises Sylvia so much that she reacts strangely. Oh, yeah? He introduced her to you? She pretends she had met her already and adds a nod of the head when her grandmother says she seems like a nice girl. Sylvia thinks that Lorenzo's interest in meeting her boyfriend and finding out about her relationship was just a way to open the door for him to introduce her to his own new partner.

She's shocked to discover that her grandmother is wearing a diaper. Her grandfather comes in to change it and makes her leave the room. Sylvia peeks through the half-open door of her grandfather's studio. The piano lid is open and there are scattered scores. Your grandfather's going to start teaching his student again, Aurora had told her with excitement.

Her grandparents' home conveys an atmosphere of illness and lack of life. Even the stairs of the building are sad like worn tears. She had promised her mother she would spend this weekend with her. That was before Ariel got injured. And now she doesn't want to leave him alone. When she calls her mother from the street and suggests postponing the trip for next weekend, Pilar responds with an extended silence.

I knew this would happen, that we wouldn't see each other for weeks. And it sounds more like she's punishing herself than recriminating Sylvia. Come on, Mamá, we talk on the phone every day. I just have to do some work for school, with other kids in the class. I swear I'll come next weekend for sure. It's not such a big deal, is it?

Yeah, but I'm not seeing you grow up, isn't that something?

Sylvia laughs into the telephone. Relax, Mamá, I promise I haven't grown up. I don't grow anymore. If anything, only my ass is growing.

14

It's the third time in ten days that the bus drops him in the plaza, beside the jardinières glistening from recent watering. From there he walks three streets, to the blocks of apartments with small balconies and green awnings. Móstoles is a remote and unfamiliar place to Leandro, a man raised in old Madrid, ignorant of those margins, cities around the city. Osembe gave him the name of the street, the number of the building, and the apartment. He wrote it down and then searched for the most accessible route in the street atlas, put together the itinerary as if it were an adventure. He left from the traffic circle under construction in front of the old North Station, and the bus went along the highway to Extremadura.

It was a shared apartment, divided into small rooms, originally designed to house a conventional family and which thirty years later held seven people. Osembe had told him that she shared the apartment with six girlfriends. It was quite messy. The kitchen was a corner filled with furniture and junk. At that time of day, they were alone. They cross through the square living room, where the blinds are down, and light from the outside barely enters. She leads him directly to the room. She says, this way, and then, how nice to see you again. She is wearing jeans with a gilded design along the hem. She seems younger and more cheerful than in the chalet. But when she closes the door and invites Leandro to sit on the bed, she regains her old serious expression and her mechanical style. The money first, of course, she says. She wears pink slippers with thick soles.

Love on the clock, thought Leandro. Because Osembe could go from licking his stomach to lifting the alarm clock to check the time without changing expressions. When the time was up, she became slinky and sweet again and she said, stay another hour, and if Leandro handed over the money, another 150 euros, then she went back to killing time indolently and chatting a bit and she got up to talk or send messages on her cell. Leandro was aware that she stretched out the time to make more money. She didn't want to spend a second with him if it wasn't in exchange for cash. He didn't deceive himself about that. But he didn't do anything to avoid it. She, for example, would lick and dampen his ear, something that bugged him and made him worry about getting an ear infection like he had in the past, but he couldn't find a way to say, stop, it bothers me. He let her do it, like a puppet on a string. He hadn't seen her for weeks and now he focuses on her skin again, her hands, the calf muscles of her legs when she leans over him.

A noise is heard in the apartment. A roommate coming back. Do they have the same job as you? asks Leandro. No, no, and they couldn't even imagine that I do this, but Leandro knows she's lying. Only with special clients like you, she had said a little earlier, and then she had smiled. She kept the money in a drawer of the night table. The same place where she hides the condoms. On the table are a fashion magazine and scattered clothes. Also perfumes and lotions. And a large bottle of body oil that she rubs over her skin and which Leandro suspects she uses to interject a film of distance between their bodies. Photos are stuck into the frame of the mirror on the wall, of her with friends and maybe her boyfriend, a young smiling guy sitting with her on the outside table of a bar. In spite of the lowered blinds, the unbearable noise of the street comes in. There is construction nearby that causes an annoying rumble. When the sexual activity quiets, Leandro is cold, but she doesn't invite him to get beneath the sheets. There is a thick, worn blanket on top of the bed. The place is dirty and Leandro finds it unpleasant.

Days earlier his friend Manolo Almendros showed up at his apartment with his wife. It was almost lunchtime. They convinced Leandro to go out to eat with Manolo while she stayed behind. They strolled to a restaurant on Raimundo Fernández Villaverde. From there they could see the black skeleton of the Windsor Tower, which had burned on the night of February 12, with immense tongues of flame. There were still speculations about it. Someone had recorded images of shadows inside the building during the fire; there was talk of ghosts, later of firemen ransacking the safes of the many companies in the skyscraper. The workers took apart the remains in a fenced-in area.

During lunch Leandro was about to confess to his friend about his dates with Osembe. They had known each other for a long time. Unlike him, Almendros was still enviably vibrant, able to get excited about a book or a new discovery. It's strange, he told Leandro that day over the meal, we lived through the café period, when we were young and the only way to discover the truth about things was to put your ear to the bar. You remember? Now all that has disappeared. There's a giant virtual café and it's called the Internet. Now young people have a peek in there, and it's not like, let's see what Ortega or Ramón is saying, no, everything is anarchic and over the top, but that's just the way things are. You know, in this country nobody wants to be part of an association or a group, but everybody wants to be right. That is the old café. And then you can find a lot of information, but that's all chaotic, too. I already told you I'm writing a piece in praise of and in answer to Unamuno, right? Well, I go to find some new information and when you type in Unamuno the first page that comes up is about Unamuno, but all jokes about his name, rude jokes, some of them fun, all making light of his name. Imagine. Leandro was familiar with Manolo's passion for Unamuno. Manolo used to quote entire paragraphs of his tragic perspective on life, shared his passion for origami, but also made jokes at his expense and speculated about the phimosis operation he had when he was already an old man. Has anyone wondered if there is a before and after in his painful view of the world? Spain hurt him and maybe what was hurting him was something else.

Then the conversation about the Web turned to pornography. Almendros had been completely taken aback by the things one could find with just the click of a mouse. It's like a huge erotic bazaar devoted to masturbation in all its forms. There are girls being spied on, exhibitionist couples, perversions, humiliations, aberrations. Sometimes I think it's better that we're going to miss out on what's coming next. People will live in cubicles and never step out onto the street, we will be a planet of onanists and voyeurs.

Maybe, answered Leandro, but street prostitution hasn't decreased, it's gone up. People still need to touch each other. Well, we'll see. I think humans are going to touch each other less and less, until one day we don't touch each other at all. Those women who put in plastic tits and plastic lips. You tell me, they don't want them to be kissed or touched, they just want them to be looked at.

And you, you never?

Almendros lifted his shoulders. I find that world depressing. Who would be so stupid as to pay for something faked? And give money to the mafias that traffic in women. No, it disgusts me. I think anyone who contributes to that market is swine. Then, during that second, while a Polish waitress brought their first course, Leandro didn't confess to his friend out of shame, out of fear of not being able to explain himself and not having enough of a justifiable reason. Did he have one? There wasn't even love, which justifies everything. I fell stupidly in love with a girl, but it wasn't true. That wasn't it.

He didn't tell him that he had spent three mornings walking aimlessly around Coimbra Park in Móstoles. Curiously watching the people who passed, those who stepped out onto their balconies, anyone driving by in a car. He stopped to carefully observe the African women walking by with their grocery bags. On a few occasions, when one of them was alone and in spite of the frightened expressions his approach provoked, he dared to ask them about Osembe. Do you know a Nigerian girl named Osembe? And they shrugged their shoulders, suspicious, and said no.

He didn't tell his friend Almendros that the third morning, sitting near the park, as he read the newspaper, he saw a black girl get off a bus. Her hair was different, shorter, but it was her, no doubt about it. She was walking with two other women and wore a very striking red leather jacket and high-heeled shoes at the end of her jeans. He followed them for a while, to see if they parted at any point. He couldn't hear their conversation except when they erupted into laughter or an exaggeratedly loud sentence, and in the end, screwing up his courage, he dared to raise his voice and call her, Osembe, Osembe, and after the second time she turned and saw him. She showed a sarcastic, but dazzling, smile.

Osembe separated from the group and walked toward him. Well, well, my little old man. Leandro explained he had been looking for her in the neighborhood for several days. Ah, but I don't do that work anymore, no, no. Not anymore. Leandro looked at her with interest. Can I buy you a cup of coffee? Chat with you for a minute? No, I'm with my friends, not now, really. She must have sensed Leandro's devastation because she said, call me, call me on my cell. And she dictated a phone number that Leandro didn't need to write down. He memorized it. It was filled with even numbers and that made it easier for him. Even numbers had always seemed friendly to him, ever since he was a boy; he found odd numbers, on the other hand, objectionable, awkward. Her number floated in his head as Osembe returned to her friends, who received her with giggles. What would she tell them? That's the old guy who can't get enough of me, the one I told you about?

He let a few days pass before calling her. Osembe's absence had made him feel better. Getting her out of his sight was the end of a nightmare. One afternoon he dialed the number from home. Aurora was being visited by her sister and Leandro spoke in a soft voice. She laughed, as if their meeting put her in a good mood, gave her power. And then she said, but, honey, why don't you come see me?

Osembe shows off her muscles for him. It amuses her to tense and relax areas of her body. She laughs like a teenager. She's vain. That afternoon she won't agree to take off her bra. The only thing she doesn't like about her body, she had told him many times, are the lines on her breasts. Stretch marks, Leandro tells her. They look like an old lady's, she says. Leandro tries to take off her bra, but she won't let him, she laughs, they struggle. She has small nipples and white lines that run along where her breasts meet her chest. He tries to kiss them, but she says it tickles and she pushes him away again and again, as if she wanted to be the only one in charge of the game.

Leandro likes her dawdling. He doesn't mind her gaze constantly shifting to the alarm clock. When they talk, they tell each other simple things. He asks what she spends all her money on, she says that's my business, I like to be pretty for you, and other lies so obvious the conversation grows grotesque.

I don't want to see you here again, Leandro tells her. I don't like coming here. It's very far, it's dirty. I don't want to bump into your roommates. Nobody's going to say anything to you, we're comfortable here, no one orders us around, she says. The next time I'll find someplace else, says Leandro, ending the conversation. He doesn't shower there. He is repulsed by the plastic covers on the toilet, the rusty little tub, the worn bathmat and the pistachio-colored tiles.

The street is jam-packed with people. There are children playing ball. Almost all of them the children of immigrants. The trip home takes Leandro almost an hour. Aurora's sister, Esther, is still beside her bed. They kid around and try to remember, with absurd doggedness, the name of the chocolate shop where their father used to take them for fried dough strips after Mass when they were girls. They say names at random and Esther laughs with her dynamic, horsey smile.

In the hallway, before leaving, Aurora's sister starts to cry in front of Leandro. She's dying, Leandro, she's dying. Leandro tries to calm her down. Come on, come on, now we have to be strong for her. Esther speaks in a bereaved whisper, but she's so good, my sister has always been so good. There's nobody like that anymore.

Leandro waits for Aurora to fall asleep and then dials Joaquín's number. Jacqueline answers. They speak for barely a second. He can't come to the phone right now, but call back in twenty minutes. When they finally speak, Leandro tells him that he's made a date with the biographer for next week. Ah, perfect, he's a charming kid, don't you think? And Leandro tells him the reason for his call. I wanted to ask you about your apartment. If I could use it one of these nights. Joaquín's silence is thick and tense. Only if it's not a problem, of course. Of course, when do you need it? I don't know, it doesn't matter, maybe Friday. Sure, sure, tomorrow I'll talk to Casiano and you can come by and pick up the keys, before eight, okay, the doorman goes home at eight. Perfect. You want to impress someone? Joaquín asks him with a laugh. Well . . . At this point, what can we do. But please, do leave the sheets in the washing machine. There's a woman who comes by to clean on Mondays. Yeah, sure, says Leandro, it'll just be this once, eh. That's good, because if Jacqueline finds out . . .

I found the letters, the letters you sent me from Paris and Vienna, they might be interesting for the book. Leandro knew Aurora had kept them, surely he could find them. Joaquín's voice regains its enthusiasm, fantastic, that'd be fantastic, although they must be infantile, well, it will be amusing. Of course.

Leandro feels a stab of cowardice again. Why am I doing all this? Why do I dirty everything around me? He asks himself questions he can't answer. He knows the weakness of others almost as well as his own. And yet that's no consolation, and doesn't stop him.

15

He had gotten up so early that he was exhausted by nine. His stomach was growling and he suggested stopping somewhere. They were in the middle of a move and they had filled the van with boxes and furniture. Wilson brought his two usual friends to lend a hand. Chincho, a young man whose neck was wide enough for four heads, and Junior, a strong, thin man with slanty eyes. Lorenzo elbows up to the bar. He orders the coffees and a slab of freshly made potato frittata. The others have a look at a sports newspaper. They seem familiar with Spanish soccer teams and had chosen to root for rival teams, so they joked around and argued. Junior was from Guayaquil and had switched the Barcelona there for the Barcelona here. I like the team colors, the blue represents the ideal and the red the struggle. You have to show your affection for Madrid, that's the city you live in, says Wilson. He had become a fan of Lorenzo's team. Even though they're having a bad year, he says. When they get to talking about players, about Ariel, Wilson says, a lot of *guaragua* but that's it. A lot of swerving and bobbing, he explains, even though he's the best at it. In Ecuador he was a fan of the Deportivo Cuenca, this year we won the national title, with an Argentinian coach, Asad "the Turk," and this is the first time we've won it. Over there we call the team the Southern Express. You have to see Cuenca, it's beautiful, the cathedral is incredible, and the university. The two friends start messing with him, Wilson knows the cathedral and the university really well, but only from the outside. They also bring up some acquaintance who last week won the competition for best Jabugo slicer in Spain, it's incredible, fifteen months ago he had never even seen a leg of cured ham.

Lorenzo had opened up a local paper and he flips through the pages without paying much attention. He sees a photo of Paco in a small box beside the image of a chalet. There is only vague information about a band of robbers arrested by police. They were described as extremely violent and the police believe they were the ones responsible for the murder of the Madrid businessman Francisco Garrido, several months earlier.

Lorenzo skims through the lines searching for information. Albanians, hired thugs, armed, cold cruelty. The bitter smell of espresso and milk from the bar hits Lorenzo's nose. He doesn't know what to think. Now he reads the entire news story, dwelling on each sentence. Everything sounds circumstantial, vague. It could be an effort by the police to pin unsolved cases on someone or just the journalist's invention.

Relief and panic. Can those feelings be mixed together? Paco's face in an unflattering photo. Maybe from his ID. He always said no one should ever allow a bad photo and tore up any he didn't like. He definitely would not have accepted that one. How ironic. It didn't in the least reflect his magnetic personality, it actually made him look common, like an insignificant victim. Lorenzo thought the arrests would open up criminal proceedings and then someone would be forced to look for conclusive evidence. Nothing is closed.

They go back to work. Lorenzo and Chincho make the first trip in the van to the new location with the furniture. The others finish packing up. The street is jammed solid. In Ecuador you must not have traffic like this. Chincho shrugs his shoulders, hiding a centimeter of his immense neck. I drove a taxi in Quito and the downtown is rough, it's super-hard to drive around there, worse than this. The move is exhausting and doesn't end until almost two. It is Wilson who receives the money and distributes it among the four after settling accounts in his little notebook. Lorenzo has the strange feeling of being just an employee. They say good-bye. As Lorenzo approaches his building, he is filled with a certain euphoria. If the crime was committed by someone else, then he had nothing to do with it.

He goes up in the elevator to his apartment, but he changes his mind and goes up one more floor. He knocks on the door of his fifth-floor neighbors. Daniela opens it. Lorenzo doesn't give her time to say anything; he slips into the apartment. She closes the door and makes a gesture for him to keep quiet. The boy is sleeping. Lorenzo kisses her, hugs her. I needed to see you. You can't be here. They're not coming home until later. But it's not right. I can help you, what were you doing? Don't be silly.

Euphoric, he pulls her further into the apartment. It's identical to his, but set up very differently. He doesn't have time to realize that the main difference is the familial warmth. Lorenzo pushes her into the main bedroom. No, no, whispered Daniela, somewhat amused and somewhat embarrassed. Lorenzo gets her onto the mattress, and lies on top of her to kiss her and caress her.

Three days earlier, Lorenzo had undressed that body for the first time in his bedroom. The moment had little in common with this one. It was a slow labor, between passionate and prudent. Daniela was passive. They had gone out for the night, but it was intensely cold. She was the one who suggested, can we go to your place? Of course, he said, he didn't think about Sylvia, she definitely wouldn't come home until later.

They sat on the sofa. He put on some soft music, brought out something to drink. He kissed her and they talked very close together. He pushed her hair out of her face with the tips of his fingers. He told her about episodes of his life and he let on that they had met when he had hit bottom. Daniela seemed to like Lorenzo's confidential tone. She bit her lip when he told her about Pilar, I think we were the happiest couple in the world for a while. Every once in a while, he interrupts his words to kiss her lightly or touch her face. Daniela looked around the house. The bookshelf in the living room, the television.

Take me to your room, she said when Lorenzo kissed her intensely, as if putting an end to the conversation.

On the bed, he removed Daniela's clothes. Her skin had a gray tone and was soft. Her flesh seemed oppressed by her clothes. The bra strap, the tight pants. She had enormous, electric-pink nipples and generous breasts that when freed produced an expansive wave of eroticism. On her back, Lorenzo discovered some pink scars at shoulder height that she covered when she lay down on the mattress. She crossed her arms above her breasts as if she were protecting herself, or as if she were handing herself over. He took off her shoes and then lowered her pants along with her panties, which were curled up inside themselves. He had trouble getting off her clothes, as if he were removing the top layer of skin. Her belly and thighs rippled seductively. Lorenzo moved to kiss her sunken belly button. She was tense, but immobile. The mark from the elastic of her underwear was imprinted on her trembling skin.

Lorenzo wanted to go down on her, but she pressed her thighs together and said no, not that, that's dirty. Lorenzo crept up to find her face and neck again. She didn't undress him, so he took it all off without neglecting her body, which he kissed and stroked relentlessly. The light was turned off, but through the window filtered in a glow that allowed him to appreciate Daniela's flesh. Lorenzo lay down on top of her and bit by bit Daniela's thighs allowed him in. Her hands found a place to rest on Lorenzo's back. He took that as the moment to penetrate her and she moaned intensely.

It had happened on the most unexpected evening. Maybe the cold of the street, maybe the time had simply arrived. Daniela had a dark birthmark on her skin, above her hip. Lorenzo came very close to her, after pulling out of her body in an accelerated twist.

There was a moment of silence and then she said, that was what you wanted, wasn't it? Why do you say that? Didn't you want it? I don't know . . .

Daniela's words sounded sad and forced Lorenzo to be more affectionate. He spoke into her ear about the first time he had seen her, in the elevator. Of the impression her almond eyes had made on him, the mystery they emanated. No other woman except Pilar had been between these sheets, he told her. He didn't talk about how dissimilar their bodies were, the different sensations. He was now a different man, too.

Don't you ever think about her? About your wife? Sometimes. Daniela's hands were very careful not to go near his sex. She had them intertwined on her belly and Lorenzo stroked them calmly.

This is all so weird, me here, with you, she said. Why? I don't know, I guess you got what you wanted, to have me, and now you can feel satisfied, victorious. Why do you say it like that? Don't you trust me? Everything can be so ugly or so beautiful. But that's it, you've slept with me now, fine.

Lorenzo was silent. He didn't entirely understand Daniela's attitude. Her flesh, on the other hand, aroused him.

For men having sex is the end of the conquest. No, for us it's the beginning. I saw your face when you rushed to come outside of me, but you, you didn't look at my face.

Daniela . . .

You didn't even ask me. Maybe I would have wanted you to finish inside me. To at least have something left when you disappear from my life.

Lorenzo kissed her as if kisses were the best way to refute her doubts. Her lips were dry, but they tasted good. Come here, get under, you're gonna catch cold. Lorenzo lifted the sheets for her.

They heard Sylvia come in, go to her room, and shut the door. In a whisper, they talked about his daughter, let's not make much noise. Lorenzo told Daniela that she had brought over her boyfriend the other night, I pretended to be asleep. She already has a boyfriend, so young, and they sleep together? No, well, I don't know about that, said Lorenzo. How can you not know? She's your daughter.

Later they made love again, or more accurately Lorenzo made love to Daniela. He let her hair get tangled in her face. He tried to place her on top of him. He had a hard time overcoming her resistance. He felt possessed by the cadence of her breasts swaying above him. Daniela rested her hands on Lorenzo's face. I'm no sex goddess, you know? Lorenzo laughed and stroked her breasts. He told her that they were very nice. She said thank you. Daniela barely moved on top of him, she moaned, but she wasn't enjoying the moment. Lorenzo forced himself to not take his eyes off of hers.

Daniela insisted on going home. She didn't want to spend the night there. She slipped from between the sheets and started to dress. He watched her; the undulation of her flesh aroused him. She begged Lorenzo to stay in bed, but he leaped into his clothes and drove her home in the van, even though he knew full well that it would be hellish finding a parking spot when he got back. They parted with a short kiss on the lips. Her smile seemed frank and happy for the first time. Lorenzo felt that there was still an abyss between them, but he said to himself, I love her, she is beautiful and fragile, perhaps I'm not yet worthy of her, but I could be someday.

He wanted to take her right there on his neighbor's neatly made bed, with the stuffed animals placed between the two long pillows, on the bedspread with white and orange flowers, between the night tables where each of them piled their reading, but she drew a hard line. No, no, not that. The day before they had gone out together, but Daniela hadn't wanted to go to his house nor did she invite him up to hers. Come, says Daniela, and she forces him to stand. Lorenzo remains lying down for a second on the bed and points with his hands to the lump between his legs. Look at this, it's not my fault, what do you want me to do with this? What nerve. She smiles.

She takes Lorenzo's hand and brings him to the bathroom in the hallway. Beside the sink, she lowers his pants halfway down his thighs and jerks him off with emphatic arm movements. She looks at his face and smiles defiantly while she does it. Lorenzo caresses her breasts through her clothes and hugs her when he comes, splattering the faucets. He composes himself quickly. She just says, now go, you can't be here.

He leaves the apartment, glancing first through the peephole to make sure he doesn't run into any neighbors. He goes down the stairs to his landing. I love you very much, he had said to Daniela a second before leaving. Very much. But all he got out of her was, get out of here already. Nothing was going to be easy.

He understood that Daniela didn't want to announce the relationship to her friends, be seen strolling around the neighborhood with a Spaniard. Someone might start spreading rumors if they saw them together. Daniela liked to feel respected. As she had said to him, I'm not one of those girls who think a man is going to solve all her problems, I'm one of those who think that he's just going to make things more complicated.

They would see each other again that evening, when she finished work. They could have dinner together, but she was never hungry. Maybe he would bring her over to his place. The time had come to introduce her to Sylvia. He didn't want more time to pass without them meeting. He didn't want to be sneaking around his own house, his own life. He wouldn't say stupid stuff to Sylvia like, I have a right to remake my life, too. He'd just say, this is Daniela.

16

They like that café because they can watch the street through the large rectangular window. Sylvia pointed it out one afternoon. Look, it's like a movie theater. Through the glass, real life passed by like a performance projected just for them. Often Ariel is the one who shows up later, and she greets him from inside with a smile. But today he is the one waiting, prepared to see her walking down the sidewalk in his direction. Ariel rests into the chair's back, ready for the pleasure of seeing her.

Luck and pigheadedness, the masseur had told him that morning. If I had to define what you need to succeed here, that's how I'd sum it up, luck and pigheadedness. If one isn't dead set on tackling obstacles when they arise, he's better off just leaving, because that's when you have to grit your teeth. He said it as if he weren't talking to Ariel, as if he were addressing the injured ankle, and it could hear him and take his advice. Half of the injuries are up here, and he pointed to his forehead. Ariel appreciated the powerful hands on his body. Here, years ago, there was an Italian fullback who always had an expression for these things. *Non piangere, coglioni, ridi e vai . . .* And that's it, there's no point complaining, he said to end the massage.

Pujalte's tan was intriguingly perfect. It was applied to his entire face in a hyperprecise way. It matched his gelled hair and contrasted sharply with his immaculate teeth. Too perfect to be a former player, thought Ariel when he saw him. He wore expensive shoes on the damp grass. The hems of his suit had gotten wet pacing the field during practice. Ariel came out of the weight room. He walked over to him, still carrying the crutch. Pujalte didn't take a step, he just waited.

We'll be more comfortable in the office, Pujalte told him, and he took his elbow as if he were helping him. It's March. He opened the small fridge and took out two little bottles of ice-cold water. Ariel doesn't drink his. I wanted to talk to you ahead of time, I wanted to let you know that as it stands today we aren't counting on you for next season. Of all the things Ariel had imagined hearing that week from his superiors, this was the most unexpected. And he felt bad about his inability to see it. He didn't like to be surprised, it seemed a sign of stupidity, of lack of foresight. It was important to anticipate others' decisions so they didn't catch you off guard. It actually had a lot to do with his attitude on the playing field, predict your opponents' options.

But Ariel didn't show his surprise. The sports director looked around the room or at his chest. His eyes never searched out Ariel's; sometimes they went to the door or to the wall, but never to Ariel's face. Neither the staff nor the fans feel that this team is the good bet for the future we were hoping it would be. Words. Words are always smoke screens. Ariel didn't listen to them. He chose instead to search out Pujalte's eyes, which he didn't manage to find. All this is to say that we are going to be hearing offers, you can do some looking around yourself, but discreetly, the worst thing we can do is let the press start to muddy the whole thing.

But I have a contract. Ariel would rather not have heard himself say that sentence.

Our only contract is with the fans' enthusiasm. The sports director's comment must have been pulled from some manual, from some anthology of brilliant, empty phrases. It couldn't be his own. Enthusiasm was too big a word for him. When their hopes aren't met, why stick to contracts.

The coach . . . Ariel tried to say. The coach is aware that we're having this conversation. He approves it and the president approves it, even though he never intervenes in these things anyway.

They're firing me, thought Ariel. Like giving away old clothes. It bothered him that they were doing it on a week when he couldn't defend himself on the field. When he couldn't even use his rage as a motivating force in the game. Injured, he seemed to have fewer arguments in his defense. And he didn't want to defend himself. He heard Pujalte talk about the future, about a more ambitious team. Ariel thought, it's my fault, I didn't try hard enough, things didn't go well.

Don't get worked up about it, I know what a player feels when he hears these words. I was like you not long ago. It would be a mistake to cling to your contract and lose the best years of your career, things might go better somewhere else and you can come back more mature, more formed as a player.

Are we talking about a transfer to another team?

We're not talking about anything, you're twenty years old, we have to see how things go, this is a meaningless stumble.

I don't know, there's something I don't understand, said Ariel. I look at the team and I don't think my contribution is where the biggest problem is, in fact, I see things going well for us out there; the fans like me. You haven't got the crowd eating out of your hand, Pujalte said. That counts for something, too. Things in Spain aren't like they are in Argentina. Here the crowd doesn't believe in the team colors or in the mushy stuff, you have to convince them at the start of the season that we're gonna take on the world, otherwise it takes us on. We can't tell them that this year is a good investment for next year or the year after that, they want it now. I'm going to be honest with you. We have another player lined up for your position, a name that will get people excited, someone new. I'm not saying you don't do a decent job covering your position, but I don't think you're a player to keep as a substitute. That's why I'm being frank with you, man to man, I don't want you to hear about our negotiations somewhere else.

Ariel nodded. It seemed he had to show appreciation for the deference. And maybe that was the case.

There'll be plenty of teams interested, give me a few weeks, let me check out the market and we'll meet again, okay? Ariel felt stupid getting up with the help of the crutch. Disabled. They definitely chose an ill-timed moment. I'm afraid this isn't my conversation to have, it would be better if you spoke with my agent. I'm paid to show my worth on the field, not to deal with meetings in offices, said Ariel before leaving.

Perhaps it's just that, you need more rest, more focus, less distractions, to feel like a soccer player . . .

The sports director spoke to his back. Ariel was about to burst out crying and he didn't want to turn around, or question him to find out if he was referring to something in particular. He called his brother from home, told him everything. Charlie calmed him down. They just say those things. Let other people take care of it, me included. But are things that bad? Why didn't you tell me? That's what most gets to me, Charlie, I didn't think things were going so badly.

That evening he relaxed, stretching out on the sofa and letting time pass, not getting into a conversation with Sylvia, just stroking her curls while she looked at her school notes. He envied her busyness. He didn't want to tell her anything. She asked, do you have Easter week off? I don't know yet, he said.

He was left with a bittersweet sensation, when he found himself being consoled by her after he had spent the last few days planning to distance himself. After seeing her bedroom, on tiptoe so as not to wake her snoring father, Ariel had realized how crazy it all was. She's sixteen years old. Posters on the wall, a stuffed animal on the bed. There he was, in the hotel before a game, going over notes from class and joking around, while she confessed that she had her period. Days later Marcelo arrived in Madrid to do a concert for his new record. He called him and said, you can't miss it.

Ariel went to the concert hall, the Galileo. Marcelo had reserved a table for him. Ariel didn't want to invite Sylvia. He had decided to take some space, put a stop to the madness. Ariel waited at the bar until Reyes arrived. He had gotten her phone number from Arturo Caspe. Excuse me, I don't want to be a bother, but the other night I made a fool of myself and I wanted to apologize. He now knew she was a quite well-known model. Oh please, it's not necessary. Ariel explained that a friend of his from Buenos Aires was performing in Madrid. I would love it if you came with me. She smiled on the other end of the line. She's an interesting girl, thought Ariel, with that almost suicidal way she smokes. You still have that beauty mark on your face? she asked. Yeah, I think so. Then I can't say no, answered Reyes. Was she flirting with him? Ariel felt encouraged, that was what he needed. You can bring your boyfriend, of course.

But she came alone.

The place was filled with people, most of them Argentinian, which Marcelo later expressed frustration about. I don't come all the way here to sing for people who already know me, where the fuck are the Spaniards? To be successful in Spain, I'd have to come live here, he said to Ariel. And I refuse to do that, because then the Spaniards look down on you because they consider you one of their own. But all this was after the concert. At the beginning, Marcelo appeared exultant, accompanied by a group of four good musicians, dressed in a black suit, white shirt, and a tie with the San Lorenzo colors.

It's funny to perform in a place called Galileo, he said after the first two songs. I hope I don't get burned at the stake. And it's hard not to end up in the burn ward of music history, right? Let me tell you, I'll be forty-five in September. Now I'm going to sing a respectful cover of the song I've woken up to every morning for almost twenty years now. That was how he presented his rendition of "Chimes of Freedom," one of Dylan's old classics, which Marcelo sang in Spanish for eight long minutes.

Ariel leaned over Reyes. Do you like it? he asked. She nodded. She was lovely, her breasts gathered in a fine black bra and peeking out through the open buttons of her white shirt, so sculpted that Ariel wondered if they weren't plastic. Toward the end of the concert, Marcelo dedicated a song to Ariel, after a long introduction in which he spoke about their friendship. Be good to him over here, he appealed.

They had a drink with Marcelo, but after that Reyes said, I have to get up early tomorrow. Ariel made a date to have lunch with Marcelo the next day. Reyes called a cab and Ariel offered to take her home. As they went out, a photographer surprised them. The camera flashes were like shots in the dark. Ariel lifted his crutch to get rid of the guy, but he backed up. They got into the taxi and left. The photographer kept shooting through the cab window. The driver said something Ariel didn't understand. I see you're very famous. I'm afraid they're after you, she said. I don't know, he said. She lived near the center of the city. Ariel apologized again for the other night. Come on, you didn't scare me or anything, she joked. It's even kind of flattering in the end, maybe you're the one who's not used to getting rejected. Ariel smiled. Does your boyfriend work in this, too? Yeah, he's a photographer, but not like the kind we just saw. Yeah. Ariel was nervous, and what do they do with those pictures? They usually show up in a magazine with a made-up interview where we say we're just good friends and that you want to recover quickly from your injury so you can give the fans more goals. The usual shit. My boyfriend has already been warned, but he gave me permission since he knows soccer players aren't my type. You might have more problems. Are you dating someone?

Ariel hesitated before answering. No, well, I'm breaking up with a girl. I don't know, it's a weird story. Reyes looked at him with interest, Ariel was silent, somewhat uncomfortable. You want to have a last drink? Near my house there's a mellow bar. She directed the taxi driver, who muttered something again, but this time Ariel did understand him, that's the way to recover from your injury, these good-for-nothings, what a life. Ariel lifted his eyebrows in Reyes's direction, and she smiled. You're more interested in girls than in the ball. Obviously, aren't you? answered Ariel. I think all women are bitches, especially my wife. Reyes coughed as if something were stuck in her throat. That's what I call speaking your mind.

They went to an Irish pub on a corner. Sitting at a wooden table, Ariel told her part of his story with Sylvia. He didn't hide the fact that she was sixteen years old. When I was sixteen, I was still falling in love with my gym teachers, she said, and I was sure George Michael was going to come pick me up after school. I guess you made one of her fantasies real and that could be dangerous. It scares me to death, he said. Even though Sylvia isn't the kind of teenager who lives in some fairy tale. Be careful, we girls are good at hiding things, warned Reyes. A little while later, she left him there with a half-finished beer, gave him a kiss on each cheek, and promised to get together another day. Ariel waited for a taxi on the street. He would have liked to sleep with her, lose himself in someone else's arms and someone else's body, to keep him away from Sylvia.

The next day, he ate lunch with Marcelo at a restaurant on Cava Baja. He invited Husky and there was instant chemistry between them, even though Husky started off strong. Before the first course arrived, he had already said, I can't stand those typical Argentinian singer-songwriters, the pretentious long-winded ones who think they're the heirs to that Catholic bore, Dylan. I like Neil Young. People who aren't poseurs. Dylan is a hamburger-eating egomaniac who thinks up songs that are too long while he's riding his motorcycle. Marcelo laughed thunderously. Is this guy nuts? Dylan is God. Marcelo was working on a rock opera. I know it sounds terrible. Yes, they assured him. It's about a twenty-eight-year-old Swiss tourist who was traveling through Argentina alone and disappeared after taking a walk in Pagancillo, in La Rioja, disappeared without a trace. They hadn't heard a thing from her in six months. Marcelo wanted to focus the songs on her father, a retired German professor who had come to the country to find her. His perspective could be perfect in summing up Argentina, that's what we need, the Swiss view. He could talk about the natural beauty, the social crap, the corruption, everything.

Shortly after, Marcelo cursed the piece of meat they had served him. This garbage is what Argentine meat is going to turn into if they keep opening up soy fields and closing pastures. Cows need to live free and not fattened up with injections like here in Europe. And when Husky disagreed again, he said, but, kid, you have a lovely voice, you have to do a duet with me on my next album, what a voice, it's crazy, it sounds like you got sent through a broken Pro Tools.

During dessert Marcelo mentioned Reyes, congratulations on the girl from last night, the one you brought to the concert, what a hot mama, but Ariel made it clear that they weren't dating. Husky asked about her. Ariel told them about the photograph. No doubt about it, if Arturo Caspe knew where you were going, he's the one who called them, declared Husky.

That son of a bitch lives to sell favors. I told you before, they're vampires, they need virgin blood every night.

Marcelo had found Ariel more serious. He blamed the injury. He didn't want to tell them about the bad news with the club or about his relationship with Sylvia, which he had decided to end. But Marcelo could be a persistent man. From the restaurant, he called a friend of his who worked as an analyst in Madrid and sent Ariel to see him that same afternoon. Husky laughed heartily. Spaniards don't go to shrinks, we get drunk in a bar, and all the barmen have psychiatric degrees from Gin and Tonic University.

Ariel sat in front of a doctor named Klimovsky who wanted that first session to just be a relaxed chat, which translated into an avalanche of information about his own life. He was an analyst, but he also wrote film scripts and painted. The paintings decorating his office were the terrible result of that supposedly harmless hobby. He barely let Ariel get out a word with more than one syllable, and even though they agreed to meet the following week, Ariel wasn't sure if he was going to come back. In one of the paintings a fish emerged from the vagina of a woman with her face painted like a harlequin. The image gave Ariel nightmares for most of the evening.

The next day, he caught the end of practice and kicked around without a crutch. He felt good after the massage and he wanted to find out the coach's opinion. Yesterday they told me they're not counting on me for next year. Who told you that? His surprise sounded fake. The club has its demands, if it were up to me I'd have other priorities, Requero tried to convince him. They say that there's someone signed for my position. This is the first I've heard of it. That was one of the things Ariel liked the least about these situations, the cowardice. He would have preferred more authority or at least an ounce of sincerity, even if it wasn't in his favor. But the coach was evasive.

I just wanted to know if you were counting on me, because I'm going to fight to stay on the team. The coach looked at him with an insignificant smile and nodded his head, as if he appreciated his spirit. He even made a stupid comment, I like people with character. While you're still on the team, don't ever doubt that you're my player.

Ariel automatically put him on his list of despicable people. It wasn't a very long list, but it included those who avoided taking responsibility when they should've owned up, those who had been fake, self-interested traitors in the moments when he was most helpless.

Amílcar invited him over for lunch. In the car they talked. He sensed something was going on. Don't get involved in it, Amílcar told him, listen to what they have to say to you and give up the noble attitudes and stuff like that. If they offer you a good team, leave, take the money, and enjoy the game, 'cause life is short. You may come back a star, it wouldn't be the first time. Ariel looked up at him. You know as well as I do that there are teams you never come back from, that only offer you a step down on the ladder. Maybe I'd rather go back to Buenos Aires than do that. They haven't even given me time to prove my mettle.

Time? Amílcar let out a mocking laugh. Time? We're talking about soccer. Here the sports newspapers come out every morning. You want time? From here to the next game is more or less an eternity. Ariel kept quiet. He knew Amílcar was right. He drove an enormous car.

Why so serious? asked Fernanda, Amílcar's wife, during lunch. Problems with the club, he didn't make the cut for next year. She had a serene beauty she tried to envelop Ariel in. Well, they're still thinking about it, he said. And don't you have a three-year contract? Five-year. So what? interjected Amílcar. Come on, sweetie, if a player wants to leave he does, if a club wants to get rid of you, they get rid of you, the contract is just a piece of paper. A piece of paper that means a lot of money, she said. The money is the least of it. They'll pay him, they'll sell him, they'll transfer him. Contracts are broken as easily as they're signed. It was easy for Amílcar to talk like that, thought Ariel. How many years have you been here, Amílcar? I didn't come in as a star.

Amílcar's harsh tone hurt Ariel for a second. He focuses on the plate in front of him. Amílcar's wife shakes her head, incredulous at her husband, and she scolds him with a look. It's the fucking truth. No one paid me millions or put me on magazine covers or sent me out on the field to win a game in the final minutes. You wanna switch places with me? Amílcar, please, you're talking to a twenty-year-old boy, don't take on that cynical attitude, insisted Fernanda. No, no, I understand him perfectly, murmured Ariel. I think he came to you looking for help, not so you could tell him all the shit that this business sweeps under the rug . . . Amílcar's expression soured. All right, sweetie, that's enough. This is serious, not a chat over coffee, okay? When someone makes what he's making, he can put up with being treated like merchandise. Well, I don't agree. Just because they pay you a fortune doesn't give them the right to treat you like shit, she said.

Okay, okay, don't start arguing now because of me.

No, don't worry. We love arguing, said Fernanda. She likes it more than I do. Amílcar's wife smiled and then brushed her husband's hand. *Meu anjo das pernas tortas*, she whispered to him, and he wagged his head, won over by her sweetness.

They ate leisurely. They only touched on the subject again briefly and they didn't delve into it. When it was time to go pick the kids up from school, Amílcar stood. You relax, I'll be back in half an hour, he said to Ariel. He disappeared shaking the car keys, his legs bowed like parentheses.

Ariel stayed with his teammate's wife. She served coffee. Do you nap after lunch? Since I've been in Spain I've gotten used to taking a siesta, she explained. I sleep barely three minutes, but it makes me relaxed all afternoon. A blond lock fell over one eye and Fernanda blew it out of the way, a childlike gesture that made Ariel smile. She was very lovely. When you finish your coffee, come up if you feel like it. She smiled warmly. My room is the first door on the right, at the top of the stairs.

She turned and went up the steps. When she got to the last one, she looked at him with her clear blue eyes. Ariel coughed. He almost knocked over the coffee mugs. The maid, a short, smug Moroccan woman, appeared to take away the tray. Ariel sat there alone. He wanted to flee. But also to take Amílcar's wife in his arms, to enjoy her beauty, which seemed to promise an icy surface, with fire inside.

Going up the stairs was torturous for Ariel. It all seemed perverse. He barely knew her, but ever since that first day he felt a mutual attraction floating in the air. Would he be able to go through with it just for a postlunch craving? Without taking anything else into consideration? Maybe it was all just a perverse game Amílcar was in on. He was about to run back downstairs. The veteran player who brings new team acquisitions to his wife. Too messy.

He knocked on the door. I won't do anything. Everything that happens will be her fault. I won't lift a finger, Ariel said to himself as he opened the door after she invited him in. He noticed his erection beneath his pants.

The electricity of the moment seemed to come from her perfect, straight hair, layered around her face. Fernanda was lying in the bed, still dressed; she had only taken off her shoes. She placed a hand on the mattress, inviting him to come closer. From the first moment I saw you, I felt a positive vibe, I know you have things in you that you haven't yet found ways to express. Ariel thought it was the moment to kiss her and he couldn't take his eyes off of her lips. But she leaned to reach the drawer on the bedside table and grab the handle. She's going to take out some condoms, thought Ariel. She extracted a thick book from the drawer. She flipped through its pages, deeply focused. When she found what she was looking for, she handed the book to Ariel. Read, read out loud, she asked.

Ariel read: "In sorrow, God is the only consolation. Nothing quenches your thirst, tiredness, doubt, and pain forever. Only the voice of God. He is the answer to all questions, the medicine for all ailments . . ." Ariel stopped reading.

She took the book from him delicately. She read slowly, with her sugary Brazilian accent. The energy she put into uttering the phrases revealed the importance she gave each word. Ariel felt his cheeks burn, but he didn't move. He heard individual words that held no meaning. Coexistence, truth, devotion. He understood what a fool he had been. He was glad in the end that he hadn't thrown himself onto her or whipped out his cock right as he crossed the doorway. He laughed at his own idea. He imagined Fernanda defending herself from the attack of his erect penis, her hitting him with that hardcover Bible-type book. She stopped reading for a second. The bizarre situation unfolding in Ariel's head didn't seem to affect her emotional intensity.

Take the book. You can give it back to me later. Take it with you. But I want you to know we would love to be able to help you.

Was it a sect? A delusion? Was Amílcar involved in this? He obviously was. He had left him alone with her for the recruitment ceremony. He stood up with the book under his arm. He could have cried or laughed right then. She spoke again; her face was lovely, not tense in the least. Don't be ashamed, we've all come from places that would shock you, you are no worse than I am. The man who came up the stairs a moment ago was just a normal man, perhaps the one who goes down them now is a better one.

Ariel nodded his head and backed out of the room. Before he closed the door, she folded her legs and Ariel could catch a glimpse of her tanned, attractive inner thigh through the slit in her dress.

When Amílcar arrived, he was sitting on the sofa leafing through the book. He had asked the maid for two more coffees and was about to start climbing the walls from caffeine. They didn't talk about the book. Was Amílcar some weird athlete of God or like that Chilean center halfback in San Lorenzo who recommended a psycho-wizard to his teammates, one who read your future in your asshole? The same one who told a player who was losing his hair from the stress of the competition to rub his own feces on his head, which didn't bring any results? He and Amílcar smiled, each for a different reason. They joked a minute with the kids and then Ariel called a taxi. He had a date with Sylvia at the café. He uses the waiting time to look at the DVDs they rent on the lower floor. He knows he won't break up with her in spite of his efforts to distance himself. Outside everything is strange. He is so lonely without her. Why is it always like that?

17

Sylvia sensed his need to talk and she let him get things off his chest. So Ariel abandoned his usual hermeticism. Beneath his hair and behind his light eyes, he kept his thoughts locked in a safe. Would you come to Buenos Aires with me? Would you come with me?

What would I do there? Ariel lent her some thick wool socks. She has her feet up on the sofa.

On Friday she brought a backpack with some clothes. Three pairs of panties. Sportswear from Ariel. Every week he gets huge bags from the brand he endorses. They spent the weekend holed up at his house. Another fake trip with Mai, but her father didn't give her a hard time about it. She seemed happy. For Sylvia it was a pleasure to wile away the evening together, wake up beside each other. When Ariel went out to buy the newspapers, Sylvia feared the worst. He had gotten a call from his friend Husky a little while earlier.

One of the sports papers had written a harsh, relentless article about him. It listed his failures, his inability to adapt, his

470 | DAVID TRUEBA

lack of commitment, and the inopportune injury that had left him, to top it all off, out of commission for the three decisive games of the season. The harshness was unusual. Too young to lead a team that needs wins. The end was enlightening: "The president would do good in finding him a team where he could get toughened up, and find a substitute who's not a potential but a reality. It's always better if the promising player is still promising in a couple of years, instead of just adding to the long list of failures." It seemed to already be fated. Ariel threw the newspaper down.

Barely a minute later, Sylvia heard the murmur of Husky's voice on the telephone trying to calm him down. Come on, that guy is on the club payroll, he's just another employee. They call it journalism but it's just a branch office. Ariel told Husky about his conversation with the sports director. Sylvia heard the story for the first time, even though it was being explained to a third party. Seeing her interest in the conversation, Ariel put it on speakerphone, and she listened to Husky say, they showed you their sophisticated working style, but they could also show their other face and throw you into the river with cement shoes.

Look, last year the president forced a sports newspaper to change both journalists who covered the team. In exchange he made sure to filter them the signings, the important news, before any other media outlet, what do you think, that the journalists aren't part of the game? Husky let out a sardonic laugh. Here everybody has to sell what they have. They need each other, fuck, I can't believe I have to explain this business to you.

Ariel tossed and turned in the armchair. Sylvia tried to calm him down after he hung up. He confessed all his frustrations about the team to her. That evening Sylvia heard him talking to his brother in Buenos Aires and noticed Charlie was able to pacify him. In their conversation, his original accent came back, the old expressions that little by little he had set aside because they were strange to Spaniards. He read paragraphs of the article and Ariel seemed to take pleasure in the things written against him, as if it were some sort of masochistic exercise.

The day before, he had run into the sports director again during practice and they had talked about some French team's interest in him. Monaco is a perfect place, don't you think? Pujalte said. Ariel had then showed his defiant side. I want to stay and I'm going to fight to stay. It seemed obvious that the article was an emphatic response to Ariel. The fight is going to be unevenly matched, get ready. A message aimed straight at his jugular.

Sylvia didn't really understand the sports reasons or the contractual difficulties. She was only thinking about one thing. If Ariel left the city, it would surely mean the end of their relationship. However, he denied that possibility. When she heard him talk, reflect on the problem out loud, Sylvia wanted to ask him, and what about me? What's going to happen with me?

Sylvia heard him say things to his brother in Buenos Aires like, the money is the least of it, it's a question of dignity. When he tamed his rage after talking with friends and his agent, Ariel lay down on the sofa, beside her. He seemed like a different person. Talking calmed him down, he lost the tone in his voice he'd had during the calls, like a caged beast. He now used a more broken, fragile tone, which was tender and made Sylvia feel useful, closer.

Now she listens with a pillow hugged tight against her belly. He says, I'm no good, I wasn't good enough, I can get as mad as I want, but that's not going to cover up the truth. No one will come out to defend me because I haven't done anything outstanding, they always have to find a guilty party, everybody was expecting something from me that I wasn't able to give them. This is a game, if you play it well, you give the orders; if not, then they have control of the situation. It happens all the time, there are players with promise, but things don't go right, and five years later they're a pathetic shadow on third-tier teams and you ask yourself, wasn't that guy going to be the new Maradona? And you feel sorry for him, or you don't even care. Well, now I'm gonna turn into someone like that. Sylvia is afraid to interrupt and say something well-intentioned but stupid, so she just looks at him with enormous eyes and tries to understand him.

Which is why she is so surprised when he changes his tone and asks, would you come to Buenos Aires with me? She doesn't answer right away. She doubts he has stopped to think, for even a second, about how all this affects her. Sylvia sees herself as the companion to a soccer player, the partner with the suitcases always packed. She looks at her backpack with the changes of underwear placed at the foot of the coffee table. The two distant, foreign, incompatible worlds come back to her, but she doesn't say anything, she knows it's not the right moment. It's time to console him, it's selfish for her to think of herself. They are talking about his career, his profession, not his feelings. That's why all she says is, and what would I do there?

Damn people. I'm not leaving here, I'm not leaving you. Sylvia knows he isn't thinking about what he's saying. In a little while, his team's game will start on television. They sit down to watch. Sylvia hopes they lose by a scandalous margin. That they make fools of themselves, that the fickle, cruel public will miss the injured player. Don't say that, we have to win, he says to her, this game is really important. Sylvia now thinks their relationship may end with the season, that he'll vanish and she'll go back to being the same gray high school student she was before she met him. She feels a fear she can't wipe away.

As soon as I'm playing again, I'm going to bring them to their knees.

18

Wait, lie down here, feel the music. Leandro takes Osembe's hand. He helps her climb up on the piano. The pink sole of her foot produces a dissonant chord as it steps on the keys. Her body lies on the shiny black wood of the piano. She is naked, except for her bra, which once again she has insisted on keeping on. She gathers her legs in a protective gesture, managing to make herself comfortable as she smiles. Leandro sits in front of the piano and starts by playing a slow improvisation. The resonance is magnificent. Osembe rests her head and looks at the ceiling. The light comes from a distant lamp and from the large window where the streetlights' glow sneaks in. But Leandro doesn't need light to play. Without consciously choosing it, he is playing a Debussy prelude, leaving out many notes along the way. She closes her eyes and he slows down the rhythm of the music.

The moment gradually loses the ostentatiousness of the staging. They forget about the clothes piled up any which way on the nearby sofa, about the sneakers overturned on the rug and the tiny white socks that stick out of them. The music covers it all. Osembe's thigh is just a few inches from Leandro's eyes. He doesn't know if the vibration of the music goes through Osembe's spine and manages to affect her, but he is suddenly surprised to notice his eyes filled with tears. The piece had always moved him.

He suddenly knows that he will carry out with Osembe all that life didn't let him have with Aurora, when they were both splendid young bodies, filled with desire, wanting to take the world by storm. How absurd. Who is to blame? Is there even a guilty party? In his old age, he gives this private fantasy to someone who isn't able or interested in appreciating it. A scene reserved for the woman of his life, but played by a substitute who charges to carry out a role she doesn't understand.

Play something, I can hear you from here, Aurora still asks him some nights before sleeping. And he carefully chooses those pieces that he knows she'll recognize and enjoy. He remembers the not so distant occasion when she told him, when I hear you play the piano and I'm doing something else, in some other part of the house, I think that's the closest to happiness I've ever known. For years it had been hard for him to come home from the academy and sit at the piano, he associated it with work, and only during his private lessons with students was it heard in the house. The masseuse who comes some mornings says, play for her, you have that touch, I'm sure it'll help her. Aurora's pains seem to have spread and in the last few days Leandro has seen her stifling a wince when she changes position and closing her eyes as if she were suffering horrible whiplash. When he cleans the excrement from her backside with the sponge and bucket of warm water, he does it delicately, because the slightest brusqueness makes her cry in pain.

On the last visit to the hospital, the only thing the doctor dared to prescribe was rest. If the pain is unbearable, we'll admit her, but while she can be at home, she'll be more comfortable. You know how hospitals are. I prefer to die at home, Aurora had said to Leandro as they left, with a terrifying calmness.

It had snowed that week in Madrid, hiding spring's proximity. Many trees that had flowered in the previous sunny days received the snowstorm with surprise. Leandro told his son, I wish we lived in a building with an elevator, at least that way I could take her out for a walk every day. But sitting was very painful for Aurora; she prefered to lie in bed. Sometimes she watched the television in her room and Leandro sat by her side, to keep her company, and she said, less television and more looking at the trees is what I need.

Friday I'm going out for dinner, can you sit in for me? Lorenzo was about to answer, but Sylvia beat him to it, offering to sleep over with her grandmother. Leandro explained that he was collaborating with Joaquín's biographer. You don't know how hard it is to remember such an awful period. At that point, he had already arranged a date with Osembe in Joaquín's apartment . . .

How many hours? The whole night. That's a lot of money, she warned him over the phone. No problem. Two thousand euros. You're crazy, I'll give you what I always do for every hour, that's it. Okay, honey, but no funny stuff, just you and me alone.

They were alone. Leandro stops playing and stands up. He brings his lips to her body and runs them along the rough skin of her thighs. She puts her hand on his head and musses his hair. You're an artist. Leandro realizes he has never given her pleasure, just those overacted orgasms she fakes to excite him.

She has never let herself go. Leandro places his mouth between her thighs, but Osembe stops him immediately. No, no, I suck, I suck. Take off all your clothes. Leandro insists. He brings his hand to her shaved, sandpapery pubic hair. She fakes a few seconds of uncontrollable pleasure, making a somewhat grotesque spectacle before sitting on the piano top. She steps on the keys again and amuses herself with the dissonant sounds she makes. She unbuttons Leandro's shirt with a white smile.

She gets down from the piano and leads Leandro through the apartment by the hand. It's beautiful, is this where you live? No, no, I only practice here. A lot of money. She stops to point to an abstract painting. How ugly, eh? she says. She pushes open the door of the bedroom and discovers the large double bed. Osembe walks to the closet and opens it. She brushes her fingers along the elegant women's clothes, the two or three suits hanging in their designer bags. There is a bathroom opposite the bedroom door. There are barely any traces of life; everything is precisely ordered.

Osembe goes naked through the entire house. He leaves his pants there, on the floor. So you're a millionaire pianist . . . Well, I give concerts around the world. You must know women much more beautiful than me. Leandro smiles and shakes his head. He hugs Osembe and tries to kiss her on the mouth. It had been a while since she stopped avoiding his kisses. But she reciprocates in a very contained way, the way she does almost everything with him. Leandro sometimes has the feeling he's kissing a damp object.

She unmakes the bed that he would have preferred to leave out of their games. But he doesn't say anything. They've opened a bottle of champagne from the fridge. I'm going to get my bag, she says, and leaves the room. As always, the wait drags on. Leandro lies on the bed, relaxed. He knows they won't be there all night, because in a couple of hours he'll want to be alone, he'll feel guilty and dirty again.

Leandro thinks he hears Osembe talking on the phone. Shortly after, she comes into the room again. She carries a condom in one hand and a small plastic bag hanging from her forearm. The image, together with her nakedness and her bra, is pleasing to Leandro's eyes. He likes when everything isn't just a calculated, professional erotic experience. Deep down, he thinks, what he'd like to do is just sit down and read the newspaper and have Osembe watch TV, or just have dinner, one in front of the other.

You've got the money, right? Of course, he replies. Leandro runs his fingers over her hair, styled hard. You like it? I like it better when you wear it without so much stuff, it's like a rock. She laughs. You're so fickle.

Osembe's movements are as unbelievable as ever. Her routine is half gymnastic and half erotic. Leandro lets her do it. Today he gets easily excited. The space helps. He tries to free her breasts with his hand and finally Osembe allows it. He manages to get her bra off over her head. He never could open the clasp, because of his arthritic hands. She tries to jerk him off but Leandro orders her to stop, there's no hurry. Sure, you're the one paying, honey.

Leandro is asking her for something impossible. For her it must seem sad, pathetic, this romantic and perverse staging I've set up. Why do I do all this? Leandro enjoys the mere play of his skin against hers, touching the hardness of her muscles, feeling how her abundant sweat soaks him, sometimes even managing to get rid of the smell of cheap cologne. He knows this will be his farewell to Osembe. There will be no more nights after the fantasy of owning this apartment, owning these picture windows, this woman's body, this mirage of eternal life. He drinks from his glass and spills a bit of liquid on Osembe's shoulder, which he immediately licks off. She smiles.

He hadn't even wanted to think about or calculate how much money he had squandered in this inexplicable torrent. The last time he checked a bank statement, the bite out of his loan was considerable, so much so that he tore the paper in pieces as if he could refuse to be aware of it. Every time he pays the masseuse or the cleaning lady or buys medicines at the pharmacy, he feels relief that the money also slips out through other, nobler, outlets.

His erection has disappeared and Osembe seems to have grown tired of her mechanical movements. She gets a message on her cell phone. She gets up for a minute to make a call. Leandro likes to watch her walk. She's picked up her bra off the floor and is heading toward the living room. He imagines her spending her free time glued to her cell phone, which she keeps in a colorful cover. It's almost like her pet.

Leandro follows her to the living room a moment later. He is naked and he sits at the piano. It bothers him to notice his flaccid arms as he lifts his hands to the keys. When she hangs up the phone, she touches him on the shoulder. Do you wanna fuck or not? Leandro smiles. She sits on the keyboard and interrupts his music. Leandro strokes her thighs. Are you going to stay in Spain forever? She shakes her head no, I'm going back and I'm going to start my own business, I'll have my own house. And I'll find a man who loves me and works. You like your country better than this one? Osembe nods without hesitation. But there democracy is bad, all the politicians are thieves. It would be better to have soldiers, a strong hand, people could be safe.

Leandro smiles at the unexpected analysis of Nigerian politics, at her almost completely naked, with her muscular rear end resting on the keys, speaking in defense of military dictatorships. In what other moment in history could someone like you and someone like me have met? Does it seem like a miracle to you? Leandro felt like talking. He didn't really mind showing his nakedness in front of her. Where would you have met an old man like me? A dirty old man, she says. Someone must have taught her the expression.

Exactly. An old man who's hooked on spending his money on a surly black girl. I'm surly? Yes, very, that's why I like you, I hate friendly people. Osembe asks him to explain the meaning of surly. He gives her a few synonyms. She looks at him with challenging eyes. We could get married, we make a good couple. You're romantic today, cheerful, she says to him. You wanna fuck?

Leandro is amused by her efforts to arouse him on the sofa. He stretches out his hand every once in a while to drink a sip from his glass. Don't drink any more, she says. If you drink you can't boom-boom. Suddenly their roles are switched. I'm cold, she says, bring a blanket. Leandro stands up and goes toward the bedroom. He pulls the comforter off the bed to bring it to the living room. It is pleasant, not very heavy, filled with down. Leandro tosses it carelessly onto the sofa. He notices that the champagne is starting to affect him. It will be a pleasure to sleep against another body. Osembe covers herself with the comforter. Stay and sleep here with me. He places himself on top. He starts to move as if he were going to make love to her.

But barely a few seconds later the front door opens with a violent shove. The man who comes in closes it behind him without making any noise. He looks around and walks toward the sofa. Before Leandro can say anything, the guy grabs him by the arm, lifts him in the air, and throws him across the room. Leandro hits the wall, in pain. The guy has a shaved head, he's black, well built, not very tall. He is wearing a leather jacket. Osembe has gotten off the sofa. The man walks toward Leandro and gives him two kicks in the stomach. Leandro folds, afraid. The man picks up Leandro's pants from the nearby chair and empties his wallet of money, then tosses it.

Osembe has started to get dressed. The man says something to her that Leandro doesn't understand. His fragile, whitish, scared body doesn't want to participate in the scene, not even to hear what's being said. She points to the bedroom and the man goes over there. He hears drawers and closets being opened, rummaged through. He comes back with coats and some more clothes that he tosses to Osembe.

He lifts up Leandro's head. More money. Where? Jewelry? His mouth is pink inside, his tongue like strawberry chewing gum. He doesn't speak very loudly, he has a funny voice with a strange timbre, but Leandro doesn't laugh. There's nothing, it's not my house, really, it's not my house. The man lets Leandro's head drop and now kicks him twice right in the face. They aren't brutal kicks. They're moderate. But they split one of his eyebrows, which bleeds. The warmth of the blood is about to make Leandro faint. His eyes search out Osembe to try to get her protection. But she is putting on her sneakers.

The man is now in the kitchen. He is rummaging through everything. The sound of cups and plates breaking is heard.

The man comes back to the living room with an enormous knife. Leandro fears he will kill him. How absurd. Osembe says, let's go. But the guy starts to stab the sofa cushions, tears the intense red curtains. Osembe seems to be smiling. The man passes in front of Leandro, but ignores him. He goes to the piano and starts to stab it as if it were an animal. The wood resists his violence. With the tip of the knife, he starts to carve into the varnish along the entire piano, leaving a conspicuous trail on the black shiny surface. Then he throws the knife and rips out a DVD player from beneath the television and a CD player from one of the shelves. He wraps them in one of the coats.

Leandro lifts his head, trusting that he will see him leaving. Then he gets a kick in the thigh. It comes from Osembe. He looks toward her, but she doesn't look at him. She kicks furiously with her sneakers three or four times. He remains immobile, shrunken. The man has opened the door and gestures toward her, she joins him, and they leave. They close the door with unexpected delicacy. Leandro, on the floor, spits out his own blood, which has slid from his eyebrow to his mouth. He feels his body, trying to calm the pain in his side. He sits up on the wooden floor. He hugs himself and discovers that from his glans hangs the useless condom, amorphous, like a dead hide. He looks around and feels panic.

19

Lorenzo waits for his father by the door. I'll stay with her, there's no rush, you can even stay out until after noon, Benita had told them. Aurora sleeps. She had greeted her son wordlessly, with a stroke of the hand. She is hot, although her cheeks have no color. Lorenzo readjusts her pillow and strokes her hair. She has lost a lot of weight. Can we go out for a walk? he suggests to his father. He doesn't want to say more, in spite of his seriously worried tone.

The first sign was the wound on his father's face. I fell in the stupidest way, Lorenzo told him. He had a cut through his eyebrow. I didn't want to say anything because I didn't want to worry you, I must have slipped on the ice along the sidewalk. Did you go to a doctor? Yes, yes, there's nothing broken. When was it, after Sylvia left? No, that night, coming back from dinner. I didn't mention it to her so she would go to the station without worrying. Sylvia had gone to spend the weekend with Pilar. Your mother got scared when she saw me, but it's nothing, insisted Leandro.

On Monday Lorenzo worked with Wilson from early in the morning, a trip to the airport and moving an old refrigerator and a sofa from one Ecuadorian's house to another's. That night he received a call from Jacqueline. She introduced herself, I'm Joaquín's wife, I don't know if you remember him. Of course, said Lorenzo, but he couldn't hide his surprise. They agreed to meet the next morning, it's important, it's about your father, she said with a strong French accent.

Leandro puts on the coat hanging from the rack and follows Lorenzo out of the house. They go down the stairs, not saying anything until they reach the street. Let's go this way, toward the park, indicates Lorenzo. No, it's really dirty, there are benches in the plaza. The kids usually get together in the park on weekends and they aren't cleaned until Wednesday, they're filled with bottles and plastic cups, cigarette butts. Lorenzo doesn't really know where to begin. That same morning, he had met with Jacqueline in an apartment near Recoletos. She had him come in and, barely saying a word, she showed him the living room. The stabbed piano, everything upside down, the gutted sofas, the curtains on the floor. I arrived yesterday from Paris, the doorman called me, obviously I slept in a hotel last night. Lorenzo could only express a puzzled face. He didn't dare ask, why are you showing me all this? He sensed that nothing good could come from the bitter curl on the woman's lips. Joaquín chose not to come, to save himself from seeing this, even though it's all his fault.

Lorenzo remembers Joaquín. As a boy, he saw him often when he visited from Paris and his sporadic visits were always celebrated events. When he made his First Communion, Joaquín sent a Belgian bicycle with a backpedal brake. There wasn't another one like it in the neighborhood. It was Joaquín who asked me to talk to you instead of your father. My father? Jacqueline looked up and fixed her light eyes on Lorenzo's. What's behind all this? A fit of insanity, Leandro getting carried away with envy? Why would he do something like this?

She told him what she knew from Joaquín. Leandro had asked to borrow the apartment to bring a woman there Friday night. Then, on Monday morning, the doorman, Casiano, a completely trustworthy man, had the keys picked up from the mailbox, as agreed, and went up to have a look at the apartment, as a matter of course. And this is how he found it. Someone will have to take care of this disaster, clearly.

Look, all this is taking me a bit by surprise. Let me talk to my father and don't worry, there must be an explanation.

I don't want explanations, I'm not interested in that, I just want someone to take care of the repair costs, for everything to go back to the way it was. Besides, in addition to what you see, there are clothes missing, things broken.

The French accent, with those impossible *r*'s, was risible, but Lorenzo didn't laugh. Perhaps stifling it was making him feel more and more resentment toward Jacqueline as she spoke. He just nodded, took down her phone number, and left without even showing any emotion. He was turning over in his head the idea of his father in the borrowed apartment on a date. Had he lost his mind?

When Lorenzo listens to his father, he has the feeling that everything he's telling him is a big lie. He can't believe it. They walk along the street and stop in the middle of some sentences, but without looking each other in the eye they continue in no particular direction. Leandro has adopted a neutral tone, he speaks in a liberating way, without dramatizing. He talks about Osembe without using her name; he refers to her as just a prostitute, someone he called from a newspaper ad. I thought of using Joaquín's apartment for the meeting, you understand, I don't know, it was a stupid idea, and then everything happened so fast, it was so unexpected. I guess they took advantage of me and I was absolutely unaware of the risk I was taking.

Let me get this straight, Papá, they beat you up, they robbed you, they could have killed you. You have to report it.

Leandro shakes his head. He does so insistently, without saying anything, as if he wants to reject the idea with his head. We can't do anything. Tell me how much it costs and I'll pay it.

Lorenzo understands his father's silence. He realizes he's a victim. He imagines him beaten, treated badly, humiliated in that apartment. The image is more powerful than the one of his father as a mere client of a prostitute, while his wife slowly dies in her bed. Well, I'll talk to the French lady and work it all out.

Should we go home? asks Leandro. Lorenzo feels pity for his father, a man he once feared for his strictness, his firm convictions, that he later ignored and even later learned to respect. His humbled father moves through the hallway and Lorenzo watches him go into his room. Who am I to judge him? If we could expose people's miseries, their errors, missteps, crimes, we'd find the most absolute dearth, true indignity. Luckily, thinks Lorenzo, we each carry our secret defeats well hidden, as far as possible from others' eyes. That's why he hadn't wanted to dig into his father's wound, to know all the details, humiliate him any more than he must have already been at having to tell his son the truth.

From the kitchen comes an intense smell of potatoes and onions frying, probably a frittata. You staying for lunch? asks his father. He understands how hard it can be for a father to show a child his most shameful, pitiful face. He can't even conceive of children judging their parents; they owe them too much. Lorenzo wants to console him, show his father that he's even worse. Papá, you should see me, what I've done.

Lorenzo says, no, I have work and then he brushes his father's elbow. Don't worry about anything, he whispers, I'll take care of it, you just take care of making sure Mamá's comfortable, okay?

That's all you need to take care of now.

20

Ariel holds the photos up to his eyes, feeling like he's looking at a stranger. He's not the one in the photos, and it's not him sitting in the club office having another conversation he never imagined. Yet in the photos he recognizes Sylvia and finds her beautiful, young, and exultant. It's her curly hair, her expansive smile, the cheerful way she hangs off his neck. He sees her in Munich, in a snowstorm, holding hands, and in Madrid, too, kissing on the street. They are foreign, dirty photos, devoid of beauty. They are stolen photos that don't capture the value of the moment; they are just evidence of who knows what crime.

It might bother people to know the girl is a minor, you know how everyone turns into a moralist when it comes to judging others. Ariel looks up toward the sports director. The manager is there, too, a guy he barely knows, with gray hair, a sky-blue tie, and an absent expression, as if only numbers excited him, not human passions. Ariel is about to respond to Pujalte, to use the word blackmail, but he doesn't. He chooses to keep quiet. Beside him is the young agent they chose to negotiate with the club, thinking he would get Ariel out of any uncomfortable meetings. But that same morning he had called, alarmed, I think you'd better come with me.

Yesterday as Ariel left practice, the journalists looked for him with their microphones and their cameras. He lowered the car window and answered their questions for a moment. There were rumors of his possible transfer to another team. I'm committed to this club and its fans, so I'm going to give it my all. Soccer is played out on the field, not in offices. Give me a little time and I'll prove it was no mistake to bring me here.

Words fill the sports pages every day, saturated with sensational, emotional, passionate declarations that no one pays much attention to anymore. Emphatic quotes are ashes the next day. Naïve, Husky told him, as much as you insist on playing the role of the good boy, you're just naïve. Ariel mentioned that in a few days he would be ready to compete again and he was already planning on defending himself on the field. That morning, after his statements, someone called into a radio sports chat show to defend him, he's the best on the team, he shouldn't leave, all the others should.

But in a sports paper from Barcelona, a journalist let slip the rumor that Ariel's Italian nationality was in question, along with some other players' origins, and that the public prosecutor was looking into the matter. If it was revealed to be a hoax, he could no longer occupy the spot of a European player and his departure from the team would be irremissible. No one is happy with the performance of a player they expected much more from. One after the other, the club knew how to deliver direct blows to convince him to obey their order. Accept what they decide. On the Web site of an Argentinian newspaper, there was already talk of the scandal over the *trucho* passports, as they called the forged birth certificates used to pass off Argentinian players as Europeans. Ariel's name appeared on a list with four or five other names.

Now they forced him to sit at that table to contemplate what could turn out to be the final staging of real power.

As you will understand, no one is interested in this continuing, says Pujalte. There are a lot of things to hide on your side, more than on ours. Not to mention how your brother left the country. I think that in everything, and I mean everything, you have the team on your side. These are innocent photos, they were brought to us by an agency that wants us to have them, and you are lucky they want to maintain a good relationship with the club, they put us before their news interests. This happens every day. Last year we had some pornographic photos of one of your teammates that some girl wanted to sell. What did the magazine do? They bought them for us. Well, they know that we both need each other. Without our umbrellas, you players would be prey, like partridges in the field, and, at the end of the day, who cares about one more or one less partridge in the bag? We are the only ones protecting you.

The sports director crossed and uncrossed his fingers as he spoke. Ariel slowly opens a bottle of water. He drinks a sip. Pujalte continues without letting Ariel's eyes meet his at any point.

What's happening is that you're trying to get the fans on your side. The executives, we're the bad guys, and you players are the good guys.

I only said I want to stay here, the same thing I said to you.

Look, if your Italian credentials are finally annulled, everything gets more complicated. I'll tell you one thing, without moving a finger, you'd lose your status as a member of the European Union, then forget about finding a team easily. It also works against us, but if you think we give a shit . . . If that's what you want, I already told you the press only gums up the works.

Ariel wants to get up and leave that room where the walls are adorned with the exploits of the club's legendary players. The manager has barely said anything; he gathers the photos from the table and puts them away in his folder. Ariel's young agent tries to lighten the tone of the meeting. We are in favor of a sale, not a transfer. Perfect, Pujalte cuts him off, give us some asshole willing to pay the termination clause, we're not going to give away a player. We can negotiate. That's what we've wanted from the first day, to encourage an elegant exit.

Ariel remembers Pujalte the day he gave him the club jersey to wear in the press conference announcing his signing. In just a few months, their relationship had changed. But Ariel is wrong to judge him and he knows it. Everyone plays their part: surely Pujalte is only trying to save his ass and his salary after a bad year. The same things that today seem loathsome to him could have been charming if things had gone well.

Let us talk with your agent, you forget about the whole thing. You still have some games ahead of you, we have a lot at stake, and that's what you should be focusing on. I'll tell you one thing, that's what you should have been focused on from day one.

Ariel doesn't respond. The sports director talks to him about the possibility of going to the Italian, the French, the English league. Ariel asks, why not to another Spanish team? And he answers, no one likes to strengthen rival teams with their own players, I don't know why but they're always particularly motivated the day they play against you. People don't understand that kind of transfer.

Ariel wants to ask him if there is a possibility of going back to Buenos Aires, but he'd rather leave it all in the hands of his agent and Charlie. He knows that in Argentina no one would be able to pay his signing price. He sees himself in Russia, on a shady millionaire's team, like so many others.

He hasn't seen Sylvia in a few days. On the weekend, she went to see her mother. The day before, he traveled to La Coruña for an Argentinian friend's birthday. Players from all over the country were there. Those days had given him time to think about their relationship, distance himself again.

Several of them had met up in the lobby of a hotel on the outskirts of the city, many of them Argentinians scattered throughout the Spanish teams; three even came from Italy. They were picked up at the hotel and taken to a house in the countryside. Some didn't know one another, but they all had friends in common. Many had met on the field, had chatted during halftime or at the end of a game; others had exchanged a few words at the door to the locker rooms after a shower. A kind of school camaraderie quickly developed.

It was a big house with a huge yard right on the beach. They prepared an enormous barbecue and there were plenty of coolers filled with cans of beer and soda. They didn't sit down to eat until late in the afternoon. There were still some players arriving after their morning practice. The idea was that they would all leave early the next day, catching planes to different destinations, and let the party go through the night. The celebration was already almost a tradition. Yeah, like Thanksgiving, joked the host, Tiger Lavalle, a veteran player with a short beard.

The absence of women was absolute. Some players joked about it. The host's family lived in the city, and they used the beach house on various weekends. His kids were at school, already grown, I gave the world a couple of Spaniards, Tiger would complain. A fullback who played on an Andalusian team asked Ariel for his jersey, I have a kid who collects them from every Argentinian in Spain, he's wild about it, he doesn't have yours or that son of a bitch's, but I'm not gonna ask him, he said in a voice loud enough for the guy to hear and laugh at the comment.

There was constant music playing from the speakers aimed at the yard. The temperature was pleasant. Python Tancredi came out of the house with a guitar and started singing Vicentico songs. Others joined in, some pathetically off-key. The song was about a boat and it was sentimental and sad. There were three Spaniards as well, good friends of the host, and also two Uruguayans who ended up being the butt of jokes. Ariel asked Python if he knew any Marcelo Polti songs. You like that guy? Gimme a break. But then he played part of "Cara de Nada," Marcelo's most famous song.

There was food left over and the entire table was filled with bottles of rum, whisky, and gin. One of the Spaniards, who was an executive on Tiger's team, insisted on bringing girls. He was funny, short, had an infectious smile, and smoked a short, stout cigar. He called up a former player and friend who after retiring had opened two enormous whorehouses not far from there. They all listened to him talk on his cell phone without knowing for sure whether it was a joke. Yeah, yeah, thirty girls is fine, but good-looking ones, don't just send me any old thing. Then he went out to give the minibus driver directions to a place on the highway he called Venus or Aphrodite or something similar.

An hour later, when pretty much everyone had forgotten about it, they heard the minibus approaching the gate. He promised me the best whores in the area, said the executive, he's a fantastic guy, he was a player on our team, came out of a little town in Orense.

Thirty-odd young ladies came in and joined the party. They divided up into groups. There were some Latin Americans, but most of them were Eastern Europeans. Thirty-three, someone counted. The men took care of serving them drinks, handing out chairs. There were people sitting on the steps of the terrace, those more sensitive to the cold were in the living room, scattered over the sofas, a few were even lying out on the grass although it had gotten cooler once the sun went down.

They brought out the birthday cake with candles, a surprise they had been saving for Tiger, and some went to get the presents they had left by the front door. Almost all of them were joke gifts. There was a blow-up doll, several bibs, two hats, a box of cigars, three cocktail shakers, you guys think I'm an alcoholic, he shouted to applause, a jersey from the Argentinian national team, and a small Argentine flag. Ariel had brought him a book, which provoked widespread confusion, who was the asswipe that brought this guy a book, he's famous for never reading anything. Ariel raised his hand and everyone cheered.

The night progressed and the sound of music and voices continued steadily. There were men who got intimate with women selected from the group. Others stayed on the sidelines; I'm happily married, fuck off. Some danced or changed the music every so often. Ariel found himself exchanging glances with a girl with a very delicate face and light eyes. When he found her on the staircase on the way to the bathroom, he sat down to chat with her.

Her name was Irina and she spoke good Spanish. She was twenty-three years old. In a corner of the living room, one of the girls was sucking off the executive as he reclined on the floor among cushions. The cigar had gone out between his lips, his head leaned against the wall. Ariel moved away with Irina.

They found an empty bedroom. The girl took condoms out of her purse. She was extremely thin and wore a very fine silver chain with a tiny heart around her waist. She had been working in Spain for almost four months, first on the Costa del Sol, but every month they switched her to a different place. She ended up in Galicia last week, she explained to Ariel as she spread a dilating cream on her vagina.

Ariel escaped from the party when he heard someone announce that a taxi was arriving. There were still people scattered through the yard and lounging between the living room sofa cushions. He hugged Tiger good-bye and shared the cab ride with two friends. On the way back, they talked about the party. Last year's was better, the girls took some of the charm out of it. It's awful, that asshole fucking it up by bringing them. Well, did you sleep with one? How was it? Bah, fine. But you're young, you have to take advantage, life lasts as long as a fart in your hand.

Ariel had offered Irina money, but she said everything was already paid for. Even so he left a bill in her bag when they said good-bye. In the hotel, Ariel checked his cell phone. He had a message from Sylvia. She always managed to pop up, her simplicity, her purity like a smack in the face. "I love you," said the message, "I want to be with you."

When Pujalte sees him stand up, he asks, how's that ankle coming along? Fine, he answers. Those photos could hurt an innocent person, Ariel dares to say before leaving, don't think that . . . Forget about the photos, the manager interrupts, they don't even exist. Ariel nods, about to thank him, but luckily he stops himself.

Ariel leaves the office with his head bowed. He puts weight on his ankle without any problem. Tomorrow he'll have normal practice. He'll start hitting the ball around again. He missed it. When he was a kid, his father used to punish him by locking the ball in a bedroom closet. When the sanction was lifted, Ariel would get back the ball and spend hours kicking it against the brick façade where for years there was a message no one painted over: PERÓN LIVES. If the ball is in motion, everything is easy.

21

Sylvia turns in her test with indifference. She doesn't meet the teacher's eye as he divides the papers into stacks on the table. She goes back to her desk and gathers her things. She doesn't feel Don Octavio's gaze on her back, his surprise at getting a blank sheet. At the end of the hall, some classmates have congregated to discuss the questions. Sylvia joins them, but doesn't participate in the conversation. After leaving school, they gather on the benches of a nearby park. Someone has bought some beers from the Chinese guy at the corner store. It's nice to just relax in the sun.

They talk about Easter break. One group wants to go camping, at least for a couple of days. Another student says his father is forcing him to go to his provincial town for the processions, I'll do it for him, for him and for my grandfather, but boy what a drag. I'd like to see you with your pointed hood on, someone kids. And are you going to continue the tradition by forcing your son to go, too? I guess it grows on you, it's a ritual, he says without much passion.

Sylvia spent the weekend at her mother's house. She had a good time. It gave her a chance to distance herself from Ariel's problems, to not feel so dependent. She was comfortable with

Santiago, Pilar laughed at his jokes, relaxed around him. During lunch downstairs at Casa Hermógenes, when Sylvia told them the school year wasn't going very well for her, he added that it must be that you're devoting your time to more interesting things. Must be, said Sylvia. Her mother tried to draw her out about the boy she was dating. Sylvia was evasive. She turned the tables, as Ariel had shown her how to do in soccer, when there's pressure on one side of the field, the best thing to do is shoot the ball to the opposite side, you force the defense to fan out in the other direction. Papá is the one with a girlfriend, said Sylvia. He already introduced her to Grandma and Grandpa. Sylvia tried to evaluate if that caused a reaction in Pilar, but if anything, all she noticed was a relaxed sigh.

The night before, she had slept over at her grandmother's. Aurora had insisted she lie down beside her. It's been a long time since I've had a warm body next to me, that warmth. Lying still, so as not to hurt her grandmother or make her uncomfortable, Sylvia remembered needing her mother's warmth as a girl. She ran to her mother's bedroom when she had nightmares, or sometimes Pilar curled up on one side of Sylvia's bed when she put her to sleep, their faces pushed close together, sharing a warmth that could be the same one her grandmother was referring to.

On Saturday afternoon, they went for a walk by the bridges, near the river. They visited the Virgin of the Pillar and the Aljafería Palace, then they had dinner in a nearby restaurant, Casa Emilio, where they were barely able to carry a conversation because in the attached dining room there was a literary gathering accompanied by constant shouting and banging on the table. The regulars, a group of drunks, shouted threats at the waiter about ordering a pizza. One of them sang a folk song, bemoaning, "they told me a thousand times but I never wanted to listen." The painfully discordant voice resonated throughout the restaurant. At first Sylvia and Pilar listened with a mocking smile, but the singer conveyed such impressive neglect and abandonment that in the end they were moved.

They walked home. Pilar hated the clusters of people who insisted on having fun as if it were their vocation, you can't imagine how downtown gets. They took refuge on the sofa and watched a celebrity gossip show where everyone lectured as if they were talking about something essential to humanity, even though the topic was the anal fistula of some survival contestant on a Caribbean island. Pilar went to bed early. Sylvia stayed up a bit longer. On TV a blond woman appeared, insignificant beside her operated lips and breasts. After this brief break, she is going to reveal the long list of soccer players who have been in her bed, announced the host enthusiastically. So don't go away, we'll be back in three minutes.

Sylvia had a hunch that was confirmed after the commercials, when the woman on television let drop that among the famous soccer players she fucked was an Argentinian player on a Madrid team who has the same name as a detergent brand. Sylvia sent Ariel a message on his cell phone. Turn on the TV, to Telecinco. Barely a few seconds later, Ariel called her. Did you really fuck that monstrosity? Ariel shivered, is that what she said? She gave clues. No shit, I'm gonna sue her, this is incredible. It doesn't reflect the best taste, honestly, she said. But it's a lie, she hooked up with my brother Charlie, he brought her up to the hotel room, we had just gotten to Madrid. So you hadn't met me yet, right? Of course not, answered Ariel. Then Sylvia asked him, and since you met me have you fucked a lot of girls? Don't be silly. No, no, I don't care, well, I'd prefer they didn't look like this pathetic ho bag, but . . . Can anybody just go on TV and say whatever runs through their head? protested Ariel. That's how people are, said Sylvia halfheartedly.

During their walk beside the river Ebro, Pilar told Sylvia that she had started an adoption process. Santiago wants to have a child, he says he envies me when he sees you. Sylvia wasn't expecting her mother to want to get involved in family life. And you want to be mixed up in that mess again? Pilar laughed heartily, that mess is now you and you're great, why wouldn't I want to experience that again? Doesn't it appeal to you? Sylvia only answered, I'm not the one who has to like it, you do.

And what if things don't work out with Santiago? Why wouldn't they? Because sometimes they don't. But when you're with someone you can't be thinking, maybe this isn't going to work out, you have to invest in everything going well, trust, otherwise . . . Pilar didn't finish the sentence.

Sylvia was envious of her mother's attitude. In her relationship with Ariel, she always had an alternate plan ready in case of catastrophe, an escape plan, an evacuation route like the flight attendants pointing to exit rows. Although most times, when tragedy strikes, no one reaches the exit or it's blocked, locked tight as drum. In her relationship with Ariel, there was something that told her, all this that you are experiencing will be over tomorrow and you won't be able to cry about it or tell anyone about it. She had never deceived herself. That's why her mother, with one painful defeat on her record, was a model in the way she took on her new life. Having a little brother or sister could be good, she felt obliged to say, which got a smile out of Pilar.

Mai had suggested to Sylvia that they go on vacation together. Come with me to Barcelona, this way you can get to
know the city. To the squat? No, no, we'll find a little hotel and
if Mateo wants to go out with us one day that's fine, but there's
no way I'm going to be tied down. In that case, why are you
going to the city he's in? Let's go somewhere else. Yeah. Mai
was left speechless. Then she said, well, you've never been to
Barcelona, it's a trip, nothing like Madrid.

Sylvia and Ariel had made plans to go somewhere during the
three days off over the Easter week. But it all depended on the
situation with the club. His time off for the injury had been exhausting. When we don't play, we're like disabled, he had explained to Sylvia. Now I understand those retired pro players
who come to watch us train, they want to chat with us, they
need to maintain contact. They put together teams of former
players and they still compete between themselves, as if nothing changed. They turn into regulars at coffee shops, recalling
anecdotes. They still sign the occasional autograph and someone might ask them about the next game as if they knew the
secrets better than anyone else. And, of course, they agree to
participate in chats and commentaries on the radio and television. Soccer players without soccer, Dragon used to call them,
a dangerous breed, like singers without songs or businessmen
without business. Stopped watches.

Sylvia found his confessed uselessness for civilian life moving. It also terrified her. She didn't want to be a victim of it,
didn't want to become the shadow of someone like that. The
shadow of a shadow. Perhaps that's why, when Ariel goes down
to the gym, she chooses to stay with her notes and the novel
Santiago gave her.

When the math teacher handed out the test questions, Sylvia understood the results of a bad school year, of the laziness, the lack of concentration. She felt terror at the thought of being left with nothing, without Ariel but also without herself. This is why she stretches out time on the street bench with her friends from school. She offers to go with her friends to buy more beers and more bags of pork rinds at the corner store. She suddenly enjoys paying the Chinese guy who furiously adds up the purchases and then distributes the bags among them. So when her cell phone buzzes in her backpack with a new incoming message, she doesn't rush to read it.

Only a while later, on the way home, does she look at it. "Should we do something together?" Everything, she wants to reply, but she doesn't because she knows it's not possible. Sometimes she says it jokingly, I'm jealous of the ball, that instead of thinking of me, my boyfriend has his head filled with thoughts of a leather ball with futuristic designs.

No one is home. She eats some slices of boiled ham that she finds at the back of the fridge. She's too lazy to cook. She lies down in her room and listens to music. Then she answers the message. In an hour, Ariel will come by to pick her up and she'll feel like another person again, far from that lazy teenager who now stares at the ceiling and whose voice repeats the chorus of a song she knows by heart.

22

He tried calling Osembe's number twice in the last few days. Now he gets the same automated response, this phone has restricted incoming calls. His eyebrow looks better, the swelling has gone down and it scabbed up normally, dissipating his fear of not having gone to the emergency room. A trace of the bruise remains, more yellow than black and blue, around his eye socket. The pain in his right side could be from a cracked rib, but it only bothers him when he sleeps on it.

That night Leandro left Joaquín's apartment hurt and afraid. He had only gathered the bedsheets and put them in the washing machine and pushed aside the broken glass on the kitchen floor with his foot, piling it in a corner so no one would cut themselves. He ran his finger over the marks on the piano. He locked the door and left the keys in the doorman's box.

He didn't really know what would happen. He couldn't do anything about it, either. He would wait for Joaquín's reaction. He would explain to him what had happened.

He didn't have money for a cab, so he walked in the cold, which seemed to do him good at first, but later hurt his face. The pain in his abdomen made him think of Osembe. Did she hate me that much? In one of her trips to the living room, she must have left the door open, ready for the guy to come in. Was he her boyfriend? Maybe her pimp.

There were a lot of people on the street, at the entrances to bars, wandering from one place to another in search of fun. It was Friday night. He went into his apartment stealthily, not wanting to wake up Sylvia, who was sleeping beside Aurora.

From her medicines, he chose a painkiller and lay down to sleep. It took him a while.

The next day he went downstairs for breakfast. In the bar, he had to explain to his neighbor that he was mugged for his wallet. Was it an Arab? No, he was black, said Leandro, African. These people, fucking hell. In the police station, he reported his ID and cards stolen. Do you want to file a report for assault? asked the youngest of the policemen. No, no, that's okay. Do it, for fuck's sake, do it, said another from a distance, so that it shows up in the stats, no one around here wants to admit what a disaster we live in.

On Monday he waited for Joaquín's call. He tossed around the possibility of beating him to it and telling him everything. But once again cowardice won out. There was still the possibility that Joaquín wouldn't reproach him at all. He could solve it discreetly and in exchange they would never have to see each other again or talk about it. Always the most cowardly solution. On Sunday he had spent a long time calculating the possibilities of being run over if he hurled himself from the edge of the sidewalk into oncoming traffic. But he ruled out the possibility after imagining himself badly injured in the hospital when Aurora needed him most. He found suicide a pretty honorable way out of his situation. Yet he suffered from an atrocious physical fear.

Suicide didn't vanish from his thoughts until midday, as he fed Aurora with slow spoonfuls. He picked off the odd noodle that stuck to her chin and then cleaned her face with a napkin. He told her that he had hit himself against the kitchen table, after stooping to pick something up off the floor. A little while later, as Aurora slept, he took refuge in the bathroom and cried in front of the mirror, bitterly, unlike how babies cry, knowing they are going to be comforted. No, he cried with the deaf containment of someone who no longer expected to be consoled.

Aurora talked to him about Sylvia. She's at that horrible age and yet she's fabulous. She had left for the station early. Leandro avoided her, in spite of hearing her go out. She says that this year her studies aren't going well, how could we help her? Maybe you could give Lorenzo money to hire a tutor. Leandro nodded. I'll do that.

Chatting with his wife helped Leandro regain his composure. This is what my life has been like, coming home terrified and finding calmness here, the solution to fear, letting Aurora's love of life rub off onto me. She's been the engine driving me, this spineless vehicle. Leandro knew he wouldn't take his own life, he wouldn't do that to Aurora; maybe when she died, he'd gladly go with her, but not before. Surely she would blame herself for being sick, judging her entire life, her personal failure, based on that ending. Suicide is an incurable stab in the back to those who love you and survive you. Leandro realizes that his relationship with Osembe has something of a suicide about it, private suicide. At least he saw himself as dead.

All these feelings skyrocketed when his son Lorenzo came to see him. I called a prostitute, he explained, I know it was stupid. He didn't want to give more details. Lorenzo offered to take care of it all with Jacqueline, those rich people don't know what money costs, we could talk to the police. Leandro feigned a last fit of pride, no, no, let it go, but he knew his son would never look at him the same way again. Are children capable of forgiving their parents when they discover that they didn't meet their expectations, either?

He had no problem writing out a check to Jacqueline for the amount she and Lorenzo agreed on. It bothered him that Joaquín had taken himself out of the equation. He also hid himself. Jacqueline settled for eighteen thousand euros, but she hadn't held her tongue in having the final word, you can't put a price on ruining a lifelong friendship.

They will polish the piano, paint the walls, put the curtains back up, change the sofa and the carpet, and among the other belongings that are now gone, old Leandro would also disappear from their lives and with him the last traces of a forgettable past.

Lorenzo worried about his father's finances. Are you sure you have it? That's a lot of money. Yes, yes, of course, answered Leandro before handing him the signed check.

Leandro hung up the phone. He wouldn't know what to say to Osembe anyway. Maybe she fears the police showing up and has even moved out of her apartment. Would all that be worth the euros she stole? Euros she would have gotten out of him in a much less violent way, or maybe the act itself was a settling of scores. That also mortified Leandro. She knew I would do nothing, that I wouldn't go through the shame of reporting her. Leandro just wanted to ask Osembe in whose name she gave him those cowardly kicks. In her own? Did he deserve them? Did she hate him that much? Or was it just an act in front of her boyfriend, to avoid misunderstandings? What did it matter? It would only help him to complete the map of human nature, something that fascinated Leandro and that he would never grasp entirely. People do things without really thinking about them. There isn't a motivation for every action, it's a mistake to think of it in those terms. Could someone imagine me? Explain me? Of course not.

He goes into Aurora's room with the bucket of water and the sponge. He helps her lift her arms and fixes the bedsheets. As he does it, his side hurts where he received one of the kicks, or was it from the fall? As if jumping from one train to another, he forgets Osembe and focuses on Aurora. She smiles, she wants to talk, but she doesn't have the strength. Leandro leans over and thinks that she wants to kiss him. He draws his cheek close to her lips, but Aurora speaks in a whisper.

It would be good if you called an ambulance, I'm not feeling well.

23

It's important to Lorenzo that Sylvia meet Daniela. She already exists as a shadow, as an idea, as a real presence even, but they still haven't seen each other. Am I going to be the last one to meet the woman you're dating? No, no. Lorenzo choked on his breakfast toast. I'm waiting for the right moment. Are you that afraid of me? Lorenzo just smiled.

Dealing with his father's situation, the grueling signing of the check and its delivery to the unfriendly doorman in a solemn gesture, for Mrs. Jacqueline, had kept him away from Daniela and her house. He had wanted to stay close to his father, who was obviously capable of doing something stupid. He found Leandro in low spirits, his gaze sunken. The next day he was thinking of going over to the bank and finding out the balance of their accounts. In all these years, he hadn't given his parents a hand with administrative matters and maybe it was a good time to give everything a once-over.

He hadn't enjoyed any intimacy with Daniela in several days, but Lorenzo wanted to find a moment to introduce her to Sylvia. It wasn't easy. She spent less and less time at home. She vanished on weekends, justifying it with vague excuses. She had a boyfriend, but soon vacations would be here, allowing for a less strict schedule. That afternoon she was going to be home studying for exams, she said, and Lorenzo went upstairs to tell Daniela.

She opened the door. Come on in, but no funny stuff. The boy was watching the television hypnotically. We're going out now, she told Lorenzo, she was going to the Corte Inglés department store with the boy, she was meeting some other women there, the floor was clean and the kids played while they chatted or did a little shopping. It was too cold for the park. This afternoon I want you to come by the house, Sylvia's going to be there and I'd love for you to meet her. Daniela didn't like him coming up to see her there and she forced him to leave quickly, she didn't want the episode from the other day to be repeated, so even though he embraced her obstinately and she noticed the erection glued to his thigh she resisted and got him out of the apartment with stifled giggles.

Lorenzo had a lunch date with Wilson. They went over the matters in Wilson's little notebook; he finished jotting down some details in his schoolboy's hand. Lorenzo asked him, does it bother you I'm dating Daniela? Why would it bother me? Would it bother you if your daughter went out with an Ecuadorian? Lorenzo raised his eyebrows. I never thought about it. I guess not. Well, then, why would I butt in?

Lorenzo was silent. Wilson smiled as always, with a lopsided expression. So you pulled it off, I could tell you were stuck on her. I think she likes me. Then what's the problem? And in Wilson's smiling gaze, with his crazy eye as he called it, Lorenzo finally found someone he could confess aspects of his relationship to that he hadn't shared with anyone else.

Lorenzo knocks on Sylvia's door. He finds her lying on the mattress, headphones on. This is how you study? She waves her notes in the air. What concentration, he says. Is she here yet? Lorenzo had warned her they would meet that afternoon. Sylvia jokes, do I have to think of her as my stepmother or just one of Papá's flings? Lorenzo takes a step back and shrugs his shoulders, a fling, of course, a fling. Because, you know, it's not the same thing. How is anyone going to be your stepmother, look at you, you're frightening, you are going to run a comb through your hair, right?

Lorenzo hadn't told Sylvia he was dating the woman who takes care of the neighbors' son. Daniela always mentioned the times she passed Sylvia on the street or in the stairwell, she stuck out her tongue at the boy, she looks pretty, today she was writing a message on her cell phone, have you seen how fast she writes with her thumb? It's funny to watch. Maybe his daughter would have the same prejudices as everyone else. Do you want me to make dinner? No, no, we'll go out somewhere. Lorenzo seemed nervous, Daniela was late. Something's going on, you're nervous, maybe you didn't tell me the truth, maybe she's my age or something like that. She's older than you. Lorenzo checks his watch again. Daniela is usually punctual, often they're running to the phone booths because she wants to call her home in Loja on the dot. He waits outside for her and her phone calls almost always last the same number of minutes.

The doorbell rings. Sylvia smiles, bites her nails in mock nervousness, pulls her hair back. Lorenzo leaves her in the middle of the living room and goes to the door. He opens it. It's

Daniela. But it is Daniela with a sports bag over her shoulder, her pale blue double-breasted coat on and her eyes filled with tears. She doesn't say anything. Lorenzo invites her in. Come in, what's going on? Daniela shakes her head. She gestures hello to Sylvia, who recognized her instantly and hasn't moved from her spot. Let's go down to the street, I have to talk to you, excuse me. She directs that last part to Sylvia, apologizing for not coming in. Lorenzo looks at his daughter, grabs his jacket, and goes out onto the landing. Right in the doorway, Daniela collapses, crying. Her first intelligible words are, they fired me, they fired me, Lorenzo.

They gave me the boot.

24

Husky says, don't ask me to do this kind of stuff again, I was about to puke in there. He gets into Ariel's car and they leave uptown Madrid through jammed streets, only to be blocked by a delivery van. The driver jumps out, holds his hands out, asking for a minute to bring a couple of demijohns of sunflower oil and sacks of flour to the door of a cheap restaurant. When the row of waiting cars grows and the honking gets more intense, the van starts up again. Husky has just come out of the agency that owns the photographs of Ariel with Reyes. It's rough facing the reality that I'm in a profession filled with vipers, says Husky. I'm spoiled, my boss is one of the very few journalists who do their job well, he's honorable, decent, and, what's more, writes like a god.

Ariel found out about the photos from Arturo Caspe. Don't think that I had anything to do with it, the agent said arrogantly. These girls are models and there are always photographers following them around. It's part of being famous. And it's not going to hurt you, soccer fans like their players to be virile ladies' men. Ariel wasn't in the mood to argue or stay on the phone very long. I just want you to tell me what agency the photographer works for, that's it, was all he said. Half an hour later, Caspe called to give him a name. In the car, before Husky went up to the agency, Ariel signed a blank check. You're crazy, I could run off to Brazil with this.

Why did he do it? The photos weren't compromising. They weren't going to do him or Reyes any damage. But right now, with the negotiation of his future hanging in the balance, he didn't want the club to use his nightlife against him. They always did that when things were going badly. That beach party in La Coruña, after the local team had two losses, was used by the club's president to suggest that the players weren't taking the end of the competitive season seriously, and the executive who had brought in the girls leaked it to a radio commentator. And then there was a deeper reason, one he didn't admit to Husky: Sylvia. Ariel didn't want this issue to poison them. First the stupid woman who went on TV to brag about screwing soccer players. They were even kidding about it on the team. Husky told him, you good-looking guys can't afford to get involved with scum like that, you have to raise the bar, it's a moral and aesthetic obligation to the world. Sylvia had also found out about Marcelo's concert in Madrid and asked him, did you go? Yes, but with Argentinian friends, Ariel told her, and she was annoyed because he hadn't invited her. I didn't think you liked him. You've got me hooked, you play it all the time. Once again he was dirtying what in her was clean, free of deceit.

Husky had taken a while in the agency. He explained how they worked. Apart from professional photos, they dealt with couples who were at odds, looking to exploit each other. It was a rare week when someone didn't show up to negotiate over some photos of a model, an actress, a TV hostess naked on the beach or on the terrace of her house, or, as Husky told him, sticking her toothbrush up her cunt, pictures taken in the intimacy of a relationship that weeks, months, or years later were only good for scamming some money or sullying the reputation of the person who dumped you. Husky told him, when the prince got married, the agencies were anxious to buy photos of his wife from old schoolmates, ex-boyfriends, they were selling her medical records, her gynecological files, her school papers, a painter even showed up selling paintings she had posed nude for. Then they use them to negotiate, exchange favors. This country gobbles up tons of celebrity gossip every day. Like every other country, corrected Ariel, you think mine is any better?

When he appeared after the long negotiation and got into Ariel's car, Husky was in a teasing mood. I was expecting something erotic, spicy, a full-scale scandal. You want to buy some crappy photos of two good-looking kids in a taxi? What's going on? She snagged a millionaire and doesn't want the photos to fuck things up? Or he's marrying the president's daughter for her money and this could ruin his career? That's what the guy in the agency asked me and, honestly, I didn't know what to tell him. Ariel didn't say anything, he just listened with a smile, waiting in the wings. Are you going to tell me, are you going to say what the hell is going on and why we had to give two thousand euros to those sons of bitches?

I'll just introduce you to Sylvia, said Ariel. And he starts the car.

Don't mention any of this to her, warns Ariel later. They're on the way to pick Sylvia up at her house. But right at that moment Ariel gets a message from her. "My grandmother is in the hospital, I'll meet you in two hours." Change of plans, we have two hours to kill. Well, after dealing with those skunks my body demands alcohol. What are you in the mood for? Husky directs Ariel to a place he swears serves the best gin and tonics in the city. They're artists. Gin at five in the afternoon? Can you think of a better time?

They drive to a place near the Castellana. It's a bar that has seen better days; it's half empty and the walls are covered with deep-red fabric. There are a couple of women at the back tables. It's a classic joint to bring dates. Husky greets the barman and they sit at a table. This is what's known as a piano bar. An Asturian midfielder who used to play on your team arranged to meet me here for one of my first interviews, while he made out with a woman who wasn't his wife. Those were other times, I was just starting in the business, and he was on his way out. I got a fabulous interview, which they never published.

Ariel and Husky talk over a drink. The lemon slice floats among the ice cubes and the tonic's tiny bubbles. Ariel had gone back to practice that morning. He barely exchanged a word with Coach Requero. I didn't think this was so complicated, he confesses to his friend. Here winning over the fans is a matter of one nice play, sometimes luck, Husky explains to him. There have been mediocre players they've loved to death and geniuses they never understood. Then there's the populist type, who always goes over well, who runs with all his heart toward an unreachable ball, the one who asks the crowd to cheer him on, the one who gets pissed off at his teammates when they're losing. There should be a penalty for the players who sweat the most in games. Sweating is overrated. And I'll tell you something else, in Madrid foreign players with light eyes have never been successful. No, this is a distrustful sport, and people always find light eyes suspect. Here breaking legs is appreciated more than dodging and weaving. And it's the same in journalism, they want leg breakers. People believe that the journalist who insults is freer, more independent, but they don't see that they always insult the powerless. They spit downward. I swear it would take you twenty seasons to even begin to understand how insane everything is around here.

It's the same over there, believe me. It's the same everywhere.

Yeah, maybe you're right. You know what your problem is, Ariel? You think. You think too much. And a soccer player can't think. A soccer player can't have an inner life, for fuck's sake. It destroys him. It beats you down, it paralyzes you. Shit, you'll have time to think when you're retired. Don't keep running things over in your head, play. Just play and see where the swell takes you. Should we order another gin and tonic?

Ariel talks to him about Sylvia. I've been trying not to fall in love with this girl ever since I met her. Maybe the alcohol or Ariel's passion when he talks about her leads Husky to confess. You know I was only in college for a year? Then I got an internship and said, fuck it, to my mother's dismay. I met a girl there. She was a really special chick, she wrote poetry. You get the idea, right? And she was pretty, you can't even imagine. We were born to never cross paths. In those days I was into the Who, I had seen *Quadrophenia* a hundred and three times and had sideburns as long as table legs, but I fell for her like a drooling fool.

Husky pauses, such a long pause Ariel starts to wonder if that was the end of the story and so he asks, and? We went out, for a month or so. Then we broke up. Maybe we were too young, I don't know, or it was the absurd feeling that if you meet the love of your life at twenty years old the best thing to do is run away. You should meet someone like that at forty, and even then it seems too early. At sixty. Two years ago, I ran into her on the street. She has a kid, she's married, she's in charge of media relations in I don't know which ministry of those jackass things politicians spend their lives doing, Justice or External Affairs. It was weird because I asked her, do you still write poetry? And she turned beet red. I was super-embarrassed, because she didn't want to talk about it, can you believe it? Well, they were horrible poems, of course, like all poems.

Don't be an ass, how can you say that?

It's the truth. When you've worked the Regional Third and every fucking soccer field all over Spain, after meeting the real people out there, I can assure you that if they put Lorca or Bécquer or Machado in front of me, I know what I'd tell them. Imagine they went out to recite their masterpieces in the middle of a soccer field, how long would it be before people jumped in to stomp on their entrails? No, dude, no, poetry is a lie that we invented to make ourselves believe we can sometimes be tender and civilized. Well, when I saw her blush, I realized I knew her secret, more than that, she had been as in love with me as I was with her, something I always doubted, even though she wrote me a poem once.

You? She wrote a poem about you?

Is it that strange? There are people who have written poems about Stalin or about a blind cow. Yes, about me. And I still have it memorized. Do you want to hear it? Ariel nodded enthusiastically. Husky began to recite with heartfelt pauses: "You aren't handsome, you aren't perfect, and that red hair, what's to be done about it, you're afraid of thinking, you're afraid of caressing, you'd rather be called an idiot than to be told I love you, which is why I now write you: you're an idiot, you're an idiot, my love, you're an idiot." Isn't that the most beautiful declaration of love you've ever heard in your life?

Ariel burst out laughing, mostly because of the importance with which Husky recited the verses. The girl knew you well, you are an idiot. You didn't get it, "you'd rather be called an idiot than to be told I love you," and she says I love you by calling me an idiot, what ignorance.

Ariel can't stop laughing. A little while ago, he wouldn't have thought that someone would be able to make him forget what he was going through. Now he wipes away the tears with a paper napkin while Husky insists, you brute, idiot means my love in the poem, it's not literal, it's a metaphor or whatever . . . Do you even know what a metaphor is? Right, how would a fucking soccer player know what a metaphor is?

They pick up Sylvia at the hospital's side door. She greets Husky, who forces her to get into the backseat. Sorry, but I'm not getting into that hole, my feet don't fit, he apologizes. Besides I've always found sports cars disgusting. Me, too, she says. I'm going to switch it, I swear, I'm going to switch it, says Ariel.

Husky chose the restaurant. To get there, they had to leave Madrid, cross a high plateau filled with offices, malls, and knots of highway. It's far, but it's awesome, and we won't run into anyone there.

It's a Galician restaurant. The owner's wife comes out of the kitchen to kiss Husky and say, my boy, my boy, you're so thin. The fact that this restaurant is open, he explains when they sit down, is proof that this country hasn't totally gone to shit. Now you'll see how things really taste, it'll blow your mind.

Husky goes to the bathroom. On the way, he shows them a slice of a large round loaf of bread in its wicker basket, look, look at this bread, please, there is still something authentic left in this world. Ariel brushes Sylvia's hand. How is your grandmother? Terrible. Sylvia is silent. If you want, we can forget about the trip. Have you thought of somewhere? she asks. Ariel nods with a smile, we men in love are like that. Sylvia looks into his eyes. You guys are both drunk.

Husky comes out of the bathroom and returns to the table. Sylvia, when this crappy loser is playing in the Siberian Third Division, please, don't stop calling me to go out, okay, keep calling me.

Maybe I will.

part four

IS THIS THE END?

1

Venice is tinged with the burnt sienna of its houses. There isn't much to do except look at this place, says Sylvia. Be amazed that someone could actually live here. They had sat in a cobblestoned square. They went into a store that sells handmade bracelets and necklaces. There were two cats lying beneath a magnolia tree. During the gondola ride, he hugs her. Sylvia curls her head into his shoulder. Music plays in a nearby house. From the canals they see the roofs of apartments, they pass postcard-perfect tourists, they hear the whistles of the gondoliers before taking the curves. Sylvia feels Ariel's hand on her shoulder throughout the whole ride. It won't be easy for her to forget. As they pass beneath a bridge, a group of Spaniards recognize Ariel and start taking photos of him and shouting. We're the best, oé, oé. The gondolier frees them from the onslaught by veering into the canal.

They visited a museum and looked at store windows with luxury designer names. They ate ice cream in the Piazza San Marco, watched the children opening their arms and letting the pigeons cover them as they landed. The night before they'd had the last drink at Harry's Bar and Ariel didn't let her look at the bill. It'll depress you. Across the table, Ariel handed her a gift. Inside a small case were two necklaces. Is it gold? He nodded. You're crazy. There are two small chains that each hold one broken half of a soccer ball. When you put them together, they make one complete ball. He's just a boy, thought Sylvia. It's lovely, she said. A jeweler from Rosario made it for me, *ha tardado un huevo*, it took him forever. Sylvia smiled. It amused her when he used Spanish expressions, they sounded strange coming out of his mouth. Sylvia put one of the chains on him and he helped with the clasp on hers. They were staying in a hotel on Lido Island, and they walked until they found an old taxi driver who offered them a drink from his bottle of vodka while he drove the boat. When they woke up the next morning, they pulled back the curtains to see the ocean, with the rental shacks on the beach.

Ariel had picked Sylvia up on her corner, and they drove to the airport. Above the check-in counter she read VENICE and that marked the end of the secret. I can't believe it. They talked me into it at the travel agency, I thought it was a little corny. Corny? You have no idea. They boarded together. Am I your sister on this flight or have we just met?

At the airport, a driver was waiting for them with a sign that had Sylvia's name on it. He took them to the wharf, and from there to the island in a boat. How can all this survive? It's magic. What a smell, right? As they go through the city in a vaporetto, they see the façades covered with scaffolding, restoration jobs. They go down to the market and stop in the middle of a bridge to look at the canal. Noisy conversations in Spanish pass closely by. Ariel wears sunglasses and a golf hat. You're disguised as an undercover famous person, everyone will look at you, Sylvia tells him. He doesn't stop signing autographs until he takes off the glasses and hat. An Argentinian family with a boy wearing a San Lorenzo jersey keeps them under the Bridge of Sighs for almost twenty minutes; the father is an economist and tirelessly explains his theory about globalization and the state deficit. At a stand selling soccer jerseys, Sylvia asks for Ariel's, the vendor checks with two or three younger employees, yes, Ariel Burano, but the vendor shakes his head. Sylvia turns toward Ariel to gloat over the humiliation.

Ariel hired a boat to take them to the island of Burano. Supposedly this is where I come from. At least that's what the club made up. The houses are painted in pastel colors around the canals; it looks like the set of a musical. The skipper explains to them that the colors help you recognize your house on foggy days and then he makes a gesture meaning drunkard, it helps them, too. They were only planning on spending a little while on the island, but they are there almost the entire day. They end up eating in a restaurant with outdoor tables that serves a fish-of-the-day special. They stroll beneath a portal of a virgin surrounded by flowers. It reminds me of La Boca, he says. There's a school where kids play basketball and two old guys greet each other in the street. They must be your relatives.

Maybe I could come to an Italian team next year, says Ariel during lunch. Would you like to live here? Sylvia shrugs her shoulders. Too pretty, right? The waiter shows Sylvia how to use the oil, he pours it on a plate for her and then sprinkles a handful of *fleur de sel* over the olive-green puddle.

In two months, the season will be over. They both fear the end. Sylvia wants to ask him, what will I be to you? but she doesn't. She knows it will be difficult to leave this whole life behind. Husky is really nice, why didn't you introduce me to him earlier? I thought he would scare you, he's insane. And that voice, at first I thought he was faking it. It's because of nodules, Ariel explains, he told me that as a kid they took out a ton of them from his throat and he couldn't talk for weeks, he just wrote in a notebook. Sylvia looks toward the canal: fishing boats are moored all along it. She's not hungry anymore. Maybe we should separate slowly, bit by bit, so it's not so sudden.

What do you mean? asks Ariel.

I don't want to say good-bye on the last day at the airport, turn around, and see you've disappeared forever. Ariel looks at her and wants to hug her. It would be better if we started doing it in installments. Like a countdown.

Why do you say that?

Sylvia has a knot in her throat. Her eyes suddenly fill with tears and she lowers her head in embarrassment. She runs her hand over her cheek. Ariel touches her knee. He is ashamed of his inability to hold her in a public place. Why are you thinking about this now? We came here to enjoy ourselves, right? Look at this. Don't think about anything else.

Sylvia nods her head. She's sixteen, Ariel seems to be thinking, she's just sixteen. He tells her, you are the best thing that ever happened to me. Aw, man, she replies, as she bites her lip to keep from crying, with that Argentinian accent you have to be careful what you say. And she wipes away a tear. I'm sorry, I'm spoiling the trip, I'm an asshole.

Maybe Venice wasn't a good idea. Venice is a place where lovers the world over come to swear eternal love. There are other places, many others, in which to later betray the pledge. But not Venice. Sylvia looks up, refuses the grappa Ariel sips. In two days, she will be gone from this place, back to the poorly ventilated classroom where her schoolmates slap each other on the back and talk loudly. Don't forget that all this is just a car accident, it's about surviving it, that's all.

Every night she called home from the hotel. Her father gave her the report from the hospital. Grandma is still there, without much hope of leaving. Lorenzo spends the nights there, so her grandfather can rest a little. Sylvia asks about him, he's seemed depressed the last few days. She asks about Daniela, everything okay?

Yeah, yeah, everything's fine.

When Lorenzo returned home the day of their frustrated introduction, Sylvia was watching a movie where a woman trained in martial arts gave her ex-husband a beating. He explained the situation to Sylvia, before she had a chance to ask. They had fired her from her job when they found out she was dating Lorenzo. Some neighbor had seen him go up to the apartment. Did you go into their apartment? A couple of times to talk to her. Lorenzo didn't tell her about what took place in the guest bathroom. I'm going to go up there, it's a misunderstanding. Sylvia held him back. Papá, wait, don't get involved. Even though Daniela had spent the whole evening saying she deserved to be fired, that she had betrayed the couple's trust, that she should have told them about it before they found out from some nosy neighbor, he insisted it was worth the effort to clear it up. Papá, Sylvia told him again, don't get involved. She takes care of their son, you're a neighbor, it makes them uncomfortable, and that's that. Don't keep thinking about it. Lorenzo grew pensive, sat on the arm of the sofa. A viscous monster was now attacking the girl in the movie. It's not fair.

Papá, it's after eleven, don't go up there now. But Daniela does her job well, that's how she makes a living. The person who takes care of their damn kid can't be in a relationship? They need a virgin maid to wipe their kid's ass? Sylvia leaned back on the sofa. When her father talked like that, he seemed like a pressure cooker about to explode. He didn't usually curse in front of her, and when he did it was because he had lost control. She's very pretty, Sylvia said to deactivate his rage. You think so? She's Ecuadorian, right? Yes. I'll tell you something, Papá, it's better for you, too, that she doesn't work upstairs, she'll find something else, for sure. Lorenzo seemed to calm down. Sylvia smiled at him. I should have gone up to meet them before, obviously. Knock on the door and say, I have come to ask for the hand of your maid. What kind of a country do we live in? This country is springing leaks everywhere. Do you really think she's pretty?

Desperation.

Why did Sylvia look at her father in that moment and see a desperate man? It could be the nervousness, the agitation, the guilt. Also his inability to soothe Daniela. She had wanted to go home, we'll talk tomorrow, I want to calm down alone. Frustration, maybe. But Sylvia didn't have the feeling it was a momentary desperation. No. Sylvia saw her father as a desperate man. He had found a woman in the stairwell. That's how reduced his field of action had become. He seemed like a shipwreck survivor clinging to a plank, worn out, overwhelmed, fragile.

Ariel and Sylvia go up early to their room. The hotel is filled with boisterous Americans with white-white skin. They don't feel like having dinner. In the huge bed, beneath the art nouveau lamp, they watch television. There are game shows and a biopic about Christ, with a long beard and a languid gaze. Ariel whispers into her ear and she smiles. Then he tickles her and she tries to get away as she laughs, until she clumsily falls off the bed to the floor, unable to grab the bedspread. Ariel sees her fallen pale body on the red carpet and he leaps to pick her up, take her in his arms, and place her on the sheets. Where does it hurt? Everywhere, she says. Ariel starts to kiss her on each part of her body.

Sylvia lies still, the nape of her neck and her back against the mattress and their clothing all in a mess. You are a very dangerous girl, did you know that? A very, very dangerous girl.

2

The days in the hospital are exhausting. Aurora is separated from another patient by a green three-piece folding screen. There are two chairs by the bed, their seats sunken from use. In one usually sits Leandro, who crosses and uncrosses his wiry legs. He holds vigil over his wife's unconsciousness as well as the periods when she wakes up and is a little more lively for company, or pretends she's listening to the tiny radio placed on the bedside table, or thanks the nurses for their visits from the country of the sane and vital. They come in like a whirlwind, carry out their tasks, change the IV drip, inject her with pain-killers, take her temperature and her blood pressure, change the sheets, as if their job were some gymnastic routine.

Leandro knows every inch of the hallway's mosaic floor, the sound of the elevator doors opening at the end of the hall, the moans of some patient dying in a nearby room. Dying is a rit-ual interpreted with the cadence of a musical score on that floor of the hospital. The doctor brings him up-to-date on the illness advancing through Aurora's body. There is a word that sounds horrible and that Leandro identifies with the shape of death. Me-tastasis. She isn't suffering, we have the pain threshold controlled so she won't suffer and can maintain consciousness for the lon-gest possible time. But Leandro is left with the desire to ask him about that nonlocalized pain, which doesn't appear on graphs or in specific complaints, but can cut through you like a knife.

Sometimes he studies Aurora's face to see if that profound illness has taken over. She had always been a brave woman who looked toward the future. When she was about to die after giving birth to her son, when she had to be moved urgently because she almost bled to death, she still had time to warn Leandro, remember to lower the blinds before too much sun can get in, that way the house stays cooler, because it was summer in the city. Aurora's sister came to help her take care of the baby boy in those days of uncertainty. Leandro went to see her at the hospital and she reassured him, you don't think I'd die now, when we have such a beautiful boy.

Is it now? wonders Leandro. Is now her time to die? Is there no longer anyone to hold her back? At nights her son, Lorenzo, who is a now a middle-aged man, beaten and bald, comes to relieve him and he lies down to sleep on the sofa, which opens into an uncomfortable bed. Leandro has some dinner in the café near his house, which he prefers to the hospital cafeteria, filled with comments about funerals and sorrowful gazes. At home he had begun to put his belongings into boxes. He was preparing to move into Lorenzo's apartment, he still didn't know how they would arrange it. Bring only the essential, his son had told him. He organized the records he would listen to again and the books he still needed for his classes. They aren't many. He stored his notes, study scores, reports, and student files in boxes for incineration. He will give away or destroy the essence of what has made up his life. He still hasn't gone into Aurora's room, he doesn't dare go through the photo albums, the old correspondence, the objects of sentimental value, her clothes. He will travel, when this is all over, with the least number of things possible. The essential? Is anything? He will be a nuisance for his son and his granddaughter, in the way. Life without Aurora looks leaden and empty.

The first night, his son arrived at the hospital and in the hallway he said, I didn't know you mortgaged the house. I've been by the bank. Leandro was silent. He listened to Lorenzo ask for explanations about the amounts of money squandered in a constant drain. There was no rage in his son's words, no indignation, he wasn't scandalized. I guess he's lost respect for me even for that.

I'm not going to ask you what you spent those thousands of euros on, Papá. I'm not going to ask you.

Leandro felt weak. He walked to the little waiting room, where there were some empty seats at that time of day. A nurse at the back made a shushing gesture. Leandro let himself drop into a chair, beaten. His head in his hands, his gaze at his feet. Lorenzo approached him, but he didn't sit down; he preferred to watch from a distance.

Don't say anything to your mother, please, don't tell her anything. Or to Sylvia, either.

How could I tell them anything, Papá? What do you want me to tell them, huh? You tell me, what do I tell them? Leandro sighed deeply. Nothing, admitted Leandro. Fuck . . .

The silence extended for so long that it was more painful than any recrimination. Leandro wanted to say, I don't know what got into me, I lost my head, but he didn't say anything. Lorenzo bit his tongue, paced around the room to release his rage. Finally, the financial matter came to his rescue. Lorenzo spoke to him. And you let the bank talk you into signing a mortgage that's a rip-off? Don't you understand? They pay you until you die, but they scam you. If you put your apartment on the market, you'd get twice what they're paying you, and on top of it all they act like they're helping you out.

They didn't tell me that.

And what do you want them to tell you? That they're bastards? Have you ever seen a bank advertisement that says, come see us and we'll suck you dry?

Lorenzo seemed satisfied. He calmed down. We'll work it out, but you'll have to move in with me. We've got to stop it, I'll figure out how. Leandro nodded. He didn't want to say some typical nonsense like, I don't want to be a bother. It would be more honest to say: I accept being a bother. He stood up. When he started to walk along the hallway, Lorenzo said something to him that hurt him deeply, shouldn't you see a doctor?

So that was it, thought Leandro, I'm sick. Nothing a few pills and a horrible-sounding diagnosis can't cure. Maybe it would be better if he went to a psychiatrist, a rehabilitation cure. Get over his addiction to life. There was something else, learning to be old, passive, a shadow. Leandro wanted to reassure him, he wanted to tell him it had all been a fit of insanity, a transitory stupidity, and he would learn to respect himself again. But he only said, it won't happen again.

In the hospital hallway, he had met another old man who was there with his wife. I was sure I would die before her, the man said, as almost always happens. Leandro hadn't ever thought about their departing order. In the last few months, he had time to prepare himself, to get used to the idea of being alone, of losing her. A number of times he heard Aurora say to her granddaughter, when they chatted, will you take care of your grandfather? Will you take care of him? And the girl promised that she would, of course.

Will I reread Unamuno or Ortega to repeat the same old conversations with Manolo Almendros? Perhaps the poems of Machado or Rubén could be some comfort? And the flesh that tempts us with its fresh bunches of grapes, and the tomb that awaits us with its funereal branches. All of Bach, what about Mozart? Or give them both up? And Schubert? What would be his measuring stick? Undoing the tangled web of a life, taking what had gotten twisted up over the years and now undoing it, walking backward. Taking only what I brought to this house when I came to live in it? This last idea amused him. But he soon realized it canceled out what had given Aurora pleasure, what they had shared, bought together, listened to together, both read. Retracing the steps of an entire life. His threw out his retirement plaque that read "for your years of devotion and training, to our teacher," because the only thing he did during all those years and with all those students was to try to bring Don Alonso back to life, to maintain his rectitude, his polite manner, his rigorous challenge to the most promising students, even intoning some Latin phrase that he now wouldn't dare say out of a fear of sounding pedantic like Joaquín.

He lingered over some scores, reciting the place and the period in which each was composed, you can't play something without knowing its history. He repeated the anecdotes he had learned from his old teacher, it is a job, gentlemen, don't forget that the author wrote every note with calculating coldness, it should be played with an iron discipline, but without forgetting its end goal was to provoke a bishop's pleasure, or a count's, or an emperor's. Haydn composed for the Esterhazys and

Beethoven composed the Sonata in B Major while recovering from a bout of jaundice, that is important when playing it. And Schubert composed the great Sonata in C Minor with traces of the "Pathetique" because Beethoven had just died and he felt himself a worthy heir. He could repeat some of his old teacher's sentences word for word. It's lighthearted, the composer was twenty years old, don't play it as if it were composed by a mummy, a statue, take off that two-hundred-year-old tombstone and remember, too, that it was written in the month of May and from the window the composer could see a garden of birch trees surely filled with butterflies unimaginable today, so play it like a celebration, not like a punishment.

Notes plus mood. Rigor plus intuition. Expressive freedom. We are what we convey. Let's not betray it. That was what he would say. He dragged the old teacher along with him until he himself became an old teacher, similar yet different, an updated version. But he doesn't know if someone is traveling around out there with the memories of his classes. Leandro thinks that life lasts longer than its players, like music, everything answers to a chaotic clock mechanism, to a fine-tuned device devoid of even the slightest precision.

The closet was filled with old metronomes, music magazines saved for some forgotten article, press clippings, programs from every concert he had ever attended. He never kept a diary, but he has the feeling he is reading one over. The shirt I still wear some Sundays, the vest I use so much in the spring, the umbrella in good shape, one of the visor hats, the leather wallet, the best pencils, two belts, the less worn-out jacket, the scarf that was a birthday present, the handkerchiefs from the last Three Kings Day.

This morning Sylvia is also at the hospital. She can barely speak anymore, he warns his granddaughter. He looks out the window. The sun alights on the trees and makes the greens pop. It is early. He has an idea. Should we take Aurora out for a walk? We could bundle her up and put her in the wheelchair. It might be dangerous, says Sylvia. In the sun it's so nice. We have to do it now because your father would refuse flat out. Should I ask the nurses? No, go ask the doctor. Sylvia leaves the room while Leandro prepares Aurora's things, her coat, which is in the built-in closet. Then he opens the wheelchair. Sylvia comes back, the doctor's gone out, he's not on this floor. They ask a nurse, who is against it, please, don't even consider it. Are you crazy?

When the nurse leaves, Leandro releases his bitterness, hospitals swallow you up, they finish you off. You enter through those doors like into the mouth of an animal that devours you whole. People used to die at home. Sylvia lets her head drop. She knows, thinks Leandro, that Aurora is closer to death than life. Death is something new for someone as young as his granddaughter. He likes the childish lightness with which Sylvia moves, her vague way of speaking without finishing her sentences and the way she shakes her hair and her whole body every time she walks. Compared to the prudent gait of the elderly, the shaky walk of those who peek out onto the hallway, Sylvia is an almost insulting breath of fresh air when she heads toward the elevator or accompanies him to the cafeteria with her long strides.

Do you want to have breakfast with me? I've already missed my first class. Then go, hurry. And they say good-bye at the elevators. Some other day we'll take her out, okay, Grandpa? Without saying anything to anyone. But Leandro suspects it will never happen. Among the customers crowded at the hospital bar is an African family. Leandro watches them carefully.

There are two women with three small children. They have trouble explaining what they want. The waiter lists the beverages while they order. A coffee, yeah, with milk, okay, and what else? Leandro notices the gesture with which the man takes the exact change from the woman's open palm. When he finishes charging her, he looks around to see if anyone is watching and Leandro looks away. The hospital bar is a mosaic, a small city, the aristocracy of doctors in white coats, the employees, the patients' family members. Leandro considers himself a relic of another time, ready to disappear. Like when he looked into Osembe's eyes and discovered a world that could no longer comprehend his own.

The world of the living.

3

Like the first few times, like in the beginning of their relationship, Lorenzo goes to the church to meet up with Daniela. Now he doesn't arrive early, but rather when he knows the service has already begun. He sneaks in through the back door. He finds a spot in the last few rows, under the curious gaze of people who turn around when they hear the noise of the street.

He has the feeling that everything he's built has fallen like a house of cards. The process of decomposition has been quick. In the last few weeks, every meeting with Daniela had been a step backward. First the firing. From the very beginning, Daniela had adopted the position of guilty victim. Don't say nothing happened, Lorenzo, of course something happened. We did something wrong. You came into the house without any right to do so, I let you in without permission. Don't lie.

The recriminations grew. It was your lust that made me lose my job. I provoked you and wasn't able to keep you out of the house. Lust? What century is that word from? Why don't you say love? Because love is respect. And I don't respect you? Of course you do, but we didn't respect their house.

It was perhaps a terrible coincidence that these discussions took place during Holy Week. Daniela seemed to be steeped in a martyr spirit. It was impossible to find a new job during the holidays, and that gave her more than enough time to fret. Lorenzo's mother was in the hospital and it kept his nights filled. Wasn't that a sacrifice? During the day, he looked for Daniela, he tried to piece back together what was broken. They went to his apartment; Sylvia had gone camping with some classmates. They had three days to themselves. But Daniela was worried about being in the building, being so close to the couple she had worked for, what if I bump into them? You have nothing to be ashamed of. You really believe that? Why would I lower my head if I saw them?

During lunch at his place, they worked on a strategy for finding another job. There is a nun that has a placement agency, she helped me the first time. I'm sure Wilson could find you something, he has hundreds of contacts, suggested Lorenzo. I don't like Wilson's contacts, she said, abruptly closing the chapter. He takes advantage of people, it's ugly. Well, he also helps them, interjected Lorenzo. No, helping is something else.

Daniela continued to have a devastated outlook. They had started helping me with my papers. I'll take care of that, don't worry. I have to send money home. I can lend you some. Don't even say that. Lorenzo felt a real desire to hold her and make love to her, but he held himself back, he didn't want to be rebuffed. Your daughter must think I'm crazy, seeing me cry like that, she said to Lorenzo. No, not at all, she told me you were very pretty.

When they finished eating, she insisted on washing the dishes. Lorenzo embraced her from behind. He played with her hands under the water and foam and then he wet her bare forearms. He remained glued to her. You're aroused, warned Daniela. Very much so, he responded. Come on, wait for me in the bed, I'll be there soon.

Lorenzo obeyed. He went to his room and undressed. He got between the sheets of his unmade bed, which he straightened with two flutters. Then he thought better of it and put his underwear back on. She took her time coming. For a second, Lorenzo no longer heard the sound of dishes in the sink and he thought she had gone. But then there was a sound of the toilet flushing. When she opened the door to his room, Lorenzo smiled at her from the bed. Daniela went to the window. She lowered the blinds. The room was in almost complete darkness. Lorenzo felt the mattress sink when she sat down. She took off her sneakers, then her pants. Then her T-shirt, which she folded and arranged beside the pants on the floor, on the little rug. Lorenzo hugged her. He kissed her on the shoulders and ran first his fingers and then his lips over the marks on her back. Are they injuries? My father was very strict, until he left us, was all she said.

Lorenzo caressed her body, you're so lovely, but Daniela said nothing. She didn't stop him from taking the straps of her bra off her shoulders or removing it, after a struggle unhooking it that made them both laugh. Lorenzo caressed Daniela's sex over her panties and then beneath them. She seemed aroused, willing. When Lorenzo lay on top of her, he heard her whisper, yes, come on, give it all to me, let's go. Following Lorenzo's rhythmic movements, her hands invited him to speed up. Like that, like that, you like it? I'm your whore, I don't mind being your whore, give it to me.

Lorenzo had never heard her talk like that. Twice he tried to lie down and put her on top of him, but Daniela's hands clung tightly to him. She turned her face and panted with closed eyes. It was so different from her usual attitude that Lorenzo even wondered if she was faking it. He stuck his thumb in her mouth, Daniela bit it without hurting him. She kept repeating obscenities into his ear. Lorenzo pulled out to come onto her belly, they remained there, damp, stuck to one another.

You're afraid, right? You finished outside of me, she added a moment later. I don't know if you are taking anything. What does it matter? Are you afraid of getting me pregnant? It was the first time Lorenzo thought, with the detachment of a recent orgasm, that she was crazy. But her tone was sweet and affectionate. It wasn't psychotic or threatening. I thought that was normal, he said. It's easy to have sex without going all the way, as if it were just a game, but it's nicer to have sex and go all the way. I would have really liked you to finish inside me.

I don't know, it's better to talk about these things first, discuss them calmly. You never asked me. Okay, Daniela, please, let's be straight with each other, does this have something to do with religion?

What makes you say that?

For the first time, Daniela acted offended. You don't understand anything. Did I force you to do anything? Did I ask you to go to church, to believe in anything? I went to bed with you without getting any promises out of you . . . Excuse me, I don't understand.

Beneath the sheets, Daniela took Lorenzo's hand and placed it on her still damp belly. She dragged it from the top of her breasts to her pubic hair. All this is yours, I am giving it to you.

Daniela turned her back to Lorenzo. He turned over and took her by the shoulders after a moment, which was a relief, because his hemorrhoids were killing him, but he didn't say anything. He started to brush up against her again. He said, do you want to have a baby with me? Is that what you want? Well, let's go for it, let's do it, come on, I want it, too. But Lorenzo stopped, fell back onto the mattress. This is ridiculous, he said, I can't have a child now, I'm sorry.

You're a coward, Lorenzo. You still have so much to change.

They stayed there for a long time, without moving, without saying anything. Daniela stood up sometime later and dressed. Are you leaving? Don't you want to shower? No, I like to take you with me. Lorenzo wanted to keep her, pull her back down beside him. When he stood up he asked, what do you want from me? What can I do?

Pronouncing the words with a firm but sweet musicality, Daniela told him, I only ask that you don't turn me into your whore. That's all I ask of you. Respect and love.

Days passed. They saw each other again as if nothing had happened. They went out for a walk one evening, took the metro out of the neighborhood, and Lorenzo took her by the waist. He liked to do that in front of everyone. He believed it made her feel good. A group of teenagers came into the car, there weren't more than five girls, but they made a scene and attracted the passengers' attention. Profusely made-up, coiffed with dubious taste, several of them wore miniskirts above their thighs. Daniela looked at them with a certain displeasure. One of them, the most willowy, drank from a liter bottle of beer that she carried inside a white plastic bag. Nobody said anything to her, but she spoke loudly. She was talking about boys in a crude way. Lorenzo always thought of his daughter when he saw a group like that. Maybe when she was out of the house she acted the same, but he doubted it. He had been lucky with her. Lorenzo looked at the group of girls sadly. Time will crush them, all that defiance they now spit disdainfully in our faces will dry up one day and they'll turn into what they most hate.

Lorenzo and Daniela went to the Retiro, they looked at the kids on the swings, on the ropes, on the slides. Neither of them brought up the conversation that had been interrupted. What can I offer her? Where am I going wrong? Her last comment in his bedroom had remained in his head, unsettled. The moral abyss between them was so vast that the couple he longed for seemed impossible.

Lorenzo accompanied her to a job interview in a house on the outskirts of the city. He waited for her in the van. It wasn't far from Paco's neighborhood, from where he had died. Lorenzo thought of him. Sometimes he was tempted to tell Daniela the truth, to open up to her. What would he say? She emerged from the interview with her head bowed, they want someone who knows English and can teach it to the children. Lorenzo wanted to take her to the old folks' home where he went to visit Don Jaime. She thought it was a good idea. He's a curious guy, Wilson and I emptied out his apartment, now he lives in a home.

He's alone, he doesn't have anyone, sometimes I pass by and sit with him.

The visit wasn't different than other times, the same polite phrases, the same absence. Don Jaime smiled when they came in, or at least Lorenzo thought he did. Daniela stroked his hand when they stood up to leave. Why do you go to see him, Lorenzo? she asked on the way home. I don't know, I honestly don't know. But it makes you feel good. Right?

Yeah, I guess so.

That night, like the previous ones, he invited her up to his place, but she didn't want to come. Then he suggested taking her home and sleeping there together. She said no.

No, not tonight.

4

Ariel wasn't surprised the day his name didn't appear on the blackboard listing the eighteen players chosen for the final game. In the previous match, in Vitoria, he had spent the best minutes on the bench and the coach only conceded him the last ten to overcome a score of one to zero. His substitution was justified. He was coming back from an injury. And it wasn't the ideal field for a vulnerable ankle. It was as muddy out there as a stable. Every stride forced two movements, the forward one and the one to extract your foot from a puddle of mud. But Ariel remembered something Dragon used to say, in the worst conditions, on the worst fields, the best is still the best. Husky tells him about the statements the coach made in the press conference postgame. At this point in the championship, I also start to think about the upcoming season and the players who are going to continue with us.

Days earlier Husky had devoted an article to him. He interwove his praise with the idea that nothing on the team had worked out the way they expected. "Ariel Burano Costa was a jewel stolen from San Lorenzo. A team that's not working undervalues all its parts, just as a team that's winning does the opposite. This is a good player devalued by a broken system."

Ariel appreciated his comments. At the same time it bothered him that it had to be a friend who praised him. He preferred the silence. He was hoping the executives would value his performance and put a stop to the war that had been unleashed. He was uncomfortable about the personal information Husky revealed. "For a young man from Buenos Aires, it was hard to integrate into a team filled with veterans, a young man who listens to music with intelligent lyrics, watches movies with subtitles, who visits the Prado regularly, and even reads! It wasn't so long ago that this same team punished kids for reading during prematch preparations with a double gym session. He came alone, without any family, without knowing the country, without enough time to understand a very different kind of soccer, which is as similar to the Argentinian game as a walnut is to an orange. He has run hard along the touchline, but he hasn't won over the stands. Perhaps he will return at a better time—after all, there is rumor of a lovely young Madrid native who gives him good reason to never completely leave this city."

You could have kept that last paragraph to yourself, reproached Ariel. Sorry, I had a poetic hemorrhage. And I only went to the Prado for half an hour the whole year I've been here, don't make me out to be some fucking intellectual. Well, compared to your teammates, they could give you the Nobel

Prize for literature and nobody in the First Division could argue. Tell me the truth, it got you a little emotional, didn't it? I don't cry easily. Do you know what my boss told me? That it was the most spectacular display of ass kissing since Mother Teresa died. Your boss is right. You forgot to say that I played like shit the entire championship.

Ariel clipped out the article and mailed it to his parents. He showed it to Sylvia first. Your friend is a softie. Does that last sentence refer to me? I think you made an impression on him. Yeah. And as far as I know, you only went to the Prado once. I told him, but that's just how he is.

He watched the game in which they were eliminated from the European competition at home with Sylvia. He didn't travel with the team because the coach considered him to be in poor form following his injury. But we've got the season at stake, please. The coach shook his head. Ariel left the locker room with a huge slam of the door. Ariel was infuriated to see the season go down the drain without being on the field. Beside him, Sylvia was amused to see him punching the sofa cushions, cheering them on, come on, keep it up, you gotta attack, let's go, there's time, there's still time. When Sylvia said, fuck them, those assholes kicked you off the team, he turned and said, that's my team, can't you understand that?

The loss depressed him. He grabbed a bottle of vodka from the freezer. Wlasavsky had brought one back for everyone on the team from his trip to Poland. It was white liquid scented by a little herb branch inside and had a mammoth drawn on the label. They both drank. They heated up some empanadas.

They went out with Husky a couple of evenings. Suddenly, when their relationship seemed doomed to a dead end, it became more stable than ever. They could share a friend, walk along the streets of the city without caring about onlookers' curious gazes. Husky served as the third man and that guaranteed them peace. If Ariel was surrounded by a group of teenagers who wanted to photograph him with their cell phones, Husky would dissolve them authoritatively or entertain Sylvia with comments on the people's looks, their way of speaking, of addressing a famous person. He teased Ariel all the time, he told him he'd soon be playing on some Russian millionaire's team, dribbling stalactites. He also said to Sylvia, you don't fit the Lolita mold, and then he recommended the novel to her, although I warn you it ends badly, Lolita grows up.

When the conversation inevitably turned toward soccer, Husky confessed to Sylvia, soccer is a very strange sport played by brainless perennially teenaged millionaires but they propel a mechanism that makes hundreds of thousands of brainless, not-as-wealthy people happy. He told her about the guy who, after his father died, kept bringing his ashes to the field inside a Tetra Pak, and many others who asked to have their ashes spread over the grass of their favorite team's stadium, fathers who bought membership cards for their sons the very day they were born, or tried to sneak their dogs into the stands, collectors of cards, jerseys, balls, people who took away pieces of the goal and the field on the day of the final game.

Husky made them laugh. He relaxed the tension that sometimes accumulated around them. He went with Ariel when he dropped Sylvia off at her door at night. Often Sylvia complained bitterly, why didn't I meet you sooner. Yeah, before you met Ariel. Husky drank beers, sweated, and wiped his forehead with paper napkins that he balled up and threw to the floor. You could use my sweat to water the African continent daily.

When are you playing your last game? Sylvia had asked two evenings earlier. Ariel checked the calendar he carried in his wallet, along with the photo of his parents he had shown Sylvia several times and his juvenile league card with his twelve-year-old photo that was good for a few laughs. Saturday, June 6, at home, he answered. Why? No reason.

Ariel feared Sylvia's reaction to the end of the season. He would say, we'll have the summer to spend together. And she nodded, as if she knew better than anyone what was going to happen.

The masseur comes into the locker room when the players were finished picking up their things. He approached Ariel. I saw that you're not traveling with the team. Do you want to come to the bullfight with me on Saturday? Okay, said Ariel. A promise is golden, I've got season tickets at Las Ventas. At that moment, a gesture of affection or support was hugely valuable. Ariel watched him head off, walking with a comical limp.

In the hall, Amílcar was waiting for him and Ariel told him about not being in the lineup. They walked together to the parking garage. Did you read what my wife gave you? I'm working on it. Don't give up, don't be stupid, any help will do you good. Don't give in to it. No, no, of course.

At the fence where the walkway ended, like every day, there was a group of fans asking for autographs or taking impossible photos. According to Husky, hundreds of thousands of rooms around the world were adorned with out-of-focus photos of the back of some idol's neck. Many of them followed the players' expensive cars with their eyes until they vanished onto the highway.

Driving back home that afternoon, Ariel thought the route he had traveled so many times would soon be a fuzzy memory, substituted by other facilities, another temporary home, and most likely another loneliness. He understood more and more why many players started a family with kids in their early twenties. They needed to put down roots in the quicksand, grab on to a passing cloud. If he could drag Sylvia along with him, it would all be different, but how could he force her to pay such a high price? It was enough for him to be a slave to this profession, albeit a highly paid slave, but asking her to change her life would be too selfish. Without knowing why, he felt that his drive home was the start of a journey that would take him far, far away, that he would soon leave all this behind.

But then, what was all this?

5

Once in a while a small detail changes everything. The language class is over and the classroom empties out at a dizzying speed to shake off the lethargy. Sylvia's classmates go down to enjoy midmorning recess. It is hot. Sylvia takes off her thin sweater and pushes it into her backpack. She slouches down at a desk and checks her cell phone. She turns it on and waits to see if any message has come in. Barely a week has passed since Ariel's fate was sealed. He will leave, transferred to play on a British team. His current club will have to pay a third of his salary and he'll remain their property until the end of his contract. Four more years. Sylvia doesn't understand and doesn't want to understand the business details of the operation, but it seems clear that Ariel's future will lower his value. She hasn't said anything, but the name of the city he's heading to, Newcastle, sounds like *cárcel*—prison—Newcárcel.

They surfed the Web for information. The place is only five hours by bus from London, and it has a university. I still have two more years of high school. You could learn English. They say that in the next few years a lot of money is going into British soccer, Ariel told her.

In the front desks, near the blackboard, there is still a small group of four students whom Sylvia doesn't know that well. They are talking about a television program from the day before that she didn't see. It seems they mistakenly invited a middle-aged man into a debate about new technologies. He was really just on his way to a job interview at the station offices. The guy responded intelligently to the questions during a good part of the broadcast, until the confusion was revealed and they took the guest off the set.

The last one to leave the room is her friend Nadia. You coming? she asks. I'll come down later, answers Sylvia. After the suspense of hoping for a new message to fall like a drop of rain, there's nothing on her cell. Sylvia puts it back into the pocket of her backpack. The math teacher, Don Octavio, walks through the hall with his outstretched neck and his lopsided gait, passing by the open door. Sylvia sees him greet her with a lift of his eyebrows. But a second later he retraces his steps and peeks through the doorway into the classroom. You're Sylvia, right? Sylvia nods. Do you have some time later this morning to stop by the department office? Sylvia says yes and he leaves with, well, I'll see you there later then, and disappears again.

Sylvia wonders why the teacher wants to see her. She doesn't jump to any conclusion, it seems random, he obviously wasn't looking for her. She passes by the open door of Mai's class but she isn't inside. When she turns, she bumps into Dani, you looking for Mai? She's in the cafeteria. They go downstairs together, but when they get there Sylvia changes her mind, it's nice out, I'd rather go out to the yard. Should I go with you? Sylvia just shrugs her shoulders.

They look for a place to sit in the sun. Did you see that show last night? Sylvia shakes her head. My mother was watching and called me over. The hostess was halfway into the program and someone must have warned her that they'd messed up. She turns to the camera and says, it seems there's been a misunderstanding and one of our guests is sitting in on the debate by accident. They all looked at each other, I think they were scared shitless. The guy in question was a pretty chubby Guinean, he seemed charming. He apologized, I'm sorry, I told the hostess that I wasn't sure if I had to participate in the program. He explained that someone at the front desk took him to the set and invited him to sit on the panel of experts. The best part was that he seemed like the least fake of them all. If it had been one of those contests where you call in to identify the imposter, they would have gotten rid of everyone else before this guy. He seemed to have more common sense than any of the real experts. It was incredible.

Three of Sylvia's classmates joined the conversation. One of them was eating a large sandwich that he offered to the others. Dani was obviously uncomfortable for a second, until Sylvia's gaze calmed him down. It was a look that was outside of the conversation, just for him. Stay.

Sylvia is surprised every time she has a strange connection with Dani. She likes his scruffy way of dressing and moving, his shyness about speaking in front of people he doesn't know, which contrasts with his confidence among friends. There's something that keeps him on the margins of the group, as if he doesn't need to join in to exist. Sylvia likes that independence. But she's not physically attracted to him, it's more a friendly camaraderie, a kindred spirit.

When classes are over at the end of the day, Sylvia heads toward the math department with a certain reluctance. The door is closed and she waits for a moment while the students file out. The teacher appears with a handful of photocopies. Hello, come in, come in. He walks into the office and leaves the papers on the table. Sit down, he gestures to a chair while he closes the door. Sylvia puts her backpack on her lap. Well, Sylvia, I wanted to talk to you if you don't mind, what's going on with you? Sylvia is silent. She doesn't really understand the question. We're at the end of the school year and a few of us teachers were discussing your performance, it's really gone down. Things could start getting complicated for you. I mean, I don't want to put in my two cents when no one's asking for it, but there's always something . . . He doesn't finish, he keeps his eyes fixed on Sylvia's. She looks over at the bookshelves. No, there's nothing going on with me. Is it that you aren't motivated, you can't concentrate? I don't know, there must be something I can do to help you out. You were doing well, you don't need to end up with an F. You understand that, right?

Sylvia chews on a lock of hair. The teacher's moustache covers his upper lip, giving him a certain serious air, which his eyes, when you looked at them carefully, contradict. They sparkle and Sylvia is intrigued by them. She doesn't manage to give any coherent response. She hesitates over saying, my parents separated, but decides it sounds pathetic. She remains silent. Let's do something to make up some of the work, okay? To see if we can help you out. The teacher stands up and searches in his drawer until he finds some photocopies. Here are four or five problems, they're more logic games than anything else. I want you to prepare two or three pages for me, working out the solutions. Do it at home, reason it out, as if you were explaining it in class. You can use the textbook, of course, but make it clear that you understand the concepts. It's very easy and I'll grade it as extra credit. Okay?

Sylvia looks up, she can't quite believe what is happening to her. Would he have done the same thing for other students? Sylvia doesn't ask. She looks into Don Octavio's eyes. You have three days. Bring it to me here, at my office, this is something between you and me, outside of class. The teacher obviously considers the conversation over. Sylvia stands up and grabs her backpack. Thank you. Don't let it drop, don't let yourself go, all right, Sylvia, we all go through good periods and bad periods, but now it's a question of stepping up the pace these last two weeks, it's not worth quitting.

On the street, a moment later, Sylvia feels like crying. Is her private life so on display that a teacher can sense it from a distance? With some sort of X-ray vision. What moved Sylvia was his almost accidental interest. He was walking down the hall and suddenly, seeing her alone in the classroom, realized that her grades had dropped, he must have remembered her last, lame test, and instead of continuing on his way he stopped for a moment to take an interest in her. Something must have gone through his head in that fraction of a second that made him decide to stick his head into the class and talk to her. Sylvia, like most of her schoolmates, was convinced she was inscrutable to her teachers, just another face in the group that occupied a year of their lives and then vanished forever. Worlds that never crossed beyond the obligatory hour of class time.

What had left her on the edge of tears was the perception that everything had been abandoned, her studies, her family, her school friends, to get involved in a story that as it was ending left a dry, frustrating, barren hole. She had been on the other side and, suddenly, the teacher, in a professional way, not at all threatening, had brought her back to reality. We are here, where are you? he seemed to have been asking her. The hand he extended meant a lot. She, too, like the Guinean mistaken for an expert on television, had been invited into a world where she didn't belong. She, too, had politely faked it, had passed the imposter test, but it was urgent that she stop feeding the farce.

On the way home, she feels her passion for Ariel dying out, or that it must die out in order to save herself. She accepts the breakup as if it had happened in that office minutes earlier. That afternoon, before the students take over the oversize tables in the public library, she will sit down with the math pages and try to do the teacher's symbolic assignment. She will read the logic problems she has to solve, but she won't really understand what Don Octavio expects of her until the third problem makes it clear.

"Two people, A and B, are two meters apart, and A wants to get closer to B, but with every step A has to cover exactly half the total distance that remains between A and B." Sylvia will swallow hard, but will continue reading. "The first step is one meter long, the second step half a meter, the third step a quarter of a meter. Each step A takes toward B will be smaller, and the distance will lessen in an eternal progression, but what is surprising is that, if we maintain the premise that each step will equal half the total distance separating them, A will never reach B, as much as A tries."

Sylvia's eyes will be red. Perhaps that simple exercise will help to explain the theory of the boundaries that changed the history of science at the beginning of the eighteenth century. Maybe it was true, as the text on the photocopy explained with quotes from Leibniz and Newton. But Sylvia will begin to write her personal explanation of the problem and it will soon transform into a good-bye letter. The same letter that she will not know how to write to Ariel to tell him, in the most logical and simple way, that our story is over. A will never reach B.

6

Some nights, when Leandro comes back from the hospital to sleep at home, the doorbell rings and he's forced to buzz up the real estate agent who escorts some potential buyers. She is a nervous woman, with an overflowing file and a cell phone that seems to be a living animal. She always apologizes to Leandro for coming at such hours. Leandro doesn't accompany them on their tour through the house, but he can read the clients' expression when they leave. In the distance, he hears things like, the whole place has to be redone, but once you get it the way you want it, it'll be fabulous; during the day it has wonderful natural light, the neighborhood is a real gem, close to everything.

He was the one who gave Lorenzo the deed and the paperwork necessary to get it on the market. The real estate agency is owned by a friend his son has known since childhood. Lalo, a bright, cheerful kid who when someone asked him what he wanted to be when he grew up would reply, an explorer in China. Fifty million of the old pesetas is what they are asking for it. He doesn't understand euro conversions for big amounts. It's a good moment to sell, said someone in the agency to be polite. The mortgage subrogated to the bank was, according to Lorenzo's calculations, a big mistake. Another one. And his spending had taken a big, excessive, chunk out. Nevertheless, the day of the signing, Lorenzo only said, we've had to face a lot of expenses in these last few months.

I think the best thing would be for me to take care of everything, his son told him. They had transferred the money to his name. If his father refused, he could have had him declared unfit, but they never argued over it. How's the house? asked Aurora from the hospital, does Benita still come to cook and clean for you? Leandro nodded, although the truth was that he asked her not to come anymore now that he was spending more time in the hospital. Benita had started crying and Leandro remembered something she said, as she left, after giving him an affectionate hug on tiptoes, we were brought here for taming and they tamed us good, they did.

In Lorenzo's house was a small room where his father could settle in, where he'd stored papers, an old computer, and a desk that Pilar used when she brought work home. There they could set up Leandro's bed frame and his few boxes of belongings. They cleared a space beside the television for the piano. Sylvia refused to let him get rid of it.

A neighbor had told Leandro, at our age we're not up for moving. He spent his days sitting besides Aurora's bed, trying to be friendly with the visitors who insisted on coming to say good-bye, all those who found out from others, and came to try to hold a conversation Aurora could no longer maintain. Manolo Almendros started crying after kissing Aurora's cheek on his last visit. In the hallway he said to Leandro, I always loved your wife, I was so envious of you.

He had thought of Osembe very few times. One afternoon he was tempted to take the bus to Móstoles and plant himself in front of her door. If he passed some girl on the street who reminded him of her, he took pleasure in watching her, studying her gestures, her behavior, as if he wanted to understand something about what had escaped his grasp. In the newspaper, he read the news of the closing of the chalet. It showed a photo of the façade, taken at the same distant angle from which he had so often observed the house before deciding to enter. The climbing vine had grown with the springtime and hid the wall and part of the metal gates. According to the newspaper, the Bulgarian mafia in cahoots with a Spaniard was exploiting the women and had a system for videotaping what was going on in the rooms. Using the tapes, they had started to blackmail lawyers, businessmen, and other wealthy clients. One of the victims had alerted the police and two of the ringleaders and the madam were arrested, and seven women who seemed to have been forced into prostitution were freed.

Leandro imagined the tapes in the hands of the police. Maybe the officers or the civil servants had gotten together to watch the old guy who was such a regular. They would have laughed heartily. Hey, come over and check out this old dude, here he comes again.

Aurora is lying in bed, her mouth partially open, her face relaxed except for some slight momentary tension. The nurses come in. Leandro watches them work. He remembers how the downward spiral all began, with his appreciation of a nurse's bared curves. Now he admits that life requires a high level of submission. Anything else is suicide.

When they are left alone, Aurora speaks to him. Did you go out for a stroll? He nods. She suddenly mentions the canary they were given many years earlier, do you remember? When the neighbor, Petra, left for a small town. Leandro thinks it's just a fickle memory springing from the mental chaos that sometimes makes her delusional or makes her see images superimposed on the wall. Lorenzo had started to go to school and the neighbor gave Aurora her canary, because every morning through the window she commented on how well it sang. It brightens up the whole building, she would say. It drove Leandro crazy with its singing, all it took was listening to the radio or having a conversation to set off its unbearable craziness. Poor bird. Those were the same words Aurora had said when she found it dead one morning in its cage beneath the kitchen towel. Why did she remember that? Aurora repeats the phrase, to herself, in a low voice, poor bird.

Leandro sits on the mattress. The woman in the next bed is sleeping and her daughter went down to have something to eat. Why are you remembering that now? Aurora smiles. It sang so beautifully. Leandro took her hand. We've had fun, he says. We've been very happy. Aurora doesn't say anything, but she smiles. Going through old papers, I found the letters I sent you from Paris. It's incredible how pedantic and conceited I was then. I don't know why you waited for me. I would have run off after reading the nonsense I wrote you, with those airs of grandeur. Leandro wonders if she can hear him. I've failed you so many times. I ended up far below your expectations, didn't I? Aurora smiles and Leandro caresses her face. I've been a disaster, but I've loved you so much. Aurora can see him crying, but she can't reach her hand up to touch him.

That same afternoon, Leandro receives his student. Luis jogs up the stairs. Climb stairs like an old man when you're young and you'll be climbing them like a young man when you're old, that's what they used to say to me, explains Leandro as he leads Luis to the room.

Boxes now hold most of the papers and books that used to fill the walls. We are moving. Your wife . . . says the young man, but he doesn't dare finish the sentence. Leandro clarifies, I'm moving in with my son, she's still the same. I don't know if we'll be able to continue the classes there, I'll let you know. Luis hears noises in the kitchen. Leandro nods his head, they're helping me pack things up. Lorenzo had sent over two Ecuadorian guys. One of them is funny, his name is Wilson and he looks toward the living room with one eye while the other looks toward the kitchen. When Leandro saw him, he thought of a young friend who's an orchestra director and also has a wandering eye and brags about being the only director who can lead both the string and wind sections at the same time. When they stopped for a moment to rest from the packing, Wilson said to Leandro, do you know you're a lot like your son? And, seeing Leandro's surprised expression, he added, no one's ever told you that before? No, not really, maybe when Lorenzo was younger. Well, you are a lot alike, you both hold your tongue, you are men of few words, huh, isn't that right?

Leandro nods toward his student, there are things in these boxes you might be interested in, if you want them, they're yours. The boy approaches to have a look at the pile of scores, a few music-history books. That one is a masterpiece, Leandro says when he sees him pick one up. Don't even look at the LPs, I should throw them out, they're just relics. My father says that CDs don't have the same sound quality, explains the young man. Your father likes music? The boy nods, somewhat unsure. He was a student of yours, at the academy. They gave us your phone number when we were looking for a private tutor. Really? What's his name? The boy told him his father's full name. Leandro pretended to remember him. He always says that you were a great teacher, that you had them play in front of a mirror, so they could correct themselves. Leandro nodded with a half smile. And that you talked to them in Latin and, I don't know, you told them things about the composers.

Leandro interrupts him. Go ahead, take whatever you want, I can't fill up my son's house with all this useless junk.

7

The news of Wilson's death came as a cruel blow. Lorenzo had tried to reach him on the cell when he was running more than an hour late for a moving job. But no one answered. He assumed something came up and called the clients to apologize. He invented a story that they'd had a little accident with the van and he would get back to them in an hour. He had no way to reach their regular helpers. He was tempted to stop by Wilson's house, but he didn't. Throughout the morning, he tried Wilson's cell phone repeatedly. An hour later, someone called him back. Are you looking for Wilson? He died last night, they killed him. Lorenzo received the brutal information in the middle of the street. He had left for the market with a long-overdue shopping list. He didn't ask for details, but he headed over to Wilson's house.

Some friends were gathered there, along with his cousin Nancy. They told him the circumstances surrounding his death. They found him on the floor of the place he rented out at night, his head smashed in by brick blows. There were fingerprints everywhere, but the police still hadn't arrested anyone. Although on the radio they said the murderer was found, someone explains.

Lorenzo waits with Wilson's other close friends for permission from the central morgue to pick up the body. They will be able to bury him only after the autopsy has been performed. They won't let them cremate in case they have to examine the body further. Nancy cries, she's talked to his mother, who wants them to send the remains back to his country. That will cost a lot of money. He must have been carrying all his money on him, as he always did, it was too tempting to see him pull out that wad of bills, says someone. It could have been any crazy person. It was scum who slept there, the worst. I'm surprised, Wilson knew how to defend himself. The conversations overlapped. Once in a while, one of the women would interrupt them with a cry or a sob. I'll take care of sending the body to his family, whatever it costs, says Lorenzo. Daniela still doesn't know anything about it, Nancy tells him, she works outside Madrid now and only comes home on Saturdays to sleep.

Lorenzo asks Chincho about the van. The previous afternoon, Wilson had picked it up at his house. Lorenzo has an extra set of keys on him, but nobody knows where it's parked. He shrugs his shoulders. It must be somewhere near the place.

Lorenzo goes into Wilson's room and looks over the space. There is barely a mattress, a small wardrobe, and a nightstand. Resting on a lopsided lamp is a postcard of Chimborazo covered in snow. Lorenzo opens a drawer and doesn't find what he's looking for. In the wardrobe, his meager clothes are lined up. Lorenzo goes through his things. Chincho watches him from the door. If you're looking for this . . . He holds out two notebooks filled with jottings, I took them off the body, just in case. Lorenzo flips through and keeps them. His name appears on several occasions. When he goes back to the living room, Chincho approaches him. You can count on me for jobs. Of course, of course. The man leans his odd neck forward, life goes on, he whispers.

Lorenzo takes the metro downtown. Standing at the back of the car, he goes over Wilson's notes. The jobs already done are crossed out in pencil, but you could still read the information. The pages are overflowing with sums and divisions, street addresses and details, all gathered in an organized mess. There are also telephone numbers jotted on the final pages. In the second notebook is more of the same. Lorenzo gets an idea of Wilson's frenetic activity in recent days. He noted down details so he wouldn't forget them, wrote down things still to be done. Lorenzo could reconstruct his life based on the order of his notes. Once in a while, there was another telephone number and beside it he had written, Carmita, neighbor. Suddenly Lorenzo sees his name, often appearing next to some figures, the division of money, the amount owed, always as an explanation of accounts. But on one page the note has a rectangle around it and isn't related to any business. In his schoolboy's hand is written: "June 10, Lorenzo's birthday. Watch."

Surrounded by strangers in the metro car, by a woman who sits clutching her purse tightly with both hands, by a couple of Brazilians who speak loudly, two women from Eastern Europe, a mother with a baby in a stroller who could be Peruvian, a man studying a city map, Lorenzo stands, in spite of the empty seats, and feels a shiver run up his back. The texture of the notebook, its rough black cover, the rubber band that holds it closed, brings back memories of Wilson, lost but nearby. He remembers that once Wilson had noticed Lorenzo always checked the time on his cell phone. Don't you have a watch? I never wear one, Lorenzo had answered. My mother always said that a gentleman should carry a clean handkerchief in his pocket and wear a watch on his wrist. After the note, that minor conversation was now transformed into a moving detail.

He met Wilson through Daniela and now there was no trace of either of them. Wilson had filled a significant spot in his life, with that frank smile, his intelligent conversations, and that crazy eye. He had seen Daniela for the last time on Saturday. She had gone out with some girlfriends and they met up downtown. He was surprised to see she wasn't alone. We've taken a step backward in our relationship, thought Lorenzo when he saw her surrounded by friends. Can we have a drink alone? They went into a cafeteria on Calle Arenal with mosaics of Andalusian motifs. She seemed happy. The pastor had offered to help her find work, he often lent a hand to people in the neighborhood in exchange for the first month's salary.

What is happening to us, Daniela, are we not a couple anymore? I don't know what to think.

At first, when I met you, the way you got to know me, without acting superior or disrespectful, I thought, this is a brave man. Daniela sipped her juice through a straw. Is this about the children thing? You want us to have kids? Look, Lorenzo, I can't have children. One day if you want I can tell you the whole story, it's kind of complicated. Let me just say that a year ago they took a myoma out of me the size of a soccer ball and they completely cleaned me out. Does that make you feel more relaxed?

Lorenzo lowered his head and tried to reach Daniela's hand, but he only got halfway across the table. She was the one who placed her hand over his. She was wearing a little gold bracelet on her wrist. Lorenzo didn't remember ever having seen it before. Suddenly he had a pang of jealousy.

When I met you, you were a strange man. I had the feeling you were lost, alone. I felt very sorry for you, but it was a happy sorrow, because I thought you were someone who could be saved, that I could save you and it made me happy. I've seen you soar into flight, like a bird that gets his strength back. But that's it. Now that you can fly, you don't need me, don't cling to me. Go if you want. I can't give you what you're looking for.

Don't be silly, I don't want to go anywhere. Lorenzo suddenly thought, with cruel clear-sightedness, that the mentality of these young women raised in the warm glow of television soap operas was perversely deformed. He looked up at the lovely composition of Daniela's eyes. In that moment, she seemed more beautiful to him than ever. But she was talking about salvation, about wounded animals. She seemed to want to end their relationship.

I need help, too, Lorenzo, don't think I'm so strong. I'm very weak. What are you talking about, that's nonsense. Daniela, let's be straight with each other, please . . . Nonsense? Maybe. Daniela smiled. Nothing you say makes sense.

But the worst of it all is that Lorenzo did think she was making sense, which is why he didn't add anything. Daniela's smile was a challenge. Her friends were looking through the window from the opposite sidewalk. They smiled and made comments to each other. Maybe I'm just the butt of some jokes I don't even get. Daniela gave him a kiss on each cheek before standing up. And that had been the last time they spoke.

Lorenzo had a terrible Saturday night. It wasn't a good idea to go out late with Lalo and Óscar and their wives. He drank too much and sank into an uncomfortable silence. He didn't have anything to say to them. He could tell they were relieved when he left. At the hospital, that night, on the uncomfortable sofa bed beside his mother, his hemorrhoids tortured him again. In the bathroom, up on a footstool, he applied a cream the pharmacist had recommended. In a position where it was impossible for him to see his ass, he rubbed the ointment into the painful area. It was horrible to do it alone, half drunk on beer, but it managed to calm the burning.

He barely slept and in the morning on Sunday, as soon as his father showed up to relieve him, he headed to the church. Lorenzo saw Daniela's hair in the first rows and he could make out her figure, as always stuffed into tight clothes. The pastor was talking torrentially with his professional sweetness. It took Lorenzo a while to pay attention, to absorb his words.

When one looks at the world in which we live, the society, the life that goes on out there, if one could talk with God they would say: Lord, save us, convert this Sodom and Gomorrah into dust, destroy us, send a flood to cover it all, and from the ashes may a civilization more just and more faithful to your image arise. He pronounced it *sivilisation*, without the peninsular *c* and *z* sound. If it were up to me, I would tell you that destruction and disappearance are the only hope for our race. But I have God's consolation. He tells me wait and you will see. We have to know that in this life there is only one thing we all deserve: death. Everything given to us, all the small joys, the everyday, the tiny good and evil of each day, and the big Evil and the big Good that many of us cannot even reach from our tininess, all that is a gift while we await the Big Gift, death. Our only liberation. But before, from our ashes, perhaps we will manage to mold a new man, a new woman, a new girl, not as some cosmetic exercise, like those sick people on television. No, as a moral exercise.

Lorenzo dropped his head. The stocky man with the guitar played an old Dylan song with the lyrics changed. Oh, it's me, Lord, it's me you're looking for. Lorenzo stayed there almost half an hour more, inside the Church of the Second Resurrection. One resurrection wasn't enough, he thought. Perhaps, yes, perhaps the pastor was talking about him, too. Then he would be able to make a new man from the tattered remains of the old one.

But it was the pastor's words that made him leave without speaking to Daniela. Why? Now, with Wilson dead, he knows. Now he understands better why he took advantage of one of the songs, before the service was over, to sneak out onto the street, to escape that place. Why was death so essential? Why give it so much power? Lorenzo rebelled against what he had just heard. Now he understands, knowing that Wilson is dead, his head bashed in with a brick.

I killed a man, he says to himself. And the worst of it all is not how I'm suffering or how I've had to pay for it, or if I'll be forgiven or reconciled, or if I'll be able to save myself. None of it has any importance, in the face of the incontestable fact that I took a life, as if I were a god. That's why he couldn't believe in God, because he had supplanted him so easily.

As Lorenzo goes down into the metro car, he thinks Wilson also died at the hands of a murderer, in a stupid fight over a ridiculous amount of money or for a drunk's violent craziness. So should Wilson celebrate his absurd end? No, thinks Lorenzo, as he goes up the stairs that lead to the street, life is that sun, that light I walk toward, all that I am. You have to walk, keep moving forward.

Thoughts and feelings crowd Lorenzo's head. He knows that he is a murderer and he walks down the street. Maybe Wilson's death was liberating for him as well, because it added to the daily senselessness. I killed a man. I was God for him. The God that some pray to, asking for a ending, a way out, a hope, that they devote themselves to in joy and in pain, that dominating force, the holder of power. That was me.

He reaches the place, cordoned off with plastic police lines. On that floor, Wilson died not many hours before. No one can bring Paco or Wilson back to life, no matter how hard they try. Nothing better will grow from their ashes. They will no longer be anything, ever, just what they were.

No one would believe, passing Lorenzo on the street, that in his head raced confusing, atheist conclusions, which worked for him. He's an angry man, who trusts life, its accidental nature, its energy, who cries over a loss, a man's broken continuity. He also cries over the power of murderers. He doesn't confess or turn himself in. He looks for a white van parked nearby, a van with tinted back windows. He finally sees it at the top of a hilled street. He walks quickly toward it. And he finds it with a green ticket that he takes from beneath the windshield wiper. He tears it up and throws it to the ground. That's the order of men; an absurd ticket for failing to comply with the parking schedule is the only mark of his passage through life.

He has a set of keys in his pocket. He gets into the van and starts it. But he doesn't know where to go, he doesn't have anywhere. He bursts out crying over the steering wheel. He cries bitterly, bowing his head. When he rests his forehead against the wheel, it makes the horn sound and he gives himself a start and someone turns in the street and everything is ridiculous for that moment.

A little while later, he drives along the highway toward the airport. He has a pickup at two-thirty. He found the flotation ring Sylvia used as a girl, he found it at the back of the junk room, and he was using it to sit on because his ass was killing him. Along the highway, he passes the old folks' home. He understands his visits to Don Jaime as his particular way of comprehending sacrifice, or penitence, or maybe something else. He has time to spare and he swerves off to go in and see him. In that neighborhood, it's easy to find a parking spot.

He finds the man sitting in front of the window, absorbed in the rumble of some plane taking off. I'm not disturbing you, am I? Don Jaime shakes his head and Lorenzo sits on the mattress, near him. They don't look at each other.

The day after tomorrow is my birthday, says Lorenzo suddenly. I don't think I'm going to celebrate. My mother is in the hospital, dying. And I think my father has lost his mind. He spent almost sixty thousand euros on prostitutes. Lorenzo sees that the note with the phone number is still in the same place it was last time. A triangular-shaped calendar from a drug company is now beside it. I'm going to be forty-six. And I'm not going out with the girl I was going out with before. You remember her? But the man doesn't seem to be in any shape to respond. They remain in silence for a moment and then Lorenzo adds, do you believe in God?

The man moves his head from side to side, as if he is about to speak, but he says nothing. Some time later, he only asks, is lunchtime soon?

Lorenzo takes his cell phone out of his pocket and checks the time. No, I don't think so. As he puts the cell phone away, he misses not wearing a watch on his wrist. The man opens the drawer on the desk and takes out some magazines and some scissors. The pages of the magazine are cut out. Don Jaime cuts around the edges of the photographs with the scissors. He's doing it again, thinks Lorenzo. In a little while, he has cut out all the photos of women who appear on the pages as if it were an assignment he must finish.

Lorenzo has prepared a sign with the name of the person he has to pick up, on the back of an old wrinkled invoice. He holds it up high when the passengers from Guayaquil and Quito start to come out. The Quito airport, Wilson had explained to him, has such a short runway and is so interwoven into the city that the airplanes can't carry too much weight, so they're forced to stopover in Guayaquil, where they take on the fuel needed to cross the Atlantic. A man over thirty with bulging eyes walks toward him. There's four of us, the fifth didn't get through customs. Behind him are two men and a woman. They are very warmly dressed for the heat that is awaiting them outside. Lorenzo leads them upstairs. He has found a spot to leave the van in the arrival terminal. One of the men carries his large suitcase tied with rope. The woman lugs two cardboard boxes. Lorenzo offers to help her; she thanks him silently. Aren't you hot with so many clothes on?

Lorenzo sits at the wheel and sticks the key into the ignition. In that moment, someone knocks on the window. Lorenzo thinks it will be a cop and he turns calmly. But it is a sturdy man with gray hair. Behind him there are others; one of them, looking about sixty years old, is smoking. With a somewhat arrogant gesture, he indicates for Lorenzo to lower the window while he looks at the passengers in the back. Lorenzo rolls down the window barely two inches.

Do you think we're stupid? If you want work, go look for it somewhere else, all right? We're sick of seeing you around here. Before Lorenzo could respond, two of them have surrounded the van. The Ecuadorian sitting beside him hugs his bag and locks the door. Some muffled blows are heard and, in seconds, Lorenzo feels the van's four wheels deflate, cut with a knife.

Lorenzo doesn't move. He keeps his gaze focused outside the van. The men, who are probably taxi drivers, cross in front of the windshield and head off into the airport. They do so in a domineering, cowardly trot, without really hurrying. One holds down his shirt pocket as he runs so as not to lose his wallet. None of them turn to look at him. It takes Lorenzo a second to talk to his passengers. When he does, he says, well, let's see how we can fix this. And he shows them a reassuring smile.

Let's see how we can fix this.

8

The ball has a silvery pattern drawn on it and a green grass stain. Ariel reaches it before it stops rolling. He tricks the defense with a circular feint, stepping on the ball with both feet to go out toward the middle of the field. The ball obeys his control and his speed allows him to easily dribble past the center fullback, who's much slower. Ariel runs his foot over the ball, in one direction, then the other, managing to disconcert both defenders who have stepped up to keep him from reaching the top of the box. As he advances to the right, one defender is blocked by the other. Ariel then fakes with his hip, turns, and hits the ball with his instep. He shot it hard, a lefty kick aimed right at the goalie's face. It's something he remembers right then, something that dates back to a practice with Dragon almost eight years earlier. If you don't have an angle, hit it right to the goalkeeper's face. He'll move away for sure, it's a reflex. And if he doesn't, you break his mug and then apologize later. The ball enters the top corner of the goal and ends up in the net in the opposite corner.

Ariel doesn't run. He makes a half turn. He walks toward the middle of the field with his head down. In the distance, he hears a commentator shouting himself hoarse describing the goal. Some teammate comes over to hug him, but he just smacks him on the back or the arm, another brushes the nape of his neck. Ariel bites a lock of hair. The stands applaud and some sections rise to their feet. His teammates give him the space to celebrate alone, a goal that tastes of good-bye. It's my night, thinks Ariel. Fifteen minutes earlier, he had scored a goal, kicking a neglected ball into the goal area with his toes. But he didn't celebrate that goal either, because it was an ugly one. One shouldn't celebrate ugly goals. One of the symptoms of soccer's decline, Dragon used to say, is seeing players celebrate hideous goals, or even worse, seeing them celebrate the goals scored on a penalty, that is disgraceful, no one ever used to do it.

Today everything goes well. He passes the ball and runs. He receives the ball with space, it's easy to beat the defenders as he races. In the first half they tackled him in the penalty box, but Matuoko hit the penalty kick into an advertising panel. With this score, they would be fourth in the standings. This mediocre, shallow team had come up with a couple of brilliant games. When the referee blows the final whistle, the players greet each other, several teammates embrace him warmly. Ariel walks toward the locker room. One of the equipment men addresses him affectionately and the substitute goalie gives him a friendly slap. The fans applaud him. Ariel appreciates the gestures, but he doesn't lift his head. Coach Requero is in the mouth of the tunnel that leads to the locker rooms and he extends a hand to the players leaving the field. Ariel refuses to take it.

We had a bad year, the masseur said to him the afternoon he took him to the bullfights. There are good years and bad years and you got a bad one. The bullfight was horrible. Ariel was surprised by the brutal way the crowd insults the matadors in an arena that amplifies every shout; soccer players in comparison seem spoiled by the fans. Three of the six bulls fell down, almost unfit. The matador didn't know how to deliver the death blow to the fourth, the only good bull according to his companion, and he massacred it with stabs to the neck, until a jab to the nape made it fall to its knees. How horrific. The only thing worse would have been if someone in the front row had given him a frying pan and he had killed the poor animal with that. The masseur turned toward Ariel as the bullfight ended with a rain of cushions tossed onto the sand. This is like soccer, he said, one good day makes up for all the shit that came before it.

The masseur took him to have some wine at a bullfighting bar where the conversations resounded and the old waiters served at a dizzying speed. They talked about the profession and the team. There were some years when every soccer player went through my hands and those of a Sevillian woman named Mari Carmen who performed at a place called Casablanca. They ended up calling her "the Fifa" because of the number of soccer players who went to bed with her. They say she was a handjob whore on the Castellana once she lost her charms. I've compared myself to her many times, one can't think they'll last forever in this trade. You know that a few years ago some Japanese guys came to see me, I thought it was to take me to some team over there, I have friends who ended up there, playing or coaching. No fucking way! The masseur started laughing, they wanted me to give massages to the veal, you know, the Kobe veal, they take incredibly good care of them, they give them beer to drink and then they only serve the meat in very fancy restaurants. They offered me a sackful of money. Never listen to money, it gives the worst advice, when you do one thing for money you end up doing everything for money.

It was an enjoyable evening. The conversation with the veteran masseur somehow reconciled Ariel with his trade. It's about enduring it, betraying yourself as little as possible. Old friends approached, they chatted briefly in a way that amused Ariel, filled with phrases he wanted to jot down, with words he had never heard before. One of them said, bah, do you go to the bulls? How dreadful, it's dead, pushing up daisies, they've all ruined it, a catastrophe. The masseur laughed and then commented to Ariel, they've been saying the same thing for years, that it's coming to an end. They're so annoying, they're the ones coming to an end. This is like soccer, it's different now, not better or worse. Before a player lasted until he was forty, you could watch him excel in three World Cups, amazing, but now that's impossible. They milk you guys like cows, three games a week, pushing to make money, television, all that, but it pays a lot better, doesn't it? And the game has changed, before a player ran about four miles each game, now it's more than six, everything is faster, that's why a good player, now, lasts two or three years, at top level, I mean, then he holds himself back and only makes an effort when it's in his best interests. That's why most of them are faces without the slightest commitment or drive to excel. Everything's like that. Look, I'm from Galicia, I mean I'm really a "Gallego," not like you guys call every Spaniard a Gallego, no, I'm from a little town in Orense. And you know what? Now the cows produce twice the milk they did when I was a kid. You think my grandfather was stupid? No, it's that the people today are smarter. And with his hands he mimed the gesture of giving a cow an injection. Twice the milk.

As soon as he sets foot on the stairs to the tunnel, the referee stops Ariel and shakes his hand. Good luck in England. Do you want the ball as a souvenir? Ariel shrugs his shoulders. The referee hands it to him. It's a shame to lose such a handsome player. It's a pleasure to watch you run over the field. He said it with an insinuating smile. Maybe I'll get a chance to whistle at you over there, or we'll meet up in some UEFA game. A radio reporter runs toward him with a small microphone, we have the star of the game here, a man who is bidding a sad farewell to the team, but happy because he has played his best game of the year. He speaks with contrived emphasis. How ironic, right? Ariel corrects him, I don't agree, there have been less showy days, but I've played better. The journalist nods mechanically. I see that you have the ball, is that a souvenir of your last game in Spain? No, no, if you want it you can have it. Ariel holds the ball out and the reporter takes it in his hands without knowing what to say.

He showers there for the last time. He dresses and puts his clothes into the large bag with the club emblem. He empties his locker of knee socks, shin guards, a bandage, his cologne, a brush, two hair bands, a stack of photos of him to be autographed and the team's official tie, which is ugly, blue and prissy. His teammates are leaving quickly. They have set up a private lunch for the next day to say good-bye to the ones who aren't continuing with them and they'll all surely end up drunk, shouting, drinking, singing, and, of course, throwing croquettes at the fan. Like the last day of school. Ariel turns down Osorio and Blai's offer to join them for dinner that night.

He drives his car out of the stadium parking garage. There are still fans at the exit who bang on the hood to get noticed and throw photos through the windows. He calls his brother in Buenos Aires. That's it, I played my last game here. Charlie has been insisting for days that a more relaxed club in England will suit his interests better. It will be easier to stand out. At the end of the conversation, Charlie talks to him about Dragon. It would be good if you went to see him when you're here. Did something happen? Ariel asks. He always had the impression that the old coach's heart could give out at any moment. No, he's fine, it's his son. They say he committed suicide, I don't know, some drug thing, something terrible. When he says good-bye to Charlie, Ariel pulls the car over to one side of the street. He dials the home number of his old coach, but no one answers. At his country house, a precarious answering machine picks up. Hello, it's Ariel calling from Madrid. I don't know if this thing works or if the message is being recorded, but I just wanted to say that . . . Ariel takes a long pause. He searches for the right words.

Sylvia is waiting for him in the private dining room of a restaurant. She is reading a book and drinking a Coca-Cola. She has a plate of cured ham, cut into thin strips, in front of her. Ariel kisses her on the lips, sits down, and eats two, three, four slices of ham at once. I need a beer, he begs the waiter. So you did know how to play soccer, Sylvia says. He smiles and lifts the book to check out the title. How are exams going? She shrugs. I'm hoping to do what you did, shine at the last moment.

In the middle of dinner, just the two of them, Sylvia asks him, do you think that after today's game they will rethink letting you go? Ariel smiles and shakes his head. Pujalte had sent a message to his cell phone: "Congratulations on the game, you are leaving with a bang." Ariel ordered an enormous cut of well-done steak for dinner.

Ariel's cell phone won't stop ringing. It is the media, but he doesn't answer. A call comes in from Husky, asking if they should all have a drink together. I can't, answers Sylvia. Ariel says he'll call Husky back later, surprised by Sylvia's response. You can't? What do you have to do? Sylvia scratches a shoulder beneath her clothes. Tomorrow my grandfather is moving in to live with us, we have to help him get his things organized. Ariel doesn't say anything. When they finish dinner, he again suggests going somewhere for a drink. Really, I have to go.

Ariel has also used these last few days to organize his things. He wants to take full advantage of his vacation time. He'll empty out his apartment, and in two days he's off to Buenos Aires. He wants to forget about the competition there, recover his excitement about the game. By mid-July he'll have to be with the new team in England. Sylvia refused his invitation to go with him to Buenos Aires. I want to stay close to my grandmother, she said. In recent days, Sylvia's been quiet, elusive.

At his insistence, she agrees to have a drink in an expensive, elegant spot that clashes with her youth. Ariel's phone rings again. It's Husky, you talk to him. Ariel passes his cell phone to Sylvia. She says hi. She smiles at something he says on the other side of the line. No, I'd rather say good-bye now, I don't want to be one of those people who cry buckets at the airport. Today's been a lovely day and that's it. I prefer it this way, you don't mind, do you? Husky seems to have suddenly grown as quiet on the other side of the phone line as Ariel had sitting in front of her. Sylvia hangs up after saying good-bye, he puts an arm around her shoulders. Sylvia can barely hold back her sobs. I didn't want to cry, she says, and she pulls away to take a sip of her drink. Nothing's ending, you're being stubborn, he insists. Fine.

On the street, his car is brought to them. A boy shouts at them from a distance, you were hot today, man. Ariel is surprised at her refusal to yield. I'd rather take a cab. Are you crazy? Ariel opens the door for her and invites her into the car. Let's not end this badly, okay? A minute later, they are stopped at a traffic light. The red light illuminates Sylvia's face inside the car. I don't want a horrible good-bye, filled with tears, the same old story. I don't want us to call each other every night and end up promising to see each other every three weeks in a hotel. It's been wonderful, for me it's been like a dream meeting you, being with you. But it's over and that's that. No big deal, right?

The light has turned but Ariel doesn't feel like driving. He is silent. Random moments lived with Sylvia run through his head, in some sort of chaotic slide show. A section of her skin, along with a laugh, a look with a scent. Sylvia points to the traffic light with her head. Ari, it's green.

Ariel arrives at Sylvia's door. Today he brings the car closer than ever before. A guy flashes his lights at him as soon as he turns onto the street. He pulls over, settling in front of a garage entrance, but the car seems to want to go into just that garage and honks again. Ariel leaves the spot, angry. Son of a bitch, he had to go in right there. He stops again at a crosswalk. This is horrible, he says. Sylvia wants to hasten the good-bye, she doesn't want the scene to go on forever. Take good care of yourself, okay? And she places her hand on the door handle. Ariel brings his fingers to the nape of Sylvia's neck and she turns. They kiss briefly. Ariel wipes away Sylvia's tears with the back of his hand. You take good care of yourself, too, he says. Sylvia nods and leaves the car without saying a word. Here, before she closes the door Ariel hands her the CDs he has in the glove compartment. I can buy other copies. Thank you, she says. She takes them and turns quickly.

She heads away from the car. Ariel sees her reach her door. Sylvia crosses between two parked cars, gets up on the sidewalk, and searches in her pocket for her keys. If you don't turn around to look at me, I'll kill you, whispers Ariel. Sylvia seems to hear him and very slowly turns around and waves the hand that holds the keys. She vanishes into the doorway. Ariel readjusts himself at the steering wheel. Now where do I go?

9

It's Saturday. Sylvia opens the door for a young man. Her grandfather sticks his head out of his room. It's my student, Luis. My granddaughter, Sylvia. They both say hi and avoid each other's gaze. Sylvia takes refuge in her room and listens from there, to the piano class that takes place in the living room. Soon the new routines will become settled. Today they still hold surprise.

Two days ago, her grandfather moved in with them. Sylvia was used to seeing him in the hospital, when she visited Aurora. One day she'd found him sitting near the bed. With his head glued to the transistor on the nightstand. Almost out of batteries, he said, when he realized Sylvia had been watching them from the door for a little while. Aurora wasn't really there. Sylvia opened the door to the closet and searched for a coat. She put it at the foot of the bed, then opened the wheelchair. It's a beautiful day out, Grandpa. Leandro looked at her and then stood up. Let's go, she said. Leandro took the saline bag off its hook and put it on Aurora's lap. Then he did the same with the bag of painkiller fluid. Between them they laid her down and moved her carefully to the chair. She barely weighed anything. They had put her coat on while she sat up on the mattress, and Sylvia had looked at her pale nudity under the nightgown. Aurora opened her eyes but she didn't have the strength to maintain her modesty. Seeing her bare feet, Sylvia took two thick socks out of her backpack, llama wool, they're from Patagonia, she said as she put them on her grandmother's feet. Leandro took off his belt and put it around Aurora's waist to fix her to the chair. So she won't fall out on us. Aurora didn't appear to be aware of what was going on around her. The important thing is to act as natural as possible, said Leandro as he pushed the chair. Sylvia opened the door for him.

They waited for the elevator for a few tense minutes. Leandro looked at his granddaughter but they said nothing. There were too many floors in the building and the elevator would get too full. Sylvia readjusted the bags of saline solution and painkiller, making sure that they weren't moving where they entered the skin under her coat. It gets harder and harder for the nurses to find a vein, said Leandro.

The doors opened and they were able to go down and out. The entrance plaza was an enormous cement square. They walked slowly until they got to a nearby street, its wide sidewalks lined with trees. It was filled with an intense smell of soldering metal, as well as the percussive sound of nearby construction, behind the corrugated fence. They headed away from the noise toward a street thick with traffic, an enormous avenue almost the size of a highway. The exhaust pipes poisoned the air; a bus passed closely by, braking with a metallic shriek at the stop. It was hot, but a slight breeze brushed across Aurora's skin. They sought refuge on a calmer side street. Years ago all this was a vast open ground and in the summer they organized festivals here, said her grandfather.

Aurora traveled with her eyes open, although it had been several days since her words made any sense. She nodded hesitantly with her head when they asked her if she knew the people in front of her. Sylvia offered to push away obstacles in the street: when the sidewalks became narrow, it was impossible to pass between a garbage can and a traffic sign, the post of a streetlight or a tree. Without saying anything, they went around the block and headed back toward the hospital. The levels of the fluids were getting low.

At least she sees the street, said Leandro. The hospital is horrible. Sylvia complained that the stroll was frustrating. The street wasn't welcoming, the noise was bothersome, there was nothing lovely to show to Aurora's empty gaze. It's a very contradictory feeling, said Leandro. When we lived together, I always wanted to be alone, for her to go out for a walk with her friends. I loved the silence the house was plunged into. But if she was late coming back, I would get nervous and worried, pace along the hall, peek out the window. They stopped at a traffic light; the street noise forced Leandro to raise his voice. Now I know I liked that silence so much because I knew that later she would come back and fill it with her voice, her questions, her radio program. And now . . .

Leandro couldn't finish the sentence. They were approaching the hospital.

Sylvia spent the first day that her grandfather lived at the house observing him. He was a quiet man. He went down to the street early to buy bread and the newspaper and he served himself a slice with a trickle of oil as he sat in the kitchen reading the news. He washed what he dirtied and left it in the dish drainer. He watched as Sylvia played a few notes on the piano. It's out of tune, he said, from the move. I'll call Suso, the tuner, this afternoon.

The man appeared around nine. Leandro had just arrived from the hospital. Lorenzo replaced him at night. It was quite a show watching the piano tuner work. He had Parkinson's, but when he pressed the keys, the trembling vanished. Sometimes he sang over the notes, with a frightening tone. La, ti, do, fa. Leandro winked at Sylvia, who was struggling to contain her laughter. The man's vibratos created some sort of comic feeling of despair. He used to tune all the pianos at the academy, her grandfather explained, he knows the workings better than anyone. Your grandmother invited him for lunch every time he came to the house to tune the piano. He used to make her laugh. The man heard Aurora's name mentioned and only said, what rice she used to make, amazing. You don't eat that well even in a restaurant.

That same morning, Sylvia finished her classes. All she had left was a few makeup exams to avoid more Fs. She was able to push one final to September, but she thought she could pass the rest, which was almost a miracle after her lack of involvement the last few months. To prepare her father, some days earlier she told him that she thought she'd have three incompletes. Lorenzo was shocked. Are you crazy? You want to get left back? She assured him she would pull through. Just you watch, your mother is going to kill me, said Lorenzo. I should have nipped that whole boyfriend thing in the bud, with these late hours you've been keeping, but we've all got our minds somewhere else. Come on, Papá, forget about it. I screwed up and I'm going to fix it, promised Sylvia. That was when Lorenzo grew serious, staring at the tray of croquettes, and said, if only I could go back to high school. Then he stood up and opened a can of beer. Can I have a sip? asked Sylvia. He hesitated for a second and passed her the can. As she took a small sip, Lorenzo sat in front of her. When did you start drinking beer? He shook his head without waiting for a reply. Then he talked to himself, without daring to look at his daughter. I don't know, I just don't want you to turn into a piece of shit, you know? It's so easy to turn into a piece of shit. Now you're . . . Lorenzo stopped himself. I don't know, it's so easy to screw up. Do everything wrong.

Sylvia then wanted to hug him, but a physical barrier had been established between them some time ago. It was only broken when joking around. He would muss her hair, she would squirt him with the cologne he hated, he would trip her from the couch, she would grab the remote from him. A hug would be a big deal. She asked him if he was still dating the Ecuadorian girl and all he said was, Daniela? No, it got messy.

Eat, Papá, your croquettes came out awesome, said Sylvia. And he stuffed a whole one into his mouth, as if he were trying to make her laugh.

Sylvia had gone into the math teacher's office before the end of the day. I'm here to hand in the assignment you asked me for. Oh, leave it over there. There were two other teachers from the department, they were having a little wine one of them had brought. Sylvia placed her papers on the desk. How'd it go? Did you do a good job? I don't know, answered Sylvia. Don Octavio smiled at her and glanced at the pages. Well, I'll have a closer look at it and see if we can improve your grade, okay.

Before leaving, Sylvia shot a last look at the teachers in the back of the room. They seemed happy. Yeah, maybe they were drunk. There was barely three inches of cherry-red wine left in the bottle. They were celebrating the end of the year, too. Don

Octavio was sitting down and reading what Sylvia had written with a vague smile.

The nurse confronted her grandfather when she saw them coming back down the hall. You are irresponsible, taking her out without permission, we'll see what the doctor says when he gets here. But the doctor just smiled and increased the painkiller dose. Then he took Leandro out of the room to talk to him alone. Sylvia remained seated beside Aurora's bed.

Her breathing began to get erratic. She opened and closed her mouth as if she were drowning. Sylvia got nervous and stuck her head out into the hallway. The doctor entered the room with Leandro. She is dying, he told them. Leandro and Sylvia stayed by the bed, one on each side. Alone with her. Leandro held her hand and Sylvia stroked her face.

It wasn't long before she was dead. She didn't take long to die. She did it discreetly. Her breathing became more spaced out, and soon it seemed that each breath was her last, but then another, weaker one would come. And it went on that way for a few minutes. Until her mouth stopped, half open, and Leandro tried to close it for her. In the moment of her death, Sylvia felt something leaving Aurora. It wasn't her soul or anything like what you might imagine. It was as if the person she had been was leaving her, the essence of what Sylvia loved about her, her presence. And all that was left was a body, like a souvenir, more of an object than anything else. It wasn't mystical at all. Sylvia looked at Aurora and no longer saw her grandmother in her, or even a woman, just defenseless flesh and blood. She lifted her tear-filled eyes and found her grandfather, who was looking at her, too, but she smiled at him. It was now just something between the two of them, a matter for the living.

Sylvia crosses from her room to the kitchen. Her grandfather and his student stop the exercise. Go on, go on, you want something to drink? Then she leaves a pitcher of water with ice and two glasses on the table for them.

Sylvia thinks the guy has an interesting face, with an unexpected mouth that gives meaning to the rest of his features. He was dressed discreetly, as if he didn't want to reveal too much with his clothing. As she returns to her room, she notices he is staring at her.

When she hears him get up, at the end of class, she sticks out her head to say, see ya later. Her grandfather remains beside the keyboard arranging the musical scores. Sylvia escorts Luis to the door. Will you be coming all summer? she asks him. Yes, I don't have vacation until August. Oh, well, then I'll be seeing you. Luis pushes the elevator button and turns toward Sylvia, who is waiting to close the door. Don't wait for me, go ahead and close it, he says. No, no, that's okay. Sylvia waits for him to get into the elevator and they wave good-bye.

Do you want to play a little bit? Sylvia is surprised by her grandfather's question. She shrugs her shoulders and walks over and sits at the piano.

Her grandfather numbers the notes of a score from one to five with an old pencil. Then he places Sylvia's hand on the keyboard and tells her which number goes with each finger. Sylvia repeats what he has marked. No, pay close attention, play what's written there. She starts again. Straighten your back. Keep your wrists in line, don't force it. Very good. As if you had a ball in your hand. Now we are going to play it one octave higher. He places Sylvia's hands again. His arthritic fingers brush his granddaughter's young ones. This is a do, fa, sol, fa, la, ti, do, do. Her grandfather starts to sing the notes with each of her strokes.

Sylvia hangs out with Mai and Dani that afternoon. They talk for a while. Mai makes them go into a clothing store. Then she comes out to talk for almost half an hour on her cell phone while she crosses from one sidewalk to the next. They both end up sitting on the curb waiting for her to finish her conversation.

I realized something about Mai, Dani tells her. Nobody would guess it from the way she looks, but I swear that deep down she's a housewife, she can dress as modern as she wants, but in ten years she'll be married, paying off the mortgage on a terraced house, and working the checkout at a Carrefour supermarket, or something like that, you'll see. With dreadlocks and everything.

I don't know, maybe we'll all end up the same way, answers Sylvia.

No fucking way, girl.

Sylvia gets together afterward with some friends from school at a bar in Malasaña. The street is packed with drunk students celebrating the end of the year, gathered on the sidewalks and at the doors to the bars. There are police observing the benches in the plaza and boys pile up in the overflowing bars. Sylvia is surrounded by classmates. Once in a while, someone lifts their voice above the noise, with a laugh or an insult. Her cell phone rings. It's Ariel. Nice tits, he hears Sylvia say to a guy when she passes in front of a group on her way out of the bar. I'm in the airport, I'm about to board. Sylvia covers her other ear with her hand. I can barely hear you, wait, I'm going outside.

I wanted to say good-bye, I hope you don't mind. Sylvia listens to him. She has gone out to the street and leans her foot on the edge of the sidewalk. Not at all, I love it, call me whenever you want, I don't know. I can call you, too, right? Of course. How many classes did you fail? asks Ariel. Just one, I think. Next week I'll know for sure. So you shined at the last minute. Just like you, she replies. And math? I passed it, by the skin of my teeth.

Sylvia raises her hand to greet two friends from her high school. On the other end of the telephone, in the background, she hears the voice of the airport public-address system. Ariel talks to her. Are you wearing the necklace? asks Ariel. Yes. Are you touching it? Sylvia takes it out from beneath her T-shirt and strokes the small golden ball broken in half that hangs from her neck. Yes, I'm touching it. Me, too . . . says Ariel. I'm gonna be watching you, eh, Sylvia. I'm gonna be watching you. And I'll be watching you, she says.

The sound as the connection breaks is the most abrupt sound she's ever heard. Sylvia stays out on the street for a moment. She is somewhat drunk. She had to eat a sandwich a little while ago and slow down on beers. Her clothes and hair stink of smoke. In one of her ears, an uneasy, percussive ringing sounds. The asphalt is still giving off the heat of the day and Sylvia notices her T-shirt is sweaty.

A little while later, she says good-bye to her friends. She decides to walk home. She does it unhurriedly, in the road, beside the cars, avoiding the people on the sidewalk. She passes in front of Ariel's apartment. I'm going to rent it out, I don't want to sell it, he had told her. If you need it, all you have to do is ask. She wants to be alone, to walk alone. She feels some sort of pain in her chest, intense but pleasurable. It's as if there were a wound, but a slight wound, a mark on her skin that you want to stroke, acknowledge, enjoy for everything it means to you. While it's still there, because it might, soon, disappear.

ACKNOWLEDGMENTS

In the process of writing this novel, I had the indispensable help of a few people. Most of them are friends, so I won't name them. This way I'll avoid pointing fingers. I want to say thank you for the many things that belong to them in this book. Some were essential readers; others brought their inspiration to my perspiration. I am indebted to them for Argentinian and Ecuadorian expressions, reflections on the game of soccer, legal details, medical knowledge, musical notes, corrections to my syntax, squinty looks, erotic experiences, and above all the generosity to share them with me. I also borrowed a logic treatise from Adrián Paenza and his book *Matemática . . . ¿estás ahí?* and musical and poetic fragments from some teachers who are quoted or hinted at or camouflaged, like for example behind that life lesson I strive to follow: *non piangere, coglione, ridi e vai . . .* But perhaps the most important thing is to recognize the patience and support of those who were close to me during the writing process. I hope to have opportunities to share with them any happiness that this book brings us.

———

The translator would like to thank David Trueba, Javier Calvo, Doug Fielding, and Dídac.